THE KUDZU COTTAGE TRILOGY

KUDZU COTTAGE

BOOK ONE
HIDING PLACES

M. Spealmann

Published by Day Studios

Cover Art by Day Studios

ISBN 978-0-9832862-1-9

US Trade paperback

DEDICATION

This story dedicated to Audie Spealmann: woodsman, craftsman, visionary and protector.

Thank you Daddy for a magical childhood

ACKNOWLEDGMENTS

A LIFETIME OF THANKS to Suzanne Thompson for reminding me always that mine was a rare and special childhood.

Kudzu Cottage had many false starts before "Danny woke up dead". My thanks for the guidance and encouragement of my daughter Natalie Rivers, my friend Kim Jefferson, and my mentor Clark Taylor during plot development. Without you Danny might never have awakened!

Thanks to those who soldiered through the very rough first draft of what was then titled 'The Stone Shed", and still enjoyed the story: Judy Ciurca, Chrissy Moore, Mary Cochran and Stacy Flores.

A special acknowledgment to Jo Bordeau who edited the initial 600 page manuscript while making the daily train-commute to Washington, DC. Thanks Jo for fending off all those curious fellow passengers and be sure to tell them its finished!

I am extremely grateful to Gary Smith, Doctor S. Rush, Chip Filault, Tanga Ellrich, Robin DeWitt, Pat Grush, Laima Rivers and to the Thompson girls for the encouragement needed to self-publish.

Particular thanks goes to Monica Foell for meticulously dotting my I's, crossing my T's, and curbing my more enthusiastic verbiage. Monica, this would have never made it to book form without your copy editing.

And to Kathy Black, who rescued me when technical formatting errors had me in a tizzy. Kathy, you jumped in your car and drove from Virginia to Baltimore to untangle me and I will always be grateful!

My final thanks are to Danny—who was there all along.

~HIDING PLACES~

...the story begins

THE LAST DAY OF SEPTEMBER

O n Monday, Danny woke up dead.

At least there is nothing more to worry about.

The featureless darkness of the afterlife was pleasant and the stillness felt warm, soothing and comfortable. Even the utter silence was a huge relief. For what felt like a long, long time Danny contentedly drifted in this solitary void.

But eternity is a long time and human beings are social animals not really meant to be alone. Aloneness becomes loneliness, emptiness becomes boring and a pointless existence becomes punishment.

If this is the afterlife, shouldn't my mother be here by now? She must know I'm dead too! Or did I do something wrong and this is it? Am I being punished?

The panicky thoughts rocked the quiet as they resonated through the void. A corner of the darkness seemed to crack open. Danny became aware of the vague sliver of light and moved toward it. The light grew brighter and brighter, reaching into the shadows and chasing away the dread.

A smiling woman, with long black hair and love in her eyes, stepped into the light.

"Mom!" Danny flew forward.

"Hello sweetheart! I've missed you!"

"Oh, Mommy! I've missed YOU more."

"Impossible! I've come to bring you something special."

"Well I'm here now for good and you are all I need."

"Hmmm... Did you forget it's your Birthday? That calls for a very special present—a magic present!"

"Mom! What does my birthday matter now? Besides, I'm too old for magic."

"You are NEVER too old for magic Danny! Now turn around and let me stand behind you...and look! No, don't argue...just take a look. You'll like it, I promise."

Danny turned reluctantly to face a dusty, floor-length, looking-glass and was surprised to see a big eyed stranger staring back. The stranger, just as startled, blinked and stepped away giving Danny a better look. She—for it was a girl—was young, with dark, tangled hair, skinny legs, scabby knees and enormous brown eyes. And she looked a bit familiar.

"Who IS that?"

"Who is THAT?! Why THAT is YOU, Daniela Francesca, the way you looked just a few years ago."

"Before you died..." Danny said before adding reflexively, "its DANNY, Mom. I hate that other name." But she couldn't take her eyes off the mirror where the image now appeared to be subtly changing...

"You were 12 then...almost 13."

The mirror-girl seemed to be growing taller. Her chin looked sharper and her eyes not so over-large and wistful.

"I know you don't like mirrors, but look at yourself the way I see you. Today you are 14."

The changes sped up and the mirror girl grew taller still. When the unruly hair pulled itself into two tight, neat pigtails and the hesitant-but-hopeful look disappeared from the girl's face, time caught up to the present.

Danny stared in disbelief at the new, confident, capable almost-woman reflected. *THAT'S ME? I really look so calm and in control? I certainly don't ever feel that way.*

The mother's reflection winked at her daughter. "I told you it was magic." And because she knew full well what her daughter was thinking, added, "Few people really know what they look like Danny, so this mirror lets you watch yourself grow into the person you are today. And that person, my dear, is really someone special. She's so smart she frightens me sometimes. I was blessed with a very, very remarkable child, and someday the whole world will meet the very, very remarkable adult you will become."

Danny, mesmerized by her mother's reflection, unexpectedly voiced a thought she'd had maybe a billion times. "I wish I looked like you, Mom! You are so beautiful and I'm just," she searched for the best word. *Boring? Average? Forgettable?*

That's it! "My face is utterly forgettable."

"Look again my girl. You will grow taller and lovelier with every year. Someday you will have that long, lean dancer's body I always wanted." Mother dismissed her own strong, short frame with a flick of the hand before reaching out to pull back her daughter's hair. "It won't be long before your cheekbones and pointed chin really showcase those eyes."

Danny blinked and noticed something quite startling. Although her mother's face was square and her own triangular, the eyes were the same. In fact, EXACTLY the same—same shape, same upward tilt, same thick, black lashes rimming irises of an identical rich chocolate brown. *Huh! How did I never notice that before?* Danny always marveled at the way excitement showed in her mother's eyes, making them luminous, highly reflective and snapping with energy—and right now, her own eyes looked just like that!

"Sooo...you finally made the connection. Great! There is a lot of me in you young lady." Mother smiled with satisfaction...and a little sadness. "You get it now. That's the birthday present I want you to have before I leave."

"Leave? No!"

"Well, yes, Danny. We are in two different worlds and its time for me to go. I am dead. You are very much alive."

There were sparks of color trapped between the strands of her mother's long and black hair; Danny stubbornly focused on them. She refused to listen, refused to hear her mother's words. *I am **so** dead!* she thought stubbornly.

"I died Danny—NOT you. This is my world and you are just visiting. Sweetheart, you can't stay here; you don't belong. Danny, honey, you know this...you know you aren't dead. You know you are only sleeping.

"**No!** I don't WANT this to be a dream! Mom, please, I want to be with you! I can't do this alone. Mom, it's not fair...it's not!" Desperate and losing control, Danny blurted, "YOU SAID YOU'D BE RIGHT BACK!"

Her mother's soft brown eyes blackened and sharpened as the compact frame, somehow, became hard and imposing. This was a parenting trick Danny remembered well and it still worked. No more hiding, No more arguing. No self-pity. Time to listen.

"Do you honestly think I **meant** to get hit by a truck?! I am really sorry sweetheart, but accidents happen—bad things happen—and the living keep going. Life isn't fair! You especially know that. But you can depend on this Danny Girl: I will always be with you. I didn't leave you."

Like butter on warm bread, her mother's love melted away months of pent-up resentment. Danny gazed up into her mother's almond-shaped eyes and breathed deep of her mother's so-familiar orange and clove scent and felt safe for the first time in many, many months. *This is the way I want it to be; the way it's supposed to be. It is such a relief not to be alone.*

No matter what her mother said, Danny was determined to remain dead...

The animal-like scratching started faintly—right on the edge of hearing. It was easy to ignore. But the repetitive noise escalated; it grew louder, more insistent, almost frenzied. Danny thought it sounded like the skritch, scratch a cat makes in a pan of kitty-litter. *It is coming from where my feet would be— if I had feet, which I don't—and if I were lying down, which I'm not—because I'm dead.*

The scratching moved closer—became even more desperate.

Should I investigate? Be concerned? No, she decided. *It doesn't matter.* Determined to remain dead, she closed her mind to the disruption and forced her thoughts back to her mother.

But her mother was gone.

That sound again as the velvet blackness began to take on a definite blueness...

And there was an itch.

The itch was in a spot between Danny's shoulder blades. It tickled. It **demanded** to be scratched. Willing herself back into the dream, she resisted the itch and dismissed the growing lightness.

She didn't have to ignore the scratching sound. It had stopped.

And then something fat, cold, and wet splashed her square on her nose...

That's it! Danny's eyes flew open and she jerked up...or tried to. Something was holding her back, pinning her down, and for the first time she felt afraid. She began to struggle, fighting wildly to tear free from what felt like tangles of soft cottony fabric until she felt a sharp pinch on the tender skin of her lip.

Ouch!

Like it or not, the day had begun. Her lip stung and dreams had fled. Taking a calming breath helped her stop struggling. *It's okay!* She told herself, *I'm camping. I'm just tangled up in the sleeping bag. The zipper pinched me a little, that's all.*

The snaggle-toothed zipper in the heavy winter sleeping bag pinched again as Danny thought about her circumstances. Last night's dropping temperatures had prompted her to zip the bag all the way up. Only her nose had been exposed and she'd fallen asleep tightly cocooned in the bag's downy cotton. But now she wondered about that zipper—how long had it been since it was zipped up that far?

The zipper's teeth were locked in place and the zipper wouldn't budge. It was almost funny! Maybe they'd find her dead body after all, stuck inside a sleeping bag, in a tent, in the woods!

I'll have to rip my way out I guess, she resigned herself. She tore at the lining and pushed up against the insides hoping to tear loose a seam, but the old material proved surprisingly strong. *Maybe the zipper track is the weakest link,* she thought and gave it a yank on either side. The dry rotted threads began to pull free as the zipper separated from the material.

Danny worked on the weak spot and eventually made a hole big enough to free her head and shoulders. Finally able to sit up and look around her father's old, bark-colored tent, her sense of relief was short-lived.

In the dim light the space that should look familiar—didn't.

What's wrong? She rubbed her hurt lip. *It's the light! It's a weird bruised blue.* She listened. *And it's quiet, way too quiet.*

Every camper knows mornings are noisy in the woods, as creatures eager to express surprise and delight, trumpet, honk, twitter and squeak with the rising sun—but not this morning. This morning a heavy, deep, profound stillness pressed down on the little tent like something crucial left unsaid...

This time the icy drop of water nailed Danny on the neck. She flinched, shivered as icy fingers rolled slowly down the curve of her back, and glared up to the source of the annoyance...

The usually stalwart little tent roof was sagging dangerously inward—straining the double-reinforced canvas—and the seam above had sprung a leak. So far the leak was small but Danny could see another droplet building—growing fatter by the instant—trembling with anticipation...

Not this time! As the drop broke free Danny managed to wriggle out of striking distance only to watch another immediately form. She felt both sad and a little betrayed that the tough old tent had let her down.

Enough of that, she admonished herself. *It's time to find out what's causing this weird morning.*

When Danny unbuttoned the tent flap to the silent, blue morning something soggy and heavy fell inside—something that landed with a loud wet **flop**.

Snow!? How could THAT be? She couldn't remember it ever snowing this early in the season. This she'd have to see to believe and so she yanked the flap fully open on a brand new world.

Snow had fallen heavily in the night, coating the trees, muffling the ground; virtually burying the little tent. Because the trees had not yet lost their leaves much of the sodden snow hadn't made it to the ground and rafts of it lay snagged over head, disintegrating in wet clumps as a hesitant morning sun rose higher in the sky.

It was a most unusual sight.

The sky was still, the leaden gray of winter storms, but the drip, drip had begun as the unseasonable snow disappeared fast. The snow that remained around the tent was melting so fast Danny almost missed the animal tracks. A line of prints led from the tent door to a distant clump of underbrush. They looked as though they'd been made by tiny hands and small, elongated feet. *That must be what I heard last night! Those prints were made by a raccoon!*

That a raccoon had visited her last night during the vivid visit with her mother couldn't be just a coincidence. Raccoons were her dad's favorite animal. Roy Smith and his daughter had spent a lot of time outdoors—either walking through the woods or messing around in the stream—and picking out raccoon tracks was one of their favorite games.

Danny knew a lot about smart, funny and mischievous raccoons thanks to her dad. He cautioned that an adult 'coon could never be tamed as a real pet but could be excellent company and sometimes—under the right circumstances—even a good and loyal friend. Raccoons, he liked to say, were serious about two things: Play and Work.

So, Raccoon were you playing or were you working? She bent for a closer look at a curious heart-shaped depression closest to the door and her smile widened as she realized what had caused it. *That's a butt print and it's right outside my door! The raccoon wanted inside the tent and needed both hands and feet to work on the buttons of the tent flap, so it had to sit down. This was a working visit alright. An unsuccessful working visit,* she amended, thinking of the frenzied scratching that had interrupted her dream. She pictured the small, ring-tailed bandit ambushed by weather then further frustrated by an unsuccessful break in. *Dad said a raccoon's nimble fingers could pick a lock and open a jar, so he must have been exaggerating—like always.*

A loud **FLOP** as a load of snow hit the ground and sent cold air streaming into the open tent. She ducked inside and buttoned up the flap, all the while wondering what had become of her ring-tailed friend. It was still too early to hibernate.

Inside, the normally cozy space had continued to shrink under the ever-increasing weight of wet snow. She pushed up on the tent canvas hearing with satisfaction the sandpapery sound of heavy snow sliding off the rough canvas. Minus the burden, the little tent did regain some of its dignity but the bulging top seam and cockeyed walls appeared to be permanent. Danny considered her situation while idly watching drops of water seep between broken threads—*reminds me of Peter Rabbit squeezing through the picket fence.*

Plop!

It is time for a new tent.

Danny rolled her sleeping bag into a dry corner and, sitting on the roll, reached for her backpack to begin the time-consuming task of digging through it. It was packed pretty tight and, *really,* she reminded herself, *it's supposed to carry books, not clothes, food and toiletries.* No matter how she packed it she had to take everything out to find what she was looking for and it was annoying.

Time for a new backpack.

Fishing out a change of clothes, a toothbrush, a hairbrush, two textbooks, a bottle of water and a Granola bar, Danny finally touched the familiar slick cardboard of her composition book. In this book with a frayed black ribbon binding and common black and white marbled cover, Danny chronicled her life; she recorded her dreams and faced her fears. Now she would write on the next to last page.

Time for a new composition book.

Opening the journal, she retrieved a black roller ball pen from the side pocket to write:

Today is like an unidentified shape in the toe of a Christmas stocking...full of possibilities

September 30-Monday

It snowed about four inches last night, so there won't be any school. Today is my birthday, and today of all days I didn't want to wake up in a lumpy bed in a nasty house smelling of cigarettes and dirty dishes. Most of all, I didn't want to have to see the snoring, quivering mass of flesh who inhabits the couch and gets paid to be my "loving Foster Mother." The Filthy Cow!

No way!

I walked back here in the woods behind HER house, where none of these city kids ever go, and I pitched my father's old tent. Thank goodness too; I can't imagine being stuck in that Foster-Hole for a whole Snow Day!

And last night I had two visitors: my mother came to wish me happy birthday and a busy raccoon came to check up on me.

Today I am 14. Today will be different.

Danny tucked her jeans into her hiking boots before pulling the laces tight and snug. The Timberlands might be old and well worn, *but they are still waterproof!* Her father stressed the importance of applying mink oil regularly; even in his absence Danny kept to the schedule. *Lots of the stuff he taught me was good,* she acknowledged narrowing her eyes. *It will be sloppy going though,* she thought, hearing the outdoor sounds of melting snow falling into already soupy mud. Pulling on her parka she slung her backpack over her shoulder and bent to exit what she already thought of as her home.

The sky greeting her was a lighter shade of gray and trees were busily shrugging off what remained of the snow. She shivered, the air, damp and chill, lay heavy in her lungs. Steam— *or is it fog?*—rose from the ground. Clouds of it pooled in low places, swirling around Danny's boots as she walked and completely blurring familiar outlines of root, rock, and forest path. There was no visible path to follow.

She settled on the path of least resistance and hoped for the best. *Let nature point your way and guide your steps*, she thought and laughed at herself. *Silly! You sound like someone out of the Pocahontas movie!* Still, the laugh made her feel better. This was, she reminded herself, HER day; HER adventure. No school; no rules. *Heck, between sleeping, eating and 230 digital channels, my loving foster mother, doesn't know, or care, where I am.*

With the day all to herself there was plenty of time to find the townhouse development and bus stop she'd spotted once before. *How big could this suburban woods be?* Glancing over her shoulder one last time as the campsite and her little canvas tent disappeared from view Danny headed for a break in the trees.

The problem, thought the old man, *is that one empty day follows another.* He remembered how stunned he'd felt 30 years before when his daughter complained of being BORED. *How can that be?* He'd thought, *its summer vacation! There are miles to walk and places to explore and books to read and games to play.* Oh, for the luxury of all those unstructured summer hours! He'd been certain HE would never get bored.

Joke's on me! The old man accepted the irony with a tip of his balding head. *Boredom must have something to do with feeling trapped, just like I am now! I wanted her safe in the house with her mother, not outside running wild like me when I was a kid. She was a girl after all. The world is a dangerous place.*

The old man's early morning thoughts were heavy as he stood at the threshold of the doors leading to a snow-covered deck, gazing at, but not really seeing, the woods beyond. Last night it had snowed—a bizarre occurrence that was all over the morning news.

His old ears began to make out sounds of the neighborhood rousing itself. Voices. The scrape of an aluminum snow shovel on a concrete sidewalk. Those familiar, muffled snow-sounds woke up long-forgotten memories of other snowstorms. *Not so long ago I was a young man pushing a shovel through heavy snow.* Remembering how his muscles strained when he picked up too much—which he always did. Remembering how he'd hoist it up and over his shoulder—knowing, but not caring, that he'd be sore next day. Remembering inhaling long-ago-air that was sharp, clean and biting, but burned like the dickens when exhaled in a cloud of steam. He'd enjoyed the work, enjoyed the satisfaction of building the heap of snow high and higher—a mountain in his small patch of yard. And then he would cut a path right through that mountain—leaving the stairs and walkway flanked by snow cliffs—because that's the way his daughter liked it.

No matter how much snow there was and no matter how tired he was, he wouldn't stop until the job was done. Of course. It was part of taking care of the family.

The old man no longer had a family; he would never again shovel his own snow and the absolute truth of this startled him. *I'm not going anywhere, anyway. Who cares if the sidewalk is clear?* He sighed deeply. *That's the problem. I'm not going anywhere ever again. Even without snow and ice to block my path, I'm trapped.*

Danny watched the stooped figure of an old man staring fixedly out at the snow. *Or is he looking at the woods? Does he see me? Is he watching?* She nervously moved further into the underbrush separating the townhouse yards from the trees and peeked out. He hadn't moved; his gaze hadn't followed her.

If he's not staring at me, what's he looking at?

This backyard was the only one without a fence for miles and she figured she could cross it and make it to the street in less than a minute, *but not while he's standing there!*

Just then the old man swayed on his feet and, as Danny watched in horror, his knees seemed to buckle and he slumped down like a deflated balloon.

Oh no! What can I do? Who should I call? Opening her mouth to scream for help and trying to remember anything at all about CPR, Danny hurried forward expecting to see the old man dead on the deck. What she saw instead made her stop before completely revealing herself.

The man hadn't fallen; he'd taken a seat...

He's sitting in a wheelchair!

The bus pulled up in a slosh of wet snow and gutter water; Danny jumped back in time to avoid the worst of it. Brakes squealed, the doors flopped open and a young, unsmiling bus driver stared out at her, "Well git in. I need ID and bus pass, or ID and five bucks."

Danny's overloaded backpack resisted her efforts to gracefully retrieve the wallet with her ID and she could feel the driver's disapproval as she fumbled. *At last!* She straightened up to hold out the ID card plus money she'd just earned shoveling snow and tried to sound confident, "Is this ticket for a roundtrip?"

The driver, eyeing her ID, took forever to respond, "Yeah." More uncomfortable seconds went by before he looked up and smiled unexpectedly. He sounded a little guilty as he forked over her change and said "So, you must be visiting Al Smith?"

The whole experience so far was confusing! First the abrupt change in the driver's attitude and now, *Al Smith?* Her last name was Smith, true—that much was on her ID. *But what makes him think I know Al Smith?* Still, he was being friendly so the best thing might be to play along. She smiled slightly and tuned back in to what the driver was saying...*he hasn't yet paused for a breath!*

"...Old Al drove this route for years before retiring...but I guess you'd know that. Heck, he trained me—tough old buzzard! And he'd check up on me too. I'd drive by and see him standing right at this same bus stop, and I'd pick him up and right away he'd start quizzing me!" His voice went gruff in imitation of old Al. "How far from the stop should you start applying your brakes Jamaal? How far from the curb should you stop if it is raining, Jamaal? What should you do if a person gets rowdy, Jamaal? Or doesn't have money to pay? Or has an expired bus ticket?" Jamaal shook his shaggy head with a private smile. "Old man had a million questions...and answers to 'em all." Coming back to the present, he glanced shyly at Danny. "I guess you gonna tell him I sprayed you with water, huh?!"

Danny tried to make her smile reassuring. "No. You didn't get me wet, and at least you stopped. I thought you were going to drive right past me."

"Tell ya the truth, I almost did! I didn't see you till I almost passed you. Old Al was the only person ever used this stop, and I haven't seen him in about a year. Heard he had a stroke or something. How is the old fella? You gotta be his granddaughter—his daughter's your Momma, right? But your last name's Smith so I guess she never got married—no real surprise there! I guess she'd be in her what?...mid-late thirties?"

Jamaal was off on another tangent.

Danny glanced longingly over her shoulder at the rows of bus seats. *Empty.* The bus was still pulled to the side and wasn't in anyone's way, so she guessed it didn't matter that they are sitting there idling while Jamaal talked. She would simply let him believe she was 'Old Al's granddaughter.' *It doesn't seem likely he will run into Old Al anytime soon, anyway.*

By now, Danny was pretty sure Jamaal's 'Old Al' was the crippled guy she'd spied on from the woods. The neighbors she'd met shoveling snow that morning mentioned an old man in 11314 who was a shut-in; no one could remembered his full name but thought the last name was something common like "Jones." *So why not 'Smith'? Smith is the most common name of all.*

When she considered it, she supposed the whole thing **was** a rather startling coincidence. *Daddy used to say there was no such thing as a coincidence. But Daddy used to say a lot of things—like, "I'll always be with you Danny." And he left.*

The bus jerked forward and Danny gratefully took a seat. It appeared Jamaal had run out of steam and decided to drive.

A sturdy, moderate-sized pop up tent in woodland camouflage cost much more than the $30 Danny had made that day. She stared at the array of tents in the sporting goods department at Wal-Mart and willed back tears.

Happy Stinkin' Birthday! That bitter thought gave Danny permission for more: *Happy Stinkin' Birthday and welcome to the pity-party! Poor Danny. Why is everything always so hard? What did she do to deserve this crummy life? Mom goes out to get ice cream and a movie and gets herself wrapped around a telephone pole. Dad shows up just in time to rescue her from becoming a ward of the state, only to leave, with no explanation, three months later. Fourteen years old, and the only safe place is in a dry-rotted old tent in a forgotten woods. And now the tent leaks.*

Danny piled grievance upon grievance with a growing sense of hopelessness pounding like the surf in her head. *What now? What now? What now?* was the chorus.

Anyone noticing the small, slightly unkempt looking girl staring with such intensity at a shelf of camping gear would wonder about the chaotic splotches of color blazing on her cheeks. They'd be concerned by the tremor shivering through her young frame, the tight fists balled at her side, and the painful glitter in her dark eyes. But no one noticed.

No one ever notices.

Danny greatly disliked feeling sorry for herself and now she knew why—giving in to a little self-pity dredged up even more. The dam was open now! Rage, betrayal, pain and loneliness— pick one...it was all there—all descending like an executioner's hood to blind her with fear. Hysteria was next she knew, and only the thought of becoming a babbling idiot in the middle of Wal-Mart helped her regain self control. Like an archer slowly releasing the tension on a bow, she consciously relaxed her clenched posture.

She was able to keep the tears from spilling over but nothing could keep her nose from running.

Great! The too-small side pocket of her overstuffed backpack contained tissue. She jammed a few fingers in and fished around with no luck before touching a hard wafer of something. Using her fingers as tweezers, she eventually worried the 'something' up from the string-filled pocket bottom where it had laid for so long. It was a rectangle of hard yellow plastic.

It was her father's ATM card.

There is money in that account! At least there was the last time I checked, she amended. The day Child Services knocked on the door the account balance was several hundred. *But I never stopped automatic bill pay so surely the account is empty. Probably...*

There was another, more chilling, possibility. *Probably, the police froze it! They must do that to the accounts of all missing persons.* The police discovered her dad was missing on the first day of school when school authorities reported her for showing up without records. *That's the day Dad became an 'official' missing person and I became an orphan.*

That was also the day Danny relinquished control of her life to Social Services. The Children's Services Division had been in charge of her life ever since.

She tried to remember if the police asked about bank records when they questioned her. *They asked a lot of questions. I gave very few answers.* Some answers Danny didn't have, but others she just didn't want to share. There was lots of stuff the authorities didn't know. *They don't know Dad really went missing in the Spring—and I was alone for the three months of summer. Why tell them? (I'm fine, after all.)*

They didn't know that Danny handled all the finances, at her father's insistence, or that the "Roy Smith" signature on all official papers was written in Danny's own hand at Roy Smith's insistence. She didn't tell the authorities any of this and the authorities didn't think to ask.

They don't know about this ATM Credit/Debit card either.

Maybe the money **was** still there and maybe it was still accessible—or maybe the account was being monitored and maybe using it would send the police Missing Persons Unit swooping down to haul Danny away.

The yellow ATM card felt hot in her hand.

*But how many times have officials told me I am too young to be responsible; that I'm only a minor? Okay then, what's the worst that could happen to a "minor"? They could take a "minor" from her home and her parents and put her in a home! Yeah, well, **that** already happened. What else? Put me behind bars. Nah! Throw a poor little orphan girl in jail?*

She would use the card.

A Big Green Money Machine squatted in the hallway near a bank of phones and a sign pointing to the Restrooms. Danny walked toward it, card in hand just as a group of giggling girls bumped out of the Ladies Room.

Danny waited for them to pass. Then she waited a while longer...

She offered the machine her father's card and was convinced it was gone forever when the machine gobbled it up. She waited, expecting the worst. Instead the machine beeped contently and displayed a familiar prompt. ENTER YOUR PIN Danny typed in the word her dad picked as a tribute to his wife's heritage: "Iroquois."

The tent box was large, unwieldy and completely filled the cart Danny pushed from the store. How was she going to carry all this on the bus? She tore open the box but had to dig through an enormous amount of packing material to locate all the pieces to the tent. *Why such a big box?* All the tent pieces fit neatly into an enclosed nylon bag that could then be secured to the metal frame of her new hiker's pack. She dumped the tent packing material in the closest blue and yellow trashcan.

Paper also stuffed the backpack, and each time Danny removed a wad she discovered a new nook or cranny—the thing was loaded with features. *Pockets!—what a luxury!* She assigned places for her new journal, flashlight, batteries, Swiss army knife, and water bottle. There was an insulated section where a whole box of crackers plus a big jar of peanut butter fit with room left over for a dozen granola bars— once they were out of their box.

With the boxes, wrappings, padding and Styrofoam gone, and the trashcan overflowing, Danny's purchases were now reduced to a size her 14-year-old self could handle.

One last thing! She reached inside the last small plastic bag and transferred its contents to the widest outside pocket of the backpack. *Happy Birthday to me...* she hummed, pleased that TWO crème-filled orange cupcakes — *Mom said its was good to have extra birthday cake...just in case someone extra shows up*—and a plastic bottle of Yoo-Hoo, fit inside so nicely.

Happy Birthday dear Dannyyy she hummed as the bus pulled to the curb and the door flopped open.

The bus was empty, its floor coated in slush and mud, but with the heater cranked up and air warm with the smell of wet wool, it felt both friendly and intimate. *How weird is that thought?* Shaking her head at her foolish high spirits, Danny scooted into a seat at the front of the bus with a view out the big front window and slung both backpack and tent on the seat adjacent—first removing her old battered journal to make a last entry on the very last page.

Today was like discovering that the horrid lump of Coal you see in your Christmas Stocking is really a lovely Chunk of Chocolate.

Finding her way back to the campsite was easy...too easy. *This camp needs to be better hidden if I want my stuff to still be here when I get back.* Moving her camp away from houses, paths and people just wouldn't be enough; she needed a spot no one would stumble on—a place that was truly hidden—if not for the tent at least for her possessions, (Danny didn't have much to lose; that's why it mattered so much).

*It would be easier to find a hiding place to stash the hikers pack...*and she could fill it with all the important stuff...*a little inconvenient, but it would work...*then she'd carry the rest of her things in the daypack. Thinking about what those things should be, she flipped aside the tent flap, stepped inside—and startled a thief!

Caught red-handed, the outraged raccoon stood up when Danny entered the tent.

With both little legs planted defiantly in the middle of a

jumble of once-orderly possessions and black, button eyes unrepentant behind its Zorro mask, the little 'coon was obviously less concerned with the intruder than in what it was doing.

What it was doing was eating.

One wrinkled, black hand protected a box of Sugar Pops as the other burrowed in the box, extracted a single sugary orb with nimble fingers, and delicately delivered it to a hungry little mouth. One at a time, two crunches per morsel—Danny's breakfast disappeared. Between chewing and swallowing, the bandit made funny, chirring sounds.

Danny noted the little animal's brazen, but unthreatening posture and listened for anger or fear in its odd language, (something between a cat's chesty purr and a monkey's high pitched chatter) and she detected no danger signs. *Just annoyed at my interruption.*

The visitor had small front quarters and a high bottom like a small bear, but the pointed nose and triangular face resembled a fox. *A gray fox wearing a black mask.* Danny had never been so close to a wild animal and immediately forgave the trespass—she even forgave the hole now gaping in the canvas tent. Signs of feasting and exploration were everywhere. *My visitor has been here awhile,* Danny thought as she bent her knees and lowered herself to a corner of the sleeping mat—all the while maintaining eye contact.

The raccoon cautiously watched the girl sit down. The freak snowstorm had started its desperate search for food—snow signaled winter—and survival depended on growing a nice thick padding of fat. Any food would do, but this particular food tasted mighty good!

Danny pulled her new backpack through the door and opened the wide middle pocket. Under her breath she hummed "Happy Birthday," delighted she'd bought that extra cake.

The little pointed ears swiveled toward the humming sound, fumbled its crunchy treat, and risked a look down. When it looked up again, the girl was holding a shiny shape—raccoons love all shiny things. Button eyes shifted from the girl to the thing in the girl's hands. When the girl pulled at the shape and it tore open with a crinkly-crackly sound, it released a smell so sweet and enticing the raccoon forgot the cereal and abruptly rocked back onto its ample bottom, nose quivering.

Danny carefully pushed the other packet of orange cupcakes toward her masked neighbor wondering what it would make of the unopened gift. She needn't have worried!

Two eager little hands immediately snatched the treat—still wrapped in cellophane—and adeptly ripped open the wrapper. The eyes returned to Danny's while those amazing hands, seeming to act independently, busily portioned chunks of Danny's birthday cake.

"I'm flattered you can't take your eyes off me but your mother should have taught you that staring is rude," Danny said companionably. "And just so you know, you aren't getting the other two cupcakes—it's **my** birthday you know—but I'm awfully glad you could make it."

Rosemary Cooney. That's what she'd christened the visiting raccoon and just thinking about the birthday snack they'd shared tickled Danny. Could anything could be cuter than watching Rosemary guzzle that Yoo-Hoo?! The raccoon had eagerly grabbed the offered bottle, clutched it to her chest and rolled to her back. Looking much like a baby with a bottle, she used feet and hands to control the drink. Tiny pink tongue darting like mad, Rosemary drained every drop of the chocolate drink.

By playing that scene over and over Danny could almost ignore the scene now in front of her.

It was just before sunset—6:30 to be exact—and *dinnertime at the Foster-Hole*. The time and the menu never varied: a Banquet frozen dinner, Wonder Bread, Tub Margarine and Coke. Danny was an unhappy participant. She sat in her designated folding chair—hands in her lap to keep them off the sticky table—watching the ash grow longer on her foster mother's cigarette. As Mrs. Laird handed out TV dinners the trembling ash toppled into Danny's mashed potato. This bothered no one but Danny.

The CSD social workers were impressed by the Laird's 'dinner hour' routine. Not only did it illustrate the stability and suitability of the Laird's as foster parents, it also made mandatory 'surprise' inspections easy to schedule. Mrs. Laird always answered the door between 6:30 and 7:15, even though her foster kids were usually away at part-time jobs or studying at the library. "That Mrs. Laird really instills a work ethic," the bureaucrats liked to say, "...and she can deal with anything! Even with that invalid husband to care for, we can always count on her to come through."

And so, CSD regularly sent Mrs. Laird the worst teenaged troublemakers—she had three in her care now. Well, really, two troublemakers, plus Danny. Danny was a special case—young and new to the system—but not afraid to cause the CSD problems by insisting she be placed within a certain school district. The only spot open was at the Laird's. Danny's caseworker told her supervisor that Mrs. Laird was at first reluctant to take the kid, "but once I explained the situation—was a real trooper about it. The woman is a saint."

Of course the children in the CSD house had a different take on the woman they called 'Lady Lard', and they'd briefed Danny before she left. Lady Lard, they said, would preside during dinner hour like a big, greasy frog. She'd have only an ashtray in front of her, and should you ask why she wasn't eating, would explain about her "special diet." But the real truth was she knew better than to eat the stuff the kids ate and kept her own private stash of delicacies such as potato chips and Ding Dongs.

When the CSD kids talked about Mister Lard, they whispered. Apparently SHE only let him out of his room at mandatory dinner hour. He was a big, hunched, flabby man in an old-fashioned wheelchair—blind as a bat and always really hungry—who constantly smacked big, rubbery lips while devouring anything anyone placed in front of him. "What ever you do," Danny was warned, "keep away from his mouth!"

Well, so far the CSD kids have been right about everything. Danny thought trying NOT to look at the spot where all the grunts and eating sounds were coming from. She picked around the cigarette ash and poked at the mystery meat, and wondered about the other two foster kids the caseworker said were part of the Laird home. Danny had seen no evidence of them in the weeks since she'd arrived. *Maybe Mr. Lard ate them.*

Danny smiled.

Mrs. Laird, deep in the sinkhole of her living room couch, was not pleased when the doorbell rang. Dinner hour was over so it couldn't be anyone from CSD and her program was on TV, so she called out "Donna! Donna! Where are you girl? Donna, someone's at the door! Tell them to go away!" Mrs. Laird shouted loud enough for either the new girl to hear her and act, or the person behind the door to hear her and go away.

It took Danny awhile to respond—Donna wasn't her name after all—but once she became conscious of the hesitant knocking on the front door she understood the Laird summons. Closing her science book with a sigh she went to the door.

The young, stringy postman was startled when the door opened. It was his first day on the job and he was running 2 ½ hours behind. He'd already decided no one was going to answer and had begun filling out a "sorry we missed you" slip for the small registered package he held in his hand. He frowned down at the owl-eyed girl looking up at him from the doorway and hesitated. "I...I have a signature required package for a Miss Danny Smith."

Danny blinked in surprise when the stranger called her by name, before realizing he was reading the name on the package. "That's me!" She reached out, heart beating faster. *Who knows I am here? Could it be from my father?*

Again the postman hesitated. Since she seemed awfully young to be receiving a registered package he probably should ask for ID or ask to speak to her mother or something, but this was the last stop of a confusing day and, besides, he wanted to get away from the nasty smells coming from the opened door. The odor reminded him of old socks, institutional gravy and cigarette smoke and, if he didn't get away, it would surely ruin the dinner his mom had waiting for him at home. He gestured to the clipboard. "Sign here."

Danny, almost sick with excitement, signed her name and accepted the mysterious, oddly-wrapped box along with a handful of Laird mail. She would wait until she was alone before opening it, in case Mrs. Lard had questions. Stuffing the box into the backpack open on the floor next to her textbook, she moved directly into the smoke-filled Laird lair. "It was the mailman and he dropped off the mail," Danny offered a handful of envelopes and sale flyers to the figure nesting on the couch. When there was no response, she moved aside a few candy bar wrappers and stacked the mail on the coffee table before turning away.

"Goodnight," she muttered.

Mrs. Laird barely looked up. She resented interruptions when her shows were on. Just now it was reveal time on Extreme Makeover, and she never missed an episode.

The night was muggy and the ground spongy with the memory of snow. On another evening such as this, Danny might have lingered in the darkness to drink in the forest sounds and night smells; but tonight was very different. *I have a package!* She thought she could feel the outline of it riding in her backpack between textbooks and notebooks.

This night Danny hadn't tried to sneak away from the Laird's. *Why bother? I can just walk right out.* It was increasingly obvious that leaving was what foster kids assigned to the Laird's did—and that Mrs. Laird both expected and encouraged them to do just that. As long as the checks from CSD continued uninterrupted, the woman had no problem covering for any absences.

Danny unzipped the door flap of her new tent—*way better than those old buttons*—as well as the extra heavy zipper on the blackout insert that was supposed to seal out the cold and seal in the light. She made certain all openings were closed tightly against both the night and her friend Rosemary Cooney before firing up the Coleman camping lamp. The propane light bathed her home in a warm, yellow glow that felt both cozy and safe.

But the 'safe' part was an illusion, Danny knew.

Trespassing is against the law, and sleeping in the rough can be dangerous. Safety for Danny lay in being invisible but any amount of light announces itself in the darkness and any out of place sound echoes like a shout. She'd heard her father talk with his friend Red about how showing any light or making any sound even in the heavy jungles of Vietnam could get you shot. With that in mind, Danny's new campsite was tucked in a small sheltering fold of land well off the regular path. She couldn't do anything about using her flashlight to get through the woods to the campsite but at least, once inside the tent, she was invisible.

Now all that mattered was the package. *What is it? Who is it from? Is it from Daddy?*

Later, Danny wrote:

So, a guy says to his doctor, "Doc, it hurts when I do this." And the doctor says,"Well—don't DO that."

It was like that with the package. I know I'm not going to hear from my dad. I know that even if he is alive, he doesn't know where I am. But I keep hoping. I keep pressing on the place where it hurts.

The package was from Dad's friend Red. It was a belated Birthday present and...Surprise! I now have a cell phone!

Though I'm really happy with the present, I feel pretty bad that I haven't thought about Red at all! He says he's keeping an eye on the camper Dad and I lived in. Says it's overgrown with weeds, but all the stuff inside still works. The card says Red thinks about me and Dad a lot,

That is SO weird, because we never really talked or anything. Red was like this real big Viking-kind-of-guy that never said Boo. He was an old Army buddy of my dad's and we lived on his land, so they must have been very good friends even though I seldom heard them really talk. How did Red know it was my birthday? How did he know the address?

The note says the phone is fully charged and a few important numbers are programmed in. He says I have loads of minutes and says I should call and leave a message if I ever need anything.

So how about that? I'm connected again! Back before Mom was killed, I was always plugged in and text-ing or IM-ing my friends. I couldn't have imagined life without a cell phone, internet connection, and iPod. My friends! We had so much important stuff to talk about back then...discussing plans and dreams and school and music. Now I can't remember any of their numbers or online names. Not that we'd have anything to talk about anyway. But still, just having this phone makes me feel less alone...thanks Red.

Gosh, it is cold out tonight. I don't know how many more nights I will be sleeping out here even though I can't imagine sleeping THERE!

Brrr! I need a plan.

DECISIONS

The little raccoon didn't know its name was 'Rosemary' but the sound of that word woke her from her deep, almost-winter doze. Her pointed ears sprung from their tightly curled sleeping position to begin tracking the sound; she was trying to decide if getting up was really necessary...

Danny called again, "Rosemary! Rosemary Cooooney! Where are you?" Taking advantage of the hour of daylight before the school bus arrived, she'd return to the original campsite and picked up the raccoon's trail, hoping to track the home invader back to its den.

Another unseasonably cold morning in the woods. Weak autumn sunlight strained through tree branches as night lingered in the undergrowth.

Making her way through clouds made by her own exhalations, Danny scanned the ground in search of the distinctive hand and foot prints of a raccoon. *I can do this! The Iroquois tracked animals for many miles, across any surface, in any weather, and my mother was Iroquois.* The pep talk boosted her confidence until she thought: *Mom always got lost!* Her mother would get so lost she'd just give up and head home. *That happened a lot...*

Eyes moist with memories, she climbed over and under several fallen logs before she realized she was now following a heavily trafficked game trail. *Didn't know **this** was here! Look at all those tracks!* She knelt to examine the path. Cut wide, it ran straight until it disappeared into forest shadows. Dirt had been churned to mud by the split hooves of many deer and then had frozen into choppy peaks. The most recent animal to pass had flattened the peaks. *Gotcha!* Raccoon prints overlaid those of deer.

"Roseemaryyy!" Danny called.

Not far away the tidy fur donut reluctantly unfurled itself and poked its black nose out of the sleeping chamber into the frosted morning air. Rosemary took a good, long, sniff.

Head down, now hot on the trail, the master tracker nearly walked headlong into a tangle of vines, trees and undergrowth— an obstacle so impenetrable and unexpected it was like a wall built in the middle of a busy street. *Wow!* she thought. *I bet every animal in these woods lives in that thicket!*

She faced knotted vegetation of roping loops and snarls of vine and bramble that offered no passage for a human—even one as small as Danny. *The stuff goes straight to the top of the oak trees...maybe 70 feet...and some of those vines are as big around as Dad's forearms!* The sight triggered a forgotten memory of a peculiar place in the woods her father had once shown her...

They'd been hiking in some southern state and stopped to look down into a ravine, and into a landscape of shaggy, undulating, deep green leaves. "What happened to the trees?" Danny had asked.

"Oh, they're there alright, under a blanket of Kudzu vines...although they're probably dead by now." Her father replied, "Some people call Kudzu the 'Wait-A-Minute Vine' because it grows so darn fast and is so aggressive. The stuff suffocates all the other vegetation by covering it over and stealing away all light and nutrients. Give it time, it can swallow towns— and it's moving north."

Could this be Kudzu? Danny now wondered and tried the word out loud: "Kud-Zoo". Scary stuff, but she liked how the word sounded.

Defeated by the vines but convinced Rosemary was close by— probably watching—Danny took a tin-foil wrapped bundle from her parka pocket and spread it out near the path. "Bon Appetit!" she whispered, before turning away to catch the school bus.

Food! Rosemary sniffed, and clattered out of her hole in the oak tree.

Help. Danny needed help. Every time she figured out one thing, another thing came along to overwhelm her! The temperature, hovering in the upper thirties, was expected to drop to below freezing and stay there for the rest of the week. And life just kept getting harder...

The library was closing for two weeks for 'light renovation' starting today. That meant fourteen days with no computer access and no where warm to escape after school. She had even tried to call Red, but only received an away message.

What to do? I have homework. Perhaps the Laird's was the only option. She recalled her first tour of the foster home; the case worker had dutifully pointed out a dinosaur Pentium computer and ancient dot-matrix printer and said "Mrs. Laird set this up just for her fosters to use; of course there is no internet."

Of course.

With a heavy heart. she used the key Mrs. Laird had given her. *No choice! Well at least she keeps it warm.* Hot, smelly air greeted her as she opened the door and reluctantly entered

A day that ended with being trapped by time and circumstances in a nasty house with an evil woman and a slimy toad of a man couldn't get much worse—until it did. One of the missing Laird foster kids had returned. The foster had reclaimed 'his' lumpy bed and rickety dresser and evicted Danny from the closet of a room she'd been using. She would have to sleep on the third floor—in what Mrs. Laird called 'the dormitory'.

Danny called it the attic.

With sleeping bag, backpack and the one small suitcase from her room, negotiating the rickety stairs was tricky. *I wonder if Lady Lard-Butt's ever even been up here,* she thought sourly. At the top of the stairs the door creaked open with only a slight push—the latch was broken—to reveal a dusty, peeked, hall of a room. A bare bulb hung from the ceiling. She pulled the cord, fearing the worst. The dim light revealed a narrow aisle flanked by two sets of metal bunk bed frames wedged under open rafters. Eight beds. A single mattress. Nothing else.

I think I've read this fairytale.

Danny tried the thin mattress on every bunk, hoping to find one that was somewhat comfortable. *No luck. This will be much worse than sleeping on the frozen ground.* With a sigh, she turned off the light, wrapped up tight—grateful for the padding of her sleeping bag—and closed her eyes thinking, *it just keeps getting better...*

Indeed.

The sounds started the second the lights went out and quickly increased in volume and audacity. Soon unknown, unseen, creatures scurried, romped and chewed around her. Aggravated, Danny struggled to sit up and pull the light chain. Under the swaying bulb the room danced with lurking, leaping, shadows. *Just mice,* she confirmed, turned off the light and burrowed deeper into the bag—making sure her face, and ears, were covered. She willed herself to sleep...

But the attic's occupants were in a partying mood, and the primary game appeared to be 'tag'. When something bounded over Danny's legs she was forced to move to the top bunk where the biggest worry was cracking her head on the low beams. It was a very long, very noisy night. Each time a cold draft swept up the stairs the attic door creaked open; there was no way to keep it closed.

No lock. Nothing is safe.

She considered this situation in school the next day as she huddled as close as possible to the warm radiator. When she returned to the Laird's she wasn't too surprised to discover she'd been ripped off. Gone were her sleeping bag and her flashlight, both necessary for visits to the camp. She knew who had taken them...the creepy kid downstairs. No way would she confront him; at least not directly.

"Call me Oxo" wasn't the sharpest knife in the foster drawer, but he didn't know that. Danny wondered how it was that a boy named after a bouillon cube could have such a high opinion of himself!

Oxo's eyebrow was swollen and red from his most recent piercing, a gold-colored double-ring. His grimy hands fingered the sore spot for what must have been the hundredth time since sitting down to dinner. *Gross!* Danny thought, *Maybe infection will take care of my problem and his whole face will just rot off.*

The boy used a handful of Wonder bread thickly coated with bright yellow margarine to mop up every bit of mystery juice caught in the pleated foil of the TV dinner's tray. When he glanced up and caught Danny watching him he slid back his chair without a word and stomped out.

Good. Mrs. Laird and Danny both thought...*he's gone!*

Mrs. Laird had already fired up a cigarette, broken open a new bag of Cheese Doodles and settled herself deep in the couch by the time Danny had fiddled open the lock to her former room.

It certainly is Oxo's room now.

She stood in the doorway and surveyed the squalor—a little impressed that in less than two days Oxo had managed to make so much of a mess! Where did he find enough clothing to build a pile that high? She spotted her red sleeping bag— still neatly rolled—tossed in the corner. Obviously, Oxo hadn't taken it to use. *He took it for spite.*

Angrily wading into the mess, she snatched it up, tossed it into the hallway then stood, hands on hips, *now where is the flashlight?* In her estimation, the self-powered LED light with its bright yellow, waterproof body was a must-have for traveling through the gloom of the woods—even in the daytime.

And it was a gift from her father.

A tangle of blankets, sheets and pillows covered Oxo's bed. An upturned box, piled high with food wrappers, loose change and abused looking comic books, served as a side table. On the floor beneath a dingy pair of grey sweatpants, peeked a familiar yellow object. The slightly sour smell of unwashed skin made her nose wrinkle as she bent for further inspection.

It was the flashlight alright—underneath the nasty sweatpants and sandwiched between the pages of a ratty comic book. Handling the pants like a dirty diaper she slung them aside to reveal both the flashlight and the front page of a comic. The artwork on the shiny paper made her stop and gape...

Bizarre! The cover seemed to actually be alive; the characters were woven together in such a way they appeared to move. *Some kind of optical illusion?* She picked it up for a better look and some clue to its origin.

There was no title; in fact there appeared to be no words at all. She ruffled the ragged pages. *I've never seen anything like this before.* Flipping it over to the last page where she expected to find publishing information she instead found color, energy and visual trickery that made the action practically leap off the page...

Two brawny men—one dark-skinned, one blonde-haired and

> one young, confident Girl, confront a huge, drooling, grasping monster. A hopeless situation, until the Girl takes to the air to buzz like a mosquito around the beast's head repeatedly stinging it with a small whip. Distracted, the monster swats at the irritant; and the men attack.

It was like being ringside, the battle so fast and exhilarating Danny actually cheered when the good guys won. Wanting more, this time she started from the beginning...

> Page one: a series of disconnected scenes. First frames picture a dark skinned guy looking sad and lonely from in a crowded subway train. Next is a series of frames featuring a defeated-looking blonde man gassing up a broken-down car. The last frames depict a ballet class viewed through a plate glass window; a girl inside does ballet very, very badly and her classmates snicker.

Huh. Danny's own mother had insisted on dance classes and now she wondered if the other girls had made fun of her too; she'd been just as clumsy. She was tough and strong, but not one bit graceful. Thoughtful, she turned the page. *Wow!*

> A two-page spread screaming with lashes of bright color, flying bodies and billowing smoke! The character in the subway is buried beneath a collapsing building; the man at the gas pump is shot by a sniper; a car bomb blows out the window into the ballet class.

Random, unexpected, undeserved disaster was something Danny understood. Without thinking she dropped to the edge of the saggy little bed and turned the page, completely caught up in the story...

> The three storylines continue, separate but parallel. Each character manages to struggle free—alive but badly damaged. All three end up in hospital—all in wheelchairs. Each of them is alone, miserable and blankly staring from their individual hospital windows.

The old man I saw the day it snowed looked just like that...

> The next page. A doctor's office.

Or it could be a gym...there's a piece of something that looks like exercise equipment in the corner. It's a little hard to tell without any words.

The guys meet and it is soon apparent they are in Physical Therapy struggling to regain the use of their legs. They are rivals; competing to grow stronger more quickly than the other. By the second page the rivalry warms to friendship.

One of those cosmic, comic-book bonds! But isn't the Girl part of this too? She turned the page...

The two wounded weaklings can walk! Now they concentrate on building themselves into bulging men of steel. They succeed. And at the end of the next page hold up their right hands in front of a Superman emblem.

Okay. Great. They pledge to fight evil and injustice. So? Where is the Girl?

The next pages are about the Girl. Her wheelchair is pushed by a smiling mother and father headed for the same building the men are training in. It's a pleasant spring day and the three seem to be enjoying one another's company as they cross the street.

Huh. So finally, the Girl gets in on the act. Turning the page, Danny squeaked in surprise.

A bus heads directly for the crosswalk and the family! A violent, color saturated, page of graphic chaos follows, as the Girl and her parents fly head over heels in the air. The last frames are of the mother and father lying next to an empty wheelchair. No sign of the Girl.

Danny could almost hear the family's screams as she stared down at the broken bodies. *What happened to the Girl?* She opened to the next page and found....nothing...the story skipped right to the battle with the monster. *Where is the rest of the story?* Holding the scrap of magazine to the dim light in the jumbled bedroom she could now see that a handful of pages had been ripped out. *Super! A story with a beginning and an end but no middle.* Bothered—and disgusted with herself for being bothered—she dropped the ragged pages, grabbed the flashlight and headed for the door. *Comic books! A sad excuse for literature.*

But something about the story had touched a chord and her thoughts kept circling back to the startling series of accidents on the opening pages. An event could change a boring, annoying day into a never-to-be-forgotten one.

Life is like that. A person turns the page and gets hit by a bus.

Danny turned for a last look at Oxo's meager pile of possessions. *Pathetic. Kids in the system usually don't have much, and if they do they don't have it for long.* Originally she'd planned retaliation—thought she'd steal something of Oxo's...or cut the bottoms out of all his underwear...even deface his Metallica T-shirt—but somewhere along the way she'd lost her taste for revenge. She figured Oxo knew, as well as she did, what it was like to find disaster lurking around the corner.

She softly closed the door. *I'll leave it alone,* she decided, *but I won't give him another chance to snag my stuff...*

Tonight she would move into the woods for good.

NO EXPERIENCE NECESSARY

The sounds the woods makes at night are the soundtrack of my new world; I don't yet know the words...but I like the tune.

I really thought I was lost last night. Maybe I hid my campsite TOO well. I did a whole lot of stumbling along even using the compass AND the flashlight! Then this morning, I guess I forgot how much mud I'd stumbled in and I just went off the school. The backside of my shirt and jeans were bad enough for Mister Runda to say something about it. I told him I'd slipped down a slope on the way to the bus stop, but I know he suspects me of being in a fight! Gotta watch out. These teachers are super quick to report any and all kinds of stuff to child services. I don't want any more of that kind of 'help' and 'concern'!

I have a book report due next week. Since I don't have access to a computer, I am actually going to write it out longhand. Weird, I know! If I didn't keep this journal I probably would even remember HOW to do that! I hope Ms. Nassar, who is from India, knows how to read my handwriting. I'll be the only person in class not turning in the report electronically.

Tomorrow is Friday and the start of the three day weekend. I don't know what I will do with myself if it rains and I am stuck in this tent, but if it is sunny I plan to explore. It would be nice to have someone to visit. I can't figure out why Red sent me this phone and programmed in his number but then never answers the darn thing!

My freshly cranked and recharged flashlight should stay lit until I finish reading this book, even though it's not the best light for reading. At least it's warm in here and nothing is scurrying around.

I am not planning on going back to the Laird's, EVER if I can manage. I left a note in the bedroom I was sleeping in, just on the off chance someone might miss me enough to come looking. The note says I'm staying with a girlfriend and can be reached at her house, and I included this cell phone number. I've programmed voice mail to use the pre-recorded robot voice greeting: "After the beep, leave a message", so a caller won't know they reached a cell phone. Sheer Genius!

The paper taped to the side of the bank of townhouse mailboxes was dry and crisp, so it couldn't have been there long. Danny noticed it as she waited for the school bus to arrive, standing back from the curb to avoid the blackened slush. It was the Friday before a three day weekend. As usual she was alone at the bus stop, but knew that as soon as the bus pulled around the corner, seven front doors would open and seven middle schoolers would bound toward her and somehow manage to get on the bus before her. The fact that she'd probably have to share a narrow bus bench with 300 pounds of gum-cracking Leo Peel and his raging BO didn't cross her mind as she read the paper taped to the mailbox...

No experience necessary!!

Invalid needs Companion

Flexible hours. Light duties.

Contact Beatrice Renee Smith at 305-688-3771

...Danny's reaction was immediate. *A job!* Her hand shot out and she ripped the notice down, furtively cramming it into her coat pocket just as the slush-caked yellow school bus rounded the corner and her rushing schoolmates shoved their way to the front.

The hulking, snuffling Leo Peel was nowhere to be found and somehow Danny scored a seat on her own, a window seat near the front of the bus. It was shaping up to be a very special day. *A job!* She pulled the crumpled job announcement out to take a good look.

Invalid? Caring for an invalid? Uh-oh. But, just so no blood or poop was involved she guessed she could manage. *Flexible hours?* Would she be expected to be a live-in nurse? Danny was thinking she might have been a bit hasty to celebrate, when she saw the name, Beatrice Rene Smith and thought of something else. *Could the invalid possibly be the Al Smith that crazy bus driver went on and on about?* She thought she remembered some mention of a daughter. If Al Smith was the invalid AND if the invalid was the same person as the man she'd seen on the deck, then he didn't look too sick. Danny had a great deal of confidence in her own abilities to handle most things. She could certainly handle an old man in a wheelchair.

She examined the telephone number. *Not a local area code.* 305 was Florida she thought, remembering a long ago vacation to Disneyworld.

Perhaps Ms. Beatrice Renee Smith lived in Florida and was visiting her dad and using her cell phone number. She'd soon find out. She imagined lots of people would be interested in the job and the minute she got off the bus...before going in the building...she would call.

But that's not what happened.

As the bus pulled up to the school, a particularly self-important boy named Paul was waiting at the curb. Danny busily got her things together and didn't think much of it. The bright orange strap crossing his waist and pigeon chest signified that Paul was a School Safety Guard— a designation about as common as dirt in her school—but when the door sighed open pigeon-chested Paul blocked the exit.

A collective groan went up as Paul announced with as much authority as he could muster, "Good Morning!" He stepped aside and gestured to the open double doors of the school, "Please exit the bus in a brisk and orderly fashion and proceed directly to the auditorium for an assembly. We have important visitors today and expect good behavior. Hurry please! You are the last bus."

Beatrice Renee Smith— who was indeed from Florida— was right now freezing her well-toned backside off, while pacing the small kitchen of her father's townhouse. She hated it here and always had. Only a dim sense of duty had brought Beatrice back a week after a Convalescent Care Facility staffer had notified her that father's course of Physical Therapy was up and that he had been returned to his home.

It was up to her to sort out the life of a man who had been a stranger to her growing up. She didn't think that was fair, especially since she was in the middle of a big business deal and needed to get back to work before her subordinates messed things. In fact, she thought, the situation was so critical that she needed to leave right away. She reached for the telephone and called the airline...

Once the new flight reservations were made for that evening, Beatrice felt calm enough to take another look at her father's situation.

The old man had recovered very well from the stroke he had suffered last season. He had gotten all his upper body, and a large degree of his lower body, strength back. He used a wheelchair, but standing, and even taking a few steps, was in his power. Since the kitchen, the bathroom and a television were all accessible, he could pretty much take care of himself.

When she arrived yesterday she had assessed the situation. The best thing for him was a nursing home, but he had actually growled at her when she had mentioned that. It was a very expensive option, so she would make the best of the current situation. If he was to live on the ground floor he would need a proper bed and not the sofa he now slept on.

A daybed was delivered and the old sofa was removed about the time Beatrice was finishing making up a standard weekly grocery list. She placed a standing order online with a grocery store that guaranteed it would deliver the same order every Monday, and charge it to Beatrice's credit card. She had no idea what her father liked to eat— and thought it pointless to ask since the one thing he hadn't recovered after the stroke was his ability to speak— so she made the grocery list up to her own tastes.

If Beatrice paused for a moment in the cleaning and sorting of her childhood home, she might admire the irony of Al Smith being struck mute. The voice was what she knew best about her father.

Growing up, she seldom saw the man himself...he worked long and hard hours...but every night she'd listen intently for the low rumble of his voice signaling Daddy was home and all was safe.

Mother didn't like it if her father's friends dropped by— so it was rare—and always took place in the basement. This delighted young Beatrice who would listen to every word by putting her ear to the heat register in the bathroom. She'd sit there for hours, listening the men's hunting and fishing stories. Her Dad told the best ones. The long, involved, outrageous tales told in his rich, deep, confident voice made her want to beg him to please, please take her on his next adventure, even though she was just a girl!

But Beatrice didn't stop to think about any of this. What's done is done, what's passed is past, was her motto. The house was a real mess, and while efficiently putting things to right, her mind was on the campaign she was working on back in Florida.

Before long the carpets were vacuumed, the dishes put away, the counters scrubbed and the bathrooms cleaned and restocked. She then used her laptop computer to order her father some new yellow pajamas...she didn't know that he didn't wear pajamas or that he despised the color yellow...then paused her mindless activity to consider the laptop itself.

Her father owned a computer. It was in the study upstairs. That meant he probably understood email and web surfing at least a bit. *That's it!* she thought, *he needs a laptop computer! That way he can communicate by keyboard. If he needs help he can use the internet to type for help, and even, if absolutely necessary, he can contact me! Brilliant!*

Ever efficient, Beatrice placed a rush order for a fully loaded laptop with wireless capabilities. The web store guaranteed delivery within the week. She wore a self-congratulatory smile when she went upstairs to pack for her flight.

In the living room, with a bed in it now instead of a couch, Al heard Beatrice head for the stairs; he saw her smug smile. Savagely he turned up the volume on the television set hoping to drown out the sound of his own voice screaming inside his head.

He shouted at the cold, efficient woman who had once been his ideal of a daughter, in silence.

My little Bea would never dismiss me the way this Beatrice-person does! Where once there was meekness, now there was bossiness. Black silk had replaced the pink ruffles, and the child he had cherished was now a stranger prancing around HIS house rearranging things, and planning his life!

Al thought his head would explode with the sheer buildup of words unspoken. All he could do was increase his grip on the arms of the wheelchair and emit a low furious growl. He remembered all the double shifts he'd worked to get his daughter through college and now she acted as though he were invisible! She obviously thought his mind had disappeared with his voice.

He couldn't tell her otherwise.

Packing, Beatrice realized no one had yet called to answer the signs she had posted. Not good. The old man definitely needed someone to check in on him from time to time, if only to make sure he was alive. Hospice care through the state was out of the question since he wasn't yet sick enough. She could think of no charity to petition for help and her father had never had time for church. His insurance wouldn't cover visits by a health professional. And SHE certainly didn't feel obligated to foot the bill for professional care!

Zipping her suit bag closed, Beatrice came to a decision. She would wait a while longer before advertising in the newspaper; after all, the signs had only gone up yesterday. Ideally, she should meet any potential employees face to face but as she'd often heard her father tell his buddies, 'desperate times call for desperate measures!' She'd interview potential hires over the cell phone and trust her instincts. There really wasn't much in this house to steal, except the new laptop, so when she got to Florida she would arrange to have the thing lock-mounted onto her father's wheelchair.

It was time to go.

Al watched with relief as Beatrice walked out of his life. Just as she was about to close the door she paused and returned to him. Leaning down, she lightly kissed his forehead. She had never done that before.

"I almost forgot" she said and dropped a folded note into his lap. The taxi driver blew his horn and Beatrice rushed out the door.

The sound of the horn seemed to hang in the air, reverberating long after his daughter was gone. Al thought it sounded important, like the end of something...or maybe it was the beginning.

Danny started dialing the minute the long, long school day ended. She was too anxious to even think about what she would say to a prospective employer.

As things like this sometimes happen, she was not the first to make that call. She wasn't the second either. She was third and the phone rang and rang before switching over to voice mail. With a sinking heart, Danny hung up without leaving a message. She boarded the bus for home, vowing to call again once she was tucked into her sleeping bag. It was cold again, the autumn sun already sliding low into the sky. Danny shivered.

It was almost as cold as Beatrice Renee Smith's voice mail greeting.

Beatrice was feeling immensely pleased with herself as she left the meeting. So far all of today's decisions, from leaving her fathers home earlier than originally planned to calling an impromptu meeting at the airport lounge directly upon her return, had been the right ones. The meeting had confirmed her suspicions that she couldn't trust her colleagues to handle a project correctly while she was out of town. Beatrice was secretly delighted by the mess her coworkers had made of things while she had been gone.

Enjoying the satisfaction of being indispensable, she relaxed into the plush leather seat of the airport limousine and picked up her cell phone. The screen showed the most recently missed call. It was from an unknown number with her father's area code. More good news, this call would have to be the answer to the nagging problem of what to do with Dad.

Beatrice pressed the callback key and just knew the good luck she'd had all day would hold. As the cell signal bounced through four states, over two lakes and a mountain range to finally ring in a tent in the woods, Beatrice was smiling.

Danny was just getting ready to dial and stood, phone in hand, thinking over what she should say if she was again connected to voicemail, when the phone vibrated. Startled, certain she'd been electrocuted, she dropped the little phone with a squeak.

The call from Florida was Danny's first on the new phone and it was nothing like the one she and her mother had once shared. Watching the odd little phone skip and wiggle in the leaves where she'd dropped it, Danny took several wide-eyed seconds to connect its antics with an incoming call. She knelt to snatch it up and then fumbled to flip it open.

"Hel...hello?" she stammered.

"Yes. This is Ms. Beatrice Renee Smith returning your call..."

Danny felt caught and—like a kid with a hand in the cookie jar—panicky. *How did she know I called? I didn't leave any message. How did she find me?*

"...or should I say, returning a call made from this number. Did you or someone else at this number make a call to 305-688-3771?

"Yes...um...yes," Danny struggled to reply. "I made the call about flexible hours and light duties..." *What am I SAYING? I must sound like a complete idiot!*

"Yes, yes. I believe that is what the notice said. I am looking for someone to periodically look in on my father who has recently begun to use a wheelchair. I am looking for a dependable individual to give him a bit of help around the household for a few hours on weekdays." Beatrice paused her recitation.

Danny thought furiously of what she could possibly say to convince this official-sounding woman that she was the one for the job. All she could come up with was a line some anonymous butler said to his rich employer on a long-ago television show. She tried to bite back the words but it was too late, they came spinning out complete with some weird English type accent... "Very well Madam", Danny said, wincing back a hysterical giggle.

The voice had also begun to speak but Danny's word's stopped it cold. The line went silent.

Oh no! thought Danny. *What have I done??*

Beatrice couldn't believe what she was hearing. Was this person making FUN of her, or perhaps trivializing the important duties she was requesting be performed?

Scrambling to repair the obvious damage Danny babbled into the growing silence, "I mean, OF COURSE. I am very dependable and I really like wheelchairs and ..."

Not making fun, Beatrice decided, and immediately calmed down. She was just talking to some silly kid! Her voice sharpened, "How old ARE you young lady? This isn't a position for a child, you understand."

Beatrice was good at using her voice as a weapon and right now that weapon was aimed squarely at the voice on the phone. But she didn't want to shut the door completely, reasoning that, if the girl was not TOO young, she could certainly offer her much less money than originally planned.... "There will be some housekeeping duties involved."

Truth would probably lose her the job; to lie was wrong and what if the lady wanted to meet her face to face? Danny knew that while she acted much older than her peers, she looked younger. *Fourteen IS mighty young.*

Danny decided to take the middle ground, and use misinformation. "I just moved into the area, and I just started at Roosevelt." *Good answer!,* she told herself, and gave her back a mental pat. While it was true she HAD just started at Roosevelt, it was the brand new <u>Theodore Roosevelt Middle School</u>, **not**, as she knew Beatrice would think, the prestigious <u>Eleanor Roosevelt High School</u>.

Danny was pretty sure she had just outsmarted an adult.

Well, if she just started at Roosevelt then she's about 16. And she is smart, since Roosevelt only takes the top percentile of High School students, Beatrice considered... She had once employed a ten year old neighbor child to dog-sit and both she and her little poodle had been quite happy with THAT arrangement. This girl sounded mature... Sixteen was old enough...but perhaps she should speak to the girl's mother or something...although, if she did that, the mother probably would expect her to pay the little darling quite extravagantly...which would not be good business...so...*talking to the mother is out.*

The girl obviously wanted the job so much Beatrice knew she had her on the run. She'd need to act quickly so as not to lose momentum.

"I'll give you eight an hour for a minimum of ten hours a week", Beatrice said decisively. "My father will keep track of your hours and write you a check at the end of the month. He will also let me know if there are problems, so I expect you to earn that money,"

Danny stopped just short of shouting *Yes, Yes, Yes!* and considered what the woman was offering. *Less than minimum wage for just ten hours a week isn't much, but it is more than I have now.* Since a person had to be at least 15 years old in the state, AND have parental permission to take a salaried job, Danny didn't have any alternatives. She again surprised herself...

"Nine and it's a deal. My name is Daniela, by the way."

Danny wrote:

Living is an oasis in the desert of life.

Maybe for the very first time I made something happen! Before now, life just kept happening to me, and most of it was bad. Today though, I used my own phone to call about a job I found. I spoke to a very businesslike lady AND I said some really smart things (okay I said some really dumb things first) but in the end, I was HIRED! Hurray! Hurrah!

Tomorrow after school I go to 11314 Harvest Court and meet Mr. Al Smith. I get paid $9 an hour to help around the house and to sort of fetch stuff if Mr. Smith needs something from the upstairs or the downstairs since he is in a wheelchair.

Fetch and carry is no problem.

The La-Di-Dah daughter was clear that I'm not being paid to make nice, just to help out. That's a good thing because I don't need any people in my life to worry about, and I don't want any adults around at all if I can help it. Mom always said "the apple doesn't fall too far from the tree" so Mr. Smith is probably as horrible as his daughter, even though I remember the bus driver talking about him like he was great company.

I do have one big problem to solve. I am getting paid by check. How will I cash it?

Al was having a very bad day. He had already answered the door twice and received nasty surprises. The first visitor was a man delivering groceries who insisted on coming in and putting everything away.

The second visitor wore a baseball hat that said GEEK. The Geek cheerfully informed Al that he would have to move out of his wheelchair so the Geek could fit the mount and plug to accommodate a new portable laptop computer.

Al knew all of this nonsense was his daughters doing, and his jaw clenched with unvoiced rage, even as groceries he didn't want were put on the wrong shelves, and even as the Geek guy insisted on nearly twisting his arm out of the socket while attempting to help him out of his wheelchair.

From the new perspective of sitting on the horrible daybed-couch contraption, he spied the forgotten note Beatrice had dropped on his lap when leaving. He figured he'd better open it if only to avoid any more nasty surprises. Sure enough, Beatrice had laid out everything in her careful script.

Daddy,

I have arranged to have groceries delivered once a week. Please let the delivery man in.

You can also expect the Geeks to Go people to come by to deliver your new laptop. I've asked them to attach it to the wheelchair for security purposes. Email me: BeatriceReneSmith@nonprofit.com if you need anything.

I have engaged a companion to stop by on a

regular basis. Please expect this companion to clean up around the house, retrieve the mail and shovel your walk should you need it. Keep track of the hours worked and let me know by email. I will send a check for you to present at the end of each month.

Your Dutiful Daughter,

Beatrice

By the time the Geek had finished inflicting Beatrice's wishes on Al, it was well past noon. Al was asleep, his head lolled back into the sea of pillows on the daybed. The Geek knew his job wasn't actually completed until everything was put back the way he found it, so he woke up the old man and wrestled him back into the wheelchair. Then he left as fast as he could, wondering why a guy with such a cool new setup had growled at him!

Before Beatrice's visit, Al hadn't really missed being able to talk. Now he suspected that was because he hadn't really had anything to say; he certainly wanted to talk now. Oh yes! He wanted to shout. He wanted to rail against what his world had become!

If my head explodes right now, words will splatter everywhere, and that might be a relief, Al told himself. *My frozen vocal chords have made me a victim, and that's a role I've never before played. I don't like it. So how do I tell someone to go away and leave me alone if I can't use words? Maybe I should kick them in the butt! At least that would make me feel better.*

The tension eased as Al imagined his work boot making contact with the posterior of the gawky Geek guy and shoving him out the door and down the steps. For the first time in a very long time, Al smiled.

The doorbell rang.

The door burst open and Danny was confronted by a tall, gray-haired man whose ice blue eyes were folded deep into a hard, craggy face. The figure stood, one shaking blue veined hand clutching the arm of a wheelchair for support.

The man's whole frame vibrated with what appeared to be pure, volcanic, rage.

I'm not wanted here, Danny thought, turning to leave just as a boney hand grabbed her arm. With dread Danny slowly turned...

And found a completely different scene; the scary man had become a friendly man. *It makes no sense.* The anger, or whatever it was, was gone, and the ice-blue eyes now were regarding her with warmth and interest.

"Mister Smith? Your daughter asked me to come by?" she said tentatively, her voice sounding high and tight.

The old man nodded his head and dropped back into his chair. Backing up and spinning expertly, he indicated that Danny should follow him as he made his way into the house.

Weird, she thought, but at least her fear had subsided. Now she was more curious than nervous. *What is up with this guy? Why won't he talk?*

She cleaned the already clean bathroom, vacuumed out the wheelchair tracks in the wall-to-wall carpet, and relegated a breadcrumb and some crumpled pieces of paper to an empty kitchen trashcan. While she bustled around trying to look busy, she could feel those eyes watching her with a kind of friendly fascination. It made her incredibly nervous. She couldn't remember ever actually noticing a person's eye color before, but the old man's eyes seemed to actually change temperature—they were so blue!

Checking her watch, Danny realized it would soon be dark and she definitely wanted to be back at camp before then. She had that book report to write. Glancing over the breakfast bar into the living room where Mr. Smith sat she offered "I can fix you something for dinner before I go,"

Al was no longer looking at her, in fact, for the past half hour he'd had his back to her, but at the sound of Danny's voice, he cocked his head and twisted to face her.

Danny saw that he had been busy fiddling with a contraption on a tray across his lap. Earlier, she had watched him struggle to manage some mechanism attached to the arm of his wheelchair. She knew he wouldn't want her help and hadn't offered.

A bit louder this time, Danny spoke, "It's dinnertime. Would you like me to fix you some Cream of Broccoli soup? Or would you prefer Low Salt Minestrone?" She'd thought he must really like those kinds of soup because that was pretty much all he had in the cupboard.

Although a look of distaste seemed to flicker across the wrinkled face, Danny waited in vain for him to speak. The old man and the young girl stared at one another. The silence stretched and grew uncomfortable...

Then Al smiled and—just as he'd done when Danny followed him into the house—gestured her forward and turned away, sure she'd come along.

What on earth is he doing? Danny wondered as she put down the dish towel and came up behind the wheelchair. Over Mister Smith's shoulder, she could see he was furiously typing on a wireless keyboard. One step closer and the bright, wide plasma screen was visible.

As soon as Al Smith knew the girl was behind him he pressed a button and the words typed across the screen began to blink the question....

ARE YOU THE GIRL FROM THE WOODS?

THE GIRL FROM THE WOODS

No. No." Danny told the old man, trying not to sound guilty. "That's not me" she assured the old man who didn't seem convinced.

I WATCH... BORED...LOOK OUT WINDOW. WATCH BIRDS... RAIN ...SNOW...WOODS. SEE FIGURE SOMETIMES...SHORT...DARK PARKA...LONG HAIR. NOT YOU?

Danny shook her head. "Not me."

CAN'T SLEEP...SIT...WAIT FOR NEXT STROKE. I SEE A LIGHT MOVING THROUGH TREES. WHO? Al looked up over his shoulder. NOT YOU?

"Not me." By now Danny's stomach was knotted with dread. Her knees sagged, and the companionable hand she had placed on the back of the wheelchair she now used for support. The mantra, *'Shut-up Shut-up Shut-up'*, repeated in her head with the mind-erasing ferocity of a jet at take off.

Again the old man typed, while Danny watched through the noise of her own hopelessness. How sure she had been that her time in the woods had gone unobserved! How careful she had been, using the same path only occasionally, using the flashlight only when absolutely necessary.

The typing stopped but, before Danny summoned the courage to read the screen, Al's boney finger stabbed out at the Delete key. The message disappeared. He started over...

Danny fought for control of her emotions. *If HE saw me, who else has?* She willed the thought away. She remembered her father explaining the Indian technique of slowing the breath, regulating the heartbeat and achieving great stillness and peace during times of crisis. She tried to find that quiet place within her own Indian heritage.

YOU SHOVELED MY SIDEWALK, the message blinked.

Danny was startled by the change of topic. Without considering her answer she nodded yes, she WAS the one who shoveled the sidewalk. Then thought maybe she shouldn't have said that...

THANK YOU! came the reply.

"My pleasure, Mister Smith."

CALL ME MISTER AL. SMITH IS TOO COMMON A NAME TO MEAN MUCH.

"Huh?" Danny paused taken aback by his statement... *Could he know my last name is also Smith? No of course not. How could he know! I haven't even told him my FIRST name.* "Okay Mister Al. My name is Danny"

The old man looked up and caught Danny's eyes. *Remarkable eyes,* he thought, and typed: DANNI OR DANNY?

"Y." She said.

"WHY?" He typed. And smiled.

Crap, she thought, returning the smile in spite of herself. *A joke. He wants to be my friend. Before I know it he will be nosing into my business, and trying to fix my life. I certainly don't need or want friends! Keep it business. Return to that quiet place. Let all this emotion roll off me.*

The old man took a long time to consider Danny, and when his old, surprisingly nimble, fingers returned to the keyboard, his eyes were dancing with mischief.

I HATE SOUP, he typed.

Later that night, Danny wrote:

Our nourishment in old age is the Stew we make of our Past, our Present, our Beliefs and our Fears, cooked over the years, and seasoned by our Memories.

I don't think Mister Al likes stew.

What a weird day I've had. First thing: The old man RECOGNIZED me! He asked straight out if I was the "girl from the woods!" Well, actually he typed the question since it seems his vocal chords don't work because he had a stroke! ....and for goodness sakes, shouldn't Miss La-Di-Da Beatrice have mentioned her dear old dad can't talk!

Anyway, I told old Al that it wasn't me he saw in the woods.

He asked me again and I told him very definitely that <u>NO! It wasn't me you saw!</u> ...I think he believed me... He did stop asking questions...or maybe that was because he was hungry, and tired. ...Why did Miss La-Di-Da think he only needed help ten hours a week?...I fixed him four pieces of toast with extra butter and a big mug of hot sweet tea. I found some sheets, pillows and blankets and made up the daybed, before I left. I took the long, LONG way around the neighborhood before heading into the trees and that's why it is now 9:30 and I just now zipped up this sleeping bag.

There isn't much food in Mister Al's house other than soup....there is LOTS of soup...but he doesn't like soup. I scouted around and the only other stuff I found was a can of cat food, a couple of tins of very old sardines, an unopened box of shredded wheat, $\frac{3}{4}$ of a loaf of bread, butter, a carton of milk, and teabags. I think there had been a package of lunch meat and one of cheese, but all that was left were the wrappers so old Al must have eaten that.

That man is so stubborn I think he would die of starvation before he would eat something he hated as much as he hates soup!

I found a wad of paper in the garbage. It was a note from Miss La-Di-Da about having groceries delivered. I also found the delivery receipt so I know she is definitely the one who ordered that junk.

The house phone doesn't work and I think Miss La-Di-Da cancelled that service. I used my cell phone to call in a new order from a list old Al typed up. They can't deliver until Tuesday morning because of the Holiday...so until then I guess I'll share my granola bars and PB&J— and I can always call and order pizza!

I'll head over there tomorrow morning and get things sorted out for him. It's supposed to rain all weekend so I really don't have anything better to do. If I bring my book maybe I can even start on the report if it looks like he wouldn't mind. It is kind of hard to write stuff out longhand while lying down in a sleeping bag. A proper table and chair would help a lot, so maybe it will be okay for me to use old Al's kitchen table while we wait for the pizza man to deliver. I won't count those hours for payment of course.

Funny thing, I think he was real disappointed when I told him I wasn't the girl in the woods.

As a child, Al loved adventure stories, and sagas about castaways were his favorites, but imagination had been the first casualty of adulthood. Fatherhood followed and his mind firmly grounded itself in the mud of the everyday while his heart pumped to squeeze out any remaining flights of fancy.

Years went by and Al kept his head down and his responsibilities at the forefront.

One day, just as the cherry tree in Al's front yard erupted in frothy pink blossom, the hammer blow of a stroke knocked him to his knees. He looked up from the sidewalk and, slurring his surprise, mumbled, "When did it bloom?" Those were the last words Al spoke.

Over six months ago Al woke up. He was mute, crippled and suddenly an old man. He had no hopes, no dreams and no future. Convinced life had given up on him, he prepared to die. But his preparation for death was interrupted when he became caught up in a mystery unfolding outside his window. It started one sleepless night with a glimpse of a fleeting figure in the woods.

It was a girl.

What was a girl doing in the woods at that hour? Even before the stroke, it had been a long time since something interested Al this much. Confirming that the girl indeed was camping in the scrappy woods behind his townhouse was intriguing. When his vigilance was rewarded with the sight of the same young girl confidently carrying camping gear and a tent through the woods his imagination was fired. And when he saw the girl show up the next morning at the school bus stop across from his townhouse, his imagination went into overdrive.

The girl wasn't camping out. She was moving in!

Al slept better than he had in a long time and woke to the sound of a winter rain and the feel of a warm house. In light of all the activity that had just come into his life, he wondered at the nagging feeling of loss.

It was the perfect morning for a good long think.

He lay back on the surprisingly comfortably daybed and considered the mystery of The Girl in the Woods. He thought of all the silence he'd filled with speculation. He recounted the hours occupied by scanning the woods for clues. He relived the thrill he'd gotten each time he managed to spot the dark, infinitely quiet girl who moved like smoke and naturally blended into the rhythms of the forest.

I don't want the story to end! he realized, *yesterday, when I opened the door fully prepared to thrash the person knocking, the sight of that solemn girl looking up at me was both delightful and disappointing...*

*—She IS, of course, The Girl from the Woods, no matter what she claims—*he'd clearly seen her face the day of the first snow and had spent many hours tracking her progress with his hunting binoculars. And now listening to the rain, he sighed, sorry the wild haired girl was no longer a stranger. She was Danny-with-a-Why, and he could no longer watch from afar.

I am an adult. Little girls are not supposed to live alone in the woods. I must step in and contact the authorities. It is my duty.

But to insert himself into the story of The Girl in the Woods felt wrong. *I'm not qualified to run anyone's life. The last time I played adult was to my daughter. Look how she turned out! Sure, she is successful but she is also a miserable, unloving woman! My excuse and rational for everything I ever did for my daughter, and for every interaction I ever had with her was 'it's for your own good'. Now I wonder...*

...was it?

Al realized he admired Danny's maturity and competence. Obviously something pretty bad must have happened to send her into the woods in the first place, *but whatever that was it happened in the past. Right now, the girl isn't hungry and she isn't cold. She isn't hunted nor is she scared. She isn't even homeless. Not really. She isn't 'on the streets' after all! While she doesn't have an address, she has a home. Sure, her home is a tent, but it is HER tent and it is in a place of her own choosing.*

She has more control over her life right now than most adults do; certainly more than I do! All the 'system' could give her was a chance to become just another boring kid with just another boring kid's problems, and for that she'd have to sacrifice her unlimited horizons.

Where is the magic in that?

The rain slowed to the steady drip of a cold gray day.

A knock at the door startled Al just as he finished shaving. Wiping the last bit of shaving lather from his face he backed the chair out of the small bathroom and hurried to the door. Al was of the opinion that 7 am was much too early for visitors and was surprised that Danny didn't know better!

The next knock rattled the door frame.

Al yanked open the door to find an impatient little brown man on the other side. The diminutive fellow was busily scribbling away on a clipboard, his form engulfed in a rain splattered brown vinyl jacket, the hood up and sleeves too long. The legs on the matching over pants were unevenly rolled, and puddled around a pair of giant rubber boots. *He looks like a rubber Monk!* Al thought.

The visitor turned his little raisin face to Al. A thin, nasally voice announced from the shadows of the deep hood, "I have a delivery for Mister Aldo Smith," and handed over a package.

The yellow pajamas had arrived.

YELLOW PAJAMAS

Danny found them when she arrived. Bag, box and plastic wrapped PJs were unceremoniously stuffed in the kitchen trashcan. She fished them out as the old man watched her from the kitchen doorway.

I HATE YELLOW! he typed, as though that explained everything.

What a grumpy Gus HE is today, Danny thought, but out loud she said, "I see. What ELSE do you hate?"

The gray head dipped to the task of typing and Danny noticed just how sparse the hair was. There was dried shaving cream behind both his ears and his razor had completely missed an asymmetrical patch of whisker under his chin. *Dad used to do that...*

BROWN, he typed.

The old man's eyes were twinkling now and Danny was glad to return to the present. "So you hate brown. I hope that doesn't apply to food since peanut butter is brown and that is what we are having." As she spoke she put the unloved yellow pajamas on the counter beside her backpack and picked up the two plates containing peanut butter and jelly sandwiches. She put them on the kitchen table along with two big mugs of hot, sweet, milky tea made just the way her dad used to like.

Al rolled up to the kitchen table thinking how long it had been since he had eaten a peanut butter and jelly sandwich. The tea was a nice touch too. He'd had it for the first time just yesterday. Picking up a sandwich he realized Danny hadn't finished speaking.

"...bothers me most is waste. I reuse those little plastic sandwich bags. I refill water bottles. I really hate it when you buy something and it comes with acres of plastic packing material stuffed in a box that's way, way too big. All that stuff goes into the landfill you know..."

Al took a satisfying slurp of tea and listened with half an ear. He was hungry and had forgotten just how good peanut butter and jelly sandwiches were. The sensation of the soft bread and the sticky peanut butter on the roof of his mouth was delightful. *Just TAKE the pajamas,* he thought, *I know that is what this is all about.*

"...just this gy-normous field of enormous, fluttering blue flowers...or maybe they looked more like flags..."

Okay. Now I'm paying attention. Gy-normous? What word is gy-normous? And wasn't she just talking about recycling or landfill or something such as that?

"...but they aren't flags or flowers...they are blue plastic bags! You know, like the ones they give you at the grocery store?...Well, those bags were everywhere...stuck on weeds and twigs and under rocks and flapping loose because the wind was really blowing hard. And I'm looking around... thinking how the blue bags seemed to be GROWING from the landfill...when the wind changed, and hundreds of them ripped away from where they were snagged to come tumbling and sailing and blowing and rolling right toward me...along with the most awful smell of rot!" Danny chewed her sandwich reflectively, memory fully engaged. She focused on the long ago incident that started with a trip to the landfill to drop off an old pressed wood computer desk.

Al stopped chewing to watch Danny intently. Clearly this story was more than a way to justify taking a pair of yellow pajamas!

Reaching for her tea Danny caught the old man's curious stare. *That's all you are getting,* she thought, *it is MY story.*

The day at the landfill had been pivotal for Danny. It was the day she had decided she wanted to make the world a better place by becoming what her mom explained was an Environmental Engineer.

"Anyway," she concluded, "that's why you can't just throw away those yellow pajamas. I'll give them to someone who can use them," she paused and looked at he old man. "Okay?" she said and waited until he shook his head yes.

Al pointedly looked down at his empty plate, then at his empty mug and gave Danny a deliberate Thumbs Up sign. He enjoyed the smile he received in return. He supposed she would leave now and his day stretched before him blasted and empty. A thought crossed his mind that least the dead landfill had lively bags...and he felt guilty for that thought. But, really, what was there for him to do? Only a few days ago he'd been able to lose great blocks of time by gazing out the window and looking for the Girl in the Woods.

The sound of the old man's sigh reached directly into Danny's chest and squeezed her heart. *He sounds so tired and so hopeless! I guess he is pretty bored just sitting all day in that chair.*

"Would you like to play a game or two of cards Mister Al?" Danny asked, and saw the old man's eyes regain their sparkle. *He really does have the most expressive eyes!*

He nodded yes. Danny cleared the dishes and retrieved a pack of cards from a kitchen drawer.

They decided on Rummy.

"Mister Al, it's not that I don't LOVE losing every game, but I have a book report I have to write," Danny said, throwing her hands up in surrender and pushing back from the table. A glance outside told her it was still raining.

Al looked at her questioningly and typed, HOW LONG COULD THAT TAKE?

"Yeah, well I have to write it all out long hand, and I haven't done that in forever..." *uh-oh* Danny thought, *maybe too much information.*

Al noticed Danny's discomfort but was unsure of the source. USE THE COMPUTER UPSTAIRS. I HAVEN'T USED THE PRINTER SINCE I INSTALLED A NEW CARTRIDGE SO THERE IS PLENTY OF INK AND THERE IS PLENTY OF PAPER.

Al didn't notice how big Danny's eyes had gotten. He continued: GO TYPE YOUR PAPER AND WHEN YOU ARE FINISHED MAYBE I WILL LET YOU WIN A HAND OF CARDS.

Al rolled into the living room and flipped on ESPN. Danny was just passing the living room on her way to the computer room upstairs when the **"Beep Beep"** signaling a special announcement turned her around. Al and Danny focused on the television.

We interrupt this program for a weather advisory. The National Weather Service has just declared a state-wide weather emergency.

Within the last hour, unprecedented rainfall, up to five inches in some locations, has paralyzed transportation.

Flash flooding is occurring in many locations. The majority of secondary roads are now closed. Barely 12 hours into the Event, fast rising waters have stranded motorists, washed away bridges and undermined the foundations of entire blocks of homes near waterways. Rushing water has toppled trees and knocked out electricity. An estimated 52,000 homes are in the dark. Emergency calls to 911 are threatening to overwhelm the system.

State Police officials instruct all residents to stay off the roads until further notice and to monitor emergency channels. Residents of low lying areas should prepare for evacuation.

Stay tuned to this channel for updates.

Danny glanced out the sliding glass doors as another wave of autumn rain pounded down, completely obliterating her view of the woods. *I could be out there right now*, she thought with a shiver of gratitude.

During a long, cold rain all forest creatures, pelted by rain and soaked by standing water, search desperately for shelter. Those unable to find a dry place to hole up, group together for warmth and protection, or hunker down alone in abject misery. Human beings fold their campsites and go home if they can, because the only thing more miserable than a rainy day in the woods is a rainy night in the woods.

Danny considered her situation. Real winter wasn't even here yet and already the weather was stealing her independence. She believed her tent would shelter her from heavy snow and even sub-zero temperatures, but rain was a different story!

Al couldn't take his eyes off the emergency messages crawling across the TV screen...

Seek higher ground if housed near a water source or a flood plain. Stay off the roads. Don't attempt to cross standing water. Call 911 only for life threatening emergency.

Obviously Danny can't go out in weather like this! What do I know about the land behind these town homes? Somewhere back in those woods, there is a stream. Large areas were fenced off last time I walked those woods, and much of the flow from the stream had been diverted, but in this weather, what once was a trickle will now be a flood and if Danny has pitched her tent in a low area, she might not have any type of home to come back to!

The question was, what was he going to do about it?

Danny finished her book report in record time, saved it to her memory stick and sent a copy directly to her teacher's in-box. She had missed playing on the Electronic Superhighway, where life was just a matter of arranging Ones and Zeros. Plus, the old man's internet connection was hi-speed, and the desktop setup was sweet. Danny felt like she had fallen into yet another alternative reality.

But it was a false reality, she reminded herself. At some point she must leave this warm house and slop through the mud into the woods. She would be soaked to the skin by the time she made it to the tent. She would get ready for bed in the damp and cold, trying to prevent her wet clothes and muddy boots from dripping everywhere. Even so, her sleeping bag would be damp from the moisture in the air.

Danny called up the Google News page and idly read about disastrous rains up and down the east coast. The predictions were dire, the rainfall unprecedented. Locally, the reservoirs were full and the Kenilworth Dam was showing strain; a controlled release of floodwaters seemed likely...*where exactly IS Kenilworth Dam?*...with evacuations mandatory.

She thought of the trench she had dug around the perimeter of her tent to channel away rainwater. Although she had deepened and widened it just this morning in anticipation of a full day of rain, it probably wouldn't be deep enough to handle this kind of weather, which would mean the nylon floor and plastic ground cover would be flooded.

Her clothes and the sleeping bag were always stored in giant zip lock bags, and Danny had taken the added precaution of bagging the Coleman lamp, her radio, and a few other items.

Thinking about the situation she figured that, as long as the bags remained watertight, the bulk of damage would be to the tent. Still...

Danny remembered her dad saying the one thing in Vietnam that could not be fought... could not be defeated...and could not be prepared for, was the rain. With a heavy heart, she acknowledged she might be forced to return to the Laird's attic, which probably leaked.

Learning to live with no one to look out for her safety and comfort involved more than being tough and self sufficient. Even Mother Nature was getting in on the act. Outside the early October rains continued.

The computer screen flickered.

Power surge! She'd started the computer shutdown process and now dug in her backpack for the flashlight.

Downstairs, Al felt the beginnings of panic. He'd been operating on battery power, and the power icon was now blinking critically low. *Stupid! Stupid! Without electricity I'm back to being mute...can't communicate, still can't hold a pencil—without lights I'm blind anyway. Where is the flashlight? Didn't my wife keep candles in a kitchen drawer?*

Where is Danny?

The computer had almost completed the shutdown process when the printer hummed to life and spit out a page. Surprised, Danny caught it as it fluttered to the floor. *What a cool old man!* she thought, reading the message sent from downstairs:

TOO DANGEROUS TO GO HOME. MUST STAY. CLOTHES, BED, SHOWER UPSTAIRS.

The lights went out.

THE FREAK STORM

The Weather Emergency meant a whole lot of people were working overtime. At the State House an emergency meeting was underway. The most immediate topic was Kenilworth Dam. Reporters busily took notes.

The governor scratched his head and wondered if he could get the state to pay for having the basement pumped out in his vacation home. Of course, state funds would take care of anything he claimed as storm damage to the governors Mansion so that was an angle... But now he supposed he should focus on what the 'experts' in front of him were saying...

"...diverting the natural flow of many creeks in the area means we can predict the path any water released from the dam will take, and act accordingly."

"So, what are you saying? We WILL have to release water from the dam?" the governor snapped his question at the person he thought most easily intimidated.

The short, round-bellied bureaucrat, known in the office as 'Toad', stammered, "...well, yes, yes sir. That's what we've been telling you." He looked to his colleagues for support but none would make eye contact. Toad took a deep breath and continued, "When the dam was built about 25 years ago, it diminished the flow of the three streams we marked on the map," he gestured to a map projected on the wall..."When we open the flood gates, which we must if we are to keep the dam viable, the water will flood the stream beds and any properties nearby."

The governor didn't know which he liked less, the bug-eyed little guy or his message. Voters always blamed the government for natural disasters anyway, and next month he was up for re-election. He supposed he could ask for Federal Disaster relief on behalf of those flooded out. "How long will it take to evacuate the targeted areas?" he asked as if he cared.

At first, the woods welcomed the rain, sucking it into topsoil crisscrossed with thirsty roots, tubers and subterranean growing-things then passing it on to the subsoil, where it strained through layers of sand, clay and porous stone to reach, and fill, the aquifer—an underground water reservoir hundreds of feet below.

And still it rained.

With the earth fully saturated, water began to collect above ground. Streams slipped from their beds and united with water pooled and puddled in low lying areas. Insects and animals climbed trees or drowned as the forest floor leveled out into a vast lake of water. The area around Danny's tent liquefied into mud; the stakes anchoring it to the ground gave way, the trenches crumbled and disappeared.

Rain kept coming.

Un-tethered and buoyant with trapped air, the pop-up tent began to lift and, for awhile, it seemed it might float away like a big balloon—but then the water discovered a seam in the tent flap...

Stitch by stitch, the seam ripped open and the incoming rush of mud and water tumbled the contents of the nylon dome. Fortunately, the contents were sealed inside waterproof bags— which bobbed and bumped on the current—but kept Danny's possessions dry. As the rush of water subsided, the largest bag was caught in the backwash; it drifted out through the hole in busted seam and floated completely away...

Communicating by flashlight with hand signals was sort of fun Danny decided—like playing Charades. So far, she and the old man had played two games of cards and eaten the last of the peanut butter and jelly. Both pantomimed that they would die of starvation before resorting to SOUP. Danny was the only one who could laugh out loud at that— but it got the old man to thinking...

A thought kept tickling his memory—flapping around in his head like a moth batting against a light. *Something*—it was—he tried to make it hold still so he could have a look—*Food? Something about food...don't I remember a chest freezer downstairs that my wife kept meat and stuff in? Did I get rid of it?... I can't remember getting rid of it...I think I used it as a sort of extension to my work bench. After she died I don't remember ever emptying it out. It's been years...but I think it's still plugged in! Maybe something is still in it and just maybe it is something we could eat.* As the rusty cogs of the old man's brain began turning again, his memory immediately coughed up another thought, *The electricity is out, but I have a gas stove, and a gas oven— even though I've never used it—so we can cook!.*

Okay, next problem. How do I explain that in Charades?

Pot roast. Was it possible? The fragrance coming from the oven was amazing, especially to a nose that hadn't smelled real home cooking in months. There were two such noses in a townhouse closed up tight against the cold rainy night. Unaware of the water rising around them, two people prepared to sit down to eat by the light of a candle and a flashlight.

The old man was amazed by how good a twelve year old piece of beef tasted. *Danny must have added something to the pot to make the gravy.*

Danny thought, *I guess he likes Cream of Broccoli Soup after all!* She had added two cans to the bit of beef she had salvaged from a larger freezer-burned chunk. It WAS tasty, and she was very hungry....

The knock at the door startled them both.

The girl and the old man looked at each other before both heading to the door.

The officious **rap rap rap** came again, sounding a whole lot like trouble.

The old man, with Danny close behind, opened the door into a night pouring with rain. The policeman looking in on them seemed as surprised to find someone home as they were to find him standing there.

Danny's stomach clenched. The unwelcome sight of an officer standing at the door was so like the night authorities came to the door to announce her mother's death and take her into child custody! She held her breath, practically overcome by a powerful combination of anger, fear and dread.

"Sir. Miss." the policeman courteously inclined his head toward Al, then Danny and began to read from a card laminated in plastic against the rain: "This area is being evacuated. Heavy rains have forced Kenilworth Dam to open all emergency floodgates. Our hydrologists predict all of Rockaway Estates will soon be flooded. The governor has ordered an evacuation. Evacuation vehicles will be on this court within the hour. Please take all medications, and important documents plus anything else you deem essential with you as you exit your home. You will be taken to the Red Cross shelter. Pets will be evacuated separately." The officer returned the card to his pocket and looked up expectantly.

The old man caught Danny's eye and frowned. *He looks positively fierce!* she thought. A zing of hope went through her, *He doesn't want to go with this guy either!*

The old man shook his head emphatically 'no', steepled his hands like a mountain and gave a thumbs up. Next, he nodded 'yes', made a waving gesture for water, followed by the football gesture signaling an incomplete pass. Finally he pointed a finger at his own chest while shaking his head 'no'.

The pantomime confused the officer, but Danny translated. "He says: That won't be necessary officer." Danny caught the old man's toothy smile from the corner of her eye and continued, "this house is on high ground, so even if the waters rise, it won't reach us." Danny faltered, flashing on an image of New Orleans following Hurricane Katrina, before putting in her own two cents, "As far as water seeping up from below, the basements in this block of town homes are aboveground."

Good! Al thought. *She's a smart one!*

Looking both annoyed and frustrated, the officer glared at the old man and his young companion. He addressed his reply to Danny, "Miss, I repeat: evacuation is highly recommended, and absolutely mandatory for the infirm, elderly and young. So please get ready to go."

Jerk! both Danny and Al thought at the same time.

Al's fist came down hard on the arm of his chair, the sound startling even him. He was not going and that was that! He understood the lay of the land in this area and was certain that the only way the homes on this block of the estates would flood was if the roof blew off and let the rain in. Now that they had a freezer full of rapidly thawing food to eat, he wasn't going anywhere.

The officer was cold and tired and facing a full night of work. He looked from the girl to the man and saw faces set against him and hardened with determination. "If you absolutely insist on staying, you must sign a form releasing the county from responsibility for your welfare, and absolving us from any future rescue attempts," he snapped and pulled some papers from under his jacket. Glancing at the top on he went on, "It says here that this is the home of record for Mister Aldo Smith."

The old man gave a curt nod of the head. *Yes.*

"And who are you young lady?"

Danny pulled herself to her full height, which wasn't very tall. "I", she said in her most mature voice, "am Daniela Smith. I'll sign the papers for my..." her voice caught "ah...for Mister Smith since he can't manage at the moment. "

Noticing the hesitation, the officer sharply looked up, "Is she a direct relative?"

Al's blue eyes were steely as he caught the policeman's eye and nodded once, twice, *Just hope he doesn't ask for identifica...*"

"Then I'll have to see your identification, Miss."

Ah-oh...not good, thought the old man.

Danny said "Fine, officer," and reached into her back pocket for her wallet. "Will a school ID do?"

"Fine," the policeman checked the photo ID. "Daniela Francesca Smith" he read.

Danny winced—she hated that name.

Snapping the ID folder closed he turned away. "You are on your own," he said and thought, *The whole family is crazy!*

As flood waters rose throughout the night, the Smiths remained unaffected. This could not be said for the rest of the neighborhood.

"Have you lived here long, Mister Al?" she asked, saying the first thing that popped into her head as she surveyed the waters encroaching from the woods now visible in the morning light.

Al, too, had been staring at the waters. He was getting just a little concerned about how long the electricity would be off, and

Danny's question was a welcome distraction. He signaled, yes, he had always lived here.

The sun was finally out, weakly streaming through the sliding glass doors and illuminating the faces of these last two occupants of Rockaway Estates. The fragrance of ham fried for breakfast lingered, making the cold house seem somehow warmer. But it WAS cold. The heater had been off for 17 hours now. The temperature outside hovered just above freezing. The old man and the young girl both clutched mugs of tea, more for warmth than for taste, since there was no milk or sugar left to put in it.

"You mean you were born here? These townhouses are THAT old?" she teased.

Funny girl! Al shook his head vigorously and gave Danny a little smile. He made the now familiar 'follow me' gesture and rolled away from the table and into the living room. He went to a bookcase; it was dimly visible in the morning light, but he could have found what he was looking for in the dark. He briefly stood to pull a thin volume from the top shelf. It was the <u>History of the County</u>. Flipping to a chapter simply headed: ROCKAWAY, he showed the book to Danny.

She was delighted. *Knowledge is power*, she thought, and right now Danny knew nothing about the area. She and her mother had moved to the Kenilworth Township after her parents' separation so Danny could be close to the best public school in the state for Engineering.

The old man handed her the book. She knelt beside the wheelchair and he shyly pointed a gnarled finger at the small print under the chapter heading. Danny read: **as told by Aldo Smith.** Confused for a moment, she remembered that the policeman had called Mister Al by that name. She glanced up at him with a question in her eyes.

Al nodded 'yes', trying very hard to keep the satisfaction off his face. He motioned Danny to have a seat in his old recliner.

Danny pulled the heavy chair closer to the window and bent her head to the print. She tried to imagine the old man at her age, living in the olden days, uncomplicated by laws and regulations. *Mister Al was around before television and computers, maybe even before indoor plumbing and automobiles. He knows stuff. Lots of stuff.*

Al Smith felt the stirring of pride. Danny was genuinely interested in his knowledge of the area! His father had been the local barber—and the barbershop was the local gathering place. 'Smitty-the-Barber' had the inside track on everything and every person in town—and entertained his family with colorful stories. Young Al soaked up every word—gossip, fact and speculation— and he retained it. He'd explained this mix of fact and fiction to the author of the book—but the man called it the 'area's back-story', said Al had a gift for telling it— and transcribed every word.

The Rockaway chapter was a first person account transcribed in the same charming, folksy and interesting way it had been delivered. Danny was hearing the voice of Al Smith for the first time:

> **Rockaway is the story of a family named Rickenbocker. Local legend says the first Rickenbocker was a stowaway on the Mayflower—which of course was ridiculous if you thought about it for more than a second—but it WAS true that the Rickenbocker's had a reputation for good luck and for succeeding by default.**
>
> **'By default' is how Rickenbocker's came to own the acreage known as Rockaway. Joseph Rickenbocker was a stone mason and he signed on to build a stone house for a family, whose name has been forgotten. It took him several years but the result was the lovely and gracious mansion the family named 'Rockaway Manor'.**
>
> **Just about the time the last shingles were being nailed up, that family took sick. And they died, every one of them, one by one. Soon, the only person left alive in a 30 miles radius was Joseph Rickenbocker. That's how Rickenbocker came to own Rockaway Manor and its surrounding farmlands, his good luck being someone else's bad luck.**
>
> **Joseph Rickenbocker was a stone mason—he knew nothing about farming. He hadn't a clue what to plant but one day he found a canoe wedged under a fallen tree in the stream where he watered his horse; in that canoe was a bag of corn. No one showed up to claim the canoe or the corn so he took the corn home and planted it.**
>
> **Turns out that sack of corn was from an experimental**

strain of super-hardy, fast-growing stock and it pretty much grew itself. With Typical Rickenbocker luck, Joseph Rickenbocker soon had more corn than he could handle locally.

In those days, only one road crossed the state from east to west, and that was the Cumberland Road. Cumberland Road formed the northern boundary of Rockaway Acres and Rickenbocker wagons loaded with corn took to that road in force! Rickenbocker corn was soon famous throughout the state.

When the railroad laid track parallel to Cumberland Road, the train station was built next to Rickenbocker property, Joseph Rickenbocker's accidental fortune again soared.

The railroad brought people and the train station brought families anxious to build homes close to the station. A settlement grew and the citizen's named it 'The Town of Kenilworth'.

Joseph Rickenbocker was by far Kenilworth Township's wealthiest resident. His donations built both the school and the firehouse. He married, had three children and became increasingly eccentric. Everyone loved him and around town he was affectionately known as 'Daddy Rickenbocker'.

Although the money kept rolling in, Daddy Rickenbocker had no interest in improving his farm or expanding his business. When his wife died, he took the same distracted approach to raising his children—he left them alone and figured they'd be just fine.

My father said Daddy Rickenbocker was absentminded— a bit of a dreamer—but he did have one all-consuming passion: making Beer.

Rickenbocker beer was made from grains and hops special ordered directly from Germany. The recipe was secret but the whole town could smell when Daddy was cooking and fermenting a batch! His hobby was a bit of a scandal even though he made only enough to last the season.

To keep his avocation away from the main house he built a little stone shed under the trees and near a clear, sweet stream. The area between the stone shed and the stream was fitted with long, wooden tables and a stone, outdoor fireplace. Inside the shed was a gas cooker, lots of counter space and shelf after shelf of storage for the copper tubing, glass bottles, kettles and drums. Raw ingredients and kegs of beer were kept cool in a shallow root cellar. Daddy Rickenbocker had everything he needed to make excellent beer.

And the beer he made WAS excellent. My father looked forward to any invitation to visit the stone shed—but I don't know what impressed him more, the wonderful beer or the beautiful surroundings! He described the little stone shed as 'a cottage located on the most lovely, peaceful place on earth', It was built of the green stone native to the area and it snuggled back in amongst majestic chestnut trees like in had grown there. Surrounded by sunny daffodils in the spring and dappled with sun and shadows when the trees leafed out in summer, it looked enchanted, according to my father—who was not a poetic man.

For the men of Kenilworth, sitting under the spreading trees, listening to the burble and splash of the stream, and sampling the season's brew at the stone shed was the highlight of the year.

The town of Kenilworth continued to expand outward, but Main Street truly became a bustling business district when the Classing family moved in. I guess you would call Randal Classing an 'entrepreneur', but back then he was known as a 'go-getter'. Soon, my daddy's barber shop, the town Post Office and City Hall were the only establishments NOT owned and operated by Randal Classing or one of his many brothers.

Classings produced big families. And for as far back as anyone could remember, only boy-children—so, when a girl-child was born on August 5th 1914, the unprecedented event knocked the start of World War One off the front page of the local paper! She was named Nola Eve Classing, and some joked that her birth actually CAUSED the war. Truth be told, everyone did take Nola's birth as a sign...opinions only differed on whether it would be a good sign one or a very bad one...

Nola Eve was an original all right! Her daddy went to fight once the United States joined the war and never returned, so Nola was raised by her mother, and about a hundred uncles. She was what passed in our isolated part of the world as a 'flapper'. You know, she wore those shortened skirts with fringe, crimped her hair, put on lipstick and flirted with the boys. Nola turned some heads but she lived in a small town, surrounded by family, so how bad could she really be, right? Besides, everyone knew Nola had her heart set on Daddy Rickenbocker's oldest boy, Bobby.

In 1920, Congress passed laws prohibiting the manufacture, transportation, distribution and/or consumption of Alcohol on U.S. soil. Because this state included beer in the ban, Daddy Rickenbocker's pastime suddenly became a federal crime.

"Prohibition killed that man!" the town doctor declared the night of Daddy Rickenbocker's fatal heart attack. "His heart couldn't choose between destroying the stone shed or becoming a felon."

Prohibition was repelled in 1933 but by then the Rickenbocker fortunes had changed forever...

The light from the window had slowly faded as more clouds rolled in and Danny's eyes burned from squinting at the print. When she leaned back in the chair to close them for a moment, she could clearly see a small clearing beside a dancing stream. The grass was long and silky and shot through with nodding daffodils and a soft breeze combed it in waves lit by flutters of light filtered through the emerald leaves of graceful shade trees above.

Danny could just make out a small cottage, almost invisible beneath the biggest of the trees. Unrestrained by geometry, the irregular outline of its rough hewn walls and slightly uneven set of its windows, suggested a structure built by nature rather than by man. Splatters of sunlight picked out the glint of window glass, the mossy green of the roof and the chipped red of an open door. Danny felt welcome.

She listened to the *shhhh* of breezes at play in the leaves and smelled the tart sweetness of spring. Taking a step forward she thought she heard distant conversation and a snatch of laughter. Danny turned to glimpse the blue of the sky mirrored in a deep, still eddy of the stream...

Al rolled over to the little figure tucked up in the Lazy Boy. Her eyes were closed, but she clutched the book still open on her lap. *Is she asleep?*

Danny's eyes opened slowly. She wasn't surprised to find the wheelchair parked at her elbow. *His eyes are the same blue as the stream.* She was starting to like him very much.

Al had something to say.

It had come to him while Danny read. He'd been looking out the window and thinking about the increasing cold when he saw the first raindrops and thought: *The rain is back, so the electricity will stay off. Wish I had a generator...or even a spare battery for the laptop. Wait a minute! I DO have a boat battery in the basement.*

Danny was so wrapped up in reading she hadn't noticed when Al crossed to the bookcase, drew out a large volume, took it to the kitchen table, and went to work. He finished about the time she closed her tired eyes.

When Danny opened her eyes, the old man was beside her with a large book in his lap, with playing cards inserted to mark the pages. He pointed his finger at her.

"Okay. Me. You want ME to do something. Right?"

Al nodded yes, and walked his two fingers down an invisible slope.

"You want me to...go...downstairs?"

A nod.

"Okay. Why? For what?"

The mysterious book turned out to be a dictionary. Al opened to the first playing card bookmark and poked his finger at a word: BATTERY.

"BATTERY. You want me to look for a battery? I thought you said you didn't need any because you didn't have a flashlight to put them in."

Al's hands described a large box shape then flipped forward to the word: BOAT, and back right away to: BATTERY.

"You have a big battery down there that you want me to find? Any hints where to look?"

Al's hands described a tabletop and legs, then motioned that the battery was under it. Then he held up one 'wait a minute' finger. He flipped to the **I** section and pointed: INVERTOR, then flipped to **P**'s and the word: POWER, then returned to INVERTOR. *Does she understand?*

Danny thought she understood what he wanted. "You want me to get the battery from under your worktable and to ALSO get something called a Inverter Power…"

The old man stopped her. Both fingers of both hands measured out a few inches.

Danny understood the gesture from the game Charades, and said "Its two words…"

The right and left hand switched places.

"…and you want me to switch the words around… Okay… so its NOT 'Inverter Power' you want. What you want is a 'Power Inverter'! Picky! Picky! Sounds like pretty much the same thing to me….and anyway, it doesn't matter how you say it, I wouldn't know one if I fell over it. Don't forget it is dark down there and all I have is a flashlight." As she spoke she shook her head.

Al's eyes crinkled with a smile though he tried to look stern, and waggled a finger at his young guest with the wild hair. Then he returned to business, his hands describing a smaller box shape. He signed that she should look on the wall… across from the workbench… up on a shelf? *Maybe?* He scratched his head and shrugged his shoulders to indicate he wasn't absolutely sure WHERE she might find it.

"I'll try Mister Al, but I really could use more clues…"

Al looked momentarily distressed, then his face lit up and he zoomed out of the living room and into the kitchen. That was where Danny had left her backpack wasn't it?

Danny followed, noticing as she extricated herself from the Lazy Boy just how cold the house had become. On her way to the kitchen she glanced out the sliding doors and saw the rain. Her mood, hopeful since the daydream visit to the cottage, plummeted. She turned the corner into the kitchen.

The old man sat there, holding up bright yellow pajamas as though they were a trophy fish. His eyes flashed happily from a network of crinkles. Ta-Da! He seemed to say as he presented yellow pajamas.

Danny cracked up. This might be the funniest thing she had ever seen! Her building tension broke apart and tears of laughter sprang to her eyes. The old man looked like Vanna White turning over a new letter on the Wheel of Fortune!

Again Al gestured toward the yellow pajamas, a bit more insistently this time. *Will she understand?*

Danny swallowed a mouthful of laughter that hurt going down like a too-big-swallow of fizzy soda. She couldn't keep the smile off her face though, knowing this whole thing COULDN'T be about a pair of pajamas (*but what if it was*)! She giggled, she snorted; she got it! "YELLOW!" Danny shouted. "The power inverter is yellow... like the pajamas!"

The bright yellow box was easy to spot in the dark basement even with the limited beam of her flashlight. The old man was anxiously waiting when Danny returned cradling the heavy battery in her arms along with a bright yellow inverter box.

The old man indicated she should leave both objects on the daybed, and return to her reading. He sat next to his equipment and began connecting this to that. *I feel so alive!* he thought, *I'd almost forgotten.*

Al soon had the battery cables from the power inverter connected to the battery posts. *Just as I hoped, there is still some juice in the battery!* he observed as the inverter's power gauge lit up— indicating power was now flowing from battery to inverter where it was converted to household current.

The yellow box had four electrical sockets on the side. He looked over at Danny who was squinting to read in the watery window light. *There is life in this old war horse yet!* thought the old man, as he located the appropriate plug.

The reading lamp flickered to life over Danny's shoulder. She glanced up, thinking the electricity had been restored and saw Vanna White, again! ....this time the old man held up the bright yellow power inverter displaying the socket where he had plugged the lamp.

With a flourish, Al reached for the plug to his computer. Danny watched with fascination as the plug went in the socket and the computer began to recharge.

"Wow!" she said, and went over to look at the set up. Carefully she examined the battery, noting it was a Deep Cell Marine Battery and a bit bigger than a regular car battery. *He must have once owned a boat.* Spotting a promotional sticker on the top of the battery housing she read: FULLY CHARGED Electric Outboard– 4 hour operation. Small Voltage Refrigerator – 5 day operation. Danny looked to the old man for confirmation. He pointed at the 'Fully Charged' note and sadly shook his head.

Next, she picked up the power inverter and read that it turned DC battery current into the AC needed to operate most home appliances. *Cool!*

Danny went to the kitchen and returned with her backpack. She pulled out her dead cell phone, unspooled the charger and motioned her intention with the plug.

The old man nodded his consent, and the cell phone plug joined the lamp and the computer in drawing juice from the battery.

Danny gave the old man's hand an impromptu squeeze. *He really is quite a guy.* Then she noticed the crank flashlight she'd returned to the side pocket of the backpack. It too was bright yellow. That got her to thinking about energy and how it was generated. "Mister Al, if I can recharge my flashlight battery by turning a crank, then shouldn't I be able to recharge that battery," she nodded her head toward the big Marine Battery now sitting on the floor, "...the same way?"

Al gestured that it just wasn't that easy. Outside, the rain was falling with increasing speed. He wished he knew how much energy was left in the battery. Although it had been stored with a full charge last year when he'd given away the little runabout boat he'd kept for fishing. *It will be nice if we have enough battery power to charge the computer, and keep the light on for a bit longer. Best of all would be having enough juice left for the little ceramic space heater to take the chill out of the air.* Then what Danny had just said really sunk in. *She is right,* he thought, *if a little bit of elbow grease can charge a small battery then a lot of elbow grease, and a lot of time, should be able to charge a large battery.* Al began to think, his imagination opening like a flower in sunshine...

Danny returned to the Lazy Boy and tucked one of Mister Al's blankets around her. The cold distracted her, until she began to read...

Some say Daddy Rickenbocker took the easy way out by dying, but that could be hindsight since no one could have guessed then at the troubles to follow.

With their father not around to look out for family interests the first thing the Rickenbocker children did was divide up Rockaway Acres according to the will.

The daughter inherited everything on the western side of the property—a full half of the land. But she really didn't get much, as my father explained it, just acre after acre of 'junk' land unsuitable for farming, and shot through with streams, swamps and rocky outcroppings. The most usable portion was a strip on the far western edge, so she broke that into parcels and sold the parcels to townspeople anxious to build homes of their own outside of town. Ten parcels sold and she took the cash, left the deed to the remaining property with the lawyer/real-estate agent in lieu of payment and left town for good.

All the good land to the east went to the male children, as was the custom in those days. A stream, crossing from east to west, intersected the eastern section roughly at the mid-point; Daddy Rickenbocker saw this as a natural property line to further divide his inheritance.

He willed Bobby, the eldest, everything north of the stream. This included Rockaway Manor, the stone shed and easy access to town. Again, this was the custom, because Bobby was the oldest.

Little brother Tommy seemed mildly suited to farming, so it seemed right that he get the lower acres. His father willed him all of the Rickenbocker farmland which was everything south of the stream, (this land was so rich that some local farmers felt Tommy had gotten the better deal).

Bobby and Tommy had always gotten along just fine as long as they weren't forced to spend any time together. Now that both had their own property they didn't see one another at all and a few peaceful years went by.

On the day of Nola Classing's sixteenth birthday, she married Bobby Rickenbocker and set about enjoying life.

Not to be outdone, young Tommy took a sudden shine to the daughter of an itinerant preacher passing through town. Tommy married the girl and they set up a storefront ministry on Main Street under the names of 'Brother Tommy' and 'Sister Irma'. Apparently, farming was not for Tommy after all.

Nola Eve, free of her families censure, encouraged her new husband's wild streak. She was determined to become a real flapper, and real flappers went to big elegant parties, where they danced, drank and flirted the night away. So Nola and Bobby began to throw big parties. Encouraged by Nola, Bobby reopened the stone shed, ignored the law and began to make beer.

Nola rejoiced in her social success. The secluded stone shed was in an ideal location, buffered by trees and empty farmland; with no one disturbed by voices lifted in song and laughter that lasted way into the night. The beer flowed freely and Prohibition was just an annoyance; the Roaring Twenties had finally come to Rockaway!

Now, the Rickenbocker brothers traveled in very different circles so, by the time word of the goings on at the old stone shed reached the little storefront ministry on Main Street, the party was going on seven days a week. Brother Tommy was outraged by reports of his brother's behavior, and staged an early morning visit to Rockaway Manor. He woke his brother with shouts, banging and threats of eternal damnation. Bobby just laughed.

That night, Brother Tommy gathered the members of the Kenilworth Temperance Society on the stream bank directly across from the stone shed. The idea was to sing hymns and quote scripture into the night, disrupt the party and shame the participants.

Hours went by and it seemed the more hoarse and discouraged the Society became, the louder and more outrageous the revelry on the opposite bank grew. Sister Irma's anger increased, as one by one, Tommy's group broke away. The devil's work had gone way too far to be stopped by gentle persuasion; only a swift and brutal act would stop the evil from spreading! But when she spotted the town's Sheriff among the partiers on the other side, Sister's fury knew no bounds.

Sister Irma persuaded Brother Tommy to call the federal authorities and turn his big brother in for making, distributing and drinking alcohol. It was his duty.

The Law showed up one dozy afternoon just as Bobby was filling a keg with Summer Brew. With righteous wrath, they pounced. Federal Revenuers destroyed the equipment, emptied out the stone shed, poured away the brew and carted Bobby off to jail. Bobby's lands and properties were seized by the Federal Government.

The party was over. Nola's husband was in prison and she was penniless.

Brother Tommy and Sister Irma packed up and left town soon after. Folks around here figure young Tommy lost his taste for the area once he succeeded in ruining his older brother.

The land on both sides of stream was left untended. Weeds grew up in the litter of devastation outside the stone shed while rabbits played in the furrows and fox hunted without restriction. Deer multiplied into herds. Birds brought in seeds. Once-clear acres of farmland soon bristled with scrub trees that grew fast, died young, and were slowly replaced by hardwoods like Maple and Oak.

The forest was back.

In 1961, the lower acres abandoned by Brother Tommy were annexed by the Federal Government and designated an 'off-site Government Research Agency'; Bobby's more northern properties were deeded to the State.

These days, State College holds the 100-year lease on Bobby's lands—including Rockaway Manor. Any stone mason who takes his craft seriously has heard of Rockaway Manor, but few know it was designed and built single-handedly by the man Joseph 'Daddy' Rickenbocker. Still, the building is considered this state's most beautiful historic home and appears in books on American architecture nationwide. State College takes in a lot of money conducting tours.

To the west, the ten families who bought land from Rickenbocker's daughter built large, clapboard homes side by side. You'll still find seven of those homes along Cumberland Cutaway Road; the other two, plus a goodly chunk of the daughter's northern properties, were annexed over thirty years ago, by the township, then cleared to build the bypass road around Kenilworth.

The remainder of the daughter's 'junk' land made a local developer a lot of money. He filled in the low spots, raised the overall elevation and built the sprawling townhouse community known as Rockaway Estates.

Although Kenilworth Township owes much of its local color to 'Daddy' Rickenbocker, the name Rickenbocker has completely fallen off the map and Rickenbocker's story has largely been forgotten. In town, the complexity of its founding father is represented by a seldom-used road, connecting at an odd angle with Main Street and leading to the back door of Rockaway Manor. Daddy Rickenbocker named that the 'Good Luck Road'. The name has stuck—there is even a sign. It's not much of a legacy really, but perhaps it's something!

The last line made Danny smile, *funny old man*, but on the whole, the story made her sad. She laid the book down, closed her eyes and leaned back in the recliner to think about what she'd read and to try to make Aldo Smith's geography fit with the world she knew.

Since Rockaway Estates was where she now was, and her tent was pitched on vacant land she must be in the part owned by either the Federal Government or State College. *Okay*, she thought, *so what—who cares?* She guessed it really didn't make any difference to her who owned the land.

She thought about the warring Rickenbocker brothers. *The whole feud thing sounds so childish. And here I always thought brothers and sisters could count on one another in time of trouble! Instead, during what should have been good times, they turned AGAINST one another, or maybe the Rickenbocker luck just ran out. Still, I do think we make our own luck...I'd hate to think it just followed us around like a little cloud.*

She thought about the stream, figuring so prominently in the tale and so clear and pretty... A source of water might come in handy, Danny thought, but there was no stream in the parts of the woods she knew. *Was it possible it had dried up?* No, she decided, she just hadn't found it yet.

Danny promised herself that, if it stopped raining, she would start her search in the morning. She would look for the stream and for evidence of the stone shed.

INSIDE-OUT THINKING

The unaccustomed ringing of a phone woke Danny from a deliciously deep sleep. It took her a minute to find her newly charged cell phone in the pocket of her jeans beside the bed. It took another minute to remember how to answer it. "Hello?"

"Is this Daniela? " the strained voice of a woman asked. "This is Ms. Beatrice Renee Smith."

Danny was fully awake now, "Yes Ma'am?" She felt a little guilty somehow, just waking from her second night in a room that had probably once belonged to Miss La-Di-Da herself.

"I'm calling about my father. What is his status? I understand there has been flooding in the county and that some areas have been evacuated."

"That's true, but the flood didn't reach his section of Rockaway Estates. I have seen him everyday. He's fine."

Great! Beatrice thought, *I won't have to come up there and sort things out!* "That is good news. I haven't been able to reach him on email so I was a bit concerned— even though I know how the news media exaggerates everything."

Right you are. You don't sound the least bit concerned! Danny thought and decided a reality check was in order. "Oh, by the way, I put in a lot of hours because of the storm. Nine hours over the last three days, in fact. There were a lot of things your Dad needed help with during the storm. But we are managing. Your father is fine." *There! Now we are talking about something she seems to care about...money!* That gave Danny an inspiration. *Amazing what a good nights sleep can do.* "And Ms. Smith?" she added.

Beatrice was trying to process this combination of good and bad news, yet automatically responded to Danny's query, "Yes?"

"When you do send the check, just leave the Pay To portion blank. I will put it in my fathers name and deposit it in his account."

Beatrice hesitated. *Where had the timid girl from only three days ago gone?* She felt a little defensive. "Well I suppose that's fine...tell my father I called will you please..."

Danny felt quite smug—she had scored one for the home team AND solved her check dilemma—until she heard Beatrice's next words.

"...remind him that it was MY idea to put in the gas stove, so that even if the power goes out he can eat and stay warm. Goodbye now Daniela." With that, Beatrice rang off.

Danny looked at the silent phone in amazement. *GAS STOVE! How stupid can I be? We spent the last two days trying to keep warm and even moved to the kitchen when I cooked the roast...not because we were hungry...but because it was WARM, yet we never connected the two things. The oven is a heat source, all we have to do is turn it on!*

Danny could almost hear the voice of her mother saying, *Let this be a lesson to you Danny, we can learn from all of God's creatures. You should never let yourself feel superior.*

Danny hurriedly dressed and rushed downstairs to tell the old man that his daughter had called.

Al's wheelchair was at the top of the stairs, but he was in the basement.

He'd done it as soon as the sun came up enough to offer light. Negotiating those steps had been a slow, humbling—but relatively safe—process. By sitting on the first step and bumping down the rest supported by his arms and his bottom, he'd made it. *The way we taught Bea to do it as a baby.*

At the bottom of the steps he stood, both hands on the work bench for support, feeling a bit disoriented. The workshop had once been his sanctuary; now it was just a dark, musty room. *Another thing that's lost,* he thought with a sigh. *At least I can do something about the light.*

Hand over hand, he followed the worktables running down the side wall to the rear. In the back wall was a door. *Let there be light!* he thought, and turned the door handle.

The rain had stopped and the sun rushed in—along with bone-wracking cold. Al tightened his scarf, pulled his hat down a bit farther and took a good long look at his once familiar workshop—then he got to work.

"Mister Al?" Danny called. The old man's bed was empty. *He must be in the bathroom or something.*

From his seat on a camping stool beside the open door, the old man looked up from what he had been working on. He'd had been so preoccupied hatching his plans he hadn't thought about Danny—that she might worry. Looking around for some way to signal he was okay and in the basement, he absently rubbed his cold hands together. *Having this door open is letting out the little warmth we have left. I think the temperature is dropping again.*

Danny heard the distant sound of metal banging on metal and was confused for a moment. Then she saw the wheelchair poised at the top of the open door to the basement. *Oh no! He's fallen down the stairs!* She rushed to the opening, her panic barely contained. A draft of freezing air rushed up the stairs carrying with it the decidedly jaunty sound of two metal pipes rapping out the 'secret knock' known by anyone who had ever been a child: Shave And A Haircut...Two Bits.

The tension left her. *He's alive. He's okay!* The depths of her own joy surprised her. *He's okay! But why on earth is he in the basement?* Then she thought, *Oh, oh. How do I get him back up here?*

The old man's face was smeared with black grease, but as she came toward him the blue eyes twinkled beneath the wool cap he'd pulled low over forehead and ears. He was bundled in a warm parka, scarf and hat. Four pairs of heavy socks had turned his feet into featureless bulbs and his every breath fogged the frigid air around him, yet his hands were bare. He sat by the open door, hunched over items spread out on an over turned crate in front of him and was lit by gloriously deceptive sunshine. Danny smiled. *Well, he obviously came down here on purpose! What's he up to now?*

Inclining her head toward the wheelchair abandoned at the top of the stairs, Danny asked, "should I bring your chair down?"

I don't actually need the chair right now, but the Geek Guy welded the darn computer to it so I guess I need both. He shook his head 'yes' and watched Danny scamper up the stairs, thinking *I can't wait to tell her about the generator.*

I can't wait to tell him about using the stove for heating! Danny thought while struggling to maneuver the chair down the narrow stairs.

Once the old man was settled back in the wheelchair he booted up the recharged computer. Before the process had finished Danny burst out with her news. She didn't think he looked too interested in hearing that his daughter had called and voiced concern, but he certainly was interested when she got to the part about using the oven for heat. The gray head snapped toward her, his eyes sharp and almost angry. Then they softened and he looked chagrined. Very deliberately he smacked his forehead with an open palm as if to say "What an idiot!!"

"That's just how I felt! How could we have not thought of something that obvious?" Danny's voiced her own chagrin. "Well, the oven is on now. I even put another roast in...pork this time...so it will be warm when we go back up. But how are we going to GET back up, by the way. Or can you walk now?" she teased.

Al typed: I'LL GO UP LIKE I CAME DOWN. SIT ON MY BACKSIDE AND SCOOT FROM ONE STEP TO THE NEXT.

Danny thought, *How simple, really. If you can't stand up and walk, sit down and scoot. If the heater won't heat, use the heat from the cooker. From now on,* she vowed, *I will try to see all the possibilities.*

IF YOU GET THE BATTERY AND INVERTER, WE CAN PLUG IN A LIGHT AND I CAN CLOSE THIS DOOR. I THINK WE DROPPED BELOW FREEZING.

Danny had just started to carry the battery and inverter down the stairs when she thought of something. She rushed upstairs to the bathroom she had been using and checked the fixtures. Yes, she was right! One of the lights was a heat lamp. Climbing up on the sink she gently unscrewed the bulb, thinking *already this new approach to problems is paying off!*

Once the bulb was screwed into the shop lamp, plugged in, and connected to the battery, the basement workshop warmed up quickly behind the closed door. With an extra pair of fully functional hands and a pair of good legs, Al's project progressed quickly.

Outside the temperature continued to fall. The progress of the receding flood slowed as waters began to thicken and crystallize.

The worst ice storm in the states recorded history had begun.

Danny was sweating with exertion by the time she climbed off the stationary bike. *But it's worth it,* she thought, *to have a few more hours of juice in the battery.* She looked with satisfaction at the contraption positioned in the living room. She and the amazing old man had built it!

In the middle of the living room, Al had cobbled together a crude power generator using an exercise bike retrieved from a forgotten corner of the computer room upstairs, an alternator dug from a box of old car parts and adapted in his basement workshop and a standard car battery pulled from his riding lawnmower. Pedaling the bike turned the wheel. The wheel in turn moved a field of magnets through the coil of copper wire inside the alternator. This action generated a current of energy that was relayed along a cable to the battery. The incoming current slowly charged the battery!

So far, everything appeared to be working; energy was trickling into the car battery slowly, but correctly. Once it was fully charged, they would see if they could juice up the Marine Cell too.

Well, Al thought as Danny rested, *my turn.* HELP ME UP THERE. I WANT TO GIVE IT A SPIN. GOOD PHYSICAL THERAPY!

As Monday night fell, the little house was fragrant with cooking smells, warm from the oven, aglow with several lamps and bursting with good will.

The little raccoon was drawn to it as though to a beacon.

Danny was the first to hear the soft scratching sound that was somehow familiar. Looking out the sliding glass door, she saw Rosemary Cooney looking in.

"Mister Al!" she cried, "Look!"

The old man didn't need much urging to stop trying to make the pedals go round. He was tired already. He looked where Danny was pointing and was delighted when a furry masked face looked back. Slowly, he moved from the bike seat to the wheelchair seat and flipped up his computer. I WONDER IF HE'S THE SAME ONE WHO USED TO COME BY. I ALWAYS KEPT A CAN OF CAT FOOD UNDER THE SINK FOR WHEN HE PAID ME A VISIT. BUT THAT WAS YEARS AGO.

Danny was already at the door, her hand to the glass. Rosemary also put her shriveled black hand up to the glass and regarded her solemnly. For Danny it was like a blessing.

Rosemary stood on the deck shiny with ice. The moon had risen as the sun was setting and its ghostly light was caught and haloed by ice that traced each twig, branch and vine.

Danny turned back to the old man, read his message and responded, "I don't think it could be the same one. This one's a girl and we've have met before...I call her Rosemary." She'd never forget her birthday celebration—and feeling that Rosemary was the only friend she had in the whole world. "Do you mind if I give her some dinner? I don't know if she likes cat food, but I know she likes people food."

FIX HER UP A BIG PLATE AND GIVE HER A BOWL OF WARM WATER TO WASH UP IN. WHILE SHE EATS, GO DOWNSTAIRS AND GET THE BIG COOLER. IF YOU PUT SOME BLANKETS IN IT, AND SLIDE IT OUT ON THE DECK, SHE MIGHT USE IT FOR A WARM PLACE TO SLEEP TONIGHT. NO CREATURE SHOULD HAVE TO BE OUT IN WEATHER LIKE THIS. I WISH WE COULD ASK HER IN, BUT A WILD ANIMAL CAN DO A LOT OF DAMAGE.

I really want to let her in. But this isn't my house and the old man is probably right. An insulated cooler would have to be cozier than a frozen wet hole in a tree. *I hope she likes Pork because it's what's for dinner!*

In fact, Rosemary Raccoon had been called from deep semi-hibernation by the smell of that pork roast cooking. With no one on the roads, and few even left in their homes, every sound and every smell was unique in the thin, icy air. Tracing the food smells to this place had been easy, but getting here hadn't been! It seemed the woods had turned into a frozen, slippery, lake that her feet couldn't properly grip.

Danny soon returned carrying a plate of food. Opening the door, she knelt to slide the meal Rosemary's way. The coating of ice made the ceramic plate move quickly across the rough deck boards and Rosemary used her hands to guide it closer; little raccoon hands immediately began relaying food to a busy little mouth. Both Al and Danny watched, observing as fingers tore neat, bite-sized chunks of meat off, popped them in her mouth, and never looked down.

Rosemary chewed with her mouth open and her little black eyes fixed unblinking on the two big faces on the other side of the glass.

The two faces stared back, grinning.

That night Danny wrote:

Happiness is easy. It is sadness that's hard.

I can usually see the black cloud that hangs over my head, but having a place to stay during this weather feels like a great stroke of luck! I might not have even lived through the last few days! Maybe my luck is changing?

I really like this job. Even though I'm getting paid to be an 'Invalid's Companion', Mister Al isn't really an <u>Invalid</u>. Sometimes I even think of him as a friend; he's interesting and very smart. Today we built a pedal-powered generator that reminds me of something I saw once on the TV show Gilligan's Island. A few versions didn't work, but he kept on tweaking this and that, explaining why every step of the way. Now it works pretty good and I plan to do the same thing once I get moved back into my tent. I could run lights, a fan, and even a little microwave oven if I manage battery output and input correctly. How neat is that?

Right now we are having more freaky weather—an ice storm this time. Mister Al told me I should stay a while longer because of the weather. I told him I would have to call home. My cell phone has a good strong signal, and I've kept it recharged. But of course I don't have anyone to call, so I pretended to talk to someone.

It is really sort of weird that Mister Al hasn't asked me any questions since the first day! We have been busy though, so maybe he forgot. I have to keep reminding myself not to blurt out stuff about my parents, or the tent. I'm especially careful not to say anything about the Laird's Foster Hole! I think he might know them.

Rosemary Cooney joined us for dinner tonight. She is so adorable I forget she's a wild animal and not my pet. As long as I don't make any sudden moves around her she lets me get real close. Too close though and she backs away— but never far. Her eyes are always looking at me like she knows something she'd like to share. Mister Al noticed the same thing, about her looking straight at him. So, since she can't be looking directly at both of us at the same time, I figure it must be a trick of the light or something. Rosemary's eyes are round and dark like black marbles. I can't see any color other than black. Maybe one day I'll get close enough to be able to see for sure.

Well, I'm going to bed now. No school tomorrow for me. (Yea!) Mister Al plugged in the radio to check.

I think he likes having me here.

CHILDREN FIRST

When the roof started leaking Mrs. Laird ignored it. On Saturday morning, water began pouring from the light fixture in Mr. Laird's bedroom in a steady stream and she tried to ignore that, too. Mrs. Laird was in a foul humor.

Her mood continued to darken into the afternoon as one emergency weather announcements after another interrupted her television viewing. When she noticed a growing bulge in the living room ceiling she struggled off the couch, retrieved a broom and took out her rage by giving the bulge a good poke with the handle.

This seriously aggravated the problem.

Water erupted from the spot and a huge gout of it sprayed into the ventilation grid at the back of her television. The television buzzed, flickered and with a sound like a particularly juicy, night bug hitting an electric bug zapper, died.

Moments later the entire neighborhood went dark.

That night, for the first time in almost two decades, Mrs. Laird did not preside over a 6:30 dinner. The microwave wasn't working anyway.

By the time the officer showed up to announce the evacuation, she was more than ready to leave.

The evacuation was the most excitement Mr. Laird had had in years. Two big firefighters linked arms, lifted him from his wheelchair, and carried him to a specially equipped van. *This is fun!* he thought and narrowed his little piggy eyes.

The wheelchair was left behind but the Laird's were assured that one would be waiting at the other end. Not so. They arrived to discover the emergency center was packed; all wheelchairs were taken. This infuriated the already furious Mrs. Laird and she grew very vocal...and quite loud.

Two different men in hospital scrubs attempted to quiet the large, obnoxious woman by assuring her that, the very next chance they had, a vehicle would be dispatched to retrieve the left-behind wheelchair. While the men kept Mrs. Laird at bay, two husky firemen wrangled Mr. Laird's bulk out of the van and into the building. They plopped him down on a vacant cot near the busy restroom. Eventually, Mrs. Laird arrived at the cot next to his. *Obviously they don't know who I am,* she thought. *They will soon enough though...*

On Monday, the governor came to the emergency center to shake a few hands and rustle up some votes and Mrs. Laird was the first in line to meet him. Although she never watched the news and never voted, she managed to play the aggrieved taxpayer to the hilt. Her narrow eyes, the color of dirt, squinted at the politician and her voice quivered with manufactured emotion as she announced, "My husband is a wheelchair-bound war hero. I myself am the foster parent of four orphaned children, and now we have been forced from our home! How will I care for my poor, dear wards, and for my poor crippled husband now?" She wrung her puffy hands, "governor, my life is about sacrifice. Always, I have sacrificed my time and comfort for the good of the unfortunate."

The words "war-hero and orphan" used in the same sentence got the governor's full attention.

Mrs. Laird noticed his interest. Her voice became syrupy and wheedling. "Now I want your assurance, governor, that my home and the home of the children this good state has given me to care for, be repaired in good time. My husband's condition is delicate, yet they brought him here without his wheelchair. And the children! These children have had enough disruption in their lives. Stability is sooo important."

Why the disgusting woman is practically cooing! The governor thought. *Still, this is a golden opportunity to showcase my humanity by helping a crippled veteran and a houseful of homeless orphans!* He then said in his deep, most sonorous voice, "This has been a tragedy for the entire community, madam, but I must admit your situation is particularly tragic. You can absolutely, certainly, count on me and my office, to help you, your husband, and those poor children, in every way we can".

Mrs. Laird thought, *he is flirting with me!* She said demurely, "Well, I certainly don't mind doing my part, but it is wonderful to know my good deeds are acknowledged". She batted her eyelashes, wishing she had applied mascara.

Does she have something in her eye? The governor wondered. *It is hard to tell from inside all those wrinkles.* "Yes ma'am. I, for one, have always been supportive of the pivotal role our foster families play in rescuing at-risk youth. Perhaps I could meet your family?" *Photo-op,* he thought glancing around for likely orphans and cripples. "We could all pose for a picture, perhaps. Something hopeful in the face of all this tragedy and loss?" The governor pictured himself surrounded by orphaned children and a man in a wheelchair. *A picture like that will make the front page of the Metro section for sure.*

"Well certainly you can have a picture", she said moving to stand beside the governor, "but my husband can't be disturbed right now, and I made sure the children were all safely out of the flood zone with friends when the rains first started. Their safety is always my first concern!" Mrs. Laird slipped an arm around the tall man and smiled for the picture.

Her teeth were green.

Her teeth look green! Oxo had lifted the morning paper from a random doorway only to find Mrs. Laird grinning out at him from the front page of the Metro section. Although he wasn't much of a reader he took the time to suss out the picture's headline— **GOV AGREES: CHILDREN FIRST!**

That old cow sure knows her way around the system, he thought as he pitched all but the funnies into the trash. *She'll probably end up with a new house courtesy of her bud, the Gov. I should have known Old Lard Butt had important friends. How else could she run that foster kid scam all these years without a hitch?*

Tossing his own newspaper aside in disgust, the little round bureaucrat his co-workers called 'Toad", couldn't believe the governor had time to hug attractive women and visit emergency shelters. *Does he think the crisis is over? The flood waters are now frozen in place and the meteorologists don't foresee any warming trends for the rest of the week. Global warming and the natural disasters that come with it, that's what he should be focusing on!*

Toad's thoughts strayed to the orphans mentioned in the article as he climbed up into the driver's seat of his Ford Expedition. He hoped they were comfortable wherever they were because it seemed they would be there a very long time. *The whole thing is unprecedented!* Toad put the big vehicle into four-wheel drive and backed out of a driveway that was a sheet of glass. The heavy vehicle took a deep drink of gas and struggled in vain to gain purchase. Just as it was about to slide into his own mailbox, the back tire hit a dry bit of asphalt and straighten out. Toad was late for work. *Blame Global Warming.*

Oxo pulled his collar up to hide his facial piercings when he saw the over-sized vehicle exit the driveway and he immediately stuck out his thumb. *No one picks up hitchhikers anymore* he thought, *but you never know....*

The huge, black Expedition gained speed as it passed the lone hitchhiker. Toad thought, *that fool will freeze to death out here...he should get himself back home right away,* before returning to the current situation. Right now the only areas really iced in were those affected by the flooding. *Good thing I forced the governor to evacuate,* he thought, and wondered who would play his character in the disaster movie that was sure to follow.

Beatrice Renee Smith scanned the paper for information on the flooding in her home state. *Nothing. Good.* She returned to thinking about a corporate takeover she was spearheading.

Oxo's body involuntarily shook with the cold as he hurried to the Laird's. He wanted to collect his sketchbooks from the room he sometimes occupied. *At least the sun is shining* he thought as, yet again, his feet slipped out from under him. Catching himself on a nearby fence he heard the sound of ripping material. Cold air immediately rushed through the tear and he imagined it drilling into his midsection. *Good thing I'm almost there!* Around the corner he could just see the shambling, clapboard, House of Laird.

The door was wide open. *Old Lard Butt didn't lock the door and the wind blew it open* he reasoned and hurried onto the porch.

The smell of gasoline was overpowering.

Skid! This was Skid's work, he was sure.

Skid, the scary, snaggle-tooth boy with the little head and long, weirdly shaped body, was **bad** trouble. Oxo stopped abruptly at the threshold knowing what he would find.

The boy himself, turned toward the open door with a menacing smile. "How ya doin' Ox old buddy?"

Oxo wouldn't have thought he could shiver any more, but he did. *Uh oh!* He shook off a desire to run and tried to look nonchalant as he stared at the weaselly teenager, with whom he had briefly shared a room in this very house. Adopting his most casual voice he replied, "Same old stuff, Skid. Ain't been caught yet." Could he manage to get his stuff out before Skid torched the place? All the CSD kids knew setting fires was Skid's specialty.

"You are just in time for the party!" Skid announced.

Bright sunlight reflected off every ice coated surface. *It IS beautiful,* Danny thought as she nervously looked out the upstairs window in the bedroom of the warm house. Although she marveled at the results of the ice storm, she had a nagging sense of impending trouble as she turned from the window—the same nagging fear that had troubled her sleep and dragged her out of bed with the sunrise.

Something is wrong. Danny knew it. She selected her warmest clothes and quickly dressed. Yesterday had been a very long, intense day and she was still tired.

Something is wrong. She tiptoed downstairs, smiling at the sound of the old man snoring. A glance onto the deck told her Rosemary had found the cooler, and was sleeping late.

Something is wrong. It was as though the air, empty of traffic and people and electricity and noise, had become a transmitter. It was transmitting a panic call. Danny felt her heart beat faster as she quietly opened the closet door and retrieved her parka. There was a pair of gloves on the shelf. *He won't mind if I borrow them,* she thought and pulled a woolen watch cap from another shelf.

Something is wrong. Gently shutting the door behind her, Danny carefully stepped out onto glassy path. Her feet began to slip; she caught herself with the railing, but barely slowed. It was as though a sixth sense had taken over, and it was dragging her toward the woods. *This is weird!*

It was slow going.

Ice had replaced standing water—even the highest spots were slick—each step was treacherous. She made better progress once she discovered she could slide along like she was on ice skates and followed the path of least resistance which seemed to be pointing her toward the back of the Laird's house. All morning she had been acting on instinct. *No reason to stop now.* Danny kept going.

Unexpectedly, her feet shot out from under her. She grabbed at a sturdy bush to stop the fall. It snapped off cleanly at the ice line and Danny and the useless branch went sprawling. *That was a heavy branch. Why did it snap off like that? More weirdness!*

Struggling to her feet she resumed her progress with more care, still thinking about the branch. *Okay,* she reasoned, *the winter weather of the last week came a month or two early. It was a freaky occurrence that probably caused a freaky reaction.*

Danny remembered her dad taking her to see how Maple Syrup was harvested. Lines of Maple trees had been pierced by wooden spigots to divert the sap as it made its way down the tree. Turn on the spigot and the tree juice ran out of the tap, into a wooden bucket where it was collected and boiled down to make maple syrup. *So, in the fall, the sap drains from leaves and branches and makes its way down the trunk to the roots underground where it's warmer. With this freaky weather the plants never had a chance to get ready for fall, much less winter. If they were full of sap-liquid when they froze—they'd become brittle like icicles. No wonder they are so fragile!* She couldn't wait tell Mister Al.

Skating on, she now consciously avoided any contact with bushes and low hanging tree limbs not liking the thought of damaging living things. She was thinking of the great damage a windstorm could do to the fragile forest when she smelled gasoline. *Something's wrong.*

Inside the house, Oxo had convinced Skid to let him run upstairs and get his sketchbooks. But could Skid be trusted when he held a match? Oxo certainly didn't want to become a crispy critter. He was moving as fast as possible when he passed by an upstairs window on the side of the house.

Danny saw the movement as she neared the house. *This area was evacuated. Who's in there?* Her thoughts immediately turned to Oxo. She sniffed, *I smell gasoline!*

Both smell and sound carry far in icy air.

"Hey man hurry up! It's cold out here!" Skid shouted. *But cold ain't nothing a great big, beautiful bonfire won't cure!* The boy was hopping up and down in his excitement. He had never done a house before and imagined the flames and the heat rising into the sky. *Just one little match and Woof!*

Danny walked around the side of the house and headed directly for the figure standing on the porch. She didn't want to scare him. She wanted to stop him. "Hey there!" she made her voice bright and cheerful. *Yeah, like we are two neighbors just outside enjoying the morning.* "Do you live here too? I'm....um... looking for a guy named Oxo, and his friends told me he was here." *What am I saying?* Even the air around the boy appeared colored by menace. Danny felt the hair on the back of her neck rise.

Caught! *I've got more company.* Skid's triumph slammed into this new reality with an impact that made his ears pop; it was like launching into a perfect dive only to find there was no water in the pool. *This is mine!* All his life he had imagined doing a big burn. Torching a dried out field or an old mattress in the woods was kid stuff really, not like what he'd planned for the Laird house. Skid nervously ran the back of his hand across his leaking nose and thought he might cry. *When will I ever get a chance like this again? I mean, how often are whole neighborhoods empty?* He tried to rally, *I could do it anyway.* But it was no good; a stupid, meddling, girl had ruined his moment.

Danny took a few steps closer to the boy on the porch.

Skid squinted down at this unknown girl. *She's just the kind to run to the Cops... it wouldn't be fun now anyway ...I'd just end up cuffed and in jail.* Skid was at heart a coward.

When the boy squinted, Danny remembered that a string of fires occurred during her days in the CSD dorm. All the kids knew who did it! Although no one would report it because they stuck together, it didn't mean they didn't talk about the firebug amongst them. They said he looked like a ferret... *And they used his name too...what was it?...something...it was some kind of nasty sounding nickname.* She looked at the boy who now shifted from foot to foot. *Pointy little rodent face with a long bow-shaped body...sure looks like a ferret to me, or maybe a weasel. They called him something beginning with S... something like...Scuzz... or maybe Snot... or...*

"Skid!" a voice from inside called. "Hey, man! You outside?" Oxo appeared in the open door, his face partially obscured by the enormous stack of comic books and loose paper he carried. He did a double-take when he saw Danny but obviously didn't recognize her. "You got company?"

Skid! That's it! That's the name...and he called his fires 'Skid-Marks'. "Hi Oxo! It's me, Danny. I hoped you'd be here." She turned her attention back to Skid and said pleasantly *as though the gas fumes aren't ready to knock us all over,* "I remember you now Skid! Don't you live here too sometimes?" She didn't wait for a response. She barreled on, improvising , "It's a good thing Old Lady Lard is so awful or we would never have this kind of freedom...I haven't even checked in almost a week and they don't care. I've got my own gig across town, so it's a good thing old Lard Butt keeps CSD off my back!"

Oxo was looking at the girl who called herself Danny with something like respect. *Saved! Skid won't try anything with two of us here, even if he does hate the Laird's. Besides, what the chick says makes sense.* Oxo's brain wasn't really used to positive thinking; he lived in a dark world.

Danny knew her scattershot of words had hit their target; the air no longer crackled with violence. The threat was gone she knew; Oxo had reached the same conclusion. From her position at the bottom of the porch steps she saw him shift the stack of papers he'd been holding high to shield his face. He transferred the weight to one hip and his free hand strayed to his eyebrow piercing.

It occurred to Oxo as he touched the pierced area that it felt a little odd, but his thought now centered on something else Danny had said....*what was it? She said some stuff about me...something about hoping I'd be here... or something...* It didn't make sense that Danny was looking for him.

Skid had lost his power; his adrenalin-rush had drained away. The manically glittering eyes were now flat and opaque with the usual dull anger he directed at everything and everyone. He thought, *Not today. Not here,* and guessed some of what the girl said was true. *The Lard-Butts do keep CSD off my back.*

The monster is gone...returned to the dark hole he came from! Danny thought. *He even looks different.* It seemed Skid's face had subtly changed. His gaze was undirected, the eyes unfocused. His front teeth appeared longer and more prominent. The elongated body, earlier taut with frightening intensity, had relaxed into in to a sort of spineless, comma-shaped slouch. *He really looks like a rodent now!* She couldn't decide though, was he a sneaky, sewer rat or a nasty, sway-backed weasel?

Skid's nose twitched. He was now in full survival mode. *Time to go, he* thought. *Let Oxo take the blame for spillin' the gas.* Turning to leave he thought, *when did it get so cold?*—and attempted a nonchalant exit from the slippery porch, having forgotten about the ice.

How could I have been scared of HIM?—both Oxo and Danny thought. Had they not wanted Skid gone so badly, it sure would have been pretty funny watching him go!

Skid's sneakers offered no traction; his feet went out from under him. He was launched down the steps onto the sidewalk; he made several unsuccessful attempts to stand up and recover some dignity, but in the end there was nothing for it but to crab-walk off the sidewalk to the grass where he had a bit of traction. He staggered down the road like his drunken old man.

Gone. Finally! Oxo grabbed the stair railing and carefully made his way down the steps, still clutching his papers and comic books, explaining as he did so, "Just came to get my stuff and ran into that crazy kid." He had an odd way of talking, sort of out of the side of his mouth like an old time gangster.

Danny was too appalled by the latest crop of piercings decorating Oxo's face to pay attention to what he was saying. Delicate gold chains connected multiple nose rings to assorted earrings, four to a side. One heavy chain ran from the lowest ear ring to a bar through the end of Oxo's chin. The effect of all those chains draping across Oxo's pimply adolescent face was bizarre, as he probably intended. But it was the eyebrow piercings that caused her to flinch. Several of these continued up into the skin of the forehead. Around the freshest site, pierced by a particularly aggressive bar entering just under the right brow and running high up under the skin of the forehead, the skin was a bloodless white-blue. Danny thought, *frostbite!*

Looking closer she noticed blue skin around many of the piercings. *IS that frostbite?* Once when she was a little girl, she had taken off her mitten to better grip a metal railing and had found her damp hand stuck tight. She worried about all that metal in Oxo's face now that temperatures were approaching zero. *Almost like the sap freeing in a tree, it CAN'T be good for metal to freeze under the skin.*

"Oxo, you need this more than me right now." Danny declared and yanked off the woolen watch cap she had appropriated from Mister Al's coat closet. She reached up and jammed the cap onto Oxo's greasy hair until it covered his eyebrows. "There ya go!" she said and felt a bit better.

Although having a woolen cap tugged over the rings and rods in his brow made the area itch like mad, Oxo didn't complain. *I can't remember anyone ever doing something that nice for me!* He was overwhelmed.

"Oh and I brought you something else," Danny said and unslung her pack. While she was digging she said "I noticed you wear yellow a lot, sooo...Ta Da!" Danny produced the pair of yellow pajamas.

Oxo loved them.

KNOW THE ENEMY

They found Mrs. Laird's stash of Hostess Ho-Ho's secreted in a box marked 'Prunes' and wedged into the farthest reaches of a kitchen cabinet, accessible only from the top step of the step-ladder. The exact location of those fabled chocolate snack cakes had been debated for years by CSD kids. Oxo now had valuable intel— sure to increase his status among his peers.

Danny and Oxo each had a mouthful of Ho-Ho as they opened drawers and cabinets in the previously off-limits Laird kitchen. The exploration revealed the source of the Lard-Butt bulk: junk food. Jumbo bags of Potato Chips lived in the lower cabinets traditionally reserved for pots and pans. One bank of cabinets contained 5 stacked cases of canned soda. The drawers were stuffed with candy of every sort. Oxo filled his pockets.

In one cabinet, Danny found several unopened jars of peanut butter, jelly and coffee creamer, plus bags of sugar and boxes of saltine crackers. She took one of each. *The old man would like a candy bar, I bet,* and she picked up one of those too. As she'd told Oxo, there was no need to be greedy.

They saved the refrigerator until last, knowing its contents would be moldy and rank with decay. Once the door seal was broken Danny had to hold her nose. *No way it got this rank so quickly—half the stuff in here was rotten already, I bet.* She found a garbage bag and dumped in the refrigerators contents. "Oxo, will you toss this outside please? It smells worse than the gas!"

Next Danny went from room to room opening windows in hope the fresh air would chase away the smell of gas. She found a big plastic trashcan full of water in the middle of the living room underneath a large, ragged hole in the ceiling's soft tile. A thin icicle hung from the hole and a skim of ice had formed in the trashcan. If water had made it down to this level, Danny knew the attic was a disaster. *Not my problem,* she reasoned and turned back to the hallway.

Meanwhile, Oxo was on a mission. *Gather intel!* He tried to be stealthy as he opened forbidden doors and gleefully sorted through the Laird's belongings. *I'm not nosey, I'm gathering valuable information,* he imagined what a hero he'd be when he told the kids at CSD what was REALLY in all those mysterious rooms! They'd had it all wrong.

According to CSD legend, old Lady Lard-Butt's room was a palace. They talked about heavy golden drapes, a huge, round, black-satin covered bed, And an enormous sitting area littered with fluffy pillows for lounging. Although Oxo couldn't imagine Lady Lard-Butt lounging in a sea of pillows...*I mean, how would she get up?*...he certainly wasn't prepared for what he found.

Squalor! He looked in amazement at the sagging, unmade bed with its dingy, yellowed sheets. Over the bed was one of the biggest black velvet paintings of Elvis Presley he had ever seen—bad art offended Oxo—a garishly, colored Elvis appeared to be looking down from heaven on the occupant of the bed. *She's rich and this is how the old cow lives?*

Just to prove he'd been there, he nicked a huge pair of grayish, cotton panties—filigreed with holes around the waistband—out of his foster mother's jumbled dresser drawer before moving on to expose the next legendary room: Old Man Lard-Butt's. Oxo was a little nervous.

The scarred, old door was closed as always; he put his ear to the heavy panel and heard a hollow, regular drip, drip. He sniffed and the smell was of old socks, unwashed hair and mildew. *Like a dungeon!* Every CSD kid knew about Old Man Laird, a man so dangerous, with such perverted habits, he was kept in chains by day and a cage at night—for the protection of others, of course. Mustering courage, Oxo slowly turned the door handle...

This was the most threatening darkness he had ever experienced. Robbed of vision his other senses heightened, the drip, drip, combined with the nasty, fetid odor, sent him dashing across the room toward a wall he knew must contain a window. *Air! Light! Got to find a window.* Oxo ran directly into dusty heavy curtains and groped to find a way to slide them open. With his efforts a slit of light appeared and he gave the material another tug; it tore with a loud rip.

Feeble light leaked through the torn curtain and Oxo felt his heart rate slow. He picked out the shape of a dresser, end table and a lumpish bed. A trashcan stood at the foot of the bed to catch the drip from the ceiling. *Well whatever money the Lard's are scamming' from CSD they don't spend it on livin' large.* The room was small, squalid and depressing.

A tarnished silver frame on the dresser caught his eye and he walked over for another look. It was a photograph, but the glass was almost opaque after years of greasy dust. Oxo energetically rubbed it with his sleeve as he carried it toward the window.

Even when the worst of the dust was cleared Oxo had to squint to make out the image. *This is really weird.* The shot was a three-quarter view of a sloppy-looking man with a crew cut in an ill-fitting brown uniform. *That's old man Lard-Butt alright, I recognize the profile.* The man's hand was palm up, his arm extended toward a poster featuring another man, also in brown and Oxo was shocked by what he was seeing. *That's a freakin' poster of Adolf Hitler!* The class on the Holocaust and the German War crimes of World War Two was one of the few lessons Oxo remembered. *Lard-Butt's a freakin' Nazi!*

Just then Danny called from the front hallway. "Oxo! Where are you?" Danny's voice came closer as she walked toward the bedrooms, "We need to get out of here. Are you ready? Where ARE you?" She paused and waited for an answer.

The voice came from behind one of two closed doors, "I'm right here and you won't BELIEVE what I got!"

"You know you shouldn't be in there", Danny scolded as she stepped into the dirty little room. "Whadja find, anyway?" She could just make out Oxo struggling with something in front of the window.

"The freakin' guy is a NAZI! Can you believe it?"

"Who is a Nazi?"

"The GUY. You know, Lard-Butt—Mister Laird—whatever you call him. He's a Nazi!" Oxo's voice was full of self-righteous indignation and, managing to free the picture from its dirty frame, crammed the evidence into Danny's hand. Once the picture was gone from the frame, several other sheets of folded paper were revealed. *Hidden?* Oxo wondered and while Danny was busy examining the photograph, carefully unfolded the first.

Wow! Danny thought, *that's really creepy. But how could he be old enough to be a real Nazi?* "He can't be a real Nazi, Oxo, he isn't old enough, but I think I've heard of the Neo-Nazi movement being big right now, especially in jail!"

"Well, he picked it up there then, because our dear foster father has a record." Oxo tossed Danny the paper he had just unfolded— "Just take a look at that!" —it was an official prison release document for a Laird, Douglas Frank and Oxo had recognized it right away. His friend at the bike store had framed his own and hung it on the wall.

This could change everything, Danny thought as she anxiously examined the document—even the small print—while Oxo attended to the next item in the frame. This time it was a thin, yellow scrap obviously clipped from a newspaper. The clipping was brittle and crumbled a bit as he gingerly unfolded it.

"It says here he did six years on a 15 year sentence." Danny glanced again at the document for reassurance before letting herself rejoice. *Yes! It is true. Thank you for being nosey Oxo.*

CSD didn't permit anyone with a criminal record to take in fosters— so Lady Lard-Butt had obviously lied to authorities. The prison release form Danny held could blow the Laird's foster kid scam right out of the water. The balance of power had changed.

*Lady Lard-Butt better not **ever** mess with us!* Danny carefully refolded the paper and slipped it into the plastic-lined, top pocket of her parka. She felt great. Maybe she would liberate some MORE things from the Lard-Butt kitchen. *Mister Al will like having some milk and sugar for his tea. He is probably wondering where I am. I should have left a note...*

Oxo had the newspaper scrap unfolded now and was staring at the headline proclaiming: **Local Man Jailed in Shocking Reversal.** The article included a grainy picture of a healthier—*well at least not crippled up and drooling*— Laird posed in front of this very house. Oxo wasn't much of a reader. He handed the clipping to Danny and watched for her reaction.

"WOW! This must be what sent him to jail." Quickly scanning the article. "It says he drove the get-away car during a bank robbery." She summarized as she read further, "Two people— bank employees— were kidnapped. They weren't found, yet were believed dead, even though there was no actual proof."

Halfway through, Danny put down the clipping and looked at Oxo. Her hair was wild and her eyes seemed bottomless. She said

"Oxo, they never caught the other bank robbers—only Douglas Laird. And Laird was to be tried for two counts of accessory to murder and one count of grand larceny." She whispered, "Oxo, that guy could be a MURDERER!".

Oxo was struggling to imagine old Lard-Butt as anything other than a helpless, grunting pervert—and he was pretty sure Lady Lard told people her hubby was some kind of War-Hero. Then he realized that anybody could say that—Old Lard DID look like he'd been through a war. *Liar, liar!*

Danny had returned to the article and read the highlights out loud:

> Laird's novel defense rocked the court with photographic evidence that the two kidnapped employees believed dead were part of the caper all along. Apparently the jury believed their own eyes, when Defense offered grainy photographs of what appeared to be the two enjoying themselves at an expensive resort in Europe. The pictures, Defense maintains, prove that the two people his client is accused of killing are very much alive and living abroad on money from the bank robbery. Defense chastised the State Prosecutor for attempting to charge a man for murder with no body, no forensic evidence and no witnesses. The DA should be looking for the real criminals, the two bank employees who master-minded the caper.
>
> The prosecutor appeared sandbagged by his opponent's tactics. In closing arguments the prosecutor could offer nothing more to the jury than his own personal assurance that the kidnapped pair were victims and that they were later murdered.
>
> Experts following the trial say they were not surprised when the jury returned a "not guilty" verdict on both counts of accessory to murder. Douglas Laird was found guilty on the remaining charge of Grand Larceny. He was sentenced to ten years in prison and is eligible for parole in five.

Oxo listened carefully as Danny read and was completely caught up in the story even as he absently fiddled with the final bit of paper hidden in the silver frame. His fingers seemed to recognize it as cheap drawing paper and he glanced down to check. The yellowed scrap contained nonsensical squiggles and lines drawn in pencil...

Danny shook her head and read the last line of the article, **"The money has never been recovered."**

—and Oxo knew what he held. *It's a map! A treasure map.* A charge of pure glee traveled down his spine and he shivered. *A map to the money they never found.*

Oxo wasn't used to feeling so alive with hope and dreams and possibilities and suddenly he desperately wanted to be alone to savor the feelings and gloat over the map. He had no intention in sharing.

Muttering "Let's get out of here," he started for the door, unobtrusively slipping his treasure map into the un-ripped pocket of his jacket. He wanted himself and the map out of Danny's sight as quickly as possible; he always felt out of his league around fast thinkers like Danny.

Just inside the doorway he stopped and turned back— something was happening outside. He clearly heard the grind of a diesel engine, and the toot of airbrakes. A vehicle was rolling on the icy road!

Both Danny and Oxo headed back to the window and peeked out through the rip in the drapes. Aware that they really weren't supposed to be in this house, they were careful not to be seen as they watched the road.

A big salt truck headed their way flinging salt pellets, willy-nilly. Its enormous tires, wrapped in chains, crushed through the inch of ice coating the road. The noisy crunching, coupled with the rat-tat-tat of salt crystals hitting and bouncing away on the slick surface, sounded alien in the silence of a frozen world.

The vehicle came closer and Danny and Oxo could see it was being followed by a truck, the side and hood of which was identified by painted crimson lettering: **WATER COMPANY**. Stuck over the lettering was a temporary, magnetized placard announcing: **ON BUSINESS FOR THE GOVERNOR**.

The salt spreader continued its slow inexorable journey, but the truck stopped two houses away at Cumberland Cutaway Number One. *Apparently the governor has some official business?* Two workers jumped out. One banged on the door while the other fumbled with a handful of keys. Inserting the correct key he opened the door and they both disappeared inside.

Danny and Oxo looked questioningly at one another. Danny pointed, "What do ya suppose THAT'S all about?" and watched Oxo's facial chains sway like the jowls of a hound dog as he shook his head in similar confusion. Both went back to watching the salt spreader advance, and the unmanned truck idle at the curb.

Eventually, the men reappeared, closed and locked the door and hurried back, obviously delighted to return to their warm truck. Oxo thought he heard one of them say "Got it", but he couldn't be sure since the salt truck was still making such an awful racket.

As soon as the men warmed up, they drove the Water Company vehicle forward a few yards to the next house. Again, they both got out, went to the door and repeated the process with the keys and the knocking while Danny and Oxo watched from the house next door. They were going house to house.

It is definitely time to go.

In the time it took for the workers to enter Number Two, do what ever it was they did, and come back out, Danny and Oxo had exited through a seldom-used back door. They crept back to the front and watched the workers move on to the Laird's Number Three.

From Danny's location she could peep out and see the porch, and just make out two pair of heavy boots stomping hard enough to shatter and dislodge the ice coating on the wooden planked porch. The ear-splitting roar of the salt truck had disappeared down the road, making it easier to eavesdrop.

"A total of seven houses on this road, right Bill?" one man said, apparently accepting the other man's grunt as a "yes" answer.

"If this is that Laird woman's house, then after we turn off the water, we gotta fetch her old man's wheelchair." More grumbles. "Yeah, but the guy is some kind of famous War-Hero."

At that, Danny and Oxo found themselves simultaneously choking with explosive laughter. *WAR-Hero! Famous!*

"Would you look at that Bill? The old bat left the door wide open." the talkative man exclaimed as he entered the house.

Both Danny and Oxo stopped laughing the instant they heard, first one window and then the other, slam shut with a sound resembling gun fire. The Water Company guys might seem silly but, they were officials and adults; it would not do for Danny and Oxo to be caught sneaking around. Neither made another sound when the Water Company boys, closed the doors, locked up and then wrestled the wheelchair across the ice and into the truck. Not long afterward, the truck revved its engine and headed around the corner toward the next home, Number Four.

The minute Oxo and Danny saw the trucks tail lights, they went their separate ways.

Danny headed back toward the woods barely thinking about the goodies she had at first been so excited to take back to Mister Al, her thoughts were now on her failings. *I opened all those windows to let the smell out, and didn't think that I was also letting the cold in. Of course water expands when it freezes, and I absolutely know that.* As she slid her way among the trees she continued to berate herself, *if those pipes had frozen and broke it would almost be as bad as a fire.* Being saved by the water company was hard to bear.

Oxo doubled back as soon as he was sure Danny was gone. He caught one last glimpse of her as she disappeared into the woods. Although this behavior normally would have intrigued him, he had trouble focusing on more than one thing at a time—and right now he was thinking about *Treasure!*

He reverently touched the map inside his pocket, almost surprised to find it actually there. He had decided the best place to think about what he would do next was somewhere out of the cold. The Laird house would have to do. He entered through the recently discovered back door and sat down at the table closest to a window. First, he pulled out the map and carefully unfolded it. Next he fished a candy bar from under his shirt and took a big bite. Chocolate helped him think.

It IS a map! Oxo's heart pounded with excitement. *Okay, next question: what is it a map of?* Examining faint pencil lines on the paper, he thought they looked a bit like one of those blueprint drawings he'd been shown in Shop class. He was pretty sure he recognized the symbol for door, window and stairs. *Yes, those are stairs. Doors, window and stairs mean* the *missing bank loot is hidden INSIDE, not in a park or under a garden rock. Where?*

He scanned the map for clues and finally saw it, almost invisible under a finger smudge: **3 C C**. *That could mean Number Three Cumberland Cutoff... THIS is Number Three!* Oxo jumped to his feet.

The loot was hidden in this very house!

HELL FIRE

That night Number Five Cumberland Cutoff burned to the ground.

Al heard the fire engines and used a broom handle to bang on the ceiling under the bedroom where Danny slept. The **ThudThudThud** woke her with a start and for a moment she was disoriented. In her dream she'd been picking daffodils in the patch of green between the old stone shed and a happy little stream...

ThudThudThud.

Okay. Okay. I'm awake already, Danny thought peevishly until she heard the fire siren screaming from the other side of the woods. *Cumberland Cutaway. Oh no. Oh no...he came back and burned it anyway!* Sick with dread and regret, Danny hurried down the stairs to find the old man trying to tune in the town radio station. The darkness in the room had a peculiar orange tint.

Danny hurried toward the sliding glass doors and looked out, trying to pinpoint the location of the Laird house from where she stood. She couldn't. It didn't matter anyway since only five houses backed the woods from this direction. *And only one was soaked in gasoline.*

The woods was backlit by the orange and red of a large fire. Heavy smoke settled beneath the trees, diffusing the angry color and making what was happening seem a bit farther away—like a bad dream or the washed-out memory of a tragedy.

A burst of static from the radio interrupted Danny's morose thoughts. She looked up in time to see Al give the radio dial one last tweak and...

.....ortunately a representative from the Mayor's office assures us the fire will not affect any properties in town, and is unlikely to spread even to any other homes on Cumberland Cutoff.

For those who missed our initial bulletin.

Kenilworth Volunteer Fireman arrived too late to save the old, clapboard house at Number Five Cumberland Cutoff. Melting ice kept the blaze contained while Engine 15 worked to keep the situation under control, but all they could do was watch it burn to the ground.

All seven homes on Cumberland Cutoff had been evacuated recently in anticipation of flooding, so no residents were ever in any danger; but fire officials theorize the empty homes may have been targeted by an arsonist.

We now return to our regularly scheduled program: The best of High School Sports.

Al clicked off the radio and looked at Danny. Her face was white and she looked badly shaken.

"I – I – I-um- thought it might be m - my friends house." Even she knew her explanation sounded lame, but her over stimulated brain was working on too many problems just then to care. There was the good news, it *wasn't the Laird's, thank goodness,* and there was the bad news, *but I bet that little weasel Skid set that fire,* and there were the questions, *what should I do with this information? If I call the police they will trace the call back to me.* Just then Danny missed her parents in a whole new way. Did she really want to be responsible for putting the little creep in jail? CSD kids had to stick together.

Danny returned to the sliding glass doors. Al soon joined her. They sat and watched the fire through what remained of the night, each lost in thought.

Rosemary tried to get the attention of the two humans sitting in front of the glass. She stamped her cold little foot and chittered her annoyance. Smoke was starting to sting her eyes and her primitive fear instincts were screaming FIRE! Run away! But she was hungry and she knew there was food just inside that door.

The girl seemed to be looking her way now, so Rosemary stood and stretched her arms as far up the sliding glass door as she could reach and smacked at the glass. When that didn't work, she bumped the glass in front of the old man and danced around until she began to feel foolish. But he also ignored her. WELL! she huffed, puffed and turned away from the people in the big glass window.

With as much dignity as a short, angry, furry animal possessed of a big butt and little head could muster, Rosemary bumbled across the deck, over the still-slippery lawn and dissolved into the woods. Rosemary was going home. It was obvious she wasn't wanted.

Danny spent what remained of the night, agonizing over what she should do. When the colors of sunrise mixed with the embers of the distant, dying blaze, the woods behind Rockaway Estates turned a blushing tangerine and Danny began to feel better. Something about the dawning of this new day helped her make a decision. *No authorities, at least until I find out what Oxo knows.*

The blue flash of the old man's eyes signaled he was awake and Danny looked at him fondly. The soft focus of morning light smoothed the hollows and crinkles of his face and made him appear much younger. "I'll fix us some tea," she said and went to put the kettle to boil. She looked forward to surprising him with a pilfered Hostess Ho Ho when she served his tea.

Al watched absently as Danny disappeared into the kitchen. Yesterday had been an unsettling day for him starting when Danny hadn't come down for breakfast. When he discovered her coat and boots missing and realized she'd gone out into the dangerous weather, his concern had intensified to low-grade panic. There was no way for him to contact Danny once she left the house and he'd run scenario after scenario of her needing his help. But even if she could call him for help, what could he really do trapped in a wheelchair?

He'd finally e-mailed Beatrice to ask for Danny's phone number. As soon as he hit SEND he realized that, even with the cell number, he had no phone to call out on and no voice to call out with.

He'd spent the remainder of the afternoon worrying and berating himself for his inadequacies; by the time Danny did return he'd been so delighted to see her, he hadn't questioned her explanation at all. The story that she'd gone 'home' and returned with a backpack of extra food was ridiculous of course, but faced with Danny aglow with cold and obviously bubbling over with suppressed excitement, he hadn't wanted to ruin it for her. So they'd eaten peanut butter crackers and a candy bar for dinner, and pedaled awhile on the stationary bike to top up the battery before, exhausted, they'd both headed off to get some sleep.

The panicky sound of fire engines ended his pleasant dreams and when Danny flew down the stairs to join him the look on her face took away any lingering feelings of well-being. He could practically hear her nerves jangling like pocket change; her eyes looked haunted and desperate. Danny was somehow mixed up with the fire on Cumberland Cutoff! Her relief was obvious when the radio reporter said the fire was almost out, but when house address was given she looked more confused than anything.

Al spent the hours before dawn working out a few things. *Danny acted more guilty than surprised by news of a fire on Cumberland Cutaway, so she must know something...maybe even how it started.* He didn't like where his thoughts were leading him...*She has some kind of connection to someone living there...I'm sure of it...suppose the fire was set on purpose...by someone she knows...* He was a little afraid Danny was mixed up in something illegal.

As the morning's tangerine sky worked its magic on Al, his dark thoughts gave way; he already knew Danny well enough to know she wouldn't do anything wrong. *The best I can do is let her know she can trust me... I am on her side.* The arrival of two mugs of sweet steaming tea and a plate containing something round and dark and chocolate distracted further thoughts.

Danny put her mug of tea on the floor and sat down beside the old man's wheelchair where she could rest her back against the glass of the sliding door. She watched with delight as the old man tore into Old Lard-Butt's Ho Ho. *Funny, he unrolls it just like I always do.*

It was a promising start to Day Two of the most destructive ice storm in the county's history.

CRIME SCENE

For the governor the jury was still out on whether the newspaper photograph of him at the shelter, benevolently hugging that woman with green teeth, was the smartest or the dumbest political idea he'd ever had. It had generated a lot of voter sympathy—definitely excellent news at the polls—but had also given that Laird woman a direct line to his office and SHE was harder to deal with than his political opponent and all three of his ex-wives put together!

He hung up the phone after assuring the Laird woman he would handle the situation and NO, taking her story to the press was NOT a good idea. *Cow,* he thought.

Apparently, it hadn't been enough that he'd sent a special team out to recover her husband's wheelchair—on a day when only emergency vehicles were permitted on the road! Now she claimed one of her Foster children had broken under the strain of being uprooted by the storm and was setting fires in the neighborhood. It was all the state's fault of course. She wanted to know exactly when the freeze would be over, her roof would be fixed and she, and the children, could move back home.

Feeling distinctly put upon, the governor gave his aide a list of tasks to handle that included: finding someone to check out that Laird woman's roof, and someone to check on the claim that one of her foster kids was setting fires.

Next, he decided to tackle the weather. *Where is the phone number for that bug-eyed, potbellied creature who caused this flooding in the first place?*

"This is the governor." A deep voice barked at Toad the minute he picked up the receiver.

A call from the governor himself! Toad was practically purring with delight until he heard what the man wanted.

"I demand to know what is going on with this weather! Exactly when will the fine citizens of this state get relief?"

Global warming immediately came to mind. Toad was not a weather man—he was a hydrologist with the State Water Department—but above all, he was a bureaucrat who's number one skill was not rocking the boat. *A successful bureaucrat never corrects his higher ups and certainly NEVER admits to NOT having an answer.* Fortunately, Toad had just checked the weather channel and so could say with some conviction, "Yes, Sir. Good afternoon, Sir. According to my latest information the State can expect more seasonable temperatures to return to the area tonight. In fact, by tomorrow morning, the ice will be completely gone. My office expects to begin cleanup of flood damaged areas by tomorrow afternoon, Sir." Toad thought it best to save mention of global warming for another time.

The governor liked definite answers, especially when delivered in a respectful manner. *Adding that last 'sir' was a nice touch,* he thought, *too bad the fellow resembles a frog or there might be room for him in politics.*

"Hem", the governor said. "Good report." He hung up and called a press conference.

The old man typed: WHO DO YOU KNOW ON CUMBERLAND CUTOFF? And Danny's mood immediately changed.

This is dangerous ground. Taking a deep breath, she answered with as much truth as she dared. "Oh...a guy from school...I think his name is Oxo...or something crazy like that..." She tried to sound nonchalant and let her voice trail off at the end like she was thinking about whether Oxo was really the guy's name. *Anything to buy a bit of time, because, next he'll ask 'what house?'...and then what am I going to say?* The feeling reminded her of taking her turn at Monopoly with nine spaces of fully developed property between her and a safe square—she'd need to roll ten or higher or be out of the game. *It all comes down to a roll of the dice.*

And then: WHERE DOES OXO LIVE?

Time to roll 'em, she thought and said, "He's um...three houses from the front. Number Three I think."

A memory stirred in the old man's head. He'd known the residents of Number Three all his life...the Laird's. *Something I recently heard about the Laird's...let me think...*

Until his stroke, Al believed he'd avoided most of the short-term memory problems associated with age but—when he tried to remember the most recent story about the Laird's—older memories were more vivid than recent ones. *I remember young Dougie Laird the puffy pervert. I remember him marrying the most unattractive girl in town...Roxanne Classing.*

He remembered Douglas Laird being somehow mixed up in a bank robbery and going to prison, but his memory was patchy on something that happened when he got out... *something? Something really bad happened to him...and there was a feeling in the community that maybe old Dougie had it coming but...I think he had brain damage.*

The memories were pouring in.

He remembered a bright sunny day with the smell of cut grass in the air; as usual he'd mowed his lawn and the lawns of all the connected townhouses on his street, but when he'd stood back to admire the results the grass had looked a bit choppy...*the mower blade needed sharpening, so I popped the mower in the truck and headed over to Cumberland Cutaway to see Chuck Classing—figuring I'd get the blade sharpened and catch up on gossip in the old neighborhood.* Chuck was still on the Cutaway at Number Two; Al had grown up at Number One. *So Chuck sharpened the blade and we talked...*

Al remembered! Chuck told him Dougie Laird was in a special hospital, leaving Roxanne alone at Number Three and she was thinking about taking in foster kids. They'd laughed, imagining ending up at Number Three with Roxanne Laird as a foster mother. *That's it! Foster kids...Danny fled from Number Three where she was a foster kid!* The thought made him shiver...*who could blame her for preferring the woods?* Then he thought about the friend she had called Oxo. *Is he for real, maybe another foster? Is he the firebug?*

Danny didn't particularly like the 'Ah-Ha look' on the old man's face. She was just about to tell him she was going back out when his computer screen flickered to life and a chime signaled incoming email.

"You have an internet connection? How? Isn't the electricity still out?

The old man was also surprised; it was a message from Bea in response to his request for Danny's cell number. He'd sent it without thinking about a connection—but he must have one because his email and her response clearly went through. *But how?*

"Let me see," Danny leaned in and clicked a WiFi icon in the lower right of the screen to display details of current connection. A new network 'Emergency Channel' had appeared and it was four bars strong. "Wow!" said Danny. "They must have forgotten to secure the channel out of the Emergency Shelter. Way to go Mister Al, you can search the web all day for free!" Danny was delighted by the fortuitous change of topic, and glad too that the old man had something to occupy him while she set off to the woods in search of clues.

The moment Danny was bundled up and out the door— which took awhile because Al had to find her another hat since she'd given the other one away— he opened a web browser and went to work.

Under the state pages link to Child Services Division a search for the name 'Laird' pulled up 27 different case numbers, spanning a period of six years. Al couldn't be sure, but if the case numbers represented foster children, Roxanne currently had four. *Four kids in that place?* He shuddered recalling his own experiences in the small, dreary house...

Dougie hadn't been born the first time Al first visited the Laird's. Mister Laird had finally agreed to contribute to the Boy Scout's annual newspaper drive and young Al, in his scratchy scout uniform with the short pants, spent a full day hauling pasteboard boxes down narrow steps to the waiting truck. All the while, Mister Ignatius Lawrence Laird watched, lurking in the shadows. The man offered neither help nor encouragement, which was actually fine with Al because Laird made his skin crawl.

Dougie Laird would have been about 8 years old and Al an adult, when Al next visited. It was the spring of 1962—a year after President John F. Kennedy urged citizens to prepare for a nuclear attack by building 'family bomb-shelters'—and the Laird Fall-Out Shelter was finally complete. Everyone else had finished the task the year before—a shelter being little more than a covered hole in the cellar floor kept stocked with water, food, flashlights and batteries—and so were curious as to what took the Laird's so long. When Laird invited some of the neighbors over for a look, Al made sure he went along.

Ten gathered at the top of the cellar stairs. Laird ushered them down the steps into a bright, clean, completely average, laundry room. It was a bit confusing until Laird pointed out a nearly invisible door cut into a side wall. Turning the door handle, he'd said proudly, "If the Japs had a place like this to go when we dropped the A-bomb on Hiroshima, none of them would have died, and we'd still be fighting the war." Then he opened the door and stepped in.

They followed Laird into an enormous, bunker-like space carved from living rock and extending well outside the house foundation. Lights hung from the ceiling, the floor was festooned with rugs and the shelves were fully stocked.

The shelter was impressive and Laird was visibly enjoying the compliments until some joker near the back of the crowd said, "Well I know where my family's going to go when the Bomb drops!"

After that everything changed. Laird stiffened, growled something about "room for only three" and hustled his curious neighbors out of the basement and out of the house. He never spoke to any of them again.

Al sat back a minute and thought about the paranoid Mister Laird and his only son. *If Dougie's dead, that's the end of the Laird line. Well, I might as well find out,* he Googled: **Douglas Laird**

He was surprised by the results. *Twelve hits?*

Al read the two lines of text accompanying each web reference noting that all but one linked to newspaper articles. The most recent reference to Dougie was a local news article posted several days before— *guess he's still alive then.*

Al decided to start with the oldest articles, and work his way forward, as a way to get to know Douglas Laird as an adult, instead of the pudgy kid he remembered.

The first eight articles were digitized from the actual pages of national newspapers and covered the 1974 robbery/kidnapping,

Laird's arrest, and Laird's subsequent trial. Al's favorite was a front page Times article, headlined: **Kidnapper Caught—Pants Down!** It detailed the surprise raid on a bathroom stall at McDonald's that resulted in Dougie's ignominious capture. The accompanying photo showed a policeman looking disgusted as he loaded a pudgy Dougie into his patrol car, Dougie wore handcuffs but still clutched his McDonald's bag. *Oh Dougie Laird, you didn't change much!*

Once Dougie was sentenced, the national media apparently lost interest and the story died out. Six years later the local paper rekindled interest with a commentary headlined: **Convict Brings Troubles Home** The author notified Kenilworth residents that Douglas Laird, a prison-hardened, unrepentant criminal, with nine years still left on his original sentence, was paroled and back in their midst.

Then, barely four months later, a short, grim article. Douglas Laird was in critical condition after his badly beaten, broken body was discovered that morning in the city parking lot. It was believed his assailant used a lead pipe, first on Laird's legs and then on his head, in an attempt to extract information about the robbery/kidnapping incident in which both the kidnap victims and the money disappeared. Laird was out on parole after serving six years of a fifteen year sentence for the robbery. Should he live, he would never recover enough brain function to provide police a description of his attacker.

The next mention of Dougie Laird came three years later in a legal announcement granting Roxanne Classing-Laird's petition to remove her handicapped husband from hospital care. The state authorized Mrs. Laird to care for her husband's special medical and dietary needs at home, with monetary help from the health department. *So, Dougie has returned to Number Three, and wife Roxanne is making money on it.*

The final article was headlined: **GOV AGREES — CHILDREN FIRST!** Dated the day after the evacuation, it included a picture of the governor with his arm around a massive woman with green teeth. *Well, hello Roxanne Classing...my how you have grown,* Al said as began to search the article for answers.

Danny crouched in a hollow between two hearty old azalea bushes flanking the porch of Number Four, and watched firemen poking around the smoldering ruin of Number Five with careful, intense scrutiny. It was clear they suspected arson.

A white utility vehicle pulled up with the familiar magnetized door placard announcing: **ON BUSINESS FOR THE GOVERNOR.** One of the firemen walked over to talk with the vehicle's occupant. He nodded, stepped back and the vehicle drove away.

"Sssttt…" the hiss was followed by a rough whisper, "So what do ya think THAT craps all about?" The voice came from the next azalea bush,

Danny smiled grimly. She knew Oxo would show up eventually—she just hoped he hadn't been involved in last night's fire. As she prepared to ask him that question, her attention was drawn back to the firemen. They were rolling out yellow plastic tape and wrapping it around stakes hammered into the hard ground. The tape read **CRIME SCENE**

Oxo said quietly, "I guess they got the message then."

"WHAT message?"

"I went to that Emergency Shelter place this morning and I seen Old Lady Lard-Butt. I tol' her you 'n me stopped Skid from torchin' her place yesterday, an' so he went 'n did Number Five instead. She got real worried…wants to know is Skid's comin' for HER, right? I say 'Sure, you give 'im the chance.' "

"Wow! So what did she say…what did you say?!"

" I tol' her to be safe an' git him caught an sent to Juvy Detention. She sez 'how?'— so I say 'ask your buddy the governor!'"

"She knows the real governor?"

"Well, yeah. Didja see the pitcher of the two of 'em? In the paper?—I figure that's why she gits away with so much—anyways, I tol' her where Skid hangs out."

"How do you know where Skid hangs out? Didn't you tell me you didn't know where he went and that nobody at CSD would hang with him? Danny asked suspiciously. It wouldn't do for Oxo to turn in Skid if he also had something to do with the fire—and Oxo didn't strike her as the kind of guy who was in to good deeds.

"I follered him, right? Once he lit the place he stuck around—watchin' it burn. He ran when them fire trucks showed up—but I follered easy 'cause he's swingin' his dumb little red gas can, right?" He shook his head in disgust. "What an idiot!"—he said more or less to himself.

Ah-Oh...Oxo was there; he might have been involved... "What were you doing here?" Danny said as casually as possible.

Great! How'm I supposed to explain that? Oxo moved further into the azalea before laying on his back and wriggling into the space under the porch—an area that in any other weather would be reserved for spiders and snakes. "Come on back— you c'n see pretty good under here an' its way warmer." He was stalling for time.

Danny took Oxo's suggestion, managing to duck-walk backward to join him under the floorboards. She gave him a long appraising look in the dim light and wondered why he looked so normal. Was it just that his spiked hair was tucked up under Mister Al's watch cap? Then she saw it, *He took off all his chains!*

Oxo looked down, more than a little embarrassed. *Why is she staring at me like that?*

"What happened to your chains? Why did you take them off?" Danny blurted and listened to Oxo mutter something about 'them getting in the way of work.' She followed his eyes as he stared at the ground and noted his particularly grimy hands. The nails were ragged and freshly torn with crescents of dark dirt embedded in the cuticles. There was dirt on the rest of him too...his old steel toed boots were extra scuffed and extra dirty....and his jeans, already ripped and grease stained, were now almost stiff with ingrained dirt. She stared.

Oxo could not ignore the force of her gaze or the questions in her dark eyes. He decided he preferred her first questions to the ones he suspected she was about to ask and tried a half truth, "Well, hey there, I weren't WITH Skid, right? I SEEN him, right? What happened was, after you ditched, I got worryin', like, what if old Skid comes back to torch Number Three? Right? Like...what happens then? ....So I goes back to sort of hang around, right? Keep an' eye on things, right? After while I got...like...cold, so I figure I'll go inside, right? In the middle of the night I hear somethin' weird, right? You know how ya hear stuff in this weather? Next thing I seen this big flash... and I know one of them houses 'round the corner, is burnin', right?"

As Oxo spoke he'd become ever more animated, and Danny was completely absorbed by his story, able to imagine the cold and the dark and the fire. Oxo didn't sound like an accomplice— he sounded like an uneducated, defensive teenager.

He continued, "Man it was weird! I go out fer a look—an before I git where I c'n see him, I HEAR him, right?"

Surprised Danny asks, "You HEAR him?"

"...man it was scary, weird! He's sort of screamin' —or maybe singin'—but he's sayin' words at the top of his lungs—but I don't know WHAT he's sayin'! When I git where I c'n see him pretty good, he's jest this black figure, right? —the house is burnin' behind him—n' he's lookin' at the sky instead —shakin' his fist— screamin' that same crap over 'n over!"

Danny pictured Skid— arm raised to heaven, his arched and oddly elongated form in silhouette against a wall of hungry orange flame—shaking with fury— like an evil demon—his little, wincey rat eyes a bright orange. "What was he shouting?"

Oxo shook his head as if to clear it of images from that night. "I finally git close enuff to hear, and the dudes screamin' 'I am the God of Hell Fire!', like somethin' outta one of them devil movies." In a shaky voice he added, "It was the weirdest thing I ever seen..."

Danny was a bit weirded out too. Absently she said, "I think that whole thing Skid was screaming, about being God and bringing Hell Fire, is just stuff he got from an old song... I'm pretty sure my dad had a record we listened to with those same words."

Oxo shuddered, "Then how c'n they call us kids crazy?"

Danny thought that was a pretty good question.

Oxo looked thoughtfully through a break between azalea branches at the scene next door. The yellow crime scene tape snapped in the frigid wind, but the people had gone. *The coast is clear,* Oxo thought and blurted in a rush, "I got stuff to do, right? Gotta-go-now-see-ya-Danny!"

Oxo low crawled from beneath the porch, dove through a gap in the bushes and disappeared from sight before Danny could catch her breath. *Didn't know he could move that fast!*

Moving slowly, she extracted herself from the hiding place and stood for a moment on protesting legs before making her way to the crime scene. In the open, with no bush or porch to block the wind, the cold was brutal. *Mother Nature can be cruel, but she's never intentionally malicious like this,* she thought as she came up on the destruction wrought by one, hate-filled, teenager.

The air smelled of wet ashes and defeat. Inside the yellow tape, tiny eddies of smoke and swirls of sparks erupted as ground and air temperature collided. The roof, walls and content of Number Five had burned to cinders.

One lone chimney poked from the rubble. Soot blackened its bottom half, but twenty-feet up the natural stone sparkled in the clear sunlight. *Green stone! Maybe the same stone as the Rickenbocker mansion.* Her eyes traveled over the impressive stone work before reaching the top—then she stood transfixed.

How extraordinary! The chimney wore a fantastic crown of glittering ice. Impossible, glassy, shapes bristled, sprouted and draped at crazy angles.

Mister Al would love to see this!

She tried to commit the sight to memory. Some icicles defied gravity by extending horizontally—*they look like glass thorns.* Other stood upright on slender stalks topped with dome-shaped sheets of ice—*ice umbrellas! And that one—draped over the side—looks just like a dove's wing! The group on the top that's all full of holes? Lace. Definitely lace.*

She was witnessing a rare phenomenon. While it is true that water sprayed in sub-zero temperatures will freeze and that chimney tops are good aiming places for fire hoses—the fire should have heated the stone chimney enough to keep ice from sticking. But it didn't. *They must have kept the hoses on long after the fire had died off—after the cold had time to reclaim the chimney...*

A shout from the Laird's ended Danny's musings. Another shout.

She recognized Oxo's voice; he sounded angry and just a little shrill. *What is his problem? He sounds like a hysterical girl!* She hurried toward Oxo's voice as fast as the ice would permit her.

Now she could make out words...

"Get out of here you...you....you furry whatever! Shooo....get away from here right now!!" the voice had gone up another octave.

Danny noticed two things as she came around the back of the house— Oxo's grammar had improved greatly—and he was brandishing a broom at a familiar little shape that seemed just as upset as he was! The scene was comical.

"Oxo! Rosemary! Both of you... stop it right now!" Danny scolded. Feeling like a mother breaking up a kids fight over a favorite toy, she strode toward the combatants,

Startled, Rosemary stopped her angry chittering— looked first at Oxo then at Danny— turned and stomped off into the forest. She never looked back.

"What was THAT?" Oxo said with wonder. His voice was more subdued but he still clutched the broom.

"THAT was Rosemary. She's a raccoon— and also a bit of a thief." Danny answered absently while trying to see the route the little coon took through the woods. "How did you two meet?"

"Well I found THAT, that little bandit sitting in the middle of the kitchen with a candy bar in its mouth and a thieving paw in a bag of potato chips! IT acted like it owned the place! I hollered at it and the thing just ignored me. So, I went after it with a broom but every time I gave it a whack it would just LOOK at me— like I was the one with a problem! So I took the broom and slid the thing right out the door on its big furry bottom—like a big hockey puck." Oxo used the broom to demonstrate his winning technique for raccoon removal.

Danny smiled imagining the scene. "You whacked Rosemary?" With a broom? She wouldn't hurt you!"

Oxo just looked at her like she had sprouted a second head.

It must have been startling for Oxo to find an animal in the kitchen. "I don't think Rosemary recognizes the difference between herself and people." For a moment her thoughts drifted.

Maybe she'd go look for Rosemary— take her the rest of that bag of potato chips.

"What are you still doing here anyway Oxo?" she asked.

Oxo felt his face go red and when he spoke, his bad grammar returned, "Old Lady Lard-Butt sez I should stay until they git back."

"But won't you freeze to death in here?"

"Naw! Lard-Butt tol' me where she hid the blankets. An' I don't feel the cold much."

Danny thought about that—the frozen patch of skin on his face, the festering eyebrow, his ever increasing pus-producing, do-it-yourself piercings— that stuff had to hurt, but she'd never seen Oxo so much as wince! *It's like his skin is numb to pain!*

Oxo tried not squirm under Danny's scrutiny. His nose began to run and he swiped it away with a dirty hand—leaving a muddy smear. *What's she lookin' at?*

Danny watched Oxo give himself a mud-mustache and thought—*if his skin is numb, how did he know that his nose was running?* Then she was struck by another thought— *HOW did he get so much dirtier in less than an hour?* —Oxo's strange face held no answers. *Not my business anyway,* she decided. She had other things to think about. "Well, if you are sure you will be okay, I'll be going."

Oxo nodded encouragement. *I wish she'd leave! I'm just about to find that money!*

Danny stopped and turned back to Oxo, a breeze stinging color into her olive skin.

His stomach turned. *Now what!* he thought with impatience.

With a sweet smile, Danny cautioned, "Oh! —and Oxo? Best be sure to lock that door! Rosemary knows where to find the chips and candy now, and she can pretty much open any unlocked door!" — *not exactly true but worth seeing the look on his face!* "I'll try to catch up with her and see if I can reason with her..." Danny was trying hard now to suppress a giggle... "Oh and I might as well take her that bag you have in your hand as a peace offering."

Oxo handed over a bag of raccoon-damaged potato chips, grumbled his goodbye and— before Danny even reached the tree line— locked himself into the old house. He took a big breath of relief before heading back to the basement.

A new smell had joined the Laird-house potpourri of stink—a smell of freshly turned earth.

Sound is deceptive in the woods, and trying to follow it to its source is the reason so many campers get lost just yards away from their own campground. *Which way?* Danny turned slowly in a circle trying to determine the general direction of the sound, but the piteous sounds seemed to come from every direction as they bounced off trees in the thin, cold air. If she couldn't decide soon which way to go she would have to guess and start walking. Once the winds started up again all hiking would be dangerous.

As she pivoted for the third time in the cloud of her own breath she adjusted the strap of her backpack and dislodged something from one of the pack pockets. She glanced down and saw the mangled, bright yellow bag of potato chips at her feet. Suddenly she knew—*it's Rosemary! Rosemary is in trouble.*

Danny knew which way to go now. Moving as quickly as conditions would allow she collected the bag of chips and began to jog toward the part of the woods where Rosemary lived—the Fortress of the Vines.

Was it possible she was lost? The need to climb over, under and around fallen limbs and branches had forced her from the path but she'd kept going by concentrating on Rosemary's cries. The distress calls had grown steadily louder until now. Now they had stopped. Focusing all her energy on picking out Rosemary's particular sound, she missed the subtle sigh rising in the trees and the tinkling of icy branches...

Crack!

Self-preservation overruled Danny's concentration and she stopped just as a massive limb broke with a sound like the shattering of a million crystal chandeliers. She watched it fall with a racing heart, aware of what would have happened if she'd been a few steps closer.

The sprawling limb hit the ground with such force it bounced and rolled to one side. The motion sent one spiny branch sweeping skyward in a complex spiral that caught the strap of Danny's pack and yanked her off her feet.

She slammed backward into the ice, dozens of flashbulbs exploding in her head. The world went black. She didn't feel the dense rain of woodchips, acorns and other detritus that followed, until one, last, jagged chunk hit her square on the nose. That woke her.

Blind with pain and choking on blood, she grabbed the back of her head, certain her skull was shattered. No brains were leaking out but a lump was forming, and it throbbed with every beat of her heart. She struggled to sit up and the blood that had been trickling down her throat began to pour from her nose. Weak, dizzy and nauseated, she tried to sort out what had just occurred but her thoughts were scattered and feverish.

Into the quiet between wind gusts came Rosemary's cry.

Danny staggered to her feet. She sniffed hard and gulped when a warm clot of blood slid down her throat. At least blood wasn't pouring from her nose and, if she remained focused on her destination, she could think just a little. *Gotta go* she thought with growing urgency.

The way ahead seemed blurry now as she entered the part of the woods where a shallow flood lake had formed. She must be very careful on the ice. Sniffing, Danny went to help a friend.

Deep in the Fortress of the Vines, Rosemary was in trouble. When the top third of the old tree she called home sheered off, Rosemary was still inside—she'd been terrified and screamed bloody murder. After the initial jerk, the downward movement slowed and then stopped altogether. It took a few minutes for Rosemary to calm down, but eventually curiosity got the best of her. She poked her head out of the hole and saw nothing but blue sky.

The top half of Rosemary's tree lay horizontally suspended in a tangled basket of vines, with the tree-hole facing straight up. Under any other weather conditions, Rosemary could have kept her home and the vines would have supported the tree top until it rotted away of its own accord—but today was different. Today, the frozen sap in the vines made even these most resilient of tethers, brittle—breakable...

One by one, the vines snapped like frozen popsicles, jolting the tree—and the raccoon—ever closer to the ground. Over and over, Rosemary tried to regain her footing, only to be tossed like dice in a cup when a vine broke. Disoriented and terror-stricken, Rosemary screamed again and again. Sawdust scratched her eyes and she could taste blood from a torn place on her ear. Her right foot hurt, but each time she tried to hold it off the ground, the ground moved. When the floor and the ceiling switched places and the tree plummeted those final feet to slam onto the unforgiving, icy ground, Rosemary's shriek seemed to go on forever.

So the tree finally fell, and— just like its neighbors had done— took out everything growing below it. The vines were able to slow the decent, so the devastation happened in slow motion—which may be why Rosemary lived.

The final crash sounded close and the long, panicky shriek was loud, but when the raccoon's cries changed to pitiful, muffled chirrings, Danny thought her heart would break. Convinced she was close, she called, "I'm coming Rosemary! Hold on Rosemary! I'm on the way!" Then listened for any evidence the little raccoon had heard her. Through the pounding in the back of her head she thought she heard a slight difference in Rosemary's crying, but it was difficult to focus.

Skating a few more feet, she finally arrived at the place she'd once laughingly dubbed 'the Fortress of the Vines'. Dismayed, she examined the huge clots of wiry-vines tangled among ropey, hanging-vines—some grew up, others hung down, while others wove in an out.

How will I get through that? Armed only with a very dull Swiss Army knife, she looked anxiously around for inspiration— trying not to hear the raccoon's sobs. At least her head felt a little clearer.

Flooding was just as extensive in this part of the woods; the Fortress of the Vines appeared part of the same lake Danny had been sliding across and the vines were rooted in rock hard ice. She allowed herself a small flare of hope. *Frozen,* she thought. *A way in! The vines should break off with a hard kick.*

Ignoring the pain in her head, Danny began to kick.

Hurt, bruised and afraid, Rosemary heard Danny's voice and redoubled her cries. If the human didn't come, Rosemary knew there would be no escape from what was left of her former home—the tree had fallen hard, entrance side down, on solid ice. When she heard the first kick of Danny's sturdy Timberlands, she knew help was on the way.

Toad had turned his cubicle into weather-central. The Weather Channel blared from the TV, the radio broadcast local traffic and weather and his computer screen had two browsers open— both tracking weather. So far, it looked good—even though he had missed the bit about gusting winds—a warm front had indeed moved in and the thaw was underway.

When he'd given the governor that secondhand weather forecast he hadn't expected the governor to quote his weather forecast moments later at a press conference. Of course, the forecast was attributed to a 'highly placed source in a state environmental agency', but since Toad WAS that highly-placed source, he was practically famous!

The local radio station had become all-weather, all-the-time. Live weather updates were interjected into a loop of repeating weather-related stories. Toad listened for the fifth time to a story about the capture of a young arsonist who's lawyer claimed he 'acted-out' because of the weather—THAT was pretty funny—but the best bit came at the end of the report, when the reporter asked the boy's lawyer, "So you claim that this all happened because of Global Warming?"—and the lawyer replied—"Yes sir, I believe the real culprit is Global Warming." The first time Toad heard the story he'd been drinking a tall latte, and sent it spraying out his nose. *Everything gets blamed on Global Warming,* he giggled.

The next local news story to air was one Toad hadn't heard before, and since it was about the governor, he turned down sound on the TV and listened carefully—least he be mentioned again.

The governor was again at the shelter promising every evacuee a trip home the following morning. There was more good news. His 'experts' (Toad smiled at the mention) said the flooding was checked by the ice storm—so very few evacuees would return to damaged property. "In fact", the governor assured his voters, "by tomorrow everything will be back to normal."

As the sun climbed closer to noon, the world began to thaw. The wind that pushed away the freak cold spell died off once the job was done. Water, no longer flash frozen as it burbled from underground streams, began to push up the ice, melting streams from the bottom as the sun melted it from the top.

The sun hadn't yet penetrated to the floor of the woods, warming only the tops of the tallest trees. Under the trees, temperatures were still below freezing and Danny's kicks were effective.

Because even the largest, normally elastic vine gave way to a couple of hard kicks, it was initially easy to smash and tunnel into the heart of the brittle thicket—but soon she found herself snarled, skewered, trapped, tripped and surrounded on all sides. Overwhelmed, she was unable to move forward and had no choice but to back up. She realized she'd need a wide, clear, deliberate path if she expected to go any real distance in this tricky landscape.

*It takes so much time...too much...I don't hear Rosemary...*Danny was bleary eyed and bone-tired. Exhaustion broke over her like a wave, pulling her down. It was all she could do to lift her boot and snap a vine at the root, then sweep away more tangles from the ceiling, front and sides. Taken one at a time, most vines were tiny and frail—like little bird bones—yet the strength of their sheer numbers was formidable. *But not invincible,* Danny's swollen brain acknowledged. .

No matter how methodically she cleared the area, long sticks managed to tangle in her heavy hair. Curly sticks plucked at her knit hat—wiry vines tied up her feet—pointy vines scratched her legs—and sneaky vines snatched at her pack from behind. *At least they aren't sticker bushes* she thought as one wavy snake of a vine whipped painfully across her face leaving a trail of blood. She was beyond caring about a scratch.

Looking up, she sighted a broken tree trunk poking out of the tangle. *Rosemary's tree.* Danny was convinced, and felt compelled to struggle harder and kick faster. *Two yards to go...*

At last! She reached the broken tree and found a giant portion of it on the ground; all the vines around had been pulled down, stripped away, and crushed. *One less thing to do,* she thought and tears of gratitude stung her eyes. *Now focus.*

She walked around bristling limbs and branches to the thickest part of the fallen tree trunk. Leaning over for a closer look at the break caused blood to rush to her head and spots to form before her eyes; she felt nauseous and dizzy, and put out a trembling hand to steady herself. A slight vibration seemed to run through her hand and she became more aware of Rosemary's whimpers. The woozy feeling passed and Danny carefully squatted to examine a pile of what looked like garden mulch spilled beside the log as though it had been poured from a container. Touching the woody deposit brought her head close to the bark and this time she clearly heard chitters and scratching. *Rosemary. Is she IN the tree?*

Danny pressed her ear to the rough bark and knocked. It sounded hollow and drove the little raccoon into even more frantic activity.

Rosemary was trapped INSIDE a hollow in the tree and, from the sounds of it, was desperately trying to tear her way out by tooth or nail.

Danny imagined the little animal stuffed into a partially collapsed cavity, franticly clawing and chewing at the soft pulp in the tree's diseased heart—cramped—battered—afraid. The raccoon was whimpering now and Danny wiped away tears. Why was she so emotional? Whispering "Don't worry Rosemary, I'll get you out," and willing her sluggish brain to get to work, she thought, *I need a plan.*

The splintered portion of tree in front of Danny was as big around as a car tire; it had smashed through an inch and a half of ice and driven limbs and branches into rock-hard ground like daggers. It probably weighed a quarter ton. *This tree is well and truly stuck* Danny knew, she also knew she had to DO something.

Bracing feet against a neighboring tree and putting shoulder against the bark, she attempted to do the impossible—roll the tree forward enough for Rosemary to escape. Her leg muscles cramped with the effort and her head felt like some one was hitting her repeatedly with an iron pipe but she pushed anyway thinking about a Greek myth she had studied, where some guy who had to roll a boulder up an impossible hill...

Impossible.

In the end, all Danny accomplished was to re-start her nose bleed. Her head throbbed and her empty stomach boiled; she needed to sit down. She wanted to sleep...

High above the township of Kenilworth, the winds had succeeded in pushing arctic temperatures back to the North Pole and ushering in a warm front, as predicted. Temperatures were now well above freezing, the sun was melting any bit of ice it touched in a steady patter of raindrops.

Al heard it when he slid open the door and looked anxiously toward the woods. He was grateful for the thaw, but his mind was on Danny. The windstorm had ended forty-five minutes ago and she hadn't returned.

Could she have gotten caught in the wind storm? Maybe hit by a tree? But surely she knew to get out of the woods when that was happening...and it only lasted 30 minutes...

He had dozed off just before the winds hit. The first blast had startled him so badly that he'd actually stood and prepared to run—before he remembered he couldn't run and sat back down.

He couldn't run, but he could certainly worry. He was doing that now.

Can't slide it. Can't roll it. Danny smacked her boot heel into the ice-covered ground that bristled with broken off vines like a man in need of a shave. *Can't dig through that.*

Time for some inside-out thinking. Danny told her self, but inspiration seemed a long time coming. Her vision was more and more blurred; she could see Rosemary desperately searching for release better than what was actually before her.

Levers and wedges, the thought drifted into her jumbled mind. Her father said anyone could move anything with a long enough lever.

A lever would be like a see-saw—one strong plank or pole with something in the middle to balance it on—a rock maybe? Gingerly getting to her feet, Danny began to look around for a long straight limb that might work as a lever. Sometimes it was hard to see, and sometimes she saw two of everything—and every now and again she thought she saw Mister Al.

THE FOREST WEEPS

Deep under the ground a rare phenomenon was underway.

Toad the hydrologist, a self-proclaimed expert on anything to do with water, would call it a side effect of Global Warming.

The governor, seeking to finance his re-election campaign, would buy up the land around it—anonymously of course.

A Native American would cherish it for its magical powers.

Mister Al—whose mind had begun to take all sorts of fanciful flights— would accept it as another miracle in an ever increasing series of miracles.

It didn't matter anyway because no one ever knew it happened.

But it did.

Within the earth's middle core, an itty-bitty crack shifted ever so slightly and through it oozed blue-hot magma. Drawn like a festering splinter, the magma nuzzled its way upward, searching out the path of least resistance. It touched and began to heat a pool of underground water sandwiched between bedrock on the old Rockaway farm. The pool had always been there; it seeped up from the ground just inside the Fortress of the Vines as a scarcely noticeable spring. Well, that spring perked right up when hit with intense heat from encroaching magma and the wet spot on the forest floor was transformed into a burbling fount of natural hot water.

Danny had no idea the ice beneath her feet was actually a frozen stream or that it was melting quickly from below. She didn't notice water pooling beneath the log. She didn't hear the new note of desperation in Rosemary's cry as water began to creep up the walls of her prison and the log began to sink...

Nothing registered as she slumped against the log—her cheek and arm resting on the rough bark as though it were a pillow. In the five minutes since she'd lost consciousness, the rising water had soaked her jeans and the bottom half of her parka.

Danny was in a concussion-induced coma and nothing the trapped raccoon could do would wake her.

She dreamed of the Iroquois. She was dressed in buckskin, beside a clear stream, where she and a boy about her own age were planning to float down that stream in the canoe they were making from a hollow log. They'd stripped off the remaining bark and were using sharp stones to scrape away the log's rotten interior. It was a beautiful day and she felt very happy. Looking up, she saw a tiny woman with exotic eyes headed her way. It was her mother. Mother came toward the hollow log and squatted beside it. With one hand she probed the walls of the cavity they'd made and with the other she tapped the smooth outside. Danny and the boy stopped what they were doing and watched carefully. Mother picked up the sharp green stone Danny had been using, hefted it—considered for a only a second—and smashed its sharp edge into an apparently random spot on the exterior of Danny's dream canoe. The wood buckled with the first blow; with the next a ragged hole opened in the side of the canoe—well below what would have been the waterline...

Perhaps it was Danny's swollen brain pushing against her skull that gave her dream such a super-animated quality, possibly this dream wasn't a dream at all, but Mother's spirit paying a visit, or maybe it was a vision sent by Danny's Indian ancestors—or the forest itself. Whatever the source, Danny felt extraordinarily happy inside.

Meanwhile, her comatose body was at the mercy of the elements. In spite of warmer temperatures, the air was cold, she was wet and her body temperature was falling rapidly. At first, this was a good thing—like ice on an injury—the slowing of her heartbeat and narrowing of her blood vessels reversed the swelling in her brain. Thanks to the cold, she would not die of a concussion.

Danny transitioned from coma into deep sleep—and to death by hypothermia.

We could have died in that canoe, Danny thought as she and the boy stared down at the hole. She bent to touch the ragged wood; expecting it to be rough and splintered, she was surprised to find it pulpy and wet. *It's rotten!* Then Danny understood that rot—like a cavity in a tooth—can spread from the inside out. Now she knew why canoe-makers spent so much time hollowing out a healthy tree instead of saving time by using one that was already partially hollow. *Hmmm* she thought, and enjoyed the feeling of the warm sun on her bare arms. Somewhere a bee was droning... Her eyes closed.

Thoughts moved on—lighting here and there like a butterfly—finally stopping to again consider a dark cavity in a white tooth... Her eyes flew open and she found herself in a dentist's chair!

The chair leaned all the way back and her field of vision was filled by a man's face. He wore a white mask and he was coming toward her...she could hear the whirr of the dental drill and could hear—but not see—her own feet helplessly beating a tattoo on the hard leather chair. The drill buzzed and whirred toward her mouth...she tried to close it...she tried to turn away...but the vibrating drill kept coming...and she heard her own shrill screams. The drill touched her tooth and the vibrations went through her entire body....she thought they would never end...

Danny's body jerked. Her cheek scraped across the bark of the log. This time her eyes did open, but her gaze was unfocused. *Where is he? Where is the dentist?* There was no sign of a dentist—or a dentist chair—or a drill for that matter—but she could still feel the drill's vibration rattling her very bones... And she could still hear screams. *Pain? Fear?*

What was real and what was dream? Struggling to lift her head and shoulders and sort out what was happening she told herself, *This is not a Dentist's chair*. But again, she felt the drill rattle her teeth...again she heard the screams.

Now the shivering began. *Cold.* Unsteady and confused she pushed herself to her feet and looked around at a forest clearing, surrounded by tangled, dripping vines. It was cold but the sun was shining... *the Fortress of the Vines!*

Then two things happened simultaneously—a piercing scream from Rosemary and, deep inside her shirt pocket, a strong vibration. *The telephone.* A rush of adrenaline jump-started her heart, and temporarily chased away the cold.

Danny was alive. The world had never seemed so clear, or so clean. She felt changed somehow—different in her own skin. Taking a deep breath, she found the mingled smell of ice, earth, sap and damp leaves, utterly intoxicating.

She knew what to do—and she knew it would work. First she needed a large sharp stone and wasn't surprised to find a large green rock at her feet. Picking it up like a baseball she knocked away the thick bark surrounding Rosemary's prison. *There has to be a soft spot.* She ran her palm over the smooth place. *There.* Without hesitation she hit the place with the sharp side of the stone and felt the wood give ever so slightly. Again and the stone bit through hard, but thin, skin to the soft pulpy rot below. Encouraged, she struck again.

This time she heard a slight splash and looked down in concern. Her blows had shuddered deep into the log, breaking loose the remaining ice; water rushed through the cracks in a way that suggested there was plenty more where that came from. She needed to hurry or Rosemary could very well drown! As if in answer, the little raccoon let out a series of sharp frightened yips.

She aimed at the soft spot and hit hard. The wood crumbled, and helped by Rosemary's furiously scrabbling toenails, crumbled inward. Two frenzied black hands reached out of the opening, followed by a ball of fur that flew as though shot from a catapult.

The raccoon fled as though pursued by demons; disappearing into the net of vines without ever looking back.

Well! That's a fine how do you do. Smiling, she thought of the little raccoon's rescue with satisfaction. It had been a long strange day...

Danny turned in a circle, taking in the small area a fallen tree had carved into the sea of vines and thinking of the drama played out there. In the few minutes passed since Rosemary's escape, one end of the log had begun to bob slightly in the flowing water. The stream was several feet deep. *This must be the stream that divided the Rickenbocker property!*

A now-familiar buzzing in her breast pocket brought Danny back from thoughts of the stone shed. *The phone.* Reaching under her damp parka to retrieve it, she became painfully aware of the cold. *I'm wet.* The phone display showed she had a text message but she was now shivering too violently to read it.

She stuffed the phone and her hands deep in the parka pocket and headed for the path carved through the vines. The shivering intensified as she sped up, hoping she hadn't come this far just to freeze to death. To take her mind off of her wet clothes she thought of the text message. *Who sent it?* The phone's intrusive vibration had probably saved her life.

At the edge of the Fortress of the Vines a flash of red caught her eye and through the tangled vines she made out a large, familiar looking shape. *That's exactly the color of my sleeping bag. Could it be my sleeping bag?* In a day filled with strange and miraculous occurrences, this seemed somehow possible...

It IS my sleeping bag!! She saw it clearly now and relief washed over her; how the bag made its way to the Fortress of the Vines didn't matter, what mattered was the insulated blanket and change of clothes inside. *Salvation.*

At the townhouse the tedious waiting was getting the best of Al. To break the monotony he'd climbed on the exercise bike and willed his legs to pedal. He was just about to give up when the lights went on and the television blared to life. It was good that the electricity was finally back on.

He occupied himself by turning off lights until he heard the long-anticipated knock at the door.

Danny, at last. I must remember to give her a key... Muting the TV, the old man rolled to the door and pulled it open with an eager smile.

A red-haired boy carrying a box grinned back at him. "You must be Mister Smith. I'm Josh, come to deliver your grocery order. I'd have been here this morning, but the roads only just opened up." The boy smiled again as he juggled the heavy box, "So, where would you like me to put these?"

Al nodded and spun his wheelchair toward the kitchen expecting the boy to follow. After a moment, he heard Josh beside him, pointed out the kitchen, and returned to the living room. He listened to Josh restock his kitchen and thought about the recent series of storms and catastrophe. So much had happened in such a short time, that it was hard to believe he lived smack in the middle of a row of townhouses and not on some isolated frontier. *Now that civilization has returned I wonder about Danny...*

"Mister Smith? Do you want me to turn off the oven?" Josh peeked around the doorframe at the old man and saw him nod so he turned the oven off and shut the door before leaving the kitchen. "I'll find my own way out sir, and I'll see you next week."

Al opened the curtains in the front window and was surprised by the stream of cars entering the neighborhood. All the evacuees were returning home he supposed. According to the radio, only one group of homes near the bottom of a slope had water damage from the flood—but probably only at basement level.

Where is Danny?

Danny sat astraddle a low tree branch trying to stay out of the mud. The fresh clothes were warm and dry but her boots weren't, so she'd taken them off and circulation was finally returning to her feet. With the sleeping bag unzipped and worn like a hooded cape the shivers had finally retreated.

Now that she was high and dry she anxiously flipped open her cell phone and followed the prompts to access Text Messages.

AL WORRIED. R U OK?

ALL worried? That made no sense. She read the message twice more before realizing her mistake. *It's **AL**, not **ALL**. Mister Al sent the message...but how??? He doesn't have a telephone and—even if he did—he doesn't know my phone number.* Danny was mystified until she thought about the other impossible things that had happened since she met the old man...

She returned to the second half of the message: R U OK? — that's text-speak for: Are you okay?

Mister Al wants to know if I'm okay...and I AM okay— because of him.

LIGHTS ON

It was still dark on Cumberland Cutaway as Oxo belly-crawled through a crawl space he'd accessed from the Laird's laundry room. The batteries in his flashlight were dying, casting an ever-smaller circle of yellow light, but he was determined to examine every square inch of the hard packed clay that still bore shovel marks. The landscape was so dry and dusty that not even a spider could live there—which was a very, very good thing because he hated spiders.

He'd finished examining the last bit of clay and was turning around when a loud buzzing followed by a strobe of intense light startled him into sitting up and smashing his head into a beam. Rubbing his forehead he looked behind him.

The electricity is back on.

The basement's fluorescent lights were pulsing to life as Oxo dragged himself out of the dark crawl space to take a look at what the basement had to offer now that he could see...

Not much, he determined at first glance. The brightly lit basement of Number Two was small, featureless and much smaller than the house above it.

In the corner hulked a big metal tank, furry with the greasy dust of many years. *That must be the oil heater* he thought and, as if on cue, the mechanism behind the tank gave a loud click followed by a whoosh as somewhere deep inside a blue flame flickered to life and began making heat.

The familiar metal cylinder of a water heater occupied the far wall and beside it in the corner lurked a very old, forgotten-looking washer and dryer. Oxo found it strange that old Lady Lard had never told the fosters about this laundry room, since she didn't like them to use the one in the kitchen. Of course SHE used the one in the kitchen—which made sense since she was too big and the basement stairs too narrow for her to schlep laundry up and down.

He walked closer and looked at the washer's many knobs, *maybe they don't work.* But a flip of the ON switch sent water pouring into the basket. *Huh!* Well at least he now knew where to go for clean clothes.

Losing interest and about to turn away, he spotted an odd crack in the wall. Stepping closer he squinted at a crack entirely too straight to be just a crack.

A door.

Excitement boiled up and Oxo felt his heart begin to thunder in his chest. He managed to pull both washer and dryer away from the wall and then—with much grinding and scraping—into the center of the room. There was plenty of room for him now. He stood—heart thundering with anticipation—eyes afraid to blink—looking at the fully revealed crack in the merciless light of the fluorescents...

There WAS a door.

Flush with the wall and painted the same color, the door was obviously designed to be invisible behind the washer and dryer. Oxo's knees felt weak. For the first time in his life he forgot all the rotten things that had happened to him. Behind the door, would he find the missing bank loot? He reached out with filthy fingers and pushed, then watched, as though from the wrong end of a telescope, as the wall swung inward...

Darkness was on the other side.

Behind Oxo the over-bright fluorescent tubes—a fixture in every rotten school he'd even attended—whined their frustration at being unable to penetrate even an inch beyond the door jamb. *It's like looking into a can of flat black paint,* he thought and hesitated.

Oxo was perfectly balanced between knowing and not knowing. He knew that once he invaded the darkness of the space beyond, there would be no turning back—he would know if what lay on the other side was a broom closet or a cave full of jewels or a shortcut to the Milky Way. Then the craziest thought crossed his mind. *I'll just close this door and leave.*

But of course he didn't.

Oxo scanned the wall outside the door for a light switch. He found it at knee height in the shadow of the dryer hook-up. Flipping the switch illuminated a hanging light inside the room; the fixture's green metal shade suggesting pool halls, gangster movies and comic books set in Gotham City to Oxo, until his eyes adjusted to what he was really seeing.

A room; a BIG room—easily double the size of the rest of the basement— but rounded like the inside of a cave—and like a cave, the walls appeared cut from living rock.

Moving into the room while still dazed, he failed to notice the steps— the floor of the high ceiling room was several feet lower than the rest of the basement—and nearly lost his footing. *Not a good time to break a leg.* Four careful steps later Oxo stepped onto a floor covered with overlapping rugs—like the carpet sellers shop in the movie Aladdin, the rugs were all richly colored.

What is this place?

Several large, beautifully constructed, drafting tables stood side by side complete with gooseneck lamps and magnifying glasses for detail work. *Maybe it's an art studio.* Oxo pulled a tall stool up to the table and hunched over as though he were drawing—when he switched on the lamp, it offered just the right amount of light, at just the right angle. He imagined working on his comic book illustrations at the table.

Perfect!

On the slanted surface of the second drafting table rested a large leather bound book that reminded him of something he'd seen witches use in movies to find spells and potions. Curious, Oxo briefly opened it, but the writing was all in cursive and he wasn't much of a reader anyway.

He continued his delighted inspection.

Drawn to a heavy contraption with a wide rubber belt and roller, he touched the ornate metal wheel on its the side—and the belt moved under the roller. It looked like a torture device, but he was pretty sure he was looking at an etching press. Further investigation turned up a shelving unit full of various flat metal plates and a drawer filled with tins of the thick, sticky ink used in printmaking.

Another drawer unit held dozens of neat boxes containing different sized writing and drafting pen nibs. The artist inks were on a wide shelf above—Oxo figured after such a long time the inks were probably unusable but everything else—even the rolls and stacks of paper Oxo uncovered in a corner— seemed perfectly fine

By the time he'd poked his hand in each drawer, followed every crack and lifted every rug it became clear the room held no lost bank robbery money. It appeared, instead, that he had discovered some kind of secret print-making shop. He tried to picture Lard-the-Bank-Robber, or Lard-the-Nazi, having the deep interest in art or drafting this room implied—but he couldn't. It just didn't seem possible. He thought he might ask Lard-Butt-the-Drooling-Wreck about the room, then smiled at his own foolishness. *Yeah. Right.*

Only one item in the whole room seemed to have a connection to what Oxo knew about Douglas Laird— a massive red Nazi flag displayed prominently on the stone wall. Oxo found the sight offensive and pulled over one of the taller tables so he could reach the ugly swastika. Forcefully, he tore it down, then carefully folded it, for use as fabric in some future venture.

This was Oxo's space now and he reckoned he'd do his own decorating.

Danny hoped Rosemary wouldn't care that she ate the potato chips. Now that she was warm, she discovered she was hungry, and the battered chips were all she had. As she munched, she looked around. From her perch on the tree limb she could see none of the storm damage—but she could see the Fortress of the Vines quite clearly.

Thinking about the path she had blasted through on her way to Rosemary, she decided she would work to keep it clear. *That won't be easy once spring comes and the vines start growing.* Maybe she'd buy a machete or something— *Do they sell those to little girls?*—then she could cut deeper into the Fortress and follow the stream, maybe even find the stone shed.

The big, immediate problem was the tent. If her sleeping bag washed away it was obvious her tent did too, and that left her— once again—homeless. As she brushed off crumbs and folded up her sleeping bag she realized that she didn't feel panicky and alone, instead for the first time in a long, long time, she felt watched over and safe.

I should bump my head more often Danny thought wryly and jumped from the tree limb onto the plastic bag where her wet boots awaited. She yanked them back on.

It was time to check on Mister Al.

The old man fixed Danny an enormous sandwich and a big glass of cold milk then sat with her while she ate. Even though Danny had just gotten out of a hot shower that lasted forever he could see she'd missed a rim of dried blood just inside her nose. There were angry scratches on her face, the fingernails holding the sandwich were torn and both hands were pretty cut up. When she turned to the side he spotted a lump under her thick hair. *Yet she seems so happy!*

"I was going to wait for the wind storm to pass before I went in but then I heard this horrible screaming and I just knew it was Rosemary." Danny stopped for a large gulp of milk and noticed the old man's look of concern. *Maybe I shouldn't tell him the rest.* But Danny was having a very hard time keeping her mouth closed—she needed to talk. *I just won't tell him the dangerous bits.*

"It turns out Rosemary was in part of the woods I call the Fortress of the Vines because vines ate up all the trees and everything and made it impossible to get through. Animals like it in there though, so I guess that's why Rosemary lived there."

Al stopped her with a raised hand. His eyes were blazing as he typed: I KNOW THE PLACE. THOSE ARE POISON IVY VINES! SAP FROM THOSE VINES MAKES YOU BREAK OUT IN HORRIBLE, ITCHY BLISTERS. SPREADS EVERYWHERE! IF IT GETS IN YOUR EYES IT CAN BLIND YOU AND IF IT GETS INTO YOUR LUNGS YOU CAN DIE. ONLY IN THE WINTER , WHEN THE SAP IS DOWN, ARE THOSE VINES PROBABLY SAFE.

He remembered with chilling clarity his childhood run-in with the poison-ivy vines of Kenilworth woods— the constant itching had almost driven him insane. He'd scratched the skin completely off parts of his legs and arms. When the juicy blisters spread their oily poison to his face and the corner of one eye his mother tore up an old bed sheet and used it to tie him to the bed—for his own protection. He carried the scars on the calves of both legs...but the memories he carried were far worse. He pressed the keys harder than usual. It was important she understand...

STAY FAR, FAR AWAY FROM THE FORTRESS OF THE VINES, DANNY!!

Danny stared at the message the old man had typed so ferociously, her forgotten sandwich held in both hands. *One more weird thing.* Catching the old man's eye she said softly, "But I'm not allergic to poison-ivy, Mister Al." She added, "Dad said it's because Mom's Iroquois... Indians don't get poison-ivy I guess..." Danny's voice drifted off as—like a key turning in a lock—the importance of what she'd just said clicked home... *the Fortress of the Vines is poison to most people, but not to me. It will protect me!*

ARE YOU ABSOLUTELY SURE? I WASN'T ALLERGIC EITHER UNTIL AGE 10 AND THEN I GOT IT SO BAD I WANTED TO SCRATCH OFF MY OWN SKIN. I STILL HAVE SCARS ON MY LEGS. BELIEVE ME POISON IVY IS NOT SOMETHING TO MESS WITH!

As Danny read it was obvious the old man was upset. Wanting to reassure him she shook her head 'no'. "It's okay. Honest. I'm okay. I once camped right in the middle of a really healthy patch of poison oak AND poison-ivy and I was fine." She was pleased to see the tension leave his face, and went on. "...but I'm really glad you told me, because I was thinking those crazy looking vines were something Dad called Kudzu"

Al was thinking about Danny's references to her parents. *Danny has Indian blood...makes sense...that's where she gets that coloring.* He typed: DON'T KNOW OF ANY KUDZU AROUND HERE...YET. THE DEPT. OF AGRICULTURE KEEPS AN EYE OUT AND IF THEY SEE KUDZU THIS FAR NORTH THEY'LL COME IN AND DESTROY IT.

"I do know the difference between Kudzu and the poison-ivy leaves, but at this time of year one dead leaf pretty much looks like any other." After a short pause she blurted, "So then, you know how about the vines? How thick they are and everything? You've seen them right?"

Al shook his head yes, and felt the skin on his legs crawl with the memory. He tried not to think about the month he'd lost to poison-ivy and typed...

You'd probably need a machete or a blow torch to get through that tangled mess the way I remember it! So how DID you do it?

"Yeah, well, this is the REALLY amazing part...well, ONE of the amazing parts anyway. Remember that flood a couple of days ago?" she smiled at his reaction to her ridiculous question.

What a neat young lady this girl from the woods turned out to be! Al thought, and tried not to give her the satisfaction of a smile...

"Well," she continued, "the vines were sitting right in about two inches of water...and when the water froze, THEY froze too! Solid." she emphasized. "You know the way you can just snap off an icicle?" She looked up expectantly.

The old man nodded. He knew.

"THAT'S what it was like." she said triumphantly, "Even the big, fat vines were so brittle they just snapped! With one good kick." Danny demonstrated her technique for a moment before continuing with a sigh. "It WAS easy, and at first it was fun, but it still took forever!...I mean it seemed that way...there were so many of them...and I could hear Rosemary." It was Danny's turn to shiver with the memory, "... but I got there...finally."

"I found Rosemary, trapped inside this log." Danny struggled to describe the scene.

Al loved a good story. He imagined the cold dampness in the air... the smell of broken vegetation...the frantic sounds of a raccoon begging for release. And most powerful of all, he sensed Danny's feeling of helpless desperation—a feeling he himself was intimately familiar with.

Danny's story continued, "...she didn't sound hurt but, boy, was she freaking out! Screaming, scratching and clawing." Danny stopped to take an enormous bite of the sandwich. The groceries had arrived just that morning so the bread was soft and fresh and the tomatoes and lettuce were crisp. She really was hungry.

Al impatiently watched Danny chew. He wanted to know how she had freed the raccoon, how she had bashed her head open, and how she would explain the giant ziplock bag full of wet clothes she had hauled back. Finally he saw her swallow.

Danny finished the milk in a satisfied gulp and smiled at the old man. She appreciated his ability to really listen. "Sooo...where was I?"

Al smacked his open palm against his head in mock frustration and enjoyed Danny's giggle.

"Okay. So, Rosemary is trapped under this huge—I mean gy-normous— log. There is absolutely no way I can move it. I tried pushing, pulling and lifting just in case I was stronger than I thought...but I wasn't. I couldn't budge this thing a single inch. Besides, it hit so hard when it fell that it was almost buried in the ice! I had no idea how I would get Rosemary out... and I could hear her clawing and squealing and sort of whimpering...so I sort of laid down beside the log and talked to her."

"Then ANOTHER weird thing happened...somehow...I actually fell to sleep! I was out so completely that I didn't notice that the water was starting to rise around the log and that my clothes were getting all wet." Danny halted and thought a minute about what she should say next. She wouldn't share her vision— that was her private treasure—but she wanted Mister Al to know just how important his text message had been.

The old man was delighted with the story so far—and pictured this small girl trying to move a log ten times her size in order to save her friend— but the part about her falling to sleep was both suspicious and dangerous. He looked at her sternly, and typed his lecture: THAT'S A RECIPE FOR HYPOTHERMIA YOUNG LADY. YOU ARE VERY FORTUNATE TO HAVE WOKEN UP AT ALL! *How horrible it would have been if she hadn't returned and I didn't know what happened to her?*

"That's right! I think I WAS slipping into hypothermia...or maybe getting ready to drown...and I was having this crazy dream about a dentist coming toward me with a drill. I could feel that buzzing drill in my MOUTH, and it scared me so much I woke up. And...guess what? The buzzing WAS real. It was my phone vibrating. It was trying to deliver YOUR text message!" She looked hard into the old man's face, captured as usual by his blue-blue eyes, and felt her own dark eyes grow misty.

Oh WOW! Al thought.

"I think you saved my life Mister Al." Sappy, un-Danny-like, emotions made her voice grow thick, "Thank you!" She laid a hand—scratched and still showing spots of dirt—on the old man's scrawny forearm and gave it a warm and grateful squeeze.

This new twist in the story caught Al completely off guard. He hadn't expected to become the hero in the tale and, truth be told, it delighted him. It had been more than a few decades since he had been anyone's hero. He put his wrinkled hand over the one Danny rested on his arm, and patted. The gesture felt woefully inadequate to him but he thought she understood.

Change the subject... NOW. Danny ordered herself and managed to clear her throat which had gone all funny and tight, "Now YOU tell ME something—how did you manage to send me a text message without a phone and without my number??"

Al's old brain still struggled to keep up with his young friend's tendency to jump from subject to subject... but he was getting better. He smiled and moved his fingers to the keyboard as Danny said...

"Tell me about the text message. I can't figure out how you did it."

GOT YOUR NUMBER FROM BEATRICE. WENT ON LINE TO EACH OF THE MAJOR CELL CARRIERS UNTIL I FOUND THE ONE YOU ARE WITH. THE COMPANY LETS YOU SEND TEXT MESSAGES FROM A COMPUTER. YOUR TURN. HOW DID YOU GET ROSEMARY OUT!?

"Huh" Danny said... a little disappointed by the old man's answer. She'd been half convinced he'd figured out how to send a psychic message via cell signal. The truth wasn't nearly as complicated. Danny thought about that...she—who normally was so grounded in numbers and science—now seemed willing to believe in anything—*dreams...visits from the grave...secret laboratories... hunches...ancient ancestors...what's next?... little green men?* But somewhere along the line her world view HAD changed—it was like she was looking at the same thing from a different side of the street.

WELL? ARE YOU WOOL-GATHERING? Al jabbed at the screen to get Danny's attention. He didn't like the flush that had come to her checks. He speculated, *Concussion?* Her eyes seemed to have lost focus.

Catching herself, Danny reigned in her thoughts. "Sorry—my mother used to say that 'wool-gathering thing', too—I was just thinking about what you said. I never knew cell companies offered that feature. Neat." Her eyes seemed again to lose focus and she gave her head a rueful shake, "Anyway—I guess I'm doing that wool-gathering thing again—back to Rosemary. When the phone call woke me, I opened my eyes sort of KNOWING what to do."

"I found a sharp rock and tapped on the wood until I found a rotten place." Danny figured there was no need to tell the whole tedious tale so she cut to the chase. "With a few good bangs, the soft wood gave way." here Danny paused to savor the memory, "Rosemary left that hole like a rocket—I haven't seen her since."

I HAVE. SHE MUST HAVE COME DIRECTLY HERE AND I GUESS SHE DID LOOK UNUSUALLY BEDRAGGLED NOW THAT YOU MENTION IT. HER RINGED TAIL MUST HAVE GOTTEN WET BECAUSE IT LOOKED LIKE A RAT'S. As he typed he thought about what Danny had just told him. I GAVE HER THE LEFT OVER ROAST. While Danny's story filled in the biggest blanks, he knew there was much more she wasn't telling. *I guess she isn't going to say anything about the lump on her head...or the change of clothes...or carrying around a sleeping bag in a ziplock bag.*

Discovering Rosemary had run to Mister Al delighted Danny, and she admitted to herself that she'd been a tiny but hurt because Rosemary hadn't hung around after her rescue. *Silly* she admonished, *raccoons are wild animals not domesticated pets.* Still, she turned toward the sliding glass doors and scanned the deck for any trace of her friend. Beyond the glass the sun was shining and the world was busily dripping and draining. *School tomorrow.* Danny frowned. *Where will I sleep tonight?*

The old man thought as he watched emotions dance across Danny's expressive face. *Her thoughts are so transparent.* The frown told him Danny had returned to the present—story time was probably over. Could he draw her out just a little bit more? The danger, he knew, was that he might push too hard and lose Danny's trust forever. The girl reminded him of a wild animal— independent, easily frightened and basically distrustful. Still, he needed to warn her about Dougie Laird...

"I stopped by my house for some fresh clothes and asked if it was okay to stay here for one more night," she glanced up for confirmation and saw the old man nod vigorously. "They said it was okay and I should also ask you if I could do a load of laundry since our washer and dryer is busted. Oh, and I also brought my sleeping bag which was always too big to wash in our dinky washer—if that's okay with you?"

Al nodded assent. *You really think on your feet Daniela Smith.* Giving Danny extra credit for her balance of fact and fiction he thought, *I suppose it's even possible she DID ask her foster parents*—but he hoped not—for some reason he felt it best to stay as far away from the Laird's as possible.

Al tried to dispassionately assess the girl sitting across from him. *What would I see if I were looking at her for the first time? Hair,* he thought. The dark hair was still snarled in the back—it seemed her efforts to smooth it had concentrated only on the front—and provided a wild frame for her tanned face. The face seemed to exist only to pay homage to the truly remarkable eyes, which were almost magically luminous, heavily lashed, and exotically tilted at the corners. Her clothes were rumpled, slightly ragged, but relatively clean—she was probably the butt of jokes at school, *but then bully's pick on the weak kid and Danny's certainly not weak. Actually* he thought, *for a twelve?—thirteen?— fourteen?— year old girl she's rather formidable.*

Danny's thoughts, like dog with a bone, had returned to the worrisome topic of Rosemary's well-being. Where was she and where would she live now that her home was destroyed? *Why am I worrying about where she will live...I should be worrying about where I will live. My house washed away too,* Danny realized with shock. *I never looked for the rest of my stuff—I won't be able to start over if everything is gone.*

With a quick glance outside and a few calculations, Danny reckoned it was already close to 5:30, which gave her under two hours before sundown. Would it be enough time?

She pushed her chair away from the table with a scrape and stood up. Mister Al looked a bit startled, and it took her a few seconds to come up with an explanation, "Um, I just thought of something. I...ah...just remembered I took out my...ah...wallet when I pulled out the phone...and I left it there." *What am I sayyying?...that is the most ridiculously lame excuse EVER.* As Danny continued to silently berate herself, her mouth went right on talking, "I've got to get it before it gets dark...or they won't let me on the school bus tomorrow... Gee Mister Al, thanks for the sandwich...just leave the plates, I'll clean-up when I get back."

Al listened to Danny babbling as she crammed the sleeping bag in the washer and pulled her now-dry boots and parka from the dryer. She was trying to convince him that she had dropped her wallet in the woods, which was of course, ridiculous. *Is she going back to collect more of her things or will she check on Rosemary?* He typed as he listened with half an ear...

"I won't be long. Back before 6. It's it nice to have the electricity on again, doncha think? No more pedaling I guess...though I really think that generator thing you made is a great idea..." In Danny's desperate attempt to get out of door without answering any questions she was trying to fill the silence completely. "I'm glad the wind finally stopped...and everything...um...like...this Global Warming is real serious! You know?" *I definitely sound like an idiot!* Her words came even faster when she saw the old man was still typing. *Oh no,* she thought, *what is he going to say? I hate to lie!* Danny braced herself.

Mister Al turned the computer screen toward Danny. GET THE BIG BRANCH CLIPPERS FROM DOWNSTAIRS. YOU CAN USE THEM ON THE VINES. I USED THEM TO CUT TREE LIMBS UP TO 2-INCHES ROUND. THEY ARE HANGING ON THE WALL OVER BY THE LAWN MOWER.

Danny's smile blazed with a combination of relief and gratitude as she scurried off to the basement.

Things downstairs looked different under the these fluorescent lights, Danny thought as she flipped the switch and headed for the section of the basement Mister Al had dedicated to lawn care. *It felt like a shadowy, secret laboratory when we worked down here during the storm!* But now the inventor's workshop was gone, leaving a regular old suburban basement in its place.

As she reached up to collect the long handled clippers from their neatly outlined spot on the wall, she noticed a high shelf of lawn care items. One bright orange jug had a black skull and crossbones carefully painted on the side. Curious, she looked at the label and read: **GroundKlear —Kills Vegetation with ONE Application**. *Huh,* Danny thought and headed back up the stairs, clippers in hand.

SIGNS

Danny was unusually light on her feet as she entered the woods. The odd sensation of being sheltered and cared for returned as she walked along, avoiding the sloppiest areas of mud and reveling in the novelty of being at peace. When was the last time Danny had felt this way? *Not for a long time...not since my mother was alive...*

She remembered that long fearful night of knowing, yet not BELIVING, something terrible and irrevocable had happened to her mother.

I haven't felt safe since then.

By the time the policeman and social worker arrived to tell Danny of her mother's fatal accident, her protected carefree childhood was over and her new world was haunted by distrust and anxiety that stood ready to poison any future feelings of contentment and harpooned and any possibility of happiness. When her absentee father showed up to claim her she knew not to let her guard down, and his disappearance proved she was right. Danny accepted that, since her life was built on dangerously shifting sands, it could never be trusted — until, today. Today—even though she had almost been killed—TODAY, she felt *safe!*

How bizarre.

She stopped short and looked around. The path leading from Mister Al's backyard to her campsite in the hollow was thoroughly obliterated by debris knocked loose in the ice storm and she was a little bit lost. Hoping for the same inspiration that had guided her actions earlier in the day, she closed her eyes and opened her imagination. Deliberately she began to turn in a tight circle. *Where would the tent be now? Which way?*

Opening her eyes, Danny started walking in a direction that felt right.

The thin nylon tent hadn't fared well; once the fabric ripped and the shelter came unmoored, the storm reduced it to an unrecognizable wad of muddy, tangled material. Retreating flood waters carried the whole mess downhill to the northeast, where it snagged on a stick in the re-invigorated current of Kenilworth woods new hot spring. It trailed like a banner in the steaming waters.

Danny would have missed it, but for the sound. As she turned to walk around a hump of a moldering log she heard, what sounded like, burbling water and stepped closer to the log. Her boots made sucking sounds; the ground was soggy; the air had the rich smell of dark mud, wet mulch and something else? She examined the shadows closest to the crumbling log. *Where is that bubbling sound coming from?*

A decayed limb forked at a forty-five degree angle from the log she'd been about to walk around. Ducking under, she stared into the shadows until her eyes caught the oily glint of moving water. It was like the deep, mysterious water that lurks under piers, and Danny thought about that as she distractedly rubbed her nose which had begun to tickle. The earthy smells intensified and became more distinct as Danny stepped closer; now she could detect the odor of tannic acid, waterlogged wood, greening plants and growing roots. The smell was strangely reminiscent of spring.

Curious, she pushed deeper into the shadow, blinking to help her eyes adjust. *That's not just a puddle. There must be stream under there.* But it couldn't be a stream because nothing was visible on the opposite side of the log. *Well, maybe it's a spring— where the stream starts. That might explain it.*

She could clearly see the water now and, if she squinted, she could make out something very like fabric fluttering beneath its surface. *What IS that?*...she thought and reached into the darkness. It wasn't until her fingers closed on slippery nylon that she realized her hand was in water—hot water. *It's like bath water!* But she had other things to think about when she drew out a large, sloppy, frayed rag. *My tent. Or what's left of it.*

The weirdness came without warning. Images projected themselves inside her mind as though the inside of her skull was the screen at an old time drive-in movie theater and she found herself looking at scenery—a wooded area. *A memory? A vision?* Occupied with the mechanics of her bizarre experience, it took a moment to notice the scene contained a little canvas tent...

That's Dad's tent! And then she thought, *so where IS Dad's tent?*

She remembered taking it down, folding the old canvas into its waterproof bag, hanging the bag from a nearby limb, intending to come back for it. Instead, she had completely forgotten about it.

The bag was hanging right where she'd left it. She'd known it would be. She was just as sure about what she must do next—go to the Fortress of the Vines.

The sun had slipped closer to a bloody smear of horizon by the time Danny reached her destination. She stared.

In the crimson light, the wall of vines looked undisturbed; it was as though she'd never been there. *But I was JUST here. I'm sure I went in right here, at the end of the path. It's like the vines knitted themselves back together. Where is the opening I spent so much time making?*

This is ridiculous, she thought, squatted, and felt beneath the vines for evidence of broken vegetation. Her palm touched sharp stubs and broken stumps jutting from the ground. *Okay— this is good— I can only take so much weirdness...*a grim smile came to her lips...*and a re-sealing vine-wall would have just been too much!* She stood and pushed her arm through the matted wall where it disappeared into empty space. *It's a curtain, it only looks solid.*

Dramatically sweeping aside a hanging mat of vines revealed the opening Danny had worked so hard to create. *All is not as it appears.* Taking a deep breath she stepped inside.

As the curtain dropped, snuffing the last red gasps of daylight, the entrance was effectively sealed. *The only way I could be seen in here was if I were wearing fluorescent clothing and jumping up and down...even then I'd probably have to be making a lot of noise.*

She turned on the flashlight and sent the beam to probing the tunnel; it looked pretty sketchy in the strong white light—in fact, if she hadn't already known the way, she wouldn't have been able to go forward. *No time to think about it.* She had clippers.

Danny went to work, snapping, clipping and dragging. The path widened and was soon littered with grizzled tendons of ancient vines, bird-bone sized sticks and the spring-like coils.

With a quarter of an hour remaining before total darkness, she reached the clearing.

At last! This scene, at least, looked just like she remembered it. *Beautiful.* Wasting no time, she unfolded, unfurled, braced and staked her father's tent. Finally, holding her flashlight under her chin, she struggled to close the tent snaps properly and thought, *mission accomplished.*

The tent, perched in the clearing under a patch of stars and embraced all around by the Fortress of the Vines, seemed a million miles away from civilization. The Fortress of the Vines was a sanctuary for all creatures of the forest—and Danny had only begun to appreciate how glorious a sanctuary could be.

Shining her light toward the blacker black of the tunnel entrance Danny prepared to go. But first she turned her flashlight back—toward the scene of that morning's drama—to what she thought of as Rosemary's tree. The section she'd broken through earlier in the day had comfortably settled into the mud of the streambed. Water burbled up through the hole that had been Rosemary's escape hatch and chased along the bark on the few inches still above the water line as it searched for a way over or under the giant carcass blocking its flow.

At the edge of the stream, Danny noticed water collecting behind a growing clog of storm debris caught between the spiny confusion of limbs and branches that had once been the tree's crown. *I'll have to clear that out and cut off those branches,* Danny thought and she turned to leave. It occurred to her then, that, somehow, at some point, she had begun to feel responsible for this place—like it was her own. *Home?*

Home. The word felt exotic. It felt right. She made a decision. *I will sleep in my father's tent tonight.*

When Danny exited the Fortress of the Vines she pushed the long handle of the clippers into the mud just outside the entrance; since she planned to return in the dark of night, she felt it prudent to mark the spot. *I just hope Mister Al won't mind too much when I return without them.* Thinking of Mister Al reminded her...*I told him I was staying over there tonight.* She sighed. It couldn't be helped. *I better figure out something to explain why I changed my mind.* She sighed again. She didn't like to lie.

Grumbling silently, Al slid open the sliding door and handed over his peanut butter sandwich to the little beggar on the darkened deck. He'd resisted Rosemary's bright eyes during the process of constructing the sandwich by keeping his back turned to her. He'd even managed to ignore her when she stood on her hind legs and pressed her wet nose against the glass like a kid gazing into a candy shop.

But when he had to roll past the animal on his way to the table—well—he just HAD to look. Rosemary's little hand tapped the glass...her little black nose quivered...and Al surrendered.

Okay. Okay. Here it is. You win! he thought, secretly pleased.

Rosemary dropped to all fours and waddled toward him expectantly. She saw the old man gesture with the sandwich in his hand. It flapped enticingly.

Go on you rascal, Al thought, *take it! Oh, don't you look at me like that! I only took ONE bite.*

Rosemary snatched the sandwich directly from the old man's hand, her eyes never breaking contact with his bright blue ones. She thought: *Hmmm...Are those blue things eyes? I'd like to climb up that human and take a longer look.*

An unexpected sound inside the house broke the raccoon's concentration and she, and Al's dinner, melted back into the moon shadows.

Al heard it too. It was the key in the door.

Danny returned as a full moon prepared to rise.

"Hi! Sorry I took so long, my wallet was harder to find than I thought it would be." Danny spoke as the old man fastened her with his bright blue eyes. She noticed his hand resting on the sliding door handle and guessed, "Is Rosemary out there again?"

He nodded. *Yes.*

"I just visited her old house and I can tell you she can't go back there. It's under water." Danny walked closer and smiled down into Mister Al's wrinkled face enjoying herself immensely. "Besides, I think she likes it here better anyway."

The old man's eyes were lively but he stuck his bottom lip out in a pouting gesture. Truth was, he rather liked the idea of a pet. He reached beside the arm of his chair and flipped the computer up into his lap. He felt like a nice long chat.

Danny watched him carefully while her mind ran through all she had to accomplish that night in order to be ready—not to mention presentable—for school tomorrow. *It would be so much easier to just stay here tonight.* Then she thought, *home.*

YOU MENTIONED WATER WHEN YOU WERE TELLING ME ABOUT ROSEMARY'S RESCUE, AND MENTIONED IT AGAIN JUST NOW. DID YOU FIND THE STREAM? Al thought she might have, after all he had been tracking the stream all those years ago when he ventured into the poison-ivy patch.

"Yes. I found the stream. Do you think that means the stone shed is nearby? I'd love to find it...wouldn't it be on the north bank? What should I look for? Could anything be left of it after all these years?"

The girl is obviously excited, Al noted. Heck! He was excited too!

Back in the day, the stone shed was known as a sort of gentleman's club; Little Al had been too young to visit —but all his life he'd heard his father talk about it. Thoughts of the stone shed were woven through every memory of his childhood and painted even now by his little boy imagination. His stone shed was devoid of men and beer and parties. Even now he sometimes dreamed of the tiny enchanted cottage set in a mystical glade where perfect smoke rose from a perfect stone chimney and hundreds of daffodils nodded their heavy yellow heads to the laughter of a crystal stream. *Ridiculous.* The old man knew this. Still, try as he might, he couldn't insert tables, mugs of beer, and the rough laughter of men into the scene—the idyllic image was too firmly rooted.

Finding the stone shed had become Al's Holy Grail.

Over the years, young Al had spent a lot of time tramping through the woods, searching for both the stream and the shed—finding nothing. His search had gotten him arrested for trespassing— on three separate occasions AND by the two separate owners of the former Rickenbocker land—and that kind of cheesed him off—*after all, why should they care? Neither owner, nor subsequent owner, ever used the property for a single thing, but none the less erected fences and posted signs promising:* **Trespassers will be Prosecuted to the Fullest Extent of the Law.**

Al remembered thinking back then, that—as a three-time trespasser— his luck couldn't get much worse. He had been very wrong.

One last time, he'd thought and taken a different path—and that time he'd been right about one thing—it WAS his last time. Al's trespass unknowingly landed him in the middle of a poison-ivy patch, and those plants almost killed him. Of course he'd never gone back and part of him had come to believe the lost stone shed was somehow protected by a forest god or something. But Danny may have found it.

RIGHT YOU ARE! MY DAD SAID THE STONE SHED WAS ON THE SAME SIDE AS THE MANSION. IF IT IS UNDER THOSE VINES SOMEWHERE IT DEFINITELY SHOULD STILL BE STANDING. ANYTHING WOOD IS PROBABLY ROTTEN—THE DOOR , THE ROOF, THE FURNITURE—BUT THE STONE WALLS WILL STILL BE THERE. IT WOULD BE GREAT IF YOU FOUND IT! I ALWAYS WONDERED ABOUT THAT PLACE.

"I promise to look for it—it would be like finding buried treasure or something! But I have to go now...ummm...my parents called and they need my help with something at home...probably the computer or something...so I can't stay over after all...sorry." Danny spoke as she moved to the kitchen and tidied up a bit. She loaded the coffee pot and set the timer. "How's 7:30 for coffee? Will that work?"

Yes, Al signaled and typed, I SAVED A NEWSPAPER ARTICLE ON THE COMPUTER THAT I WANT YOU TO READ. STOP BY AFTER SCHOOL IF YOU CAN. AND PICK UP THE MAIL WILL YOU? MAIL BOX 1 1. THE KEY IS ON THE RING WITH THE HOUSE KEY. ALL THE BACK MAIL WILL GET DELIVERED IN THE MORNING AND BESIDES, BEATRICE SAID SHE SENT YOU A CHECK.

Danny had much more to say, but she was out of time. Collecting her sleeping bag and backpack she went to the door and began to pull on her boots. "Okay, I'll stop by after school and should I order pizza or do you want me to heat up one of those dinners you ordered?"

Pizza.

*Good! I know he will want me to eat half... blast! ...I probably need to figure out how **I'm** going to eat this winter. I can't mooch off Mister Al forever!* "Bye!"

Bye, Al nodded as his heart sank. *I guess her tent made it through the storm somehow. Lucky.*

Now, what to do with the rest of the evening? I'm not tired at all. The old man wheeled himself over to the stationary bike...he'd discovered that if he placed his hands on his upper thighs, he could push downward and turn the pedals more often with less effort. It was working. After only three days, he was sure his legs were stronger.

If I could walk, I could visit the stone shed. Sweat broke out on his brow and began to stream along the wrinkles in his forehead and he amended, *I could visit the stone shed IF Danny finds it.* Pushing down as hard as he could, he forced his legs through a reluctant revolution while thinking, *and IF she also figures out a cure for poison-ivy...*

Discouraged, the old man decided it was time for bed.

The first time Danny went camping in the wilderness with her father she liked it fine...until the sun went down and the moonless night closed in. Sinister sounds...buzzing and grunting, skittering and flapping, scratching and slithering...kept Danny sleepless and petrified, convinced death—or worse—crouched in wait just outside the tent flap.

Now I find everything about the forest at night soothing. Musing on this, Danny nimbly made her way among the trees in the bleached light of a full moon. She was very close now to the Fortress of the Vines but navigating by moonlight was tricky — shadows looked solid by the light of the moon and multiplied the many new blockages to the old path. Each time she came to an obstruction she would walk around it—taking care to return to the path at the first opportunity—but her progress was slow.

Identifying a rustling to the right as a sound she herself had caused by stepping on short end of a long branch, Danny relaxed and her thoughts returned to that first camping experience. They had camped for a whole week, and her father had crammed ever minute with nature lessons and camping tips. *So why,* she again wondered, *hadn't he explained away my stupid nighttime fear…instead of falling to sleep the minute he lay down? He must have been able to tell I wasn't getting any sleep.* She had endured two full nights of sleeplessness before, on the third night, overcome by exhaustion, she'd slept— deep and dreamless. She had never been afraid again.

Sleep, just thinking the word brought on a jaw cracking yawn. Head down she slogged forward, a bubble of light in the shadows.

An unusual shape snagged in her peripheral vision as she arrived at the wall of vines. *The clippers.*

Moonlight bleached the distinctive bright yellow handles of Mister Al's heavy duty hedge and tree clipper's to a nondescript gray, but with both handles in the mud, the shape stood out. Hours ago, she'd been reminded of an upside down 'V', but now through a trick of moonlight—and maybe fatigue—she saw a sentry—arms crossed, legs spread—guarding the entrance to the Fortress of the Vines.

Danny paused a moment to wrench the tool handles free of the ground, then confidently spread apart the vines and plunged inside. The moonlight didn't penetrate the tunnel and her flashlight beam fractured against the walls, but her energy had returned. She felt like a character in a book.

She congratulated herself for having the foresight to clean up and widen the passageway before the sun went down, because now following the wide, straight path was relatively easy and required only minimal light. She moved eagerly, *so close,* she thought picturing her father's battered, canvas tent, waiting for her at the end of the tunnel, nestled in a moonlit clearing next to a babbling stream.

Oxo enjoyed the solitude of what he now called The Den. With the door closed the space was light-proof, sound-proof…and snoop-proof. He'd discovered that last attribute earlier in the day when a home inspector and a cadre of day laborers showed up out of the blue—apparently sent by the governor.

Oxo had been liberating the mattress from Old Man Laird's room when he'd heard the front door open and the sound of heavy boots tromping through to the rear of the house. The sound was somehow menacing.

If the footfall had belonged to the Laird's, he would have stood his ground—*what can THEY do to me now, anyway?*—but these boots belonged to someone else.

Gestapo. he thought, *some of Lard-butts Nazi friends.* And even though he knew better, he was instinctively afraid—as though he were being hunted.

It was time to hide.

Dropping the mattress in the doorway Oxo scrambled for the basement steps—if his good luck held he wouldn't be spotted by the intruders.

He reached the basement and was slipping behind the heavy door to The Den, when he heard someone descend the stairs. A man's deep voice called out, "I'll check the cellar for any damages but I really think the roof is the worst of it... the place seems pretty well built."

It IS well built, Oxo—oddly defensive about the old house—thought. He managed to pull the door to The Den closed, just as the inspector reached the bottom of the stairs. The fluorescents were still on but he figured the guy would think they came on when electricity was restored.

And what if the guy inspects the wall behind the washer? He thought and was suddenly very nervous. With the door closed he could hear nothing—no sound penetrated The Den. *What is going on out there?* So he was left waiting behind the closed door, convinced that any second now it would swing open and he would be caught, dragged away, and thrown in prison....

Minutes ticked by.

Nothing happened, but the feeling of unease was hard to shake. *The inspection must be over by now,* he told himself but stayed put anyway, telling himself, *they might be inspecting nearby and see me.*

Maybe he could do some drawing to pass the time—he'd have plenty of time tomorrow to finish the furnishing of his new digs.

Adjusting the goose necked lamp just-so over the drafting table and then meticulously taping a sheet of newsprint to the table, Oxo gathered several sticks of charcoal and a kneaded eraser and began to sketch. Drawing usually calmed and focused him. Not this time. This time, for some reason, his thoughts kept returning to men with heavy boots.

The drawing was going nowhere so he put the stick of charcoal down.

The images and feelings rushed in.

Hate. He hated them all! Most especially the poisonous woman who had the nerve to call him, and the rest of the kids, her 'Foster Children'. Remembering the news photo of the governor and Mrs. Laird increased his fury. Politicians and bureaucrats, in his opinion, bought votes with favors, and the thought made him sick—even if it got the roof fixed.

It is all about trading favors. Adults LET this stuff happen because they don't care how things ARE, they just care about how things LOOK. All of them just pretend like they care! He clenched his fists into hard balls.

Nobody really cares at all about us kids! ...not that Lard-Woman...not the governor...

Bright blood squeezed from between Oxo's fingers, crimson pearls in the puddle of light on the drafting table. He didn't feel the bloody crescents his nails were making in his palms.

...nobody really cares...not the fathers...not even the mothers...

The sheer injustice—of conditional love and artificial concern—fueled the hurt and anger always with him and he choked, pounding his damaged fists into the table. Oxo struck again and again.

But the table could take it.

Much worse had happened in the years since the secret room was built and furnished. Through the years it had borne witness to all manner of human ugliness—raw fear, bitter hatred, violent anger...even madness. The walls...first chopped by hand through heavy orange clay, then blasted and chipped from living rock...were familiar with violence, yet the space they defined was serene. The room did not judge those within, the walls did not reflect turmoil, magnify pain, or amplify emotion...but—like a thirsty sponge —offered anonymous strength, understanding and comfort.

He raged. He howled. The pain his body never felt, burned like acid in his veins and drove him wild with fury. For a very long time nothing, and no one, stopped him. Then something did—or maybe that level of rage is unsustainable—and Oxo felt something inside break and, like the lancing of a boil, the poison drained away. For a while he feared his soul had gone with it. *Empty.*

He cried then—and he didn't even know he COULD cry—tears of loneliness, inadequacy and humiliation. Like a dirty, overgrown baby, Oxo lay on the cold floor, sobbing, blubbering every child's mantra..."not fair! It's NOT FAIR!" He might have said other things too but no one was there to hear; this drama was between Oxo and walls, ceiling and floor.

How long did it last? The room had no clock.

Finally, nothing at all remained but a room with a past and a boy with a future. Oxo felt hollow and imagined a spring wind whistling through his emptiness. Like loosing a tooth, he couldn't help but probe the hole left behind... *there is an empty place and it is the weirdest feeling.*

He looked around then—at the order, simplicity and solitude of this forgotten place—and was content, clear-eyed and focused. Picking up the charcoal, Oxo began to work. The hours flew by, even as a new, foreign, sensation began to slowly drip into the empty place—it was the feeling of HOPE. Oxo felt— *like somebody*—and that made him smile.

FOG

Danny splashed handfuls of water into her face, reveling in the beauty of the stream and unexpected warmth of its waters. It looked clean enough to drink...but she knew better than to risk that.

She was responsible for the clear water. She'd risen before sunrise and, by the glow of the recovered Coleman lantern, managed to clear the biggest clogs of debris caught between branches of the fallen tree. Once water began running again, currents quickly flushed the remaining litter downstream and from the sound of it, this made the stream very happy. Cheerful gurgles and chuckles issued from beneath otherworldly fog obscuring the stream and thickening in the brightening morning. The stream's laughter drifted in and out of the warm mists curling up from the warm water to meet fog aglow with the reflected pastels of dawn. Some bird, who hadn't flown south with the rest of the flock, began a complicated song of joy.

Taking it in, Danny found it hard to remember the close call she'd had right there only a day ago...

Time is passing, Danny shook herself back to reality. *School.*

Crouching close to the water and waving away the mist, she examined the dark, almond-shaped eyes staring up from its mirror-like surface, *like mother's.* She closely inspected her face, *clean, and the scratches barely show.* She dipped a hand into the water and used it to pat down the stray hairs that had worked themselves out of the tight braids she wore. Middle School, she knew, was no place to be different.

By the time she'd eaten a granola bar and packed her backpack for school, the morning was considerably warmer. The fog had burned off, everywhere but over the water where it lay thick and creamy in the stream bed. *Odd,* Danny acknowledged, slung her book-laden pack over her shoulder, and hurried off to catch the school bus.

Toad had received a call late the night before from the governor, who wanted to know what the weather would be the next morning, of all things. Again, fortune smiled on the Toad—he'd been watching the weather station and knew this area of the country was in for a long spell of perfect autumn weather and that is what he told the governor. It wasn't until the governor rang off that Toad began to doubt.

I'm not a meteorologist anyway! He lay awake all night worrying about his weather forecast, checking the clock and waiting for sunrise, but the time for dawn came and went and it was still dark. Toad opened the door to a wall of fog so heavy it blocked the rays of the sun. *Not a perfect autumn day.* When a cold, wet breeze made him shiver, Toad really began to worry. He checked his watch once more in superstitious horror. *What if the sun DOESN'T rise?*

The world lightened noticeably even as Toad stood shivering on his postage stamp of a porch. *Its only morning fog.* He comforted himself, *it will burn off.* But again his stomach bubbled. *The governor is counting on me.*

The governor slept late that morning, waking only when the sun was high enough in the sky to find its way into his bedroom. As always his first thought was of the election...*primaries in a less than a month*...and his second thought was of his schedule. *Photo-Op as I surprise the Laird woman with the repairs I had done on her house.* An image of that slovenly woman and her green teeth coming toward him to express her gratitude made him slightly sick to the stomach. *The things I am called on to do for these voters!*

The governor elected to forgo breakfast, petulantly shoving away the plate of scrambled egg beaters and turkey bacon his wife sat before him.

Roxanne Laird couldn't wait to get home! She'd spent her second sleepless night in the shelter beside her brainless lump of a husband. She couldn't escape him. Day and night the man's snorts, slurps and wheezing went on, accompanied by nauseating odors—so noxious and fetid they made the eyes water and her delicate stomach roil.

The moment she reached home she planned to wheel the man into his own bedroom and bolt the door. *Soon,* she thought as she pushed open the heavy door leading to the dark, now empty, ladies room. In the corner was a small window; she went to it and managed to bully it open.

Shivering, as much from cold as from anticipation, she felt in her pocket for the forbidden cigarettes. The lighter flared and Roxanne Laird sucked in cigarette smoke along with a blast of chill air. For a moment she felt better and idly watched as the gray fog drifted in to mingle with her blue tinged exhaust. *Shouldn't it be morning?* Putting a hand on the window ledge she leaned out and scrutinized the fog, trying to make out any change in light that might spell dawn.

She wondered which of the kids would be hanging around when she finally reached home. *At least the little firebug is taken care of.* Then her thoughts turned to her favorite characters on her favorite Soap. For two and a half days now she'd been out-voted in the TV room, and was now behind on the storyline. *Stupid trash preferred Judge Judy to good drama!*

The fog began to lighten.

"That'll teach the little snitch", the boy with the weasel face muttered and tossed the match through a misshapen hole beside the trailer's door. The door remained locked but Skid had watched his hungry, drunken father open many soup cans by punching a hole in the side and prying open a hole, so that is what he'd done with the trailer—only he'd used a crowbar on this particular can. The hole was big enough to accommodate the spout to the gas can, and of course, the match.

Woof!

A ball of super-heated blue flame shot from the trailer. It had all the fury and brilliance he'd hoped for. "Burn!" he exalted.

His long torso leaned toward the flame and his whole body swayed in ecstasy. His pink tongue darted in and out, as though he could taste the evil he had unleashed and relished it.

Inside the trailer, the fire blindly snapped and tore with the blood-lust of piranha fish in a feeding frenzy—biting everything; tasting nothing. Initially, the trailer's contents either burned or melted. This caused the enclosed space to super-heat like an incinerator; metal, plastic, and glass were reduced to ash—a development which seemed to further enrage the fire.

Skid was like the fire he'd set, craving immediate gratification, driven by a mindless need to destroy.

It had taken several days for Skid and his new red gas can to find the place; locating the trailer in the heavy fog took more hours. When he did find it, getting through the doors or windows proved impossible; everything was locked up and reinforced. Punching that hole in the side left him bruised and bleeding but he didn't care one bit—his whole being was focused on the burn. He never even wondered why a common camping trailer had such a heavy, metal door and he wasn't the least bit curious about what the trailer contained...in Skid's experience, people who lived in trailers had nothing anyway.

And, besides, Skid wasn't a thief.

At first Red mistook the smoke for fog.

He'd been awake for hours—keyed up and oddly tense, starring from the window into the blank night. The acrid smell of burning was the tip off. That reek, and oily black smoke he could now detect, came from the burning of synthetics: plastics, paint and vinyl as well as rubber, oil and...*it's the trailer.*

A flash of light blazed through the haze.

Oh my God! Red recognized the orange throb of light as an explosion. *The propane tank.* Although he was braced for the concussive thump that would follow it still rocked him on his heels. *My fault*

Red was a big man, slow of thought but quick to act and now indecision immobilized him. *Call 911? Go take a look?* He didn't know what to do; his mind jumped all over the place. *I moved that propane tank into the trailer to keep it out of the weather, and the fire turned it into a bomb. Maybe a one-percent chance the fire was an accident. Who is out there and why? Why* this *target and why now?*

Then his lifetime of training kicked in, sending Red's body toward the brightening spot in the fog while freeing his mind to visit a different time and place...

Vietnam.

Roy moved quickly and efficiently, walking with ghosts, images of bombs, fires, blood and night patrols, the faces of fallen friends and remembered enemies. *Vietnam.* And there was *Roy. Roy Smith. The kid who saved my life; the man who rescued my sanity; I promised Roy...*

The promises he'd made and the secrets he'd pledged to keep, pulled Red back to the present. The cobwebs cleared enough to allow Red one crystal clear thought: *The fire was set on purpose.*

Skid had just taken a small step forward when the tank blew.

The force of the unexpected blast picked up the boy's long, scrawny body like a rag doll and threw it into the trees. The flash singed away eyebrows, lashes and a great deal of Skid's dirty hair and blistered his skin. When his torso hit a sapling at the edge of the tree line, the immediate impact broke bones and scraped away the wet blisters. The body came to rest at the base of the little tree, blood leaking quietly into the moldering leaves.

Red found only a blackened depression where his friend's camper once stood. All evidence of it was gone—obliterated by an explosion powerful enough to blow out the fire that caused it. *At least the fire is out.*

Ugly black smoke mixed with the fog and the oily mud it created hung in a cloud that coated everything.

Red tried not to gulp the foul air as he surveyed the scene but his escalating panic forced each breath to come faster. *Concentrate,* he thought and narrowed his focus. *Look around.*

No part of the trailer was visible from where Red stood. The blast site must be massive...*could a half empty tank of Propane have caused this kind of damage?*

Intrigue began to outweigh fear, and the big man's galloping heart slowed to the normal rate as he used old skills to help him understand the destruction. Delicately he sipped at the air, tasting and assessing its different components against his knowledge of explosives. In his experience, smells could overwhelm, but the sense of taste could be trusted.

Starting at the charred, still-steaming center, Red methodically searched the site. He stepped over smoldering globs of plastic, ruined components and the unrecognizable chunks of litter, but found no large pieces. *Where is the main field of debris?* He continued to search...

The morning sun had burned off enough fog for Red to see a darker shade of gray ahead; he'd almost reached the tree line. *That clearing was half the size of a football field and the camper was parked in the center,* Red knew. *I should have found some larger pieces of evidence by now.*

A weak ray of light cut through the oppressive cloud and Ray spotted a faint glimmer as it touched a nearby tree. As he stepped quickly toward it, the movement caused it to tremble and he saw a ragged artifact protruding from the tree bark at about chest-height. He touched it in wonder—*its aluminum...paper thin, razor-sharp.* He considered the elements needed to create an explosion with enough power to turn a sheet of torn metal into a Frisbee with enough velocity to bury itself in a living tree. *I've only seen hurricanes and tornados pack that much wallop.* The story of a tornado driving a stick of straw through a tree came to mind. *Clearly,* he thought shaking his big head; *this was much more than simple arson.*

Something above him moved and he crouched down in reflex, thinking, *sniper!* Fearfully scanning the tree tops, he found the field of debris he'd been searching for...

Sheets of contorted metal, flung high in the tree branches, dangled in unlikely poses, The sight was ugly and somehow threatening and Red's sense of self-preservation went into overdrive. *Focus on what you actually see. You can do this. You were trained to do this...*

He resumed the methodical search, *walk slowly, look down, look up—identify anything still in one piece.* He would have to contact Danny, and that would be much less difficult if he could recover something that was her father's—*must find something in this mess to give her; something to remind her of her father.* Thinking about Danny, and the grief she would feel, kept images of a long-ago war at bay.

At the bottom of a particularly battered sapling he saw what appeared to be a heap of torn and dirty clothing and something about it made him uneasy. He looked down at the mess, and caught the smell. Red had seen burn victims before...and was certainly familiar with the smell of cooked meat...but even standing directly over the boy, the fact of it took awhile to register.

Body.

In the swirling fog and early morning half light, Red, the soldier carefully slid a boot-clad foot into the pile of rags and lifted. He stepped back, hand on weapon, and looked down.

A boy's burnt face and sightless eyes stared up at him.

The soldier knelt beside the inert form and thought, *the enemy*. There was no satisfaction in the knowledge. He ran his hands over the contorted body, looking for things that soldiers look for. *Nothing obviously broken...no blood currently flowing...smell of gasoline...something in the inside jacket pocket...feels like...sounds like....papers.* Red opened the boy's jacket to pull out a folded bunch of paper stashed in the breast pocket. He examined them closely. *Envelopes. Odd sizes of paper.*

The largest envelope looked familiar. He turned it over and saw it had been ripped open. The original address was crossed out but still legible: **Ms. Danny Smith at the CSD, County Division**. A new, forwarded address was written to the side: **3 Cumberland Cutoff**.

The big man's stomach lurched. *This creep has Danny's mail! Why? How did he get it?* Growing sicker because he thought he knew, he stared at the return address in the upper left corner...*My address.*

The envelope was from Red; he'd used it to enclose a few official pieces of mail from the post office and library that had come in for Roy Smith, figuring Danny might want them. *And I included a note telling her not to worry, because I had 'winterized' the trailer and was keeping the grass cut in the clearing. Then I sealed the envelope and mailed it to Child Service Division –figuring they would forward it. So how did HE get his hands on it?*

But HOW the kid had gotten Danny's mail wasn't the real issue, Red knew. What mattered was that *the scum was following Danny's trail, and I led him right here through my letters. How could I have been so stupid as to put the farm address in the return address slot?*

Red felt equal parts fear and outrage as he stood over the body, staring into the distance.

He thought he could see the old demons coming for him.

Danny wrote:

Fog is the forests' exhalation—warm and alive. With each breath, each tree, blade of grass and living creature, inhales 'what is', exhales' what was', and collectively weaves a veil to hide 'what can never be'

Hmmm ... not sure where all this poetry is coming from, especially since Leo Peal's BO is about to knock me out of my seat, and I'm having a hard time writing while the bus explores every single pothole!

Mom used to say "You are a kid! School is your job." But school seems sort of silly after all that's happened. I mean, in the last five days we had flood, ice, wind, fire, adventure AND I met Mister Al.

I don't think I am going to be able to concentrate on conjugating a verb.

Right now the weather feels more like spring...sort of warm and humid. The trees never had a chance to turn colors and drop their leaves because of the freak freeze so the leaves fell while they were still green. It looks weird out there, and it smells funky too, not the moldery, pepper smell of dry leaves—more like rotten groceries. But winter will be back real soon and I need to get to the store and get a new tent, real soon. It might not be a bad idea to get a cot too, so I won't have to deal with the keeping the cold and damp from coming up from the ground.

The walls of the Fortress of the Vines will break the wind, which is the worst thing about the cold IMHO. Plus the vine-walls are so thick I won't need to be much worried about light and sound giving away my position. No one can sneak up on me either, unless they know the way in.

Maybe I can make this a real home.

I've been wondering about Mister Al's pedal-powered generator. If I could get myself a deep cell battery, a power inverter and an old alternator, I think I could make one like Mister Al did. I remember how and if I made a generator, I'd have electricity! (I just had this insane image of me in the tent...blow drying my hair....and microwaving popcorn! Just how much electricity does one of those batteries hold anyway?)

The hard part it going to be moving things in. I'll have to be patient and carry in a little at a time. Just carting the battery up from Mister Al's basement was tough because it is really heavy!

As Danny slid her journal into her school backpack she felt something plucked from her hair followed by a vicious poke between the shoulder blades. Jerking around, she found herself nose to nose with kitten–faced Donna Adagio. In Donna's hand was a leaf.

Donna looked all-knowing as she nonchalantly twirled the stem of a brown leaf between her pink gloved fingers. She sniffed. She twirled some more.

Rats! Danny fought off the sensation of being ambushed. She watched Donna Adagio twirling the leaf round and round, round and round—resigned to what was coming next.

Donna smiled that contented little lazy kitten smile, still twirling the leaf round and round, round and round. *Gotcha.*

I thought I checked my hair. How did I miss a leaf the size of that one? Still, Danny had to admire the way this blue-eyed, blonde girl managed to convey **menace** by simply twirling a leaf.

Donna Adagio was feared by all but the popular few. Her way of quickly passing judgment on others with cruel glee and cutting comment—like she was a District Attorney on some crime show—made her initials, D.A., perfect. Everyone called Donna Adagio the D.A. and Donna loved it.

The D.A. liked to make her victims sweat, but she had never had much luck with Danny...until now...and she savored the kill. **FlipFlip** went the leaf. Then came the purrr... "Did you and your Mummy sleep outside again, Smith? Where was it this time, dear, the gutter?" The soft little kitten-mouth pouted, prettily, "Or did you and your charming Leo Peal have time this morning for a roll in the leaves?"

The D.A. broadcast her poison in a sweet, sugary voice that reached every student on the packed bus.

Danny felt her ears burn and hoped her braids covered the red. She so desperately wanted to stick her fist into the other girl's pink little face...and twist. *Daddy always said 'sometimes you gotta take it on the chin'. This must be what he was talking about.* Danny had to work hard to summon a smile, but she did it. *Making-nice actually hurts,* she thought, and forced her voice to sound conversational and unconcerned. "Why, thank you Donna". She then reached forward and plucked the leaf from the D.A.'s startled fingers. *It is getting easier...* she thought, and said, "I was looking for that very leaf." *Okay, so NOT a very clever statement I guess, but better than cringing or crying. Never show a bully any fear. Dad said to look them straight in the eye.* Danny leveled her gaze at the D.A., as beside her she felt the pulpy mass of Leo Peal cringe away as though he were trying to disappear into the seat corner. *Hah!* she thought.

The D.A. was startled when Danny spoke to her as though she was an old friend of the family. And when Danny looked her in the eye, Donna ALMOST looked away. Truth was, this wild haired stranger was intimidating. Danny Smith seemed much older and more confident than the rest of the kids. *Too much trouble,* the D.A. decided, and moved her gaze to an easier target. Leo.

The fat kid is practically wetting his pants, Donna Adagio gloated and leaned forward, preparing her next salvo. But Leo was saved as the bus sighed to a stop and the doors flipped open.

Later, thought Donna, *I'll get him later.*

Danny felt the briefest triumph knowing she had successfully shifted The D.A.'s attention away from her own self, after all it wasn't her fault it landed on Leo. *Was it?* As Danny started down the bus steps she was aware of Leo right behind her. *How could I not be? He takes up so much space it compresses the air.*

Danny thought it wisest not to tempt fate; she skipped a visit to her locker that morning and headed directly to Algebra class. She had just managed to stuff her coat into her backpack and sit down when she heard Leo Peal puff into the room still wearing his jacket. *Is he following me?*

Leo had a few things wrong with him, but nothing was wrong with his brain. He knew he was offensive and decided he preferred it. Being offensive had its perks, like getting a seat on the bus to your self. He'd had a seat to himself for years until Danny showed up—and he sort of resented her for intruding on his space. But today? Well...he had to hand it to her! This was the third time he'd seen her shut down the Adagio-girl. "Well played", he said in a rusty voice, gave Danny thumbs-up, and waddled past her into class.

Surprised by Leo's unexpected attention, Danny watched him labor to the far side of the classroom and pour himself into a front seat. She thought, *Leo Peal is in this class?? Since when?*

He draped his jacket over the back of the chair and pulled out an Algebra text, identical to her own. Danny tried to pretend she was not staring. *He belongs here alright, but how could I not have noticed him before? It would be like missing a mountain. Wasn't I just saying he took up too much air?*

Slowly the classroom filled up as Danny struggled to make sense of this new information. *My plans to live alone require me to be observant, so how could I NOT have noticed that Leo Peal, of all people, was in my class?*

Class was late getting started that day, but it didn't matter. **X -2(7G) = Y+ X** equations and formulas held no interest for Danny. Her energies were focused on another formula, the one Leo used to become invisible. *He arrives early every day,* she reasoned, *so his entrance can be sloppy, noisy, even comical— but no one is around to notice. He sits at the front of the room— but on the side and out of everyone's line of sight—the instructor* *would have to actually turn his head to look at Leo. If he doesn't call attention to himself, there is no window or chart over there, and no reason for students to look toward Leo's part of the room*

Throughout class, Danny tried to think of ways to apply the observation to her situation. Her father had shown her that the woods were filled with animals hiding in plain sight using natural camouflage, but the Leo-technique took the concept a step further– *there are places where it takes a conscious effort to look. Search for a natural 'blind spot' to hide in.*

Once Oxo hauled the mattress down the steps and set up a 'sleeping area' in The Den, both physical and mental exhaustion hit him pretty hard. Reaching for the lamp he had repositioned nearby, he hit the switch and the world went dark. He loved night—but this darkness was so immediate and so utter, it seemed to change the very air pressure, and Oxo felt his ears pop. *This darkness is different!* It did not close in; it opened out. The dark made all the other stuff unimportant. It delighted Oxo, and for awhile he amused himself by projecting beautiful mental pictures into the blackness, as though it were a movie screen.

Sleep came gently, completely and lasted twelve and a half hours. The total darkness gave no clues, yet he knew it was morning, and he woke feeling as though his troubles had shifted, or maybe rolled away. He'd slept with both the basement and The Den doors partially open—so he would hear anyone enter; now he felt an unfamiliar sense of anticipation as he reached for the lamp. As his fingers found the switch he heard the distinctive click of the house door opening then closing with a slam. *Showtime!* he thought.

The Laird's had returned to Number Three Cumberland Cutoff.

Red sat on a kitchen chair that needed fixing...again. Determined sunlight blasted its way into the kitchen through a grimy window and a pair of yellowed lace curtains. The big man had shaved off his beard and most of his hair revealing a trembling face and unblinking gray-green eyes. He ran a big paw over the spiky remains of his hair and tried to bring his surroundings into focus, but the smell of death remained in his nostrils and the sound of pain buzzed around his head like a mosquito.

On the same black and white tile floor, Red's mother once knelt to scrub while Red-the-child played, waited a tightly packed canvas duffel bag and a pair of old scuffed black boots. The big man didn't remember ever being a child, he didn't remember his mother, didn't remember his father, had no recollection of his first kiss or his dead wife or even his own middle name—all he remembered was Vietnam, and promising a friend to keep an eye on a girl called Danny.

Red opened the refrigerator, flipped open the butter door and pulled out a cell phone. He hit automatic dial, waited, left a message, then tossed the phone into an old microwave oven, hit start and heard it explode.

Red didn't remember to lock the door behind him when he left that afternoon. Truth was he had been gone for hours and hours before he ever walked out.

Time is a funny thing, thought the old man, *I spent 70 plus years never having enough of it, and now, after my stroke, I have too much of it. How stupid is that? So close to the grave and wishing the hours away!*

But he was doing it again—checking the time every few minutes—thinking *hurry!* He'd even bumped his way to his long abandoned bedroom upstairs and dug out a watch. *Why? Just for a closer look at the minutes passing?* What he wanted was for Danny to finish school and stop by...there were things he wanted to tell her...and things he wanted to ask. He felt unaccountably anxious.

Again, he looked at his watch and unconsciously did the math...*five more hours of school, plus an hour give or take and she will be back! It is time to tell her I know she is the Girl in the Woods. Maybe she will let me help her, or maybe my knowing her secret will drive her away.*

He wondered what he would do if that happened.

THE BLIND SPOT

In Danny's opinion, one of the many great things about living in today's world was constantly advancing technology and she was doubly delighted by her teacher's announcement. "Ladies and Gentlemen," Mister Arnold opened computer class, "Good news! Kenilworth Township, and this very school, is finally, **really**, on the map!" He paused for effect, "Yes indeed, we are now visible on the Google Earth map. Last night, Google Earth, replaced the old, hazy satellite overviews of the county with up-to-date aerial imagery. This is amazing stuff, you guys, you can now zoom in close enough to count the stop lights on Cumberland. I highly recommend that you finish today's assignment as quickly as possible so you'll have time to check out the view."

She finished building her spreadsheet in record time and immediately went online. Entering the school address into the search engine and selecting Google Earth, she was soon descending through space to Earth, then North America, the United States, the state, the county and finally...Kenilworth Township. A red arrow pointed to the school's location in town. *There I am.* Danny selected the minus sign and the school moved closer as the area grew smaller. *Wow!! Mister Al will love this.*

Danny looked down on Roosevelt Middle from above and thought, *how close can I actually get?* She nudged the zoom-in button and images dropped to the final level of detail. *I can see the tops of the cars.* She was able to determine color and parking space, and so figure out who owned them.

Next, she typed in Mister Al's address, and the view pulled out to show the entire Rockaway Estates development laid out like houses on the Monopoly board. *I didn't know the development was that big.* At the final zoom level, decks, back yards, parked cars—even mailboxes—were quite clear. The red arrow hovered over Mister Al's house with its deck and empty parking space in front.

Danny zoomed out for a look at the area surrounding the development—*I wonder if we can use this to find the stone shed?*—but when she saw the size and shape of the woods behind Rockaway Estates she forgot all about the stone shed.

The aerial view of the woods she first camped in was revealed to be little more than a buffer of trees between Rockaway Estates and Cumberland Road. *How could that be? I entered the woods from behind the Laird's house on Cumberland Cutoff and walked a good way before I pitched my father's tent; I walked even further to get to Rockaway Estates after the snow...I guess I must have walked parallel to the road when I left the Laird's.* Danny zoomed out a bit more for a look at the rooftops of Cumberland Cutoff, Cumberland Road and Rockaway Estates. It was true—the deep mysterious woods she had fled to was nothing more than a narrow corridor of trees.

But the woods MUST get wider at some point! The Fortress of the Vines is far in—it has GOT to be in deep woods—I tried to walk around it when I went to help Rosemary and couldn't. Danny slowly shifted the view to the right—toward the East—and followed Cumberland Road until it unexpectedly made a wide swing north at the end of Rockaway Estates. This immediately quadrupled the wooded area...*I was right.* Danny breathed easier as the forested area continued to expand the farther east she went; eventually the entire screen was filled with trees. *Hallelujah!* thought Danny, *this time, for sure, I'm camped in deep woods! Now, just how big is this woods really?* She zoomed out once. Twice. Still treetops filled the screen.

Again.

Holy smoke! That is one BIG woods. It goes east, surrounds Kenilworth Dam and, after the dam, it keeps on going. Intrigued, she manipulated the view, looking for landmarks and noting familiar roads, and thinking, *I wonder if it was like this when...*

The overhead light blinked on and off derailing Danny's train of thought. She looked up to find she was the only student in the classroom. It wasn't the first time she hadn't heard Mister Arnold dismiss class because she was wrapped up in what she was doing; she knew he had blinked the lights to get her attention.

Smiling, Danny gathered up her things. She left the classroom as the next group of students began to stream in.

The rest of the day seemed to fly by.

Science was the last class of the day and today her lab partner was absent. That made it even easier for Danny to position her daypack on the top of the high counter near the conveniently located receptacle and plug in her phone charger to drain a little of the school's electrical juice without removing the phone from her bag. *When was the last time I charged it?* The phone had turned itself off when the battery flat lined.

Class today was just a review in preparation for a test. If you already knew the stuff it could bore you to death, so Danny pulled out her journal and pretended to take notes....

Perspective makes everything true, and everything false. Leo Peal is a genius; Leo Peal is a toad. To a flea the world is a cat.

I know Mister Al will be interested in the new satellite shots of this area. I saw so much just in my quick look. I'm sure Google Earth has some clues! Maybe between Mister Al and me, we can find a landmark or feature of some kind to help find the stone shed. The images were taken when the trees were really full though, so seeing anything but leaves will surely be almost impossible. I know Mister Al gave up a long time ago on the stone shed; chances are I won't find it either but I want to take a better look, anyway! Mom used to say, "Never say Never."

Can't forget to stop by the mailbox. Didn't I say pizza tonight? The groceries should be in though. I think I saw an old Crock-Pot down in the basement. I could make some soup out of leftovers and let it cook all night so he would have it tomorrow—but I better not call it SOUP since he HATES SOUP! Silly man!

It gets dark so early now. I just remembered— Thanksgiving will be here soon. I really hope I can be settled by then...the holidays are depressing enough with no parents, I hope I at least have a place I can call home. I'll bet Mister Al is depressed about that too... his only relative seems to be that Beatrice person and she sure doesn't ACT like a daughter. He will probably be home alone too, and he will probably expect me to be with my own family during Thanksgiving. I hate all this pretending! It would be much easier to be honest with Mister Al—but then he would know I lied and probably report me. He surely would report the Lard-Butts if he knew what they were up to.

I'll just tell Mister Al that I'll come by after 'family' dinner and fix him something to eat.

Maybe Rosemary will stop by too.

Danny was so busy making plans that she forgot about the D.A. until she put her booted foot on the first bus step. Then she figured it didn't matter; there wasn't anything she could do about the situation anyway.

As usual, every seat on the bus was taken except Leo Peal's— but this time Leo Peal himself was not in it. Danny looked down at the vacant seat in surprise. *No wonder no one wants to sit here.* The green vinyl bench was shiny and cracked with use while the side nearest the window sagged as though it had been hit with a cannonball *or flattened by Leo Peal's giant rear end.*

Gingerly, Danny perched as close to the aisle as possible but it was no good, the impression left by months of Leo-weight on the poorly designed bus seat was just too strong and she had no choice but to surrender to gravity and slide into the dent. The black hole had a lumpy bottom and something broken poking through. *Feels like I'm sitting on the floor.* She tried to get comfortable...*I can't even see out the window*...wriggling as the bus began to clatter out of the parking lot. *How does Leo live like this?* She felt every bump. *At least the D.A. isn't here either...she would have lots of fun with this. If she could **see** me that is! I'm so far down, I can't see over the seat in front of me.*

Something chirped sharply.

All around kids began hauling cell phones out of jacket pockets and book bags. *Cell phone?*

The chirp came again—louder and more insistent. *My phone!* It must have turned itself back on and she couldn't remember ever hearing it chirp before. Digging in a side pocket she hit the mute button and then looked at the screen. *I have a text message.*

The OK button brought up the message: CHECK MAIL OK?

Mister Al really has this communication thing licked! The phone chirped again. Startled, she looked down.

PIZZA?

I guess that answers that question. Pizza it is. Thinking about the old man, she wished she had a way to reply, but couldn't without an email address and when the phone chirped again she wasn't surprised, *Mister Al wants to talk.*

But this message wasn't from the old man.

687 3990 OXO

Oxo? Oxo wanted her to call. *What's he want?* Frowning, Danny stared at the little screen. *He's weird.* But he **had** helped her get the goods on the Laird's. *He stole my stuff too.* Then she thought of him facing off with Rosemary, holding a broom and screaming like a little girl, and the smile replaced the frown. *I almost forgot about that.*

She decided to call the number when she got off the bus. *How did he get my number? For that matter, how'd he get a phone?* She keyed in the number, pressed save and put the phone on mute. Puzzling over Oxo kept her occupied until the doors opened at her stop.

Kids jostled to be first out the door as Danny attempted to hoist herself up out of the seat. This wasn't easy to do and took a few tries. She heard whispers and giggles from the aisle and knew she looked like an idiot. The part of her that wasn't thinking about Oxo's message momentarily admired Leo Peal for getting out of this seat everyday without seeming to struggle. *Full of surprises.*

As always, Danny was last off the bus. The curtain twitched at Mister Al's window and she knew he was watching for her. That made her feel somehow warm inside. She walked behind the bank of mailboxes which hid her from the window. *First the mail, then the call*, she planned and slipped the key into Mister Al's mailbox. The box was stuffed so full it required both hands to unload.

Sure enough, one of the letters appeared to be from daughter Beatrice and it appeared to contain her check. She put all the mail into the front pocket of her backpack before picking up the phone to call Oxo. A split second before she hit the 'send' button, a tiny envelope icon in the corner of the screen caught her eye. *I thought I already checked all my messages...Oxo again?* Then she saw it wasn't a text message; she had voice mail.

The voice message was sent early that morning. It was a man. Danny listened to it twice before she identified the voice. *Red!* But Red sounded strange; he was talking fast—not in his usual slow quiet way—and his voice seemed higher than she remembered, and sort of —tight. His words were just as confusing.

Frustrated, she listened to the message a few more times. He was trying to make her understand something—without actually telling her what that something was.

"You know who this is." Red said. "I'm calling to tell you the field house burned down. Nothing is left. You understand? The-Smith-Field-House. It is gone." Red spoke the words again, more slowly, with a waver in his voice, "...The...Smith...Field...House..." but it still didn't make any sense to Danny.

The message went on, in clipped sentences. "All games are cancelled. Don't come by. There is no one here. I will get in touch if I can. Don't worry. I'm sorry." The voicemail ended abruptly.

The Smith 'Field' house? Red HAD to be talking about her father's trailer, which was parked in a field, of sorts, on Red's farm. *Is he saying our trailer burned down? If that's true, what does it have to do with any games? What about games?* Danny swallowed hard. Through the buzzing in her head she dimly heard a door open nearby. She'd been standing behind the mailboxes a long time and shook herself back to the present. *Mister Al probably opened the door to see what happened to me.*

Danny was adept at moving her troubles out of the way and not thinking about them until she had the time. She did that now.

The old man waited at the door. He had even stood up for the occasion. Danny felt better just seeing him there.

She came in chattering brightly, about the day, about the weather, about something very cool she had to show him on the computer.

The old man watched the girl drop a bundle of mail on the kitchen table and then pick up the phone and order a cheese and pepperoni pizza. He wondered about the two bright red spots on her cheeks. Was it colder outside than he'd thought? He watched as she rearranged some of the grocery items delivered that morning and thought, *something is wrong and she isn't going to tell me what.*

Danny thought, *now Dad can never come home.* And she said, "Didn't I see a crock-pot downstairs Mister Al? I think I did." Turning quickly, Danny bounded down the stairs, grateful for the cool solitude of the basement. Somewhere inside she ached.

Feeling helpless, Al watched her go. He'd forgotten how difficult trying to communicate could be. *What is a crock-pot?*

Danny stood before the shelf holding an avocado green crock-pot trying to catch her breath. *Settle down,* she told herself, *things are no different than they were before. So what if the trailer is gone? Nothing has changed. It's no big deal! I mean, it's not like I would ever go back there. Dad wasn't coming back before and he's not coming back now. Nothing has changed.*

She let the last door to her past slam shut—and for a second—wished she could die. Then it passed.

She felt better.

Danny wiped her eyes with the back of her hand and reached for the dusty crock-pot.

The door bell rang. *Pizza!*

Taking the stairs two at a time, Danny was suddenly hungry and anxious to show Mister Al the latest satellite images from space courtesy of Google.

She forgot all about returning Oxo's call.

The old man was delighted to hear Danny charging up the stairs. Her mood had been so different only moments ago when she'd seemed very young and in need of protection.

That wasn't the way he wanted to think of the Girl in the

Woods.

Danny handed the deliveryman Al Smith's credit card in exchange for a fragrant pizza.

The smell of hot, greasy, pepperoni with gobs of extra cheese brought Danny and the old man immediately to the table. *Good thing the pizza came with a stack of napkins!* Neither of them took the time to put out plates—they just dug in.

Danny was halfway through her second piece and already thinking about her third when the old man knocked on the table to get her attention. She looked up—noticing he had somehow managed to ALREADY eat two pieces—to see him keying a message onto the computer screen.

CHECK ARRIVE?

Danny nodded

DO YOU HAVE AN ACCOUNT FOR THIS DEPOSIT?

Danny's vague plan to deposit the check in her father's account now seemed like a very bad idea. Where would she even find a branch of his bank? Would the sudden activity cause the authorities to look closer at the account of a guy on the missing persons list?

Even as the old man watched her hesitantly shake her head 'yes', the look on her face told him what he wanted to know.

LET'S SET UP AN ONLINE ACCOUNT AT MY BANK, IN YOUR NAME. THEN BEA CAN TRANSFER THE MONEY TO MY ACCOUNT AND I CAN TRANSFER IT OVER TO YOURS. YOU GET YOUR PAYCHECK RIGHT AWAY THAT WAY. THEY SEND YOU AN ATM CARD SO YOU CAN TAKE OUT CASH. OKAY? I CAN DO THAT RIGHT NOW.

She smiled when he mentioned the ATM card, *if only he knew*. Thing was, more and more, she wanted him to know. She wanted to tell him everything. *This old man is probably the best friend I've ever had.* The thought made her a little sad until a more immediate problem presented itself. *He'll want an address and maybe even a parent's signature to set up an account. How should I handle this?*

"I don't know, Mister Al," she hesitated, "Don't I have to ask my mom or dad before I can do that?"

No need to trouble your family. Just use this address. It's quicker. If you need a signature I'll just sign my name—it IS Smith after all! All you really need is a social security number, a birth date and a signature card. He smiled at her obvious excitement.

You know your numbers right?

Danny nodded. Everything just fell into place when she was around Mister Al.

Run upstairs to the printer. I printed the form you need. Sign it. We can stick it right in the mail. It will take a couple of weeks to activate the account and get your ATM card though. The old man watched Danny bound up the stairs to retrieve the form.

Now he was committed to a plan of action. He would play along. He just couldn't risk losing Danny's company by challenging her story. Maybe someday she would trust him enough to tell him the truth. Until then he'd try to make her life a bit easier whenever he got the chance.

He'd spent a long, silent day piecing together what he actually knew of Danny's life. The girl had been raised by parents who cared—she was too well-manner, too well-schooled and too well-adjusted NOT to have been. Something very bad must have happened for her to end up all alone and in foster care.

Because she knew a bit about the obscure Cumberland Cut-off, he was almost certain her assigned foster parents were the Laird's. That was bad enough—but speculating about what drove the young girl out of the house and into a tent in the woods made him so angry, he'd gotten up on the bike and actually managed to get the pedals moving an agonizing ten revolutions. After that, he was so exhausted he needed a nap, only to wake fifteen minutes later as more problems presented themselves.

Winter is coming. They say it will be a bad one. She needs a tent big enough and strong enough to handle the elements. She did need his help.

The remainder of the day was busy, hatching plans and making moves to insure Danny was outfitted to face the snow and cold of winter in the woods. Setting up the bank account was just the first step—he had other surprises.

Danny looked at the old man in the wheelchair and marveled at how young he now seemed to her. His wrinkled cheeks looked a bit fuller and the sparkle of blue was pronounced next to the healthy white of his eyes. *He definitely has a glow.*

The old man reached out as Danny returned with the forms from the printer, but not for the papers. He handed Danny a pen.

Wow! It's like he had all this it planned.

She bent over the kitchen table and scanned the enrollment application for a bank account looking for places to sign her name and saw that Mister Al had already filled in most of it on-line. For residency he used his own address; he used her cell number for telephone and his name as the emergency contact. She filled in the blanks for social security and birth date, leaving just the signature black.

She caught herself just before she signed her father's name. *That would have been tough to explain.*

'Daniela Francesca Smith' she wrote, winced and handed the old man the completed forms.

He folded them into an envelope, already addressed and stamped, and set this aside. Then turned to the computer screen, DO YOU KNOW WHERE THE WAREHOUSE STORE IS?

Danny nodded yes, curious about another new direction.

NUMBER FIVE BUS STOPS ACROSS THE STREET FROM YOUR SCHOOL EVERY AFTERNOON AT HALF PAST THREE AND IT WILL TAKE YOU TO THE WAREHOUSE STORE. COULD YOU GO BY THERE AFTER SCHOOL TOMORROW?

"Don't you have to have a membership card?"

I'LL GIVE YOU MY CARD. I DEALT WITH THE MANAGER BY EMAIL THIS AFTERNOON AND EXPLAINED MY DISABILITY. HE AGREED TO TRANSFER MY MEMBERSHIP TO YOU. I TOLD HIM YOU ARE MY GRANDDAUGHTER AND TEMPORARY CARETAKER. HE WILL BE ON HAND TOMORROW AFTERNOON TO MEET YOU AND HANDLE EVERYTHING.

"Why?"

I NEED YOU TO PICK UP A FEW THINGS I ORDERED, PLUS YOU CAN GET ONE-HUNDRED IN CASH BACK WITH THE MEMBERSHIP CARD. THAT'S YOUR MONEY—TO USE HOW YOU

WANT. I WILL ARRANGE A TAXI TO PICK YOU AND THE PARCELS UP OUTSIDE AT 5PM.

"Why can't I just ride the bus back?"

TOO MUCH STUFF TO CARRY.

Danny navigated her way back to camp that night by starlight, and snuggled gratefully into the sleeping bag. *Google Earth will have to wait,* she thought while drifting off, *tomorrow I am going shopping!*

At first, the taxi driver dismissed the girl waiting near the curb as too young to be the fare he was supposed to pick up. He'd pulled to the curb, reclined his seat and prepared to wait when a sharp rap on the window startled him out of a very nice daydream. He looked out into the girl's dark, serious eyes and thought, *Ooops!*

Trunk and backseat were soon full and the taxi pulled away from the warehouse store. The driver looked over at the girl in the passenger seat to ensure she'd buckled her shoulder harness, and decided she was older than he had originally thought. *Maybe those braids, Timberland boots and puffy jacket just make her look like a kid. Her face is small and her eyes are dark and somehow exotic even without makeup. Maybe sixteen? Seventeen?* Shaking his head he stepped on the gas.

The taxi rolled out into traffic.

Danny watched the world flash by the taxi window and felt like things were coming together for her. *It's like I've got this guardian angel or a tree spirit or some kind of special mojo-magic hanging around me lately!* She stole a happy look over her shoulder at the treasures piled on the back seat. It was about time she had some good luck.

The back seats barely accommodated her new, oversized, hyper-insulated cooler-on-wheels. In the cooler she'd managed to stuff TWO large, rugged terrain tents, a gas camp stove and three small bottles of propane. She'd crammed a battery charger, dozen rechargeable batteries, and a box of Granola bars into her pack.

It hadn't been easy to narrow her purchases to what could be concealed and transported inside the cooler, but considering all the useful items she had discovered in the store it had absolutely been worth it! When she first arrived the store manager had everything Mister Al ordered ready—all she needed to do was have a picture taken and sign her new card, and he'd handed her a receipt marked PAID and one hundred dollars.

She'd had a little over an hour to look around the store. *Astonishing.*

The massive, no-frills warehouse was stocked with everything from food to deluxe tents, and from solar-powered computers to large utility sheds. Pallets— stacked ceiling high—turned wide aisles into canyons. Danny spent a long time in the aisle geared to high living RVers. She found power invertors and AC/DC converters and examined Marine Cell batteries. She thought, *this stuff is so high-tech it makes Mister Al's homemade generator look primitive—but it pretty much does the same thing.*

Bright-eyed. Thrilled beyond belief. Danny shopped.

The over-large cooler immediately caught her eye. It was designed to roll on the beach and looked to be the perfect thing. *If I put everything I buy inside, I can get it by Mister Al without too many questions.* She figured she could roll it through a winter woods.

Even with membership-warehouse prices, Danny needed way more than the one-hundred dollars. *Dad's cash card.* Swallowing her dread, she headed for the entrance where she'd seen a small ATM.

The machine was much smaller than the Big Green Cash Machine she had used at Wal-Mart, but when she offered it her father's cash card, it pulled it from her fingers and gobbled it up without incident. Her mind was so completely occupied with visions of what she would buy, that when the screen flickered to life, it took a few seconds to remember the password, IROQUIOS.

She carefully typed and impatiently waited.

Nothing happened.

Another message began blinking on the unfamiliar screen. It read: WOULD YOU LIKE TO MAKE ADDITIONAL TRANSACTIONS?

Danny stabbed at the NO button.

Waited.

What now?

She was instructed to: PRESS ENTER TO CONTINUE, OR CANCEL TO EXIT.

Danny pressed ENTER and the machine finally leapt to action, with a long and loud series of mechanical whirrs, beeps, shuffles and flips.

Come on!

New 20 dollar bills drifted, slowly, into the tray; a process that seemed to take forever. Until, *Finally!*

Danny collected the cash and, anxious to get back to shopping, turned to go.

BeepBeep The irritating ATM called her back.

She had forgotten to take her receipt and the machine was displeased.

I REALLY do NOT like this machine. Not wanting to draw unwanted attention she snatched up the receipt. The beeping stopped and she rushed off. Never glancing at the paper the ATM had labored to produce Danny balled it up and absently stuffed it in one of her many pockets. Her focus was on shopping.

In the middle of the store was a display of tents pitched in a circle on a piece of artificial turf. Danny headed to the largest, parked her shopping cart and thought, *I can replace the tent that was chewed up in the storm with a much better, bigger one.*

Very systematically she began to compare each model's merits.

The largest tent was family-sized. It was for long term camping. The material was dense and both light-proof and varmint-proof. It had windows that could be completely sealed, and was constructed with reinforced metal braces and supports.

The shelter was amazing. But it was heavy. *Too heavy to drag through the woods.* Next she examined the information printed on the box. *Wow!* She saw the price. *Expensive too.*

Danny moved on to look at contestant number two.

This one looked exactly like the first one, but at a quarter the price. *Must be a mistake but worth a look.* Danny felt the material, tried out the zippers and fasteners, compared sizes, *the same.* The difference in the two models seemed non-existent until she discovered it, (in the fine print); the internal braces and supports on this tent were made of different material. The 'bones' of this model were made of dense plastic which made it cheaper *and lighter.* She liked those options.

Although the first tent was better designed to stand against the most brutal winds, lashing storms, and temperature extremes, Danny figured it would be over-kill; the Fortress of the Vines was a natural wind-break and the lighter tent was also highly rated.

The perfect choice. She thought and felt like a bottle of soda, effervescent, bubbly, and rising up. She stepped over to the last display model.

Tent candidate number three was called 'The Weekender'. Made by the same company, it looked identical to the others— from a distance. But up close, Danny saw that it was smaller (a foot smaller in each direction), and made of simple rip-stop nylon with flexible, synthetic rib construction and tie-down fasteners. *Huh! Pretty much like my last one,* she thought, and turned away. After looking at the first two shelters tent number three held no appeal. Then she remembered something that stopped her completely.

The article. I'd forgotten. Last night, Mister Al insisted I read a boring National Geographic article about an arctic explorer who walked to the North Pole...

Danny hadn't wanted to read the article; she'd wanted to get to camp and to sleep so she could dream about the up-coming shopping expedition. She'd tried to tell Mister Al she was too tired to read and promised she'd take a look some other day. But uncharacteristically, Mister Al was adamant that she read it **before** leaving. So she had. And now the article was knocking around in her head.

The explorer in the article had cleverly fashioned a 'double' tent for protection from the sub-zero temperatures, and credited the system for saving his life. And—right in front of me—are two tents that will pair perfectly—one inside the other. If I buy both, the air trapped between two shelters will work as insulation.

How could this just be a coincidence?

Her purchase came packed in remarkably small bundles. *Better and better.* She was able to stuff both into the cooler.

With the cooler filling the taxi's back seat and Mister Al's order filling the trunk Danny allowed the magic of the Fortress of the Vines to fill her head.

The taxi driver couldn't believe how much traffic he was running into. *Where on earth are all these people going?* In his admittedly limited experience, Cumberland Road was pretty rural. *Kenilworth Township must be growing.* Then he saw the flashing lights. *Accident,* he groaned.

Two badly crumpled cars faced each other on the opposite side of the road. It appeared one had plowed into the other.

Typical, thought the driver as they inched past the scene.

Typical, thought Danny, who'd been pulled away from her dreams and plans by the flashing lights and bumper to bumper traffic. She watched the drama unfolding on the shoulder of the road and thought about her own mother's fatal crash. *How had it happened?* It was a two car accident but, according to the police, no one was at fault.

The taxi driver sensed the change in his passenger's mood. He glanced her way. Gone was the bright-eyes young person he'd picked up only a few miles ago; a sad little girl slumped in her place.

Danny stared out the window hypnotized by flashing lights and considered how a no-fault accident could ever happen in the first place. For some reason an image of Leo Peal popped into her head, which made her consider the phenomenon of the blind spot. *Blind spot. Could that be it? Could it be that simple?*

The taxi, breaking free of a line of rubber-neckers, began to pick up speed. It passed the crash site near the top of a rise on a stretch of road that ran straight through the Kenilworth woods. The driver glanced again at the girl. *She looks a bit better.*

Danny felt she'd finally located the end of the string that, if pulled long enough, would unravel the mystery of her mother's death. She began to tug at it, stretching it this way and that, preoccupied with possibilities and scenarios... *Blind spot.*

Movement in the woods caught her eye.

What's that!? She watched as a man in a red plaid jacket stepped from the edge of the trees and began to walk toward the accident, no doubt drawn by the flashing lights. *But what was he doing hanging around in the woods in the first place?* Twisting in the seat improved her view and she caught a flash of a faint dirt road. Overgrown and rutted, it led back into the shadows, stopping at a metal barrier gate. *That's a driveway.* As the taxi topped the hill to make the left into Rockaway Estates, Danny lost sight of the figure. *I travel this road back and forth to school everyday and I've never seen that driveway.*

Life just keeps getting weirder. Maybe the universe was giving her clues. *A driveway can't just appear; I just never noticed it before. Where does it go? To a house? Could there be a house back there?* The only thing Danny knew for sure was that the driveway led into the back of HER woods.

When the taxi pulled in front of the townhouse, the front door opened. An anxious old man stood, looking out. Waiting for what would come next.

TANGLED WEB

The young girl knelt beside the old man's wheelchair. Flickering blue from the computer screen was the only light in the darkening room and the electronic color danced across their avid expressions. They were exploring the world. Courtesy of Google Earth.

First they had visited the streets of New York and the lights of Las Vegas, done a flyover of London, Paris, and Rome, and traced the mighty Amazon to its source, via satellite imagery.

They'd been at it for hours.

Dinner and more surfing lay ahead.

Earlier, the old man suggested that the girl stay put for the evening and then had listened with interest as she faked a phone call 'home.' He didn't want her stumbling through the woods, pulling the mammoth cooler he'd watched her wrestle from the back seat of the taxi. *Although that is some great cooler! Wonder what she has packed in it?* Plus, she was about due for a bath and general clean-up. *Is that a twig sticking out of her braid in the back?*

There was something about being with Al that made Danny feel content. After the emotional highs and lows of her long day, she needed a friend and when he'd insisted she stay over, she surprised herself by nodding yes. Her normal way of working through troubling thoughts was to hole up and write everything out in her journal. *But,* she rationalized, *Mister Al needs some company.*

Anyway, it was already dark. She knew she'd left a change of clothes in the guest room upstairs. *And I can finally introduce Mister Al to the satellite views on Goggle Earth.*

Google Earth was a hit.

At this height, it's like having my own helicopter. The old man thought as he hovered over the Grand Canyon. He was delighted.

"Would you like a cup of milk tea?" Danny asked as she hoisted herself up from a kneeling position on the floor and heard her knee crack.

Mister Al looked up sharply. *Ouch!* He shook his head **yes** and followed behind, stopping at the sliding glass door as Danny continued into the kitchen. He flipped on the deck light and watched trees at the edge off the woods beginning to whip around as gusts of wind hit from different angles. *I wonder where Rosemary is tonight?*

Rosemary was asleep. A cold front was moving in so she'd found a warm place to bed down. Maybe she didn't miss her home in the tree at all. The strong gust of wind urged her deeper into the tight ball of sleep. The ears disappeared from view as the pointed chin snuggled into the dense winter fur of her belly and the fine, full ringed-tail draped over her eyes. In sleep, Rosemary looked much like one of Daniel Boone's coonskin caps.

The little raccoon's stomach was full of winter fat. Her coat was lush and glossy. Twice that afternoon she'd visited the blue-eyed human to demand food and he'd coughed up a couple of peanut butter sandwiches. She suspected he was holding out on her though because, each time he opened the door she could smell something wonderful cooking. She'd kept a careful eye on her provider as she ate and could see that her provider watched back.

All that work. Of course Rosemary was tired. With a cat-like purr the little animal descended into hibernation.

If it stayed cold for a few days, she might not move at all.

In the kitchen, Danny looked around while waiting for the kettle to boil. Things looked very different from the way she'd found them on her first day. On the side counter, a simmering crock-pot of beef stew filled the house with comfortable smells. The canisters were full of coffee, tea and sugar. A few loafs of sandwich bread were piled up beside the refrigerator. The cabinets were stocked—and so were several shelves downstairs— with the cans, jars, bottles and packages she had brought home from the warehouse store on Mister Al's direction.

He sure bought a lot of peanut butter. I wonder if he can eat three whole loaves of bread before they get moldy? Maybe he could. They both had two slices of bread and butter and a bowl of stew a few hours ago. *I eat here a lot. Miss La-Di-Da Beatrice probably wouldn't like that.*

The tea kettle began to whistle and Danny turned off the burner. As she poured hot water over a teabag in two oversized mugs she saw the trash can next to the counter was full. A newspaper lay on top and two familiar faces stared up at her from the rumpled front page. She slammed the kettle down and snatched up the paper.

The headline read: **Governor Gets Job Done!** The accompanying photo took up half the page. It showed a large woman with green teeth embracing a scrawny young teenager. *That's Lady Lard-butt...and she is hugging Oxo.* Danny felt her heart flutter with anxiety. Breathing steam from the hot, sweet cups of tea calmed her enough that she could read on.

The cut line identified the photo: **Reunited foster family thank Gov.**

Reunited?! Confused by this turn of events, Danny skimmed the article...

> **One full day; that's all it took the governor's appointed team of contractors to repair extensive storm damage to foster parent Roxanne Laird's home.**
>
> **The governor became aware of the Laird family's plight during his recent visit to local emergency shelter and was moved to immediate action, "I felt terrible for everyone I met at the emergency shelter—each and every one faced some degree of weather-related ruin— but the Laird story cut me to the heart! Mrs. Laird is one of those people we need more of. She gives back to this community, selflessly opening her home to anywhere from 4 to 10 orphans each year in addition to caring for her handicapped husband. When she told me about the roof, the leaks and the damage to the children's dormitory, I knew these were all things in my power to fix"**
>
> **The aid came as a complete surprise to the Laird family. When they returned to their unexpectedly warm home, the first person they saw was the governor himself, who took them on a tour of the areas repaired and renovated. Roxanne Laird choked back tears of gratitude even as she lavished praise on the governor.**

**But a knock at the door brought another surprise, a
foster child had returned! Overjoyed, Laird made this
heartbreaking statement, "I'd like to thank the governor
for making this moment possible! I don't know what
thrills me more, knowing I can now continue to provide
quality foster care to unfortunate wards of the state, or
being reunited with my eldest foster child—Oxo Pierce!"**

*Nah! PIERCE? Oxo the human pin-cushion's last name is
PIERCE? That woman made that up I bet.* Danny looked at the
picture and noticed for the first time that Oxo did not have his
chains and body piercings in. His face looked a little lumpy and
distorted from the scars and outrages he had inflicted on it, but
he was actually smiling—even though he was being hugged by the
evil Lady Lard-Butt. *So this is why Oxo called me. He must be
using the information we found to get control. But he is still
living in that house with those awful people. Yuck. I guess not
everyone can find their own place like I did.* Thinking again that
she really did owe Oxo a call, another thought danced by. *I
wonder if any of the other kids showed up? The only other I've
even ever met was that firebug-kid called Skid.*

Shrugging, Danny dropped the newspaper back into the
trashcan.

"Tea!" she announced and stepped from the kitchen balancing
a tray containing two mugs of tea and a plate of chocolate
cookies. Thinking Mister Al was still in the living room, she
passed right by the big table in front of the sliding doors and
failed to notice the old man.

Finding the living room empty, she turned back and saw him.
He had pulled his wheelchair up to the table. An empty chair was
at his elbow, and he had somehow detached the laptop from the
tray so it could sit directly on the table. *It couldn't have been
easy to do that.*

The old man smiled and pointed to the chair next to him. It,
too, had a view of the computer screen.

He wants me to be comfortable, she realized and her eyes
began to sting. *That is so sweet...* Danny sat down and focused
unblinkingly on the laptop. She listened to the old man slurp his
hot tea and managed a smile.

*Okay...*she took a breath, reached for a cookie—saw that only one was left and smiled again...*time for a look at Rockaway Estates from the sky. Who better to explain the terrain than Aldo Smith?* Mister Al would love to show her around the neighborhood.

In this new configuration, Danny had access to the mouse and keyboard and she moved the cursor to the top of the screen. "The best thing, Mister Al, is that we might be able to use satellite images to find the stone shed." With a click she closed Google Earth, returned to standard Google Search mode, and moved her hands back to the warm mug in front of her.

Al Smith loved a mystery. He leaned forward, anxious to see what she would do. His blue eyes twinkled with interest.

Danny indicated the search bar, "Okay. It is all yours. Type in your address—you just need the house number, road and the zip code."

He typed, thinking, *I already know where I live.*

She could feel her own excitement building as she said, "Press ENTER."

They watched as Google pulled up a small map of the address. Mister Al raised one shaggy eyebrow, *SO?* He said as clearly as if he had spoken.

Quickly, Danny reached across and clicked on the map to open a larger screen. She then pointed to the top right map corner where the word MAP appeared in a box. It was highlighted. Beside it were two other boxes labeled SATELLITE and HYBRID. Danny didn't have to say a word.

The old man clicked SATELLITE.

Three cups of tea later, Danny decided to interrupt—after all it was a school night. "I found out about this in computer lab today. The teacher was pretty excited about Google updating the images in this part of the county. You can get really close to the ground now, and really see stuff. Before the update only a general satellite overview came up and if you tried to get in closer the 'Image not Available' screen came up."

The old man was focused on her now, but she saw that his eyes had lost their sparkle. He seemed sort of sad.

Opening a second window, the old man typed slowly: |

THOUGHT I KNEW THIS COUNTY. BUT PLACES ARE NOT WHERE I THOUGHT THEY WERE IN RELATION TO OTHER PLACES.

"What do you mean?"

He manipulated the screen map and used the pointer to follow Old Cumberland Road. SEE THIS? He rested the pointer over a slight dent in the otherwise straight tree line beside Old Cumberland Road, then glanced her way to be sure she was following. THERE IS A DRIVEWAY HERE THAT LEADS TO THE STATE COLLEGE RESEARCH AREA.

Danny squinted. *That must be where I saw the man – on the State College Research driveway! What a weird coincidence that Mister Al should point to the exact place I've been thinking about.*

LOOK CLOSE OVER HERE AND YOU CAN MAKE OUT SOME BUILDINGS.

Lost in her own musings, it took Danny awhile to realize the old man was typing more and more slowly. She felt a hint of concern and scolded herself. *Well if I paid attention, I might just find out what's wrong.*

IF IT'S TRUE THE STREAM DIVIDED THE TWO BROTHER'S PROPERTY INTO TWO EQUAL PIECES, THE STREAM SHOULD BE ABOUT HERE, He slid the pointer side to side at the mid point of a large parcel of woods bounded by roads. BUT LOOK NORTH AT THE STATE COLLEGE BUILDINGS. SEE THE DARK GREEN STRIP RUNNING BESIDE THEM? VEGETATION GROWS GREENER NEAR A WATER SOURCE AND CHANCES ARE THAT'S WHERE THE STREAM IS. The old man turned stricken eyes on her for a moment before adding, THE STREAM ISN'T WHERE I THOUGHT IT WAS AND NEITHER WAS THE STONE SHED. IT WAS WHERE THOSE BUILDINGS NOW STAND.

The silence was deafening.

Danny understood. *He spent his whole life looking for a place that no longer existed.* She squinted at the screen to avoid looking into his disappointed eyes, and noticed something unusual. *There's another change in color—sort of a brownish green stain—that starts south of the green band and spreads down through the middle section of the forest. What could it be?*

Danny pointed the odd color variation out to Mister Al. "Do

you see it?"

A blank stare.

"There!" She pointed to the middle of the screen. "See? It's there."

Nothing.

"If you squint real hard and sort of turn your head a little to the right, you will see it...its like a large brown stain...right there!" She jabbed her finger at the area near the heart of the forest, and was gratified when she saw the old man's eyes light up as some of his natural curiosity returned. *Yes! He sees it.*

YOU THINK THAT'S THE PLACE YOU CALL THE FORTRESS OF THE VINES? He typed and saw her nod. He traced the area defined by a slight color variation in vegetation; it was much, much bigger than he had imagined. *Even Danny is surprised at how big it is—certainly it has tripled in size since my day—looks like little brother Tommy's inheritance has been eaten up.* He looked at the subtle line formed as the brown-green met the green-green at the State College property line.

Danny was looking at the same area; now that she was noticing different shades of color, the demarcation line seemed even more pronounced, *like the stain gets darker where it meets the green.* Roof tops were visible within the green-green, showing that area was inhabited, at least sometime.

THE LINE IS TOO STRAIGHT TO BE NATURAL. THEY MUST HAVE PUT A FENCE NEXT TO THE STREAM.

"Or maybe they just put up a fence and there IS no stream."

ONLY A WATER SOURCE COULD MAKE THE VEGETATION THAT GREEN. GOT TO BE A STREAM.

"Unless it only LOOKS greener because it's next to the brown!" Danny willed the old man to consider the possibility. "Don't you think the brown stain looks darker where it meets the green? Maybe the green looks greener too."

The old man responded to the excitement in the young girl's voice and began to think about what she was saying. He wanted to believe the stone shed was still out there; and so did she.

Maybe it is still out there. After all, the stream was SUPPOSED to divide the properties equally, and the State

College buildings are too far north. Like a match to a gas burner, hope reignited with a *whoosh.*

YOU COULD BE RIGHT! THEY OWN LAND ALL THE WAY TO THE STREAM, SO WHO'S TO SAY WHERE THEY PUT UP A FENCE? THEY COULD PUT IT ANYWHERE.

Danny shrugged. *Who knows why adults do what they do?*

MAYBE THEY BUILT THE RESEARCH BUILDINGS WHERE THEY DID BECAUSE THE VINES WERE JUST TOO MUCH TROUBLE TO DEAL WITH FARTHER IN. NOW THEY MUST TREAT THE FENCE LINE WITH WEED KILLER TO KEEP THE VINES FROM CROSSING OVER. He thought a moment before adding...WEED KILLER WOULD EXPLAIN THE DARKER BROWN LINE TOO.

"Well," she said, "whatever they are doing is keeping the vines from total domination. Wish I had some of that spray."

The old man nodded philosophically recalling his own near-death experience with the poisonous vines. Then he typed, I HAVE WEED KILLER IN THE BASEMENT FOR POISON IVY. IF YOU THINK IT WOULD HELP, YOU NEED TO APPLY IT IN THE FIRST DAYS OF SPRING WHEN THE SAP IS RISING.

That got Danny's full attention. "I could keep a path open with that. Ummm, then I'd have a better chance of finding the stone shed."

He nodded, welcoming the familiar bloom of excitement that always came with thoughts of the stone shed.

Danny returned to examining shades of green on the screen. Where was her camp in relation to what she was seeing?

She tried her father's trick of using the clock to give directions. *Find the approximate center of the Fortress of the Vines and superimpose a clock face over the whole thing. Now, north is always straight-up—12 o'clock and south is always straight-down—6 o'clock. East is 3 o'clock. West is 9 o'clock.*

According to the clock, the State College fence line crossed the circle from 10 to 2. If the real stream came in at 9 and exited at 3, the College had surrendered the area between 10 and 9 and between 2 and 3 to the vines.

Danny had the hang of the clock-thing now and superimposed it over more known territory. She enlarged the view to include

Mister Al's house in Rockaway Estates and considered the geometry. *When I leave Mister Al's I walk a straight line—pretty much north.* She drew an imaginary line north; it intersected with the Fortress between 7 and 8. *I have a new address. I live at 7:30!*

The old man tapped the digital clock on the bottom corner of the screen and startled Danny. *You have school tomorrow,* he reminded with a few hand gestures.

The lights were out and Danny was asleep before the old man's computer screen flickered back to life.

He had a bit more surfing to do.

Danny rose early, needing time to wash and braid her heavy hair. At least she didn't have to dry it, having discovered it was easier, and quicker, to braid while wet.

Weak morning sunlight filtered through the curtains and a strong gust of wind whistled between the town homes as Danny tiptoed down the stairs twenty minutes later. She didn't want to wake Mister Al.

Mister Al was already awake.

Just as he spotted her, Danny saw him. He was on the bike, obviously straining to move the pedals. He might have been a bit embarrassed at having been caught, but he grinned warmly, gestured as though he were tipping up an imaginary cup and pointed to the kitchen. *Coffee?* he said without saying.

Danny wished she'd made a bit more noise coming down the stairs. "Good morning Mister Al!" she said and dropped her pack by the door. "Sorry if I disturbed you."

She could smell the freshly made coffee even before she entered the kitchen. *He set the timer an hour earlier than usual before he went to bed. Really, who was taking care of whom here?*

Danny poured two cups and stepped out of the kitchen only to find the old man had pulled his wheelchair to the table. YOUR HAIR IS WET, he typed, frowning disapproval.

"It will dry." she said and sipped the hot coffee a little too fast. It burned her tongue.

Don't embarrass her, he thought. But really she was a little too old to wear her hair in two braids—and her part was crooked again. *Well, I might as well...* He took a deep breath and typed: I WAS IN THE NAVY AND WE USED TO BRAID ROPES.

Oh GREAT! This is exactly the way my Mother used to talk when she was getting ready to tell me something 'for my own good.' I am **out** *of here.*

Prepared to stalk out, she shot a disappointed look at the old man. His blue eyes were not as sharp as usual. They seemed soft and pleading...

Danny stopped herself from rushing off to an empty bus stop. Instead she sat down quietly and sipped the hot coffee with deliberate care.

HAVE YOU EVER HEARD OF A FRENCH BRAID? Al typed and raised a shaggy eyebrow. He was very aware he'd almost lost her. He waited.

Danny shook her head and swallowed.

EASY TO DO. *Maybe this last thing will convince her.* MAKE YOU LOOK OLDER.

Danny's hair was almost dry by the time she ran to catch the bus. Everyone watched as she hopped onto the first step, but she didn't mind. The weight of the single French braid slapped against her back.

Danny already liked her new look.

More good news. Three seats were open on the bus. For the third day, both Leo Peal and Donna Adagio were absent and this time Danny didn't have to take the seat caved in by Leo's butt. She moved on to a seat open beside a big-eyed first grader. The boy was called 'Chippy'.

"Hi Chip!" Danny said and turned away, planning to ignore the little boy for the rest of the journey. Danny had a lot of exciting new things to think about...

The bus soon wheeled into the school's circular driveway and stopped with its characteristic lurch. This made the more girly-girls squeal in surprise. *Like it never happened before,* Danny thought with disdain and began to gather her things. At first she didn't feel the light touch on her arm.

The big-eyed little boy tapped her again and whispered, "...Is that old m-man your daddy?"

Danny smiled down at him.

His little face lit up.

"That old man is Al Smith. I stay with him sometimes." She swung her braid over her shoulder and stood. "He's my granddad."

Just as she stepped into the aisle she felt another tap. *Now what?* With a big sigh she looked down into Chip's red, flustered, little face. *He heard me sigh,* Danny realized, and felt a little ashamed.

Chippy's stammer was more pronounced, "Lll—lll-Leo pp—p—Peal and the d-d-D.A. got sus—su—suspended." He gulped. His face turned still redder, "—f-f-f-for f-figh-fighting."

Oxo leaned back in the kitchen chair, looking first across to the massive woman every CSD kid knew was a thief, and then at the drooling man he knew was a bank-robber-Nazi and thought, *they aren't much, but they're mine. This is where I belong.*

To be sure, Oxo had made an effort to improve everyone's living conditions by making some changes. First, he refused to allow Mrs. Laird to smoke at the dinner table—*she is still a disgusting slob, but, hey, I can't fix ugly.* Next, he demanded she serve variety and better quality, microwave meals and insisted she keep the kitchen stocked with snacks, drinks and stuff for sandwiches—*an artist needs his calories to create*—and finally he insisted Mrs. Laird learn, and call, all the foster kids in her care by name, starting with him.

Oxo was very pleased with the way things had come together since the governor's visit. Oxo had gotten things rolling that day by telling the governor in front of the cameras that his dear foster parents couldn't afford a decent computer or internet connection, which everyone knew was a necessity for school these days. The governor immediately promised a computer, printer and high-speed internet connection before the week's end—*no surprise there*. But Oxo was surprised by public's response.

Gifts from local vendors began arriving the morning after the press conference. The biggest box contained a computer desk. The smallest box was a fully-loaded laptop; then came a photo-quality printer, boxes of ink cartridges and various types of paper. Oxo took the laptop and printer for his den. Then he tossed out the Laird's prehistoric computer and dot-matrix printer and installed the stuff the governor had sent over. *From now on, Lard-butt fosters will be on-line.* The walls of his den were too thick to use the house Wi-Fi connection, but he'd managed to run a cable through the door and set up his own network.

An uncommonly, wet slurp from the Nazi at the head of the table derailed Oxo's happy thoughts, so he grabbed a piece of soft white bread, smeared it with thick yellow margarine and wrapped it around the chunk of finger-lickin' good chicken. The big satisfying roll dripped grease down his arm; he liked to eat with his hands. He took a big bite—tried chewing with his mouth closed—and remembered why he'd stopped doing that. *It's like an echo chamber when my mouth is closed...I can hear all the glooey, munching sounds inside my own head.*

Oxo let his mouth drop open. *Much quieter.*

Roxanne Laird watched covertly in her muddy-eyed way as her unwanted foster son ate and ate and ate. She was dying for a cigarette and was missing one of her shows, but a combination of fear, hatred and some unknown emotion kept her pinned to the seat, silent. She'd been that way since Oxo strutted back into her life. *I am a victim.* She thought, *soon he will have this place filled to the rafters with his snot-nosed friends. He'll probably make me move in with Dougie so he can take over my room.*

On the opposite side of the table, Oxo watched a tremor flutter through the fat on Roxanne's assorted chins and thought, *Huh!* He knew she didn't like his new rules, and didn't much care. Just remembering her haughty displeasure the day he knocked on the front door—right in the middle of the governor's visit— gave him great pleasure.

He'd carefully planned his entrance that day. He'd sleeked back his hair, put on clean clothes and left the den by the kitchen door. Knocking on the front door was important, since he knew

Lady Lard-butt would open it. His timing was perfect. Reporters snapped shots of Roxanne opening the door to welcome back her foster son. They continued to snap pictures as he moved to pose beside his 'dear foster mother' and whisper the lines he'd practiced in her ear. He'd said, "I know all about you, Roxanne. I can bring you and your criminal husband down— right now—in front of all these reporters. But I'm not going to do that—because I am a nice guy. I'm your favorite foster son, right Roxanne?" He gave the large woman a squeeze and when he'd felt a quiver of alarm vibrate through her, summoned the confidence to adlib the rest, "And Roxanne, since you have no doubt forgotten my name, it is Oxo...Oxo Pierce."

He still couldn't believe he'd made up a name on the spur of the moment; he knew he was dull-witted. Now he thought about that stroke of genius as he chewed, *it was like I was James Bond or something...like maybe an actor! I know it shocked old Lady Lard-butt—yet she turned right around and made that tidy little speech to the reporters and to the governor.* He took a last bite. *I suppose she's used to pretending.*

Oxo was pretending too. *Nothings felt real since...*he swallowed... *since the storm. But now it's time for Oxo Pierce to take it to the next step. Gotta lay things out,* he decided and caught Mrs. Laird's eye. "You look worried Roxanne. Don't be, I don't plan to leave you. I'm staying right here. I am quite comfortable in the den downstairs."

Although everything he knew about blackmail was from TV or comic books, he thought it was working. *She is scared of me, and she'd better be!*

He gave Mrs. Laird a hard look and ground home the point, "You know the place I mean Roxanne? Little ole' Dougie's secret Nazi nest?" Satisfied by the naked fear in her eyes, he cut a quick glance to the Nazi himself, expecting to see Dougie Laird busily slurping his at microwave dinner.

But Dougie wasn't eating—he was staring at Oxo with an unexpected spark of sanity. His big, puffy hand shot forward and latched onto the boy's forearm.

Oxo jumped in alarm at finding himself in the crushing grip of a man who normally had the intelligence of a pumpkin! But even before he could react to the unexpected turn of events, insanity reclaimed Dougie Laird and the hand fell away. Oxo watched the spark of life die away as the big head drooped forward. It was over so fast, it was as though it didn't happen, but it did and it was a little scary.

Oxo knew his bloodless coup affected everyone in the Laird household, he took a third off all CSD checks, but since he reserved the other two thirds for actual foster care he reasoned, *the only people who might suffer, just a little, are the Lard-butts —and they deserve it.*

Already his new rules had lightened the atmosphere in the house, enough he hoped, that Danny might consider coming back— Danny was his lucky charm. Whenever he did his art, Oxo wore the yellow pajamas she'd given him.

Danny's computer assignment didn't take long at all. Finishing early gave her time to surf and she knew just what to do—Google Red's address.

Typing the number into the search box, she mused, *Why haven't I done this before?* Seconds later she was looking down on an isolated spot at the end of a dirt road. Red's farm. Although the satellite view wasn't tight enough to spot her father's old trailer, it did clearly show that Red's farm was surrounded by forest spreading out in all directions.

Danny Googled driving directions—from Mister Al house to Red's farm—then stared at the surprising results. *Two pages?* The extensive directions listed roads, turns and mileage for an estimated drive time of 1 hour 20 minutes. *It can't be that far.*

She compared the aerial view with the driving map and saw the problem was not distance—Red and Mister Al lived only 9 to 10 miles from one another. The problem was the roads—there weren't any—at least none making a direct connection. The driving route involved a series of wiggly secondary roads and complicated back tracking, that wandered all over the map.

No wonder it takes over an hour by car.

Flipping back to Satellite view, Danny saw nothing but undeveloped forest between Mister Al and Red. It seemed possible to cut through the woods and walk to Red's—but—as the search for the stone shed revealed—many things could hide beneath forest foliage. Her father's compass would send her in the right direction until she ran into some impasse—like a big swamp or wide stream or even another Fortress of the Vines— and was forced off course. If that happened she could easily get lost. And what if she came upon a man-made barrier that protected private property? She'd have to turn back.

Then Danny remembered the power lines.

Metal towers supporting hi-tension power lines marched side by side across much of the state. Danny had come across one such tower while exploring Red's property. *I called it the Eiffel Tower.* That had amused her dad who'd explained that her Eiffel Tower was part of a long line of towers that ran from Kenilworth Dam to the end of Red's property before heading east to the city. He'd called this line a 'power corridor'.

Power corridors use heavy cables suspended on tall metal towers to carry electricity from power plants to outlying areas. Every effort is made to locate towers in unpopulated areas away from public view and the power company keeps the land under them clear to give technicians access to the remote locations.

Who needs a Yellow Brick Road anyway? Just follow the power lines.

By the time the bell rang to change classes, Danny had traced the power corridor from Red's all the way back to Kenilworth Dam and found the closest access point—Cumberland Cutaway. *Hi-tension lines cross the road just around the corner from the Lard-butt's.*

Danny felt a field trip coming on.

The holidays were *supposed* to be tough, Beatrice reminded herself. All you had to do was watch the news to see how miserable Thanksgiving-Christmas-New Year made everyone. Single people drank too much. Husbands jumped off bridges. Wives lost their minds. Little kids got emotionally scarred for life. Christmas brought out the worst in everyone, Beatrice knew.

Best to ignore it.

For years, she had successfully done just that. The holiday insanity thing had washed right over her and she'd kept her head down and her nose to the grindstone. She'd done just fine.

Anyone foolish enough to ask Beatrice about holiday plans received a withering look and a two word answer, "I'm working."

So why today, when a new employee asked about Thanksgiving plans, did she have such a hard time managing 'the look'? And why did "I'm working" get stuck in her throat and send her into a coughing fit?

Her cough was so violent it sent her to the Ladies room.

Now she stood at the sink, staring into the mirror but, no matter how much cold water she splashed onto her face she couldn't manage to push away the tears.

Breathe, Beatrice, in and out, in and out...

It was much more than tears. Beatrice was losing control. And to her that meant losing her edge in the business world. She could feel herself slipping.

It had all started with the dreams—she hadn't had a decent night rest since they started two weeks ago—and now EVERY night she experienced long, colorful, *disturbing* adventures. She dreamt about absurd things, like fireplaces and Thanksgiving turkeys and Santa Claus. In her dreams, her mother was alive and her father was young and strong. *Nightmares,* she called them. Every morning she'd wake with wet eyes and a sore heart—this morning the ache was so strong she'd thought, *is this what a heart attack feels like? Did my father feel this way before the stroke? I should ask him. I've never asked him about that.*

Danny wrote:

A story has a beginning, a middle, and an end, but life consists of beginnings.

These days every morning feels like a beginning, and every day brings surprises. This morning I had two surprises when I stepped out of my cozy double-walled tent.

First: It was freezing COLD!

Second: I had a visitor.

I could see the deer clearly, because the sun slants into my clearing well before it gets to the rest of the woods. He might have been there for the sun's warmth because he stood in a pool of early light. It was really beautiful! Mists from the stream bed swirled around his legs and through his magnificent antlers and his breath steamed as he breathed.

We stared as each other for the longest time and he didn't seem the least bit afraid. After awhile, he just walked slowly into the shadows.

I shouldn't really be surprised. I knew deer lived in these vines, but he's the first I've seen. Since the water is warm here, even when it is below freezing everywhere else, the animals like it here. But how did a deer get to be his size while living so close to people?

I wonder what he saw when he looked at me?

GIVING THANKS

It was time to ask for the governor's help, but frankly Toad was scared to death of the man.

His stomach had been upset since he looked at the just-posted satellite imagery of the county—and saw close-ups of Kenilworth Dam. Toad needed those details taken off the internet immediately and thought the governor could and would make that happen if there was a political benefit.

After hours of thinking through the problem from every angle, the little man had chosen his approach. He would tell the governor that Kenilworth Dam and Reservoir was a juicy target for sabotage and now terrorists could use the recently posted satellite images to map the dam's structure, along with the location of streams feeding it, to gain access to the city water supply. "What," Toad planned to say, "would this county do if their primary source of water was blown up—or even poisoned—by terrorists with detailed maps?" THAT should get the politician's attention!

Running the scenario again and again, he refined the speech and increased the urgency by jacking up the threat-level. He needed the governor to act quickly. If his plan didn't work, Toad could kiss his government job—and probably his pension—goodbye.

Fortunately, Toad could report that the forecast for the upcoming four-day Thanksgiving weekend would bring shoppers out in droves—news that should put the governor in a receptive mood...

The phone rang.

"Yes sir!" Toad croaked.

It was the governor.

Danny came by very early Thursday morning to put Thanksgiving dinner in the oven on a delayed timer—claiming her own family's dinner was at noon.

Al acted as though he believed her—telling her to thank her

non-existent family for sharing their daughter with an old man.

Danny smiled, and fibbed—and said she would tell them he said hello. She promised to come by at 4 o'clock to take the turkey out of the oven.

Al asked her to please save room to eat again with him on her return.

When she left, they both were satisfied and looking forward to having Thanksgiving dinner together.

Both of them were getting very good at pretending.

The whole house smelled of roasted turkey. The old man breathed the holiday smell with pleasure and actually felt his toes curl in anticipation. He couldn't remember ever being so interested in a turkey dinner.

Maybe that's because I'm standing close to the oven, he reasoned.

He was leaning over the sink—steps from the oven—peeling potatoes. On the countertop were an array of discarded knives and vegetable peelers. Al picked up another potato—this time selecting a short knife—and began to hack at the spud. He'd had no luck with the peeler-with-the-metal-handle or the peeler-with-the-black-handle—and he'd almost cut his finger off with the big carving knife.

Thick peels dropped into the sink as he hacked at the fist-sized spud. He thought the little knife worked pretty well, *why would any one use a special peeler?* In seconds, a much smaller white potato clunked into the pot. As he looked down at the two, tiny, misshapen potatoes he'd produced so far he thought, *Wow, these things don't amount to much!* He reached for another.

Five potatoes later he had enough for two people—if they weren't too hungry—and the door bell rang.

"Hello Daddy," a brittle voice said, "forgot my keys!"

BEATRICE?...Al's old brain screamed until he looked up at the haggard, middle-aged face of the woman standing at his door and felt his heart break. *What has happened to my daughter?*

Beatrice noticed the old man's watery eyes; she leaned down for a brief hug and felt his arms shake. *Poor old thing!* she thought, *it's a good thing I came.* And felt better than she had in months.

Al was relieved when she pulled away— *that was like hugging a bag of chicken bones*—and then felt guilty for feeling that way. *She's my little girl. Did someone HURT her?* For the first time in awhile he wanted desperately to speak; frustration rose like acid.

Beatrice moved to the handles of her father's wheelchair and steered it toward the living room. She would sort him out in no time. *What is that wonderful smell?!* She wondered until she rounded the corner and spotted the bike and battery parked next to an unmade daybed.

Al saw her always-there frown deepen and thought *uh-oh! Trouble.* He reminded himself that this was his daughter and she might need his help.

"Well I see that the girl I'm paying an arm and a leg isn't keeping this place straight." Bea's voice was shrill and her movements were jerky; she hadn't stopped complaining since she'd stepped through the door.

Talk! Talk! Talk! He thought. *She has no business bad-mouthing Danny that way. It's MY house; MY bike, and NONE of her business.* He watched resentfully as his daughter stomped over to a pile of pillows beside the bed—his annoyance already outweighed any concern for her health. It was quite obvious she hadn't come to see him!

Beatrice began to yank at the bed sheets, never glancing at her father. She wondered why a crippled old man would need a bike, until it dawned on her. *The bike must be for the girl. SHE must have dragged it up here to use. I'll need to tell her this is NOT her gym.* Beatrice plumped the pillows as she arranged them on the daybed. *She must be a cook though, because dad never cooked anything in his life and something smells really good.*

Al thought, *I HATE all those silly pillows on my bed. I have to shovel them off every night anyway.* He deleted the long paragraph he'd just typed and started over again. It was hard to think while she was fussing around—babbling non-stop about the weather, the government, taxes, calories—anything and nothing—in no apparent order. *It's like she is emptying her head into the room.*

She still hadn't looked at him.

He typed faster and, as she finished arranging the pillows to her satisfaction, turned the screen to face her. *Look this way. READ it,* he silently shouted, watching her roll up her sleeves and begin to walk.

Without a glance, Beatrice disappeared into the kitchen.

The old man was left alone—nearly choking on unspoken words—the message—WHAT ARE YOU DOING HERE?—blinked unread on his computer screen.

Unbelievable! He realized, *she is STILL talking.*

The sky was a deep, bottle-blue with just enough wind to feather the clouds. In the Rockaway neighborhood folks were busy. Smoke curled from chimneys and the air was redolent with tantalizing smells, hints of burning wood, whiffs of basting turkeys, butter and sugar and bubbling pies.

Whispers of these smells penetrated the tangled Fortress of the Vines nudged along on an autumn breeze. The fragrance discovered a dark, loamy hollow at the base of a large oak tree, pushed its way in and curled seductively around the animal sleeping there.

The little raccoon's nose began to twitch. One sleep-bleary eye cracked open only to slam quickly shut. It was still too cold to wake up! But the breeze shifted and this time the air was infused with the rich smell of baking bread.

Rosemary was awake.

Her tummy felt loose and grumbly. It sloshed in her thick winter coat when she staggered to her feet. She followed her nose out of the warm den into the brightness of a perfect Thanksgiving Day.

The aroma of multiple Thanksgiving dinners cooking throughout Rockaway Estates surrounded Danny's tent—ready to pounce the moment the tent flap was opened. So far it hadn't been. Danny was whiling away the time before dinner with Mister Al by writing in her journal.

Danny wrote:

Thanksgiving alone is like fishing in a bathtub. Pointless.

This Thanksgiving I have Mister Al's company to be thankful for. If it wasn't for him I'd be by myself missing my mom and dad like crazy.

Come to think of it, there IS something worse than being alone on Thanksgiving Day—being stuck with the Lard-Butts! That's probably where Oxo is, in that gloomy house with those awful people. Lady Lard probably won't even serve turkey, unless she found one that fit in the microwave.

Oxo's strange—but then lots of CSD kids I met are. I should have called him after he left me that message. If Mister Al insists I take home leftovers, I'll take them over to Oxo— even though going near that house creeps me out.

I wonder if stopping by Mister Al's early would be suspicious? Maybe if I stopped by BEFORE noon I could say I wanted to check the turkey before going to my own home?

Sure hope Mister Al doesn't expect me to dress-up for dinner! I have a couple of pairs of jeans and some tops to pick from. Clothes should be next on my shopping list I guess.

Danny's phone beeped. She put her journal aside, located it and flipped it open. It was a text message from Mister Al.

TROUBLE. BEATRICE HERE FOR T-GIVE — ACTING WEIRD. DON'T COME BY. WILL TEXT LATER.

Oxo happened to spot the figure just as it rounded the corner onto Cumberland Cutaway. It looked very much like Danny, but since he'd never seen Danny walk aimlessly—head down, hands in pockets—he squinted for a closer look. The figure passed by without glancing at the Laird house. *That's Danny alright.*

The whistle was high, sharp and close enough to startle the girl out of her thoughtful mood. Looking around, she saw a boy wave from the porch of a nearby house and realized she'd almost walked right by the Laird's without a glance.

That's Oxo! She thought, *he looks different.*

Oxo sprinted down the steps, delighted Danny had finally shown up, thinking—*she looks different.*

"I'm going for a Thanksgiving hike—to the farm where I used to live." Danny shouldered her pack a bit higher, squinted up at Oxo—but continued to walk. "Do you want to come?"

Oxo shrugged, wiped his nose with the back of his hand and fell into step beside Danny.

I guess he's going. For some reason this made Danny feel better. "I'm cutting through the woods here..." she said as she stepped off the road into a shallow ditch "... and I'm following the power lines." She pointed up then shrugged toward an opening in the weeds.

Oxo glanced up and thought, *Huh. Never noticed that before.* The base of a metal tower, just visible through the weeds, was so tall it poked high above the tree tops. Giving his borrowed watch cap an extra tug and pulling up the collar of his jacket, he picked up the pace. It would be good to get away from civilization. The smells of Thanksgiving were driving him crazy.

The old man did his best to run interference, but his little visitor was simply not cooperating. Even with the curtain closed he heard Rosemary patting insistently on the sliding glass door. Picturing her standing on furry back legs, her arms leaning forward on the glass, he thought, *Oh Rosemary, Beatrice is going to see you. You better clear out if you know what's good for you.*

Beatrice was busy in the kitchen. After she'd sliced the turkey, mashed a few potatoes and microwaved a green-bean casserole, she transferred each into its own plastic container and placed them side by side up on the counter, then turned her attention to washing, drying and putting away the pots and pans and knives and wrappers. For some reason, the normally silent Beatrice detailed every step of the cooking, cleaning and preparation process—out loud; she couldn't seem to shut up.

The little raccoon began to chatter—adding to the confusion in the old man's ears.

"Time to sit down for dinner." Beatrice announced after the

kitchen was spotless. Now she opened the plastic containers and served out the cooling contents onto two plates. Each plate received exactly two slices of turkey, one tablespoon of cranberry sauce, a serving spoon of green beans and another of mashed potatoes. "We aren't having that box stuffing you had out on the counter. One starchy item per meal, that's my rule, so potatoes are it..." She drizzled thin gravy over the turkey, and headed for the dining room.

Rosemary caught the rich scent of cooked meat and smacked the door so hard it shook. She could make out the silhouette of a woman putting plates on the table and expected to be included.

Al had closed the curtain and now he backed his wheelchair against the glass door, hoping to muffle Rosemary's antics. He tried to ignore the knocking and chittering but fully expected his daughter's wrath at any moment. When it didn't come, he realized the woman was STILL talking.

She can't hear anything but the sound of her own self. What the devil is WRONG with her?

The old man wished he could make some noise to cover up the commotion coming from the deck—but of course he couldn't. *Nothing I can do Rosemary. Even Bea can't talk while she's eating and she's motioning me over to the table right now. You are on your own.*

"How do you stand it?" Danny blurted out when they stopped for lunch.

The boy paused in the examination of his wet boot and considered her question. He knew what she wanted—but didn't feel like telling her just yet—so he shrugged and said, "Ah, its okay. Me and the Lard-butt's have come to what lawyers call a 'mutually beneficial arrangement'...they don't bother me and I don't report them." Oxo pulled off his boots and sat to wring creek water from his socks.

Danny looked at his boney, white feet and saw dozens of bloody blisters. *How can he still walk?* She had set a pretty good pace and—until Oxo's foot slipped crossing a small stream—he'd kept up. She said, "I couldn't even breathe when I stayed in that disgusting house."

He just shrugged, and gave each sock an extra squeeze before putting it back on. "I don't stay in the main house. Got my own rooms in the basement."

Danny was intrigued. "What do you mean? The basement is part of the house isn't it?" She looked at him.

He shrugged again dismissively and stood up.

Point taken. End of conversation. He won't tell me anything more, Danny thought, *I know the signs.* She'd watched her father shrug just that way when asked personal questions, even when it was his wife or daughter doing the asking. *Dad had lines he wouldn't cross...* She stood, stuffed the sandwich bag she used for PB&J sandwiches into the side pocket of her pack, and started walking.

They covered a pretty good distance before Danny looked up to see the orange clay cliff marking Red's property line. "We're almost there." She turned toward the cliff and began to pick her way up the slope. Fortunately, it wasn't terribly steep.

Oxo was happy enough to climb along side her. He wasn't a big fan of nature and hoped they were headed for a town or maybe a house. He could use a cold soda and maybe a bathroom. He heaved himself the last several feet to level ground and looked around expectantly. *Nothing.*

It took Danny only a second to spot the path leading to the trailer. She glanced over at Oxo, grateful for his company—and his silence. She didn't want to explain. Her stomach felt loose. Her tongue seemed to stick to the roof of her dry mouth and she could hear her own heartbeat, **thud, thud, thud.**

Danny was scared.

Why is she walking so slow? Oxo thought and moved ahead to take the lead. It seemed pretty straight forward—just follow the path. *And look for civilization.* He sniffed, and wiped at his itchy nose. *Funny smell.*

Danny smelled it too.

They stepped into a clearing and the acrid odor surrounded them. The land here looked blasted. Broken limbs, scattered chunks of metal and other rubbish, hung from tree limbs, protruded from tree bark and littered the ground.

"Looks like something blew up, big time." Oxo was impressed. He squatted to pick up an interesting piece of melted plastic fused with twisted metal and thought, *Cool!*

Danny stumbled into the field of debris and kept walking. *How could this happen? There is absolutely nothing left...nothing at all.* She felt really weird—sort of numb and tingly—like she had when her mother died. Why was this affecting her? *Because I believed there was always a chance he would return. Now I know he can't.*

She felt the boy come up beside her and it was okay. He understood loss. He'd been there himself.

"I lived here once. In a trailer. With my dad."

Oxo watched her carefully and then he said, "Maybe we can find something, maybe there is something left. We should look."

"Yeah."

They found it sticking from blackened earth under the trailer—only now the trailer was gone. Danny recognized it right away, "That's Dad's!" She knelt to snatch up the battered metal oval. It was still warm.

Oxo saw Danny's eyes grow misty, *great! She's going to cry.* "What is it?" he asked, although he could clearly see it was a belt buckle.

"A buckle, like cowboy's wear, with a raccoon on the front" Danny turned the oval over and over as she spoke, remembering. *I thought he'd like it, and convinced Mom to buy it. We had it engraved.* "See this?" She pointed out the deeply engraved letters visible through the soot on the back. "It says **To Daddy, Love Danny**", she looked up and smiled.

Her face and hands were covered in soot, and Oxo thought she looked very young. "I'll wipe it off," he heard himself say, and took the buckle from Danny's hand. *Well, I can always wash the shirt and it's a dark color,* he thought and grabbed a shirt tail.

"Not your shirt! Here. Wait a minute. I have something." Danny dug in her pack and produced a handful of napkins.

"Maybe you better use those to wipe the soot off you face, besides cloth works better," he said as he rubbed at the metal vigorously with his shirt. The oily black came off the buckle's shiny metal face, but clung to the cracks and scratches making the raccoon on the front stand out. The same was true of the engraving on the back. he saw as he polished. Pausing to admire the effect, he noticed something... *There's more stuff scratched on here.* "What's that other stuff on the back?" he asked as he handed Danny the gleaming buckle and tucked the filthy shirt tail into his pants.

A neat pattern of elaborate scratches encircled Danny's engraved message to her father and she looked at it curiously, "I've never seen that before." She held the oval disc up to the light, "It almost looks like cursive writing."

Oxo was looking over her shoulder. Although he wasn't much of a reader he was very good at design. "Nope. It's a pattern. Some kind of decoration."

"I suppose it must have always been there and I just never noticed, but what is it?

"It is what it is." Oxo said.

"What's that supposed to mean?"

"That it's a beautiful design, and that's all it's supposed to be."

"Yeah...well..." She rubbed her finger over the surface. *He only wore it on special occasions. So he left without it. Maybe he planned to come back...*

Leaving Danny to moon over her father's belt buckle, Oxo returned to his search for more bizarre looking relics of the explosion. He'd collected some choice pieces already and envisioned a collection entitled 'sculptures of destruction' or something like that. The best piece so far was one he'd pulled from the side of a tree; a wad of ashy copper sheeting and a dagger of charred wood welded together by a blob of primary blue plastic. *Cool.*

Perceptive little beggar! The old man thought, chewing a mouthful of turkey and enjoying the silence. Some kind of survival instinct must have alerted the little raccoon, because the second his daughter stopped talking, the noise on the deck quit too.

He took another bite, wondering if Rosemary was out there right now staring in at them. *Or did she just leave in disgust?* He planned to smuggle out a plateful of turkey as soon as the coast was clear. *I should add some vegetables too...* his thought was interrupted...

"...for your health. As soon as I move to a bigger place, I can have you live with me." She was oblivious to the shock in her father's blue eyes.

Oh no! Oh no, no, no! He had to tell her. *No. I will not move.* But how? He was invisible; even as her eyes brushed across him, he knew her focus was the wheelchair— not the person.

Beatrice's mouth was full when she thought she heard something. She stopped chewing and listened. *Yes!*

Al, tuned to his captor's every movement, saw Bea cock her head to listen and thought, *Uh-oh, Rosemary's back.* He listened for sounds from the deck. *Nothing... no...wait, did something buzz?*

Again came a muffled round of buzzing from the living room where Beatrice had deposited her travel bag. The cell phone.

His daughter's normally sour face lit with pleasure and she practically turned over the chair in her haste to reach the phone.

"Oh, it is probably the office!" Beatrice tossed over her shoulder and headed for the privacy of the living room. "They can never seem to manage when I'm gone!"

Maybe Beatrice was more like him than he'd guessed. He'd once felt the same way about his profession—until he lost it. *Is that what's going on with Bea?* The hard years that followed his dismissal were awful for him—but he'd never considered the effect on his wife and daughter. Al wasn't proud of the way he'd acted then. *But things got better when I took the bus driving job.*

"Well, it looks like I'm going to have to leave in the morning." Beatrice said while striding back into the room. She pushed a non-conforming piece of hair off her forehead and sighed dramatically. "I know I promised to spend some time with you, but they have things all muddled up at the office and so, I must go in. I'll probably be working straight through the weekend."

Later that night, Al admitted to a guilty sense of relief and delight in Bea's upcoming departure. *Probably I am a very bad father*, he told himself. He quietly slid open the door to the deck and pushed out a plate loaded with turkey and green beans. A shiny button nose immediately appeared around the edge of the upturned cooler and a long arm reached from the shadows to expertly snag the plate.

Al watched the plate disappear into the deeper shadows and smiled.

Things again felt right in his world.

Danny wrote:

Some clothes we wear for comfort, some we wear because they make us look good, and some we wear not knowing they make us look bad. But, we need clothes to keep us safe and warm—and not naked. Friends are like clothes, good bad or indifferent, we need them on many levels.

Oxo was so funny today! On the way back, he was behind me mooning over the metal chunks he found. I heard something in the bushes beside the trail and I looked over and saw a big deer standing there. When the deer saw me it leapt out— right in front of Oxo! I swear he squealed! He started jumping up and down—like one of the girly-girls on my school bus—his watch-cap slid over his eyes and his legs were lifted so high I could see the soles of his long black boots! He was hollering "Help Help Help!" but hugging those metal pieces like someone wanted to steal them!

It was so funny! I wet my pants I laughed so hard! He was that way when he saw Rosemary too, I remember.

Right now I'm curled up in my 'nest' looking at the raccoon belt buckle I gave my dad years ago. We found it buried under the camper/trailer we used to live in. The soot stuck in the grooves and once it was cleaned all this swirly decoration became visible.

Finding something of my dad's makes me feel better even though the trailer is well and truly gone. Oxo says it probably started as a fire but then something big exploded, and I think he's right. Only an explosion could do the kind of things we saw; melted glass and bits of trailer were driven right through trees. Oxo says the explosion broke everything apart and turned it into 'shrapnel'; he says shrapnel kills more people than an explosion. Well, all I know for sure is that anything powerful enough to sling our heavy trailer door up to the top of an oak tree, is dangerous enough without shrapnel!

Before we left the farm we checked to see if Red was home, even though he did tell me not to in his message. The farmhouse wasn't locked and Oxo insisted on going in to use the restroom. The place smelled funky—and sort of empty—but I didn't look around. I mean Red is entitled to his privacy, I guess.

Why do grown-ups have to be so mysterious?

This was nothing like the Thanksgiving I'd expected, but it least I didn't spend it alone.

Beatrice brushed her teeth and started to floss when her phone began to buzz. Puzzled—why would someone call her after office hours?—she checked the display. It was a text message. She put the phone beside her pillow and continued to get ready for bed.

Not until she turned out the light and climbed into bed did she read the message: B. I KNOW SOMETHING IS WRONG. LET ME HELP. I LOVE YOU, DAD

Beatrice was shocked. The words sounded so familiar, *he said that to mother all the time, "What's wrong? Let me help. What can I do?"* She started to cry, remembering how the questions annoyed her mother. *She told him to go away, but he kept asking, until one day she shouted "It's my hormones Al!! Just my hormones! So leave me alone, there's nothing you can do!"*

The memory surprised the tears right out of Beatrice. She wiped her nose and thought about *hormones. A hormonal imbalance caused Mom's problems—maybe that's my problem too. It's all hormones.* Beatrice was suddenly glad she'd come to check on her father. *I'm not cracking up. I just need to go to the doctor and get my hormones checked—they have pills for that no.!*

Bea deleted the text and rolled over for some well-deserved sleep.

Danny had just drifted off when the beep startled her awake. She sat up, turned on the flashlight and reached for the phone. In her experience, calls late at night were usually bad news. Had Red discovered she'd come by the farm after he had told her not to? She opened the phone...

It was a text message: BEA LEAVES TOMORROW. COME BY AFTER SCHOOL FOR PIZZA AND CARDS?

Danny flipped off both phone and flashlight and lay back, smiling into the darkness.

A WORK-AROUND

Winter bore down in the months leading up to the most wonderful time of the year. It seemed sunlight barely managed to leak to earth, before night pulled the curtains.

The dark, still, winter woods made sleep Danny's greatest pleasure; she understood why many animals hibernate in winter. By day, the double-walled tent kept the worst of the cold out and her body heat, plus heat radiating from the propane lamp, made the space downright cozy—perfect for thinking, reading or keeping a journal.

The tent didn't begin to cool until Danny was snuggled under the covers enjoying dreams of Iroquois, stone sheds and visits with her mother. The night-world was hers...but school-day mornings were not.

No matter how early she went to bed or how much sleep she got, the alarm clock always managed to ruin her best nighttime adventures—and after it rang, there was no going back. It was time to un-zip, un-snuggle and change clothes in the frigid darkness as quickly as possible. It was all so hard, and getting harder.

In December, temperatures moved into the negatives. Advisories went out that pets should be kept indoors at night.

Mister Al began weaving elaborate fictions to justify 'insisting' Danny stay the night in the guest room; Danny responded with her own untruths and gratefully accepted. Soon, every school night was spent at Mister Al's—but not weekends.

Weekends and holidays were Danny's solitary treasures.

Without the alarm clock, she was free to wake with the rest of the creatures living beneath the vines—sometime after dawn. She liked to lie awake awhile, enjoying her warm bed and the leisurely morning. Eventually though, the mystery of what the day had in store got the best of her. She'd wrap herself in a thick blanket, pull on wooly boots and take a look outside.

There was always something new waiting beyond the tent flap—perhaps a deer, a fox or a confused opossum or maybe just the spectacular colors of a misty dawn. Animals never seemed bothered by her presence. *I'm one of you,* she'd think and feel special and protected.

The stream was bringing its own kind of magic to the Fortress of the Vines. With each temperature drop, the fog cloud over its hot water grew denser, compacted into the space between the banks by cold air acting like a lid on a pot.

The trapped air was warm and humid and magnified the sounds of the water's happy gurgles and the fragrance of growing grasses and tiny flowers decorating the mossy banks. Inside the cloud the world became a blank slate.

The effect was of the two parallel worlds. *Enchanted,* she'd think and wonder if the spell included just the clearing or embraced the whole Fortress—maybe even the whole woods. Maybe her mother had something to do with it. It was easy to have such ridiculous thoughts in such a location; it was a lovely place to dream!

In Danny's mind, only one thing marred the scene's perfection: the spiny carcass of Rosemary's tree. It stuck up through the cloud and down into the stream—there was no getting away from it—and it made her unaccountably uneasy. *Understandable,* she'd tell herself, *it almost killed me and Rosemary.*

What she didn't know was that beneath the stream's still surface, Rosemary's tree continued to cause trouble. Water pressure built up behind the new obstruction then rushed over the top with a downward force strong enough to bite into the stream's sandy bottom. Months of this hydraulic blasting had created a sizable underwater crater and sent quite a bit of excavated sand to Danny's side of the stream bank.

One day Danny noticed that the drop off from the stream bank to the water had leveled out—squinting through the thick blanket of ever-present fog, she made out a small crescent of sand where none had been before. *A beach.* And every day the crescent seemed a bit bigger. *A beach, AND it's forming practically under my feet.*

The beach building slowed. By December, the crater's depth exceeded the downward current's reach and the current was unable to stir up any more sand. Frustrated, the water began to circle inside the cavity.

Danny discovered the full extent of Rosemary's tree impact on the stream one lazy Saturday morning when she waded out to wash her long hair, Normally, she did that task at Mister Al's so she was stepping carefully, but blindly, toward the middle of the stream—when the bottom simply disappeared! Danny plunged under the white cloud and far below the black, swirling water, and panic took over.

What's happening? Which way is up? I'm going to drown!

Her feet touched bottom. She pushed off, and shot back to the surface, gasping and flailing for something, anything, to grab on to. Her hand brushed something and her fingers snatched at— and found—the thing just below the surface. A tree limb. Griping, sputtering, heart thumping, she hung on for dear life, her legs dangling in deep waters buffeted by inexplicable currents

She had to accept the impossibility of water over her head in a stream that was less than a foot and a half deep and get her bearings, but she was blind and disoriented under the heavy cloud... *I walked toward the middle of the stream, and then...Rosemary's tree.* She gulped. *Rosemary's tree caused this.* She froze; *and now I'm hanging onto one of its branches.*

Courage was required to let go of the limb and move away in the deep, strangely swirling, water. It took a long time to find that courage—but she did—and immediately found shallow water only an arms length away. Emboldened, she ran her feet along the stream's sandy bottom and explored the edges of the very deep, very mysterious whirlpool—*just like a hot tub.*

By noon, Danny's hair was washed and beginning to dry but, she saw no need to move, she was lounging in the hot, constantly circulating, water and it was wonderful. She reflected on the irony of the situation. *My own Jacuzzi —and my own beach —all thanks to that horrible old tree.* The tree had even supplied the underwater bench she now sat on. She said "Okay, Rosemary's Tree, I don't hate you anymore. Thank you."

Her words were trapped and amplified by the fog.

Danny wrote:

All truths are not equal —what we 'see' may be different from what we 'know'. The red fox wasn't surprised when he stepped into the fog—though his legs disappeared into what must have looked like a solid white surface. That fox believed in an invisible stream; he kept walking—in spite of what his eyes told him—and he got his drink of water.

Actually, I was sitting in my hot-tub-under-the-cloud-just looking toward the bank, and saw a fox's leg drop down from the cloud. Then another leg. Then the whole fox! It was so strange, like he materialized a little at a time. Pretty soon he was on my beach lapping up water! He looked over at me—his eyes golden like honey—not a bit concerned or even curious. Just thirsty.

I like to think the animals have been gossiping about me—spreading the word that a two-legged stranger has moved into the neighborhood—maybe Rosemary told them I'm harmless. When we meet, they react pretty much the way the fox did, stare a little and dismiss me.

I spent most of the morning soaking in my hot tub. The colder it is—today we have record-breaking cold—the hotter the water feels. It is the most wonderful thing! I wonder why Mister Al never wrote about any hot springs in the area. I think the hot spring must have played some role in the Rickenbocker's beer making. I should ask Mister Al.

As long as I'm under the mist its warm—but getting out is a bear! And back at the tent it is **winter!**

Guilt prodded Al to keep reaching out to his daughter. He'd committed himself to emailing her everyday—although it was tough to find things to write about without imparting details about his current life. *I can't have her poking around in my business.* He lit on the solution: write about her as a little girl.

That should let her know he WAS paying attention while she was growing up.

Within a week he'd run out of Bea-memories and caught himself writing about things he and Danny had done. He stopped writing then, and began sending cards. *Let Hallmark do it.*

A good thing was that his legs were getting stronger. Bea had left before carrying out her plan of moving the bike back to the basement, so his program of pedaling every time he felt anxious or frustrated continued. He'd begun to generate some electricity.

On the bike for the second time that day, he heard the expected knock, swung off the saddle into the wheelchair and waited. Danny always knocked before using her key. She was very polite.

"It's me Mister Al!"

With a rush of cold air and good health, Danny came toward him, carrying a massive armload of holly and pine branches. Her hair was loose and wild and he thought, it had been a long time since she'd looked so like an untamed child of the woods. *I missed that.*

She said, "It's almost Christmas!"

So it is, he thought and his heart skipped with happy.

"What do you say we make a wreath for the door so the deliverymen won't think Scrooge lives here?" She looked at him and saw approval sparkling in his eyes. "...and I thought we might bake up a few pans of those slice and bake cookies you ordered." Again she looked at him, enjoying his smile. *Good. He's been acting a little peculiar since Thanksgiving.*

The old man had been worried for weeks that Beatrice might swoop down to ruin the Christmas holidays, but just that morning he'd received email announcing her intention to work through the rest of the holidays. *What a relief!*

Now he had a great idea of his own. He typed: LET'S PUT UP THE TREE, TOO. THE CHRISTMAS THINGS ARE IN THE ATTIC.

Danny insisted on returning to the Fortress of the Vines that night —although it was very late and she was very tired. She negotiated the paths mostly by moonlight and memory, letting her mind run through the hours she and Mister Al had spent decorating.

First, they built the wreath —twisting together a slightly lopsided circle of spruce and wrapping it with wire Mister Al found in the kitchen junk drawer. When they added sprigs of shiny green holly, clustered with crimson red berries, and tied it with a velvet red ribbon, she couldn't remember wreaths her mother made being more beautiful! Both she and Mister Al were excited to hang it on the front door. *Now every time the door opens and closes, the wreath sends a breath of Christmas.*

They'd filled the house with the smell of baking chocolate chip cookies and she'd hauled down box after box from the attic before breaking to enjoy hot cookies and cold milk. *Who else would let that be dinner?*

She'd never assembled a fake tree before but it proven to be easy; the lights and ornaments went up quickly, too. To her surprise and delight, Mister Al was able to stand quite steadily to help decorate the tree; he even walked ten paces or so to tune in a station playing only Christmas music.

It was a perfect day, she thought and patted the treasures in her backpack —three strings of battery-operated twinkle lights. Mister Al insisted she take them.

Later that night she lay awake looking at up at those twinkle lights strung inside the tent —and breathed in the spicy scent of the pine bough stuck in a jar of spring water by her cot. She couldn't help feeling completely happy but at the same time guilty. *Is an orphan allowed to be this happy?*

Then she thought of Oxo.

Oxo had always been a night person and the natural darkness of his den suited him well. For the last three weeks he'd gone upstairs only to grab a sandwich or can of soda and check if the CSD had sent over any more fosters. They hadn't, so he'd returned to his work.

He was creating a new super-hero comic book—with two main characters, a girl named Sky and a boy called Crow. Oxo wasn't much of a reader —he used his drawings to tell the story and could usually avoid using words completely —but with the laptop computer came voice recognition software. He no longer had to rely on page after page of **Zocko!**...and **Powee!**...and **Blat!** *I just speak into the microphone and my words appear on the screen.*

So, in his new series, the heroes had something to say. Oxo liked it so far —yet wondered why he'd given the girl such a big role in his story.

Screwing the top back on the ink bottle, Oxo stood and stretched. He couldn't guess the time —didn't know the day —but his stomach was rumbling, so it was time to eat. He headed for the kitchen, taking the steps two at a time.

Thank goodness I don't have to go through Roxanne to get to the kitchen, he thought while raiding the refrigerator. Opening a cold soda and digging out meat for a sandwich, he heard the usual blah-blah-blah background sound of the television—but when he heard a familiar tune he stopped to listen. It squeezed his heart.

Jingle Bells?

Danny rang the bell and ducked behind the shrubbery. She certainly didn't want to be tagged by any Lard-butt. She waited, feeling the cold nibbling at her ears and edging down her collar. She hunched down farther and waited a bit longer.

The door opened. Oxo stood blinking like an owl in the daylight. He looked out—saw no one—shrugged, stepped back and closed the door.

How could he miss the wreath? Danny couldn't believe he hadn't noticed the Christmas wreath; it was resplendent with an enormous red bow and it lay just outside the door! She waited only a few more seconds before bounding to the porch, ringing the bell, and preparing to run.

Too late. The door swung immediately open and Oxo said, "Ah Ha!"

Where does he get this stuff? "Ah-Ha?" What's up with that? She smiled.

"Caught ya."

"No you didn't. I just got here."

"No you didn't."

"Sure did." She smiled and held up the wreath. "I'm selling Christmas wreaths for the orphans. Is the Lady of the house in?"

It was the first time she heard Oxo really laugh—and it was worse than his silly giggle. Deep and staccato, Oxo sounded like a dog barking. She said, "You sound just like a dog barking."

"Yeah." he was eyeing the wreath and the big tag that read 'OXO'. He stepped aside and motioned her in.

"No way. I'm not going in there. I can smell her cancer sticks from here."

Oxo sniffed. He didn't smell anything. He reached out and took the wreath, "Just come on in. I want to show you what I found downstairs."

Against all her parents' advice, she followed the boy who laughed like a barking dog through the dim house and down the stairs.

She'd never been to the basement before and was first surprised at how neat it was under twin banks of fluorescent lights. It wasn't until Oxo walked to a shadowed corner and disappeared behind the washing machine that she began to get nervous.

His head reappeared. "Come on!"

As she walked hesitantly toward the corner, she saw yellow light coming from what could only be a different room. The warm glow seemed to draw her forward. She reached the washing machine and saw Oxo disappear through an open doorway, then followed.

How can this be? Like Alice when she fell through the Rabbit Hole into Wonderland, Danny couldn't believe what she was seeing. There was a room behind the washing machine! And not just any room. This room resembled a banquet hall in a medieval castle. Carved from living rock and bathed in soft light from dozens of incandescent lamps, it glowed with mystery and opulence.

Oxo observed his first guest with glee. *She is impressed alright! I'll just let her walk around and take it all in.*

"Oxo, what is this place?" Danny drifted down the steps and

moved dreamlike to the center where she stared up at the rock ceiling. She looked back toward the entrance; she'd passed rows of wide shelves and drawer units and two large drafting tables. Nearby was what looked like a hand-operated printing press. "It's a print-making room right?" In a corner behind the old press was a neatly made bed, side table, dresser and lamp all arranged on what appeared to be an oriental carpet. "Where did you get all these nice things?" Were they here? How did you find it anyway?"

Oxo was both amused and delighted. For the first time, Danny seemed much younger than he. Her eyes were round and her voice was high. He was thoroughly enjoying himself and felt absolutely no need to answer any of the questions she tossed his way. *Let her be jealous.*

Danny turned in time to see Oxo carry his wreath across to the stone wall. She thought the wreath looked very out of place in this cavern. A shelving unit against the stone wall prominently displayed several pieces taken from the site of the trailers explosion. It crossed her mind that they did look quite intriguing.

Oxo pulled over a tall stool, stood on it and raised his Christmas Wreath to the center of the wall —securing it on a handily placed spike. He jumped down from the stool to check the effect. *More light.* He adjusted the beam of the goose necked lamp away from the 'sculptures of destruction' to shine onto the wreath above.

The light turned the wreath on the stone wall into something beautiful.

Oxo has taste! Danny was surprised. "Oxo, that's beautiful. You have a good eye for design," She squinted at him in the half light, noticing a new look of confidence in his eyes. His hair was clean and sleekly tied back in a ponytail, "You are, like, an artist who draws cartoons!"

"Comic Art," he corrected, "or Graphic Art — not Cartoons"

"Okay. 'Comic Art.' I saw some Comic Art on the drafting table over there. It's yours right? It has to be."

"Yeah. I do underground comics. Just local though."

"What do you mean 'just local'?"

Crap!

"You mean it's published? Like someone could buy it? Locally?" Danny was astonished, and trying very hard not to sound that way, but she could hear her voice go higher.

Is that so hard to believe? Am I that much of a loser?

Danny remembered the comic book she'd found in Oxo's room and blurted. "Wait, I think I saw one of them! Did you do one about two guys and a girl in wheelchairs?"

Oxo's eyes lit up. *She read my comic.* Only a handful had been printed in the basement of a now defunct head shop. *My only success.* Oxo nodded yes and tried to act successful and confident, "I'm working on a new series now though —so you will have to wait."

Christmas mornings are very sad when you live alone, the old man knew. His heart ached for the girl in the woods. *I can't ask her to stay here Christmas Eve since she doesn't know, I know, she's alone. But I can at least make Christmas Day special. She needs a surprise. But what? What do you give to someone like Danny? Has there ever been ANYONE like Danny?* And then he thought of something he often forgot about these days. *How does an old man with no car and no voice go shopping?*

A radio announcement broke into his thoughts:

> **The newly reelected governor expects December's frigid weather to bring snow in time for the Holidays, putting shoppers in the perfect mood to spend big. His statement came on the heels of early economic reports posting healthy seasonal profits statewide. Locally, with five shopping days left to Christmas, Kenilworth retailers report record sales.**

Like I need the reminder, Al grumbled silently, clicking off the chirpy announcer. He'd already heard the weather report—now he had plans to make and surprises to plan.

Work with what you have old man. So what do I have? KNOWLEDGE, The word appeared like neon inside his head. *Well that doesn't help...since SOME of what I know keeps me from telling her the REST of what I know—about her situation.* He boiled it down further: *I know she doesn't know, I know — what I know.* The word play amused him while he brewed some tea.

The shortest way to get from A to B is a straight-line —but that's not the ONLY way! Al told himself as he sipped steaming tea, *I need what we used to call a 'work-around'.* Annoyed with the sluggishness of his old brain, he put down the tea cup, climbed up on the bike and willed his legs to work. The trick was to focus on something else completely. *Like how much this still really hurts.*

Sweat began rolling down the valley of his back and the cords stood out in his neck. Concentrating on another revolution, inspiration elbowed through the pain, *Danny put her search for the stone shed on hold for the winter—but, again, she doesn't know, I know, that. So...what if what she thinks that I think she's spent every weekend looking for it? Then she wouldn't be suspicious if I gave her things to help in the search.*

The internet is an amazing place —particularly if you are armed with a high speed connection and a credit card. Most things can be delivered—even though delivery sometimes costs more than the purchase itself—but ANYTHING can be bought.

What to do five days before Christmas?

Kenilworth was still a small town but fortunately, many downtown businesses were savvy enough to also list websites and email addresses in the phonebook. He flipped to 'J' for 'Junk Yard'. Nothing. *What do they call it nowadays? Oh yeah...'Auto Salvage.'* He flipped pages... *Much more promising.*

Danny was really going to be surprised.

Hours sped by as Al typed and plotted. He hadn't been this excited about Christmas since childhood. One special Christmas memory out shone all the others and he stopped what he was doing to lose himself in it...

Snow had fallen for five days leading up to that long ago Christmas. *Snow drifts taller than me...it was a long winter that year, with winter snow on the ground from November to March...*

Those were the days before central heating and he remembered hurriedly stuffing his cold little feet into oversized cowboy boots...*I loved those ratty old things...* and clattering down the narrow stairs. The sun was barely cresting the horizon but his parents were waiting...*maybe they had stayed up all night...* He saw the flicking firelight, as he came around the corner headed for the warmth of the hearth...*and when I turned around —there it was.*

Here the old man paused, wanting to get the feelings and memories right. *The red sled. Santa Claus had propped it against the opposite wall—beside the tree. It was so shiny it reflected the colored lights and flaming fire.*

Did I know when I saw it that it would change things?

Nothing before...or since... had delighted him more than the red sled. Some days he was an Arctic explorer with a sled loaded with gear and animal pelts for trade with the locals. Other days he was the Heroic Rescuer, delivering a sled-load of food and medicine to families stranded by the blizzard.

It was like being given a Magic Carpet. The old man shook his head in wonder; *my folks never questioned where I went if I took the sled and stayed out all day. They thought I was sliding down Cumberland Hill like everybody else...heck, Dad probably got it for me in the first place, so I'd play with the rest of the kids...but for me, it was never a toy.*

Al had been a different kind of kid, a loner with a very active imagination and a romantic streak. His bedroom window looked down into the backyard and into the woods at the end of the lawn where shapes moved between the trees; he'd wake in the night certain Indians were about to attack. Other nights were animal nights, and a peek out the window showed a forest filled with hungry, yellow-green, eyes. Even in full sunlight, the Kenilworth woods was dark and snarly enough to thrill—and seduce—the young boy.

The first time he'd gone in was the day after Christmas. *The sled gave me courage.* The forest in snow was all black and white. Trees like fence posts crossed wide open spaces in any direction and he'd cut a path straight through them, delighted by the challenge and the mystery. *I had a mission: Find the fabled stream and follow it to the stone shed.*

It had been a grand winter—although he never found the stream or the stone shed.

The old man's eyes grew hazy with pleasant memories and

sleep seemed the best option. He shut down the computer, walked the two paces to the bed, and tumbled into dreamland.

It wasn't until morning that he remembered he hadn't even thought about a gift for his daughter—again.

Danny wrote:

The last day of school before the Christmas break gets to be special just because it's last!

I wonder why they made a half-day Monday the last day? I'm practically the only one here, but at least it is warm. I probably wouldn't have come in either, except last night I stayed at Mister Al's and it would have looked funny if I hadn't gone to the bus stop in the morning.

It is so COLD! Sunday morning I stayed zipped in the sleeping bag and read for most of the day—and I heard the wind kick up. It was one of those howling winds out of a horror movie, and strong enough to cut through both layers of the tent. AND temperatures dropped into the minuses! Even my hot spring had a rim of ice. That scares me most! Suppose something turns off whatever makes my hot stream hot? Then what? But I think the wind caused water to splash above the fog where it froze because, the water still felt great when I stuck my arm in.

The teachers are talking about another weather change, thank goodness! —and the likelihood of snow! Sounds good to me! I plan to get off the bus early and do a little exploring since Mister Al doesn't know I have a half-day.

Al rested against the tool bench before beginning his final search of the basement. He'd looked everywhere but between the rafters and that meant he must climb a ladder. He wasn't sure he could do it.

He must have fallen into a light doze, because the knock at the door became part of his dream. He roused when the air around him stirred and he realized an outside door had opened.

"Mister Al! Mister Al, it's me Danny. You won't believe what happened!"

The old man got to his feet, re-invigorated, and shuffled to the stairs just as Danny poked her head through the opening at the top of the stairs.

"Mister Al?" she said, "What are you doing down there? You know I don't mind getting stuff for you don't you?" Danny watched with concern as her friend began scooting up the stairs one at a time. *He looks a whole lot stronger than the first time I saw him do that.* "Well, I'll just go boil some water and make us some tea, then." She didn't want to embarrass him.

Always polite, the old man thought and scooted up one more step. About half way up he caught the flash of a familiar red and stopped —stunned. *The sled?* He saw it clearly from his spot on the middle step. *The sled!* Tucked between floor rafters and covered with dusty spider webs, the rusty sled was within easy reach. *Perfect.* He thought. *Tomorrow I'll find red paint.*

Danny brought two mugs of tea with plenty of milk and sugar to the table just as Mister Al rolled in. She looked at him carefully, delighted by the sparkle in those blue, blue eyes. *What's up?*

LAST DAY OF SCHOOL. RIGHT?

That was all the encouragement Danny needed. "You are not going to believe this Mister Al! Honestly." She paused, thought about what she should say, took a deep breath, and changed her story, "They took down all the detailed satellite views of this area! Really and truly! My Computer Science teacher talked about it in class and then I heard him talking later with some other teachers and they said it had to do with a National Security threat! Can you believe that? Wow! What are they talking about?"

The old man watched his outraged friend and considered what she'd said. *Could they be talking about the security of the dam? Has Kenilworth Dam been threatened?* He typed: THE GOV MADE FRONT PAGE NATIONAL NEWS TODAY WITH A SPEECH ON SECURITY LOOPHOLES. He frowned and shook his head thinking the world was very different now. He typed:

LUCKY WE CHECKED OUT THE AREA BEFORE THEY TOOK DOWN THE GOOD MAPS!

Danny hadn't thought of that!

I SENT SOME VIEWS OF THE RICKENBOCKER WOODS TO THE PRINTER UPSTAIRS. FORGOT I DID THAT. HOPE BEATRICE DIDN'T TOSS THEM.

Danny smiled. *What a great guy.* "I'll run up and get them!"

NO HURRY. DRINK YOUR TEA. LET'S ORDER A PIZZA. WHAT ARE YOUR CHRISTMAS PLANS?

*I plan to spend it with you, s*he thought and said, "Well my family wants to spend the week between Christmas and New Year with cousins upstate, but I don't want to go."

DO YOU WANT ME TO EMAIL THEM AND ASK IF YOU CAN STAY HERE TO HELP AN OLD MAN?

"Please!" *I can set up an email account in their names tonight. Why didn't I ever think of email?* "Oh, yeah, and you are NOT an old man. I told you we learned in Health Class that the human body was designed to last 140 years."

He watched her shake a finger at him and smiled. *She did a pretty good job on that braid today. I like the gold and silver chains wrapped around it. Very festive. Very artsy-fartsy.*

If the governor was into thanking those who did his bidding he might have started the phone conversation differently, after all, the person on the other end had been responsible for his great success in addressing the national meeting of governors. But the governor said 'thank you' only for political gain and so his voice was accusatory when he said, "You people talk about Global Warming all the time! Yet the diesel in that environmentally-correct piece of junk they make me drive FROZE last night, and YOU promised me a warming trend."

Toad gulped—this was the second time he'd been wrong about the weather; the governor was not the forgiving sort. *But I am a hydrologist — NOT a meteorologist*, he thought indignantly then reminded himself that this governor had enough clout to get all the close-up satellite images of Kenilworth Dam taken down. *That's power!* Toad felt he owed the man, "Sir, I AM sorry. I got the time wrong on when the warm front would arrive; it is only just now moving into the area—six hours later than predicted—but temperatures ARE climbing back to normal, Sir. Along with the warmer temperatures, it looks likely we will get snow by tomorrow night. We are going to have a white Christmas this year." *Great, he will rip my head off now. He HATES snow.*

"Excellent. That is really good news. Christmas snow puts the people in the mood to spend. I'll get those roads salted down and put snow plows on alert." The ringing voice trailed off before growling, "And you better be right about this!"

Toad jumped and once more checked computer monitors. Each screen clearly showed a band of snow on the way. "I'm right."

"I'll be in touch,"

"And...and...and Sir? I...I..um...thank you. I just wanted to say thank you for getting those satellite close-ups off the web."

Danny wrote:

A rock can be a weapon or tool, an obstacle or a bridge, a the keystone that holds the whole structure together or a missile that brings the whole thing down. It can be one of many or one of few. There is no such thing as 'just a rock'.

I'm all excited because school is out, and because I can SMELL the snow in the air, and because, MOST OF ALL, I made a really BIG discovery this afternoon...BIG, like a the-world-is-not-flat kind of discovery!

And I can't tell anybody.

Here's what happened: I got the school bus driver to let me off on the little hill before the entrance to Rockaway Estates near the access road to State College Research land. The road sort of hides —even if you know where to look for it—and it's just a dirt track with a padlocked barrier across it. The lock was rusty enough to break with one good kick — but it was just as easy to step over it.

The road angled and I couldn't see too far ahead, but I think I walked quite awhile before it straightened enough to see the fence Mister Al said would be there —eight-foot tall and all chain link. Well I walked over—expecting to see a solid tangle of vines on the other side... But, nope.

The fence was at the top of a steep bank and at the bottom **was a stream!** It was just like Mister Al said before I convinced him otherwise and he was right all along! I was looking at the Rickenbocker stream and State College had built beside it, so the stone shed was long gone.

I tell you, I felt pretty rotten, depressed about giving him false hope — and I even thought about not even telling him. But I decided that wouldn't be right.

I remembered how much better I felt after I found the belt buckle that was my father's, so I decided to look for ruins, maybe a pile of rocks or a crumbling foundation, anything I could take back to Mister Al to maybe make him feel better. I was walking along the fence line and got to a place where the bank wasn't as steep and got a look at the stream. It was frozen. I thought: How could a running stream full of hot water freeze solid like that?

So maybe it wasn't frozen solid. I found a place where I could wiggle under the fence and then went down to the water.

It was frozen solid alright.

I tried my best to break the ice but there was no way. I even chipped a hole in the frozen mud and worked a stick under it to pry up a piece. FROZEN! Even the river dirt came with it. That's when I started to think THIS MIGHT NOT BE MY STREAM!!!!!!!

I sat and thought about that until my butt got cold and I had to do some walking. I figured I might as well slide out on the ice. I did and saw the banks were steep, and very far apart. I could tell when I stood in the middle, this stream was much deeper than MY warm pokey little stream and must run a lot faster from the look of the cuts on the stream bank. Then something else hit me!

Maybe there are TWO <u>different</u> STREAMS?!!

That HAS to be it. Only explanation. TWO streams. My stream — the hot one — is the one in the middle, right where Aldo Smith's history says the original stream is supposed to be. His history doesn't mention a second stream — but his history said nothing about a HOT stream either —so maybe his history is incomplete. There IS a second stream and I saw it!

This changes a whole lot of things if Mister Al was looking for the stone shed beside the wrong stream all those years. Somehow I'm going to give him this information as a Christmas present. I know he loves anything about the stone shed.

I just have to be careful not to give away the surprise —I already almost slipped up and told him everything but caught myself just in time and said about the satellite maps instead.

Turns out Mister Al printed the detailed map versions before Google Earth took it down. I have the prints in my backpack. I'm going to ask Oxo to use them to do a 'comic art' version of the map, adding in the TWO streams — like a pirates treasure map — a Christmas present for Mister Al! Now that I have my own ATM card I can pay Oxo for the work. I'm sure he could use the money.

I love surprises. Three days to go!

Danny closed the journal and blew out the lantern. She lay back in her downy nest, gazing up at the colored lights twinkling above. Eyes beginning to close, she caught the so-familiar scent of orange and clove. *Mom.* She smiled and tumbled off to sleep.

In the clearing the first snowflake fell grudgingly, as though unwillingly squeezed from the sky. More followed as low clouds began to shake icy grit over the world.

On the other side of town, a bug-eyed man known behind his back as 'Toad', stared anxiously out the window. When the first flakes fell he did an awkward little victory dance in front of his window. "Its snowing!" he sang and prayed it wouldn't quit.

It snowed sporadically throughout the night.

A GIVING OF GIFTS

What little snow did make it to the leafy mulch under the vines resembled sugar spooned over corn flakes. This snow wasn't pretty.

Danny was greeted by several inches of it when she opened the tent flap. She crunched her way to the warmth of the hot spring thinking, *does a White Christmas mean a Christmas with snow on the ground or must it actually snow on Christmas to count as a White Christmas?* Playing the question over in her head she passed through the cloud into the embrace of hot water.

Sleet began to fall in fractured spits and sparks. The icy flakes that managed to punch through the protective cloud and reach Danny's warm skin stung like tiny electric shocks. Reflexively, she slipped lower into the pool as she concentrated on lyrics to the song playing in her head since she woke that morning. It was 'White Christmas'. At total peace with the world, she hummed and let her feet burrow into the pool's sandy bottom.

Her toes touched something in the sand.

No, please tell me it can't be! But she could feel the manmade object under her foot — hard, sleek and cylindrical — when she pulled it free she knew what she would find. "Litter!"

Disgusted, Danny held up the recovered dark brown bottle still dripping with sand from its hiding place on the stream bottom. She was outraged. Her un-touched, un-discovered glade had been violated. *Some fool would probably litter in the Garden of Eden.* Gripping the bottle by the neck, she prepared to launch it up on shore and deal with it later, until something about the shape made her pause and look down.

The bottle was larger and heavier than the usual bottle. It looked old; certainly older than any she'd held before. Her palm smoothed the broad shoulders of the rough glass and felt a pattern of small, raised bumps across the surface. *Interesting*, she thought and carefully ran her fingertips over the bumps in the center of the bottle.

The bumps formed an oval and inside the oval, were what felt like raised letters. Holding the scratched bottle up to the hazy, occluded, half-light she squinted and tried to make out words embossed in fancy script...

B...R....E...W. Brew? Then with more conviction, *BREW. Like brewery...brew...like BEER. Okay, I've got the hang of it now...next word...the letters are smaller but the word is longer...*

Danny turned the bottle this way and that, catching the letters in relief, reading *'R' and maybe 'I'. Definitely 'B' and a couple of 'K's and—maybe— another 'R' at the end.*

R-I-C-K-E-N-B-O-C-K-E-R?

Rickenbocker! *Rickenbocker Brew. This is one of Daddy Rickenbocker's beer bottles. Mister Al is NOT going to believe this. And I found it in MY stream so the stone shed MUST be really close.*

Now handling the bottle with the dignity given a priceless antique, Danny used her own shampoo to wash and clean it thoroughly. As she did this, she let her feet play through the sand and stones on the bottom of the pool, because you never know what else might turn up.

Nothing else did, but Danny had her prize and she thought, *now I have two great presents to put under the tree. I have just enough wrapping paper for it and the drawing I bought from Oxo.*

'White Christmas' played another round in her head as she hurried back to the shelter of the tent.

Tomorrow is Christmas Eve, thought the old man as he cut another piece of paper way too short. *How did my wife do this?* Surveying the pile of crumpled wrapping paper he'd already ruined, he knew Danny would not approve.

Christmas—all of it—had been something he left to his wife. Thinking about it now, he believed he would have enjoyed getting involved—buying gifts or decorating or something—but she insisted he stay out of it. So he did, and had no trouble finding other guys to hang with whose wives felt the same way. *She even bought and wrapped her own Christmas present.*

He eyed the oddly shaped piece of machinery in front of him

and decided he needed a box. Finding one took a bit of time, but at least it was easier to wrap.

So it was with some satisfaction an hour and a half later that he finally placed the third and final gift under the tree. Certainly not wrapped to his wife's standards—in fact they looked decidedly ratty — *Oh well, it's the thought that counts. The thought.... The thought... Oh good heaven I've forgotten my daughter— AGAIN.*

Fortunately, even two days before Christmas, with a high speed connection and a credit card— you could find something on the Internet.

He ordered his daughter a pair of yellow pajamas, smiling a little as he chose Overnight Delivery and hit PAY.

Oxo decided his ponytail was long enough for a bow and carefully arranged a red ribbon to look haphazard-yet-jaunty in honor of Christmas Eve. He looked in the mirror and saw the handsome pirate he had spent the night dreaming he was. It crossed his mind that Danny probably wouldn't see him as a pirate but, he didn't really care.

Today was Christmas Eve and he'd left Danny a message to please stop by. He didn't have his own memories of Christmas celebrations of any sort but every year felt the season's pull. The wreath on the stone wall was his first Holiday decoration ever and, also for the first time, he sort of had a friend.

He hoped she liked the gift he had for her...but even if she didn't he knew he would sell quite a few copies.

Oxo had begun using the kitchen door in the back as his exclusive entrance—it was closer to the basement door and farther away from Roxanne's toxic fumes. He'd just turned the deadbolt when someone knocked. Bracing in anticipation of the cold, he tugged the door open and looked out. It seemed warmer and there was Danny. "Hey" he said.

"Hey, yourself. And Merry Christmas!" Danny grinned, glad Oxo had called. The visit gave her something to do with the time she was supposed to be spending with her fictional family.

Oxo tried to smile in a devil-may-care way, "Merry Christmas to you, too! It's going to really snow tonight, did you know?" He turned and opened the door for Danny like the gentleman-pirate he decided he'd be.

"Snow? I thought I smelled it in the air." she reached up and touched the ribbon in Oxo's hair as she walked by him into the house. "I like that. Very festive, almost as cool as the chains you put in my braid last time."

Once the two of them entered Oxo's Den, Danny relaxed. She didn't like being anywhere near those Lairds and she found it hard to understand how Oxo stood it—even having this great place. *It really is a great place, too.* Danny looked around again, taken by the size of the chamber.

"That new comic you told me about? Did you finish?"

"Yeah," he reached behind his back. "Merry Christmas" he said, producing a big manila office envelope with a flourish. He handed it to Danny, delighted by her surprise.

"Oh my gosh Oxo, is this IT?! Is this your comic?" she stared at him, honestly excited, until she looked at down at the manila envelope he had handed her — then she couldn't take her eyes off it; it was a work of art!

The standard, stodgy, office envelope had been transformed into a delicate lace of cut-out patterns and shapes. The paper filigree was supported by a backing of deep purple velvet that made the common tan envelope appear rich and golden.

Danny honestly didn't know what to say. The envelope alone was one of the most ridiculously lovely things she had ever owned.

Oxo interrupted her enjoyment, anxious for her opinion on its contents, "Well, open it! I scanned and printed thirty-five, full color, copies last night. That stuff donated to Roxanne's fosters came with an awesome photo quality printer. I'll have this edition on the street by the New Year."

Somewhat star-struck, Danny carefully pulled the comic free of its lacy sleeve. *I always underestimate him.* She sat down for a good look.

Oxo began fluttering around. He adjusted the light, handed Danny a can of soda, moved his Sculptures of Destruction slightly to the left...and watched Danny from the corner of his eye. He was surprised by how nervous he felt.

Danny stared at the cover, thinking it looked very professional. The cover was thick and glossy with the title— 3‑Ring —slashed across a picture of a valley on fire. Backlit by orange and red tongues of flame, a silhouetted figure stood on a hilltop, overlooking the inferno and casting a long shadow into the blaze. Inside the inferno, something that looked very like a tiger—clawed upward in a bid to escape. Neither image nor title offered clues as to what the comic was about.

Danny found it unsettling, but like before, intriguing.

She opened to the first page, and was confronted by a familiar looking girl. She stared for a moment until the braid gave it away. *It's me! Oxo made me one of his super-heroes.* Her pleasure increased as the plot unfolded...

> A girl named Sky and her brother, called Crow, live with a traveling circus after their circus parents are killed.
>
> Sky, like her dead mother, is an animal trainer and Crow is a magician like his father, but Crow's specialty is levitation. The audience loves Sky and Crow—and their acts make a lot of money for the circus. But what no one knows is that they aren't acting — Crow really CAN levitate and Sky can get animals to do what ever she wants because she TALKS to them!
>
> It is night and the circus is burning. Crow and Sky must reveal their powers in order to rescue their friends.

Danny found Crow's rescue of the tiger and the Fat Lady an exciting end to the wild tale and her eyes shone as she looked up from the last page. "Oxo, I love these drawings. Every frame is like its own story." She flipped back to a remarkable drawing of a huge flaming tent collapsing onto a panicked elephant and wondered, *where did he come up with such a story line?*

Oxo said, "What do you think, really? Hooking Sky and Crow into a traveling Circus? Think it's too weird?"

"Bizarre, maybe. You know? Different. I like it and I can really see how it will make a great series. I think you can illustrate some very whack stuff with circus characters."

"How about the Fat Lady? Was okay to save her?"

Danny wrote:

Christmas is magic because we want it to be. So many people thinking so many good thoughts all at the same time. That's Magic!

Good morning and Merry Christmas World! I don't usually write before the day has even happened but last night when I was walking home I saw my first-ever Christmas Eve snowflake and this morning the world is double-dipped in white!

Maybe the special hush of the snow falling all night made my dreams more vivid, or maybe my mother really did check in on me. All I know is, in my Christmas Eve dream, I introduced my mom to Mister Al and we all talked—in the dream Mister Al could talk—about the stone shed. Mister Al told Mom that finding it now would be even better that finding it when he was a kid. Mom nodded like she understood completely and said something about anticipation sharpening appetite. They talked more about looking forward to Christmas...other stuff too that I can hardly remember.

It was so real... when I opened my eyes I really thought they'd be magically waiting for me in the clearing! I guess in a way I DID get my magic, because the biggest, most amazing, deer I've ever seen was outside this morning and he was tossing his head and pawing the ground as if to say "Merry Christmas".

Mister Al sat up through the night enjoying the view out the sliding glass window. Snowflakes drifted by in lazy spirals and he imagined the red sled's yearning to take it on. He wasn't a bit tired. He was too excited.

What a Christmas this is going to be!

According to Danny her own fictional, family Christmas would be over by eight-thirty, and she would be by at ten. He checked his watch.

At nine, he rolled to the living room and lit the Christmas tree and a pine scented candle, the way his wife always had. He checked the three gifts he'd wrapped for Danny, before letting his eyes rest with satisfaction on the shining sled leaning against the wall. *Perfect.*

At 9:30 he went to the kitchen and slid a pan of cinnamon rolls into the oven.

At 9:55 he put a kettle of water on to boil.

At ten sharp the door bell rang once, followed by a familiar knock and a young girl, in a red hat and scarf, stuck her head in and said, "Mister Al? Mister Al, it's me! Merry Christmas!"

The old man smiled as he rolled toward his visitor, drinking in the draft of cold fresh air and enjoying the sight of the fresh snowflakes, peppering red wool and black hair. When she leaned down to give him a hug, water welled in his eyes and he thought, *this is a really special girl.*

Danny headed directly for the Christmas tree, loosened the straps on her backpack, sat it down gently and reached in for the presents she had so carefully carried through the snowy woods. "I think you are going to like these, Mister Al!" she said, pulling out first one, then another, beautifully wrapped gift. She wanted to watch him open them right away.

The kettle whistled.

Oh! she thought and remembered what she had learned in last night's dream about anticipation. *There's no hurry.* Taking a deep breath and quickly tucking Mister Al's gifts beside others under the tree, she turned toward the shouting tea kettle and caught the seductive aroma of cinnamon rolls. Her stomach responded. "I'll fix us some tea, and boy does something smell good."

The pan of cinnamon rolls was out and she'd begun drizzling on the icing when Mister Al joined her in the fragrant kitchen. Danny's stomach grumbled loud enough to make the old man smile. "I guess I'm hungrier than I thought."

He nodded agreeably, collected plates and forks and rolled to the table. He could hardly wait for her to sit down because he knew what she would see when she looked toward the tree.

Danny carried out two mugs of sweet, hot, milk tea and a big plate heaped with warm, crusty cinnamon rolls. "I think this is the prettiest snow I've ever seen. It's so fluffy, I'll be able to just sweep it off the sidewalk." She sat down, "It's my first White Christmas, you know." She took a bite of roll and a sip of tea, letting the warm buttery pastry melt on her tongue, and sighed with pleasure. Leaning back in the chair, her gaze wandered to the lights on the tree...

Then she saw the red sled. A tag, visible from across the room, dangled from a shining runner. It read: FOR DANNY'.

"Mister Al!!" She jumped up.

All the colors of the glittering Christmas tree seemed to dance along the gleaming runners and across glossy red paint of the old wooden sled that was just as tall as she was. She knelt to run her palm over the flawless surface catching whiffs of fresh paint, thinking—*how many coats?* —and examining the sharp edges of the shining metal runners—*a lot of time sharpening these.*

Tears filled her eyes thinking of the old man, working alone in the basement, making her this lovely gift. Danny sniffed, stood, and looked at Mister Al.

He'd rolled into the living room and was typing on his computer.

She said, "Thank you so much! I love it! I've only seen beautiful sleds like this in Christmas cards."

IT WAS MINE WHEN I WAS ABOUT YOUR AGE. I USED IT TO EXPLORE THE WOODS HOPING TO FIND THE STONE SHED. MAYBE YOU WILL USE IT THE SAME WAY.

It really IS old, she thought, then smiled as she thought of her secret. *Time for gift giving.* "About the stone shed.... I have a big surprise.... but first," Danny picked up a flat, rectangular box and handed it to her friend, "First, I want you to open this."

Ripping into the paper with anticipation he hadn't felt in years, the old man was confused to find a large picture frame. *It's a map,* was his first thought as he stared down at an aerial view of woods. *But not a printed map,* he realized, *this is hand drawn in ink and colored with watercolor.* In many ways, the picture resembled the Google view of Kenilworth Woods with several notable exceptions. He looked up questioningly. *Where?*

"That's the surprise Mister Al! This is a <u>revised</u> map of Kenilworth Woods!" Pointing out two blue ribbons running side by side through the trees, she kept talking, "Remember that road into State College property? You thought the dark line was the stream, but then we decided it was a fence? Well I went exploring the other day and walked to the end of the road and the fence was right where we thought it would be. But guess what? You were right too. On the other side of the fence, there IS a stream."

If Danny would have paused for breath and looked at the old man she would have noticed how flat his blue eyes had become.

Growing more animated, she neared the important reveal in her story. "But here is a very best part. IT'S NOT THE ONLY STREAM!! There is ANOTHER stream farther south," she gestured to the second brightly painted blue line. "Right here." She pointed "Just where we found the greenest part on the Google map. So you see, Kenilworth Woods has TWO streams."

The old man was only half listening. He'd spent his childhood hearing about the Rickenbocker's and the stone shed and its idyllic location. He KNEW the stream that eventually separated the Rickenbocker brothers was the ONLY stream.

Danny said triumphantly, "I had a friend who's an artist, draw the new revised edition of the map just for you." Danny's words were coming so fast she began to trip over them, "...and when we find the stone shed—he will be able to ADD it in."

The old man glanced up at his young friend and saw that she absolutely believed what she was saying. *What if?* He let himself think... *No.* Again he examined the picture, holding it before him...letting memories, and possibilities tumble around in his head. *I didn't find ANY stream and I sure looked, and now she thinks there are TWO of them? Well, she seems pretty sure so she must have some kind of proof or something.* He shook his head sharply...*ridiculous.!*

"I know what you are thinking, and I don't understand it either. Look, when Rosemary almost drowned, it was because the tree she was in, landed in the half-frozen water of a stream. That tree, and the stream it fell in, are not far from here—inside the Fortress of the Vines. The stream on State College property is much farther north, near the road. And don't forget that green strip we saw on Google Satellite; it ran right through the middle of the Rickenbocker properties! Remember?"

DANNY, STREAMS DO FUNNY THINGS. THEY ARE ALWAYS TWISTING AND TURNING TO AVOID NEW OBSTRUCTIONS. ISN'T IT MORE LIKELY ROSEMARY'S STREAM CURVED BACK ON ITSELF, ONLY TO SHOW UP ON THE OTHER SIDE OF THE FENCE? I DON'T BELIEVE TWO STREAMS COULD CO-EXIST WITHOUT SOMEONE MENTIONING IT. MY DAD WOULD CERTAINLY HAVE KNOWN IF THERE WERE TWO STREAMS!

Al's logic gave Danny a chill for a few seconds as she considered how she might be wrong...*but...NO!* Danny remembered and said, "Did your dad mention a stream with hot water? I mean, like hot spring water?"

The old man's eyes shook his head NO. And scanned the folk stories he'd heard growing up, *I've heard tell of hot springs in this area, but not here.*

Danny examined her friend with concern thinking he didn't look too good. "Well, there IS a hot spring. The water is so hot right where I found Rosemary that none of it has frozen, even a little bit. And another thing, I also walked around the west side of the Fortress of the Vines and discovered where the frozen stream enters the vines. It was way too close to the road and NOT hot water. Suppose Rosemary's hot spring starts somewhere inside the Fortress of the Vines? It must. Right?"

The old man considered. He guessed what Danny said made some sense; *Natural springs DO pop up all the time. Hot springs? Outside of areas with volcanic activity? Rare – but not impossible. A hot spring-fed stream couldn't have been around when the Rickenbocker's owned the land, or everyone would have heard about it, so it's new. And if it's new, it can't be the original. Danny has it backwards.*

But Danny said, "The way I figure it, Mister Al, the only way someone wouldn't have noticed hot water coming out of the ground, was if it was diluted by more water. I'm thinking there WAS just the one stream, fed by multiple springs as it ran through the middle of the Rickenbocker property. Then one day, like you just said, something forced part of the stream to change course, because like my father always said, 'water takes the path of least resistance'. After that, Rosemary's stream was left all alone in the original stream bed."

GOOD STORY, AND YOU MAKE IT SOUND LIKE MORE THAN SPECULATION. DO YOU HAVE MORE PROOF?

Danny began ticking off circumstantial evidence. "Well, right now the temperature is in the low 30's and State College's stream has a lot of water that's frozen solid; I've been to Rosemary's stream and it's shallow, very hot and unfrozen. Rosemary's stream is wide, gentle, looks old; State College stream is deep and fast and raw looking. Rosemary's stream is in the middle of the Rickenbocker property; State College stream is farther north. The obvious conclusion is that Rosemary's stream is the ORIGINAL. What else could it be?"

The old man thought about that, staring at the framed map propped on his thighs, trying to imagine a new configuration... *My dad would say when ever I doubted the evidence of my own eyes, "Son, if it walks like a duck and it quacks like a duck...it must be a duck!"*

"One more thing Mister Al." she handed him a cylindrical package roughly the size and shape of a wine bottle. "There's **this**."

This? What could this have to do with anything? Sitting the framed map aside, but still distracted, he hefted the second present. *It's very light.*

He tore away the wrappings to discover an empty, brown, bottle. It was abraded with scratches and obviously old. *A beer bottle?* He turned the odd gift over and over in wrinkled hands, unable to make sense of it. Then, he put the thick brown glass up to daylight poking through the living room window and his thumb brushed over the raised medallion on the glass. He touched each letter, trying to make out the words printed there. B- R- E- W was easy but the smaller letters were far more interesting. R-I-C-

Danny couldn't wait any longer. She blurted, "I found it at the bottom of Rosemary's stream."

Now she had his full attention.

"It says Rickenbocker Brew...I think. Could that be right?

Parts of a dimly remembered conversation over heard at his father's barbershop came back as his thumb explored a circle of print running along the shoulder of the bottle. *Someone said something about the town dairy going out of business, and someone else said that meant the end of the bottle plant too, since they made the milk bottles. And then my father said something...something....*

Danny was growing anxious. This was not the response she'd expected. She burst out, "Because, if it REALLY says Rickenbocker Brew and if I found it in Rosemary's stream, doesn't that PROVE the stream has been there a long time?"

Now he remembered. *Dad said the bottling plant could just make a different kind of bottle. He said it wouldn't be the first time it had to start over. He said it first opened to make bottles for Old Man Rickenbocker's beer.*

Danny saw Al's pensive face transform with a bright smile. He carefully sat the bottle on the floor next to the drawing and typed:

I'D FORGOTTEN! RICKENBOCKER BREW WAS ONLY BOTTLED FOR ONE YEAR! MY FATHER SAID OLD MAN RICKENBOCKER HAD JUST BEGUN BOTTLING HIS BEER WHEN PROHIBITION CAME ALONG AND CLOSED HIM DOWN. THIS BOTTLE IS A TREASURE. AND YES, I THINK IT DOES PROVE THE STREAM IS OLD. THANK YOU DANNY! YOU CAN'T GUESS HOW MUCH ALL OF THIS MEANS TO ME.

Yes she could. She could see it in his eyes. And now they were one step closer to finding the elusive stone shed.

THE WATER IN THAT STREAM MUST BE REALLY HOT IF YOU WENT WADING IN IT AS COLD AS IT'S BEEN. THAT'S REALLY GOOD. I THOUGHT IT MIGHT BE TOO COLD TO DO ANY LOOKING FOR THE STONE SHED. THAT MAKES IT AN EVEN BETTER PLACE TO SET UP A SORT OF BASE CAMP FOR EXPLORING. I WAS THINKING A BASE CAMP WOULD BE REALLY HANDY, RIGHT THERE IN THE FORTRESS OF THE VINES. OPEN THOSE GIFTS UNDER THE TREE AND YOU'LL SEE WHAT I HAD IN MIND.

What could he possibly be talking about? Does he know about my camp or is this just another bit of the magic that's followed me since I came here? Obediently, she picked up a bulky present from under the tree. *He must have used a full roll of tape to wrap this.* She smiled, warmed by the clumsy effort. "This is really heavy. You know you didn't have to do this, besides you already gave me that beautiful sled..." her voice tapered off as she tore open the wrappings and found herself holding something mechanical and vaguely familiar. The roughly round metal object was vented on the sides. Through the vents she could see a coil of copper wire, and she knew. "It's an alternator!"

He could tell by the way she jumped up to fetch the next package that she understood, and approved, of where these gifts were going.

Package number two was shaped a bit like a small suitcase.

It's a voltage inverter box... She unwrapped a newer, more versatile, Inverter, delighted it was the same bright yellow as the one connected to Mister Al's bike. Possibilities circled in her head. *I can make my own electricity! I can stay warm!*

The third large, heavy package awaited her. *Must be the deep cell battery.* She unwrapped it eagerly, noting that it was fully charged, and saw a card attached to the side. It read: **LOOK IN THE LAUNDRY ROOM**.

Have I ever had this much fun before? The old man speculated as he watched the normally mature Danny turn into a giggling, delighted child and rush to the laundry room. When he heard her fling open the door and squeal with pleasure, no sound had ever sounded sweeter.

"Yes! Yes Yes!" Danny clapped her hands when she saw what awaited her beside the washing machine.

A refurbished bike painted the same bright red as the sled, stood upright in a special rack. Unlike Mister Al's exercise bike, this one had gears—to increase the torque, he later explained and generate more energy.

Danny jumped on board and began to pedal. Right away she could feel the air generated by the wheels. She shifted gears causing the wheel to spin faster and faster. *Electricity. The Fortress will really be home now.* It was overwhelming what her friend had accomplished from his wheelchair.

"Thank you! Thank you! Thank you Mister Al!" Danny said as she danced back to the living room.

SINCE YOU ARE GOING TO BE AN ENGINEER, I THOUGHT IT WOULD BE GOOD FOR YOU TO PUT TOGETHER YOUR OWN GENERATOR, AND IT MIGHT MAKE EXPLORING EASIER IF YOU SET UP A CAMPSITE WHERE YOU COULD STORE THINGS AND GET WARM IF YOU NEEDED TO. THE GENERATOR WILL HELP WITH THAT. MOST OF THE PARTS CAME FROM THE SALVAGE

YARD, IN CASE YOU WANT TO DUPLICATE THE PROCESS ANY TIME IN THE FUTURE. AS LONG AS THERE'S SNOW, YOU CAN MOVE THIS STUFF EASILY USING THE SLED.

Packed properly it would all fit on the sled—but they decided Danny need only take the battery home this first night. That was heavy enough. She planned to spend only one night at 'home' with her fictitious parents, then the remainder of the week with Mister Al. Everything had been worked out by email between Mister Al and Mister and Missus Smith, which delighted Danny.

Al was sorry to see her go, but they had plans to work on the generator the following day. He had something to look forward to. *I'll have to work out a way for her to get herself one of those ceramic heaters after we put together her new generator/power source.*

He watched the small figure pulling a loaded sled across the moonlit snowscape thinking, *she looks too small to manage such a large load.* The waxed, sharpened, sled runners cut a path, silently and effortlessly, and Danny disappeared completely into the blackness of the woods. *Anything is possible with the right equipment.* The knowledge that he'd provided Danny with the right equipment, filled him with pride and he yanked the sliding door open for a bit of Christmas night air. A song drifted in with the cold and he listened, not convinced he'd heard anything in the first place, until he heard it again.

Somewhere far away, a small voice was softly singing "...may your days be merry and bright ...... and may all your Christmases be white."

'White Christmas.' I love that song. The old man lifted his eyes to the moon and spent a long time smiling into the night until cold forced him to close the door and get ready for bed. But first he wanted another look at his treasures.

The beer bottle was on the coffee table and he picked it up feeling the abrasions on the brown glass—running a thumb gently over the raised letters. *This is an important find and is probably worth something. I've never seen another bottle like this.* He moved the bottle to the center of the bookshelf covering one living room wall.

Next, he picked up the picture trying his best to be realistic about what it meant. *She COULD still be wrong about the stream. I won't be one hundred percent sure unless she follows it from one end to the other. The hot spring is a completely new wrinkle.* He stopped to think about that for awhile, trying unsuccessfully to picture hot steam and boiling water belching from a hole in the middle of a winter wood. *What a find that would be, he* thought and propped the picture against the legs of an end table where he could see it when he climbed into bed.

A perfect day, he thought, *anything seems possible.*

Christmas Day has a way of moving old memories ahead of more current ones. That was happening to Oxo as he walked deserted streets toward his buyer's store in Kenilworth. He carried 33 editions of <u>3-Ring</u>, all carefully wrapped in plastic, in an old backpack; he was remembering the first time he'd brought in work to sell. That had been three years ago.

The Kenilworth Women's Club had made sure every lamp post in town was hung with tinsel and a wreath, but in this part of town it made little difference, people didn't have much to celebrate. *At least they cleared the snow,* Oxo observed. He trudged down the center of the deserted street looking at the shuttered shops and boarded up businesses and thinking, *A little ratty, a lot grimy, but at least you always know where you stand with the people here.*

General Junk & Motorcycle Shop was on the corner. It looked closed, but Oxo knew Bull Astor would come down and open up when he knocked. This was the only place Oxo had ever felt accepted.

He knocked hard. Three quicks. Two Slows. Three quicks. And waited.

Bull finally opened the door into the bright Christmas Day, squinting out from the gloom. He hadn't expected visitors.

"Got something." Oxo said as he stepped in and closed the door. He took in the store's peculiar odor of axel grease, warm beer and old books mixed with the unwashed scent of its owner then looked at Bull. *He looks sick.* The old Biker had blue hollows under his eyes, skin hanging from scrawny, tattooed arms and much less hair than he remembered. *Hope he can move these...* Bull was his only buyer and Oxo had high hopes for this comic.

"These are already printed, Bull. In color too! So there's nothing for you to do this time but sell 'em. I call this series: 3-Ring".

Bull grunted and motioned to the dim and dusty interior of the cluttered space. Most of the space was given over to motorcycles old and new, but around the edges, and in the office at the back, shelves and display racks groaned with comic books. Bull specialized in things Bikers liked... and the Bikers he knew liked underground comics. Oxo was his youngest contributor. *Kids got a good eye. I've made some money on him before—but that was when I took a 65% cut for filling in the words, doing all the printing and all the sales.* Bull tugged at his long gray ponytail and considered...

Oxo handed over a copy of 3-Ring, leaned against the counter and tried to coolly wait for the verdict. *Be confident and commanding,* he reminded himself.

Bull was too good a horse-trader to show the kid he was impressed. He'd read thousands of comics over the years—both mainstream and underground stuff—and he thought the kid had something. *He might make it with this one. Too bad I probably won't be around to see it.*

Bull settled for a 20% cut and bought all 33 copies outright. He had never done that before.

THE SAP RISES

U rge. In the woods around the hot spring, a great upward yearning was underway. Trees, bushes, plants and insects, within thirty-feet of the waters, woke to stretch. Sap climbed out of the roots and into trunks and stems and twigs with one goal in mind: to reproduce.

The feeling loose in the glade the first week of February woke Rosemary a bit earlier than usual. She wasted no time in beginning her move south to the riverside. The annual walk was longer than she liked, but the urge was strong. If she was the first raccoon to arrive, she'd be first to feast on early season crayfish.

For Danny, the changing world inside the clearing was a constant source of delight. Now that temperatures up and down the east coast had climbed above freezing, the dense fog her stream had wrapped itself in throughout winter was dissipating and the warmth was spreading into the Fortress of the Vines.

High on the banks of the stream shy snowdrops, purple crocus and dark silky grasses appeared; around the clearing the vines reddened with buds growing longer and fatter as new leaves preparing to break free.

It's still winter so don't forget your coat, Danny had to remind herself before each morning as she set off to school. The trek to the bus stop was like traveling backward through the seasons — the closer she got, the colder it was. Outside the Fortress of the Vines, trees were bare and the ground still hard in places. She always paid special attention to the early blooming cherry tree in Mister Al's yard. *No sign yet of a blossom.*

The situation on the school bus had changed so much over the winter that Danny felt almost comfortable. Much of this was because Donna Adagio was gone. The rumor was that the D.A.'s parents had moved her to a private school 'to protect her from bullies'—which struck everyone as funny since the D.A. was one of the worst bullies.

No one seemed to know where Leo Peal had gone; few even remembered his name now that the bus seat he'd collapsed had been replaced. Danny thought he'd probably like it that way. *The invisible boy.*

On the fifth day of March, anticipation of Spring Break crackled in the air and morning temperatures were so mild not one kid boarded the bus wearing a coat.

Finally, thought Danny.

Everyone's spirits were high. Voices were loud. The situation on the bus was maybe a little out of control. Danny had an aisle seat trying to ignore a game of paper-wad volleyball being played over her head, when she over heard something that got her attention.

At the back of the bus a boy said, "Crow is this awesome character that can really fly, but everyone thinks he's just doing this really good trick..."

"...mumble. mumble?" was all Danny could make out of the reply.

"No, that's the thing. He really CAN fly."

More mumbles and then...

The first speaker responded, "3-Ring, yeah. You gotta know where to go."

"Mumble?"

"I think they sold out, but I'll ask my dad. He said it was a new series and it..."

"SIT DOWN!" The angry bus driver bellowed. Apparently someone had clocked him in the back of the head with a volley-wad.

But Danny had heard enough, *they're talking about Oxo's comic! Sold out! Wow...it was pretty good, not all those muscle bound bodies this time—more of a story to it. I liked it. I wonder where I put the copy he gave me for Christmas?* She remembered how beautifully it had been wrapped. She was sure she brought it back to the tent—but then came Christmas Day and things got hectic.

As the bus unloaded, Danny stationed herself outside the door hoping to spot someone with a copy. Sure enough, she recognized 3-Ring's fiery cover sticking from a tough looking boy's backpack and stopped him with, "Hi!"

"Hi? You want somethin'?"

"Yeah, well, I heard you say something about 3-Ring. I know the guy—the artist— who did it and was hoping for a look at your copy."

The boy was a little suspicious, but pulled out his rolled up copy and handed it over, thinking, *she is SO lying!* He watched the girl with the braid carefully. *No way could she know the artist.* Yet he thought she looked familiar...

Danny examined the cover, flipped the pages, and finally spotted something new at the bottom of the title page. **Fourth Reprint** it read. *Wow! Oxo has really been busy. He must have sold out three times already...I wonder how big each print run was?*

"Hey!" said the boy, finally realizing why the girl with the braid looked familiar, "YOU are the girl! You ARE!" He was excited and his voice grew louder. "You are that Sky-girl, aren't you? From 3-Ring!! The girl who talks to animals. That's you, right? You talk to dogs too?"

"No," Danny said, "not me!"

The boy's friends now crowded in for a look at he girl who could talk to dogs. Other students pushed forward to see what the commotion was.

Oh gosh no! Danny felt her face go red. "No, no, of COURSE I can't talk to animals. I'm not Sky," she said again—shoving the comic back into the boy's hands. "I'm just friends with the guy who wrote 3-Ring." She managed to struggle away from the crowd.

But it was too late.

The linking of Danny with the author of 3-Ring made her an instant celebrity among the comic's fans—and 3-Ring had a lot of fans

Thank goodness it's Friday, she thought, as yet another boy stopped to question her about the comic. She was determined to keep Oxo's life private but did slip and mention that he was a teenager. This revelation only served to win her more interrogation.

"Are you related to him? What's he like? Where's he live? Why did he make Sky look like you? Where does he get his ideas? When is the next edition coming out?" On and on and on it went. By far, the most star-struck of the bunch was the stocky, freckle-faced, Fred.

Fred, who happened to be the biggest mouth on the school bus, was now desperate to be Danny's friend. *Anything to meet a comic-book artist.* The moment she boarded the bus for the ride home he pounced, "Hi. You're Danny right? And you live on my court?"

Al was starting to obsess about the cherry tree in the front yard.

The last time it bloomed, a stroke had knocked him flat and left him staring up into its confusion of pink flowers, unable to move or to cry out. Soon it would blossom again. *It has been nearly a year.!* He had learned many lessons since then.

The old man's bike now faced the window—he liked to keep an eye on both the cherry tree and the bus stop, while pedaling. Looking at the leafless cherry tree made him pedal faster—almost convinced he'd be strong enough to walk down the steps and stand beneath it when it finally blossomed.

The big, yellow bus pulled up as he was toweling sweat from his face, and he missed the unprecedented sight of Danny being first off. When he did look up, a knot of kids had formed near the mailboxes and the bus was disappearing around the corner. One of the kids was Danny. *I didn't know she was friendly with kids in this court.* He supposed he shouldn't be surprised, *even Bea had lots of friends at that age.* Bea's very best friend had lived right next door, *every night was a sleepover.* He wondered just how Danny reconciled girlfriends with her living situation. *She can't very well invite them over, can she?*

Danny said, "Fred, I **promise** next time I see my friend I will tell him about you. But honestly, I haven't seen him since before Christmas and I don't know where he lives! Now I have to go. Goodbye." She spun away quickly and felt her braid hit something. *I hope that was Fred's big mouth.* She walked off, forcing herself not turn around and make certain Fred wasn't following her to Mister Al's.

The old man watched the exchange. *Not friends.* He slowly walked to the door and opened it for Danny. As she smiled and stepped inside, he saw the boy wave and heard him shout, "Maybe I'll stop by later and see what you are doing this weekend."

Danny cringed.

Al motioned her to the table and shuffled into the kitchen to make two mugs of tea. That gave him a few minutes to think about her situation. *It's the classic problem of the too-friendly, nosey neighbor.*

At the table, Danny fretted over Fred's threatened visit, while part of her watched Mister Al in the kitchen. She wasn't sure how it had happened that she was sitting at the table and he was making the tea. Wasn't it her job to take care of him? She was even being paid for it.

Soon he was back with two mugs of sweet, milk tea and a plate of chocolate cookies. He handed her a mug and sat down in his wheelchair to access the computer.

THAT KID NEXT DOOR BOTHERING YOU?

The look she gave him was pitiful.

OKAY. THEN THIS IS WHAT YOU DO....

There was a line outside the General Junk & Motorcycle Shop when Bull came downstairs to open that evening. He peeked between the blinds. *It's just a bunch of kids!* Kids aren't interested in bike parts or anything mechanical, he knew...

They want comics.

Shaking his head at another lost opportunity, he checked the locks, turned off the light and slowly made his way back up to bed thinking, *I should have kept a copy for myself.*

The kids were there for 3-Ring, and he'd sold the last copy two days before. Oxo wouldn't do a fifth reprint.

Danny checked the cherry tree without much hope next morning—and was encouraged by the size of the buds. She squeezed the hard shell protecting the tender young blossom and found it softer than the day before. *Soon,* she thought and resumed walking around the block toward the woods.

"Hey Danny! Where you going?" shouted Fred from three doors down.

At least he didn't come knocking yesterday, she thought, hating the feeling of being watched. *I came in through the basement this morning, and I left way after dark last night, so he couldn't have seen me, could he?* She turned toward the boy, "Oh. Hi Fred."

Fred was staring at the equipment Danny carried. He said again, "So where are you going with all that? Is that a paint compressor? Are you going to see your artist friend??"

Oh wonderful! It's none of his business where I'm going. She thought for a minute. The pockets of her over-large coveralls were stuffed with 2 pairs of leather gardening gloves, clear goggles, and old rags; she was pulling a cylinder-type sprayer on wheels. The filled cylinder was heavy, and bristled with attachments. It was all equipment Mister Al thought she needed to kill vines at the clearing, even though Danny had argued that it was way more than she'd need.

She looked down at the assortment of equipment and decided on a half-truth, "I'm just going around back to kill some weeds for Grandfather Smith." Then she sighed and added, "I really don't like leaving him alone; he's really old and not right in the head." She lifted her eyes and gave her voice some punch, "So I see YOU and I think—why don't I ask my new friend Fred to visit the old man while I do some chores?"

Fred looked a little hesitant.

"How about it?" she urged. "Grandfather is a pretty nice guy most days, he just needs help eating and you might have to walk him to the bathroom and give him a little help sometimes. But I'd be just around the back—so close you could just stick your head out the window and call me if you need help to—like—clean him up or something."

"Clean him up?" a small voice repeated.

"Well he's old and wears adult diapers at night, but not during the day so sometimes...well you know."

T he woods held its breath as Danny entered. Utterly quiet, utterly still, the scene had the elegance and simplicity of a black and white photograph—a brittle tableau where movement was unwelcome...

Then the winds came...and things began to explode.

The first blast occurred right over Danny's head when a gust of wind forced an ice-burdened Oak to bend and it broke. When the thick wood snapped, it sent the top of the tree smashing down and Danny reacted as though she'd been shot. She jumped, fell and slid across the ice—and was almost crushed by a massive tree limb that hit the ground in an icy rain of twigs and bark.

It's okay. It's okay, the limb DIDN'T hit you, she tried to reason with her racing heart. *Remember, you said yourself that Mother Nature isn't vindictive or malicious.!* But when a second gust of wind blasted the top off a nearby Maple and another amputated branch fell close enough to send debris skittering her way—she changed her mind—Mother Nature WAS getting personal. She thought about her ancestor's belief in Tree Gods as the war escalated over her head and she sent up a little prayer for safety.

All she could do was stay put and wait it out; she'd be a fool to try to cross the battlefield now. Sitting on the broken limb to keep her bottom off the icy ground and pulling her knees to her chest to make herself a smaller target, she put her head down and listened to the forest destroying itself...

It began with a sigh and a gentle tinkling high in the trees— like wind chimes in the doorway of a Chinese restaurant. Danny's anticipation would build along with the sound...until **CRACK**— the sickening noise of a bone breaking. After that, chaos, as the shattered branches, limbs, twigs and ice tumbling to earth, crashed into neighboring trees. *It's like some invisible giant is playing pinball— TRYING to hit as many other trees as possible—TRYING to do as much damage as possible!*

Danny winced; seeing and hearing the destruction was painful. The forest was her friend— her only safe haven—now it was under attack, being violated before her very eyes. All she could do was crouch and cringe and weep.

How long it went on she couldn't say.

Rosemary was extremely annoyed at having her meal cut short and she was still grumbling about it when her feet started to slip and she was forced to pay attention to her surroundings. Things around her just didn't look right. The smoke had cleared but, as far as she could see, the forest floor was shiny with ice. She skated and scrambled along in a most undignified way as she made her way home.

Getting traction became easier once she entered the protection of the tangled vines, but she felt very wronged when she reached her Oak tree and found it, too, was surrounded by the ice. She scrambled with difficulty up the slippery trunk and within minutes was fast asleep in her tree-hole.

Rosemary was dreaming about taking things away from the boy who had whacked her with a broom, when a sound punctured her doze...

Crack!

A gunshot! Most all animals know and fear that sound, however Rosemary had lived through enough hunting seasons to know she was safely hidden, so she went back to sleep. But again and again, shots woke her. Now she was way past annoyed. Who could sleep with all that racket?

The irate Rosemary must investigate—raccoons are even more curious than cats—and she'd just begun backing out of her den when her world fell apart.

Through a lull in the wind storm Danny heard the animal's scream. She jerked upright, hyper-alert as the shrill, throaty cries filled the woods. *It's not crying like its hurt,* she decided, *it sounds terrified.*

A squirt of adrenaline overruled her fear of the forest. *Something needs help!* She stood up, ignoring the cramps and kinks in her legs, and snatched up her pack. *How long was the creature screaming before I heard it?*

Fred's freckles stood out against the sudden paleness of his skin. He backed up a step, his revulsion evident.

Danny moved closer "... yeah, I can see that having a friend like you in the neighborhood could be a really great thing, because sometimes—you know—I just really need a break..." Her smile was sharp.

Fred was as white as a spotted sheet as he choked out words, "Um, s...ss...sorry. Um...my mother told me to come right back....I promised I'd help her at the grocery store." With that he turned and ran off.

Wow! Mister Al was right! That really did work.

It hadn't been pleasant talking about Mister Al that way—even if he had practically written the script...

He'd typed: SCARE HIM. OLD PEOPLE SCARE KIDS HIS AGE. TELL HIM YOU NEED A FRIEND TO HELP WITH YOUR CRAZY, GRANDFATHER. GROSS HIM OUT. ASK HIM TO HELP YOU CHANGE THE OLD MAN'S DIAPERS.

She'd grossed Fred out alright! Pretty funny, but still... *I just wish I didn't have to lie to start with. The more I do it, the harder it gets to remember what's true, and it makes people more curious about me.* Odd behavior she knew, sparked curiosity, *just look what happened when Mister Al noticed lights in the woods.*

Danny had a lot to think about as she made her way behind the houses into the woods. It was easy to find the Fortress of the Vines these days, her comings and goings had worn down a path.

The wild grape vines were losing the first-to-leaf race to poison-ivy. Each year poison-ivy claimed a little more real estate—at the rate it was spreading it would soon overrun the wild grape vine to blanket the Fortress of the Vines. High on the Fortress wall the distinctive three-leaf clusters were beginning to sprout. *That's poison-ivy alright!* Danny thought with satisfaction. Then, like a farmer admiring his crop, she broke off a tender leaf and rolled it between gloved fingers watching the way the shine drained from the bruised leaf to cover the leather glove with urushiol oil. She knew that the slightest contact with poison–ivy transferred the oil and raised itchy, weeping, blisters on most people. *Not me though!* Removing the glove, she touched the shiny oil almost reverently with her fingertips. It would defend the Fortress and repel human intruders. She was counting on it.

Time for work. She lifted the curtain of leafless vines and walked behind into the dim, mysterious, portal—pulling her own canister of poison behind.

In the process, she dropped her leather gloves. Fortunately, Mister Al had tucked an identical pair into her back pocket.

The weather was mild enough to entice the old man out on the deck. He gazed as he always did, with interest and affection at the area beyond his back yard. Kenilworth Woods. *So many secrets hidden in that suburban patch of wilderness.* Now that Danny was part of his life, his childhood dreams of the stone shed had returned. He welcomed them back.

The raucous caw of a crow broke through his musings. Something had disturbed it. He looked to the tree line and saw movement. *That kid from the neighborhood is in the woods. What is he doing?*

It had taken Fred some time to summon enough courage to follow Danny into the woods, so he wasn't surprised that she was out of sight. Fred only liked nature, sunny and mowed, not dim and untamed and, even though there was a path, the woods freaked him out. *Did she think I'd believe she was going out to kill weeds? I can see for myself that's not true. Who needs to kill weeds in the woods? But maybe this is just a shortcut....*Fred's imagination worked overtime.

More than anything, Fred wanted to meet the graphic artist known to all fans as OK. 3-Ring was OK 's third comic—and by far Fred's favorite—so when Danny revealed she knew the artist, he'd hung on to her every word. Already he had some answers. *OK is a teenager-guy, maybe my age, who lives around here. He knows Danny well enough to make her a main character in 3-Ring.* He simply didn't believe Danny hadn't seen the guy since before Christmas.

A rustling startled him as a big black bird launched itself from a nearby tree. The bird kept rasping out its cry and circling the tree, casting an enormous shadow across the path ahead. *Like a*

Batman comic! Determined but nervous, Fred began to walk faster.

What a creepy place, he thought, glancing around in the half-light. Something huge and dark and furry caught his eye on a nearby tree. An old vine, as big around as a forearm and bristling with roots had wrapped itself around the trunk. To Fred it was a giant centipede wiggling up a tree and he didn't stop to look closer—he broke into a sprint.

Meanwhile, in the Fortress of the Vines, Danny had begun to spray the ground around her tent—moving slowly, stooping to squirt weed killer directly into any vine stubs she came across. Her phone buzzed and she straightened to lift the face mask. It was a text message:

KID NEXT DOOR IS IN WOODS. FOLLOWING YOU?

Danny stared disbelieving at the message. *Fred!*

Fred's head was down and he was running full tilt when he smashed into the wall of vines. The surprise impact knocked him to the ground and drove breath from his lungs. He lay looked up through trees wondering what just happened. *I was on a path. What could I have run into?*

Danny, who had stationed herself just inside the curtain of vines hiding the entrance to the Fortress, winced involuntarily at the strength of Fred's collision. Had he hit a bit more to the left, he might have come all the way through. *This is bad, really, really bad.* Her mouth was dry and she felt a bit sick. *What now?*

Fred was a little shaky but his shirt had deflected most of the sticks. Only his face and hands were scratched and burning. When he got to his feet the muscles in his chest and arms felt bruised but appeared to still work, so he looked around for something to blame.

A solid wall of vines stood in Fred's path. He stared at it—wondering how it came to be in the middle of such a well-worn path. *Paths don't just stop for no reason,* he reasoned, *they stop when they reach their destination. Is THIS the destination? It looks solid, but maybe...*

The boy tried to stick his hand through the tangle, but the woody vines resisted any intrusion.

Then he tried to kick his way through and succeeded only in peeling back his pant leg and his exposed skin. Rubbing at his bloodied leg, he looked at the barrier with new respect. *Not getting through there. Guess I'm wrong, SHE couldn't be in there.*

He would have been shocked to know just how close SHE was...

On the other side of the vines Danny held her breath and concentrated on willing Fred to give up. *Just go away...go away!!!* The tangled curtain had swayed ominously under Fred's onslaught and she was convinced he'd push through if he kicked again.

She waited and a plan began to form.

It occurred to Fred that if Danny didn't make the trail, something ELSE must have. *ANIMALS make paths; some little animal could probably scoot right under this stuff and keep on going.* As he stood thinking about the kinds of creatures living in a forest small enough to wiggle under the vines, he had a sobering thought, *Snake. Do snakes make paths?* "Snakes", he muttered, "I hate snakes!" The Indiana Jones line seemed to give him a bit of courage as he stepped back and glanced nervously around.

A leather glove lay in the shadows.

Fred almost missed it; then he almost ignored it. Finally he kicked at it, a little afraid to reach into the shadows. *That's a gardener's glove.* "Yesss!" he said and as he bent to retrieve it, he spotted another.

Fred was now confident he'd been right all along. *She WAS here! She probably ran into this same wall and dropped her gloves. THEN where did she go? She didn't turn back or I'd have seen her, so she must have gone around.* He was sure he was right. Now all he had to do was figure out if she went to the left or to the right.

On the other side of the vines Danny stood listening to Fred's every movement. She clearly heard his frightened muttering about snakes and heard twigs snap as he stepped back. Then he must have discovered something because he said, "Yess", and sounded excited. *What did he find? I didn't leave anything out there....maybe I dropped something?* She did a quick inventory of her equipment. *Nothing missing.*

Fred had watched his share of cowboy movies; he knew that a good tracker searched the ground for signs. So he knelt on the path for a look.

Closer than he could guess, Danny waited.

Comparing the left side to the right side, Fred thought he detected some bent grass. *She hauled that thing on wheels through here, so shouldn't there be something more obvious?* He put his cheek to the dirt and the whole perspective changed. Cheek still in the dirt, Fred looked at the vines; there was a gap clearly visible below. The few inches of empty space was tantalizing enough to conquer his fear and he tentatively slid out his hand. He met no resistance. *Empty? Empty space!* The discovery excited him so much he forgot his apprehensions and thrust his whole arm deep into the shadows beneath the vines...

Three things happened. Fred's wandering hand touched something warm and furry. Next, a wet, slimy, *something else* dropped on his forearm and began to crawl. And finally, from the dark place just inches from his face came a soft, threatening, **hissss...**

Snake! Fred snatched his arm away and frantically scrambled backward until his progress was stopped by a tree. There he crouched, unblinking, unwilling to take his eyes off the dark place under the vines. He was not exactly sure what just happened but his thundering heart told him it was very, very bad. "It bit me...it bit me....it bit me..." he whimpered and cradled his arm as he waited for the poison to stop his heart. He was immobilized by panic...until the vines began to move and rustle. *It's coming out!* An electric shot of adrenaline lifted him to his feet. *It's coming! It's coming!*

Fred ran.

The old man moved his wheelchair to the deck to keep vigil. He was sick with worry. *If that boy should stumble into the Fortress of the Vines and discover where Danny is living, there will be no shutting him up. Everyone will know, including the authorities.*

A crashing through the woods got his attention and he was

surprised to see the boy. *That kid is running like he's being chased by the hounds of hell.*

Danny's phone beeped and she read the message from Mister Al with relief: WHAT HAPPENED TO SCARE THAT KID SO BAD? HE RAN STRAIGHT HOME AND SLAMMED THE DOOR SO HARD THE WHOLE NEIGHBORHOOD HEARD IT.

Saved! She hadn't let herself believe the fur lining of a glove, some soggy wet paper, and a theatrical **hisss,** would be enough to scare Fred off—even now she wouldn't let herself feel too happy. *If Fred HAD gotten in here, it would have been my own fault for leaving such an easy path to follow.*

After Fred's visit, it was hard to think about weed killing, none-the-less Danny forced herself to work—targeting actively growing vines. She found no new growth in the interior of her tunnel but her sunny tent site on the banks of the hot spring was in danger of being overrun. Grimly bending again and again to shoot vegetation killer into sprouting vines, she was very aware that she was poisoning the very ground she lived on.

I don't have a choice, the clearing was alive with activity and she had to be thorough.

The crippling task took all weekend and for the first time, she was glad that short people didn't have as far to bend.

On Monday morning, everyone at the bus stop had something new to think about.

Danny wrote:

Fred is in the hospital.

I think I killed him. They say his face, arms, legs and chest are covered with severe poison-ivy. It's in his eyes and his mother thinks he might go blind. She said the doctors have him on heavy steroids and are treating him like a burn patient because of the blisters. He is tied to the bed and sedated so he won't scratch off his own skin. He can't have visitors.

I don't know what to do! Mister Al tells me it's not my fault but then his eyes get all weepy. I think he's remembering how bad poison-ivy can be.

Mister Al and I weren't worried about Fred, because the poison-ivy vines hadn't leafed out yet—at least where Fred touched them. But it turns out that once the sap rises, breaking a vine releases just as much oil as touching a leaf. If we'd have known that we could have warned him and got him protective shots. Another thing we found out was that urushiol will enter the bloodstream through a scratch and Fred had loads of scratches.

He could actually die.

Al was doing his best, but Danny wasn't responding. He typed: HOW ABOUT SOME OFFICIAL LOOKING 'DANGER: POISON IVY' SIGNS? I CAN MAKE THEM ON THE COMPUTER AND INCLUDE A DRAWING OF WHAT THE PLANT LOOKS LIKE.

"Okay. I also have to get rid of the path somehow. But how?" Danny responded with indifference. For days now she had felt helpless and knew she was depending more and more on Mister Al; she just didn't care. She'd decided she didn't like being an adult.

Danny hadn't been back to the tent for days.

Discovering Fred was in the hospital had shaken her confidence. She felt guilty about hiding from him, guilty about lying to him and guilty about scaring him—she wished she hadn't been so clever. The stunt with the inside-out fuzzy glove, the slimy, wet tissue and the imitation snake hiss seemed childish and mean to her now.

The old man didn't understand her reaction. He was upset about the boy too, but he didn't feel responsible. *The kid went in the woods. Poison-ivy lives in the woods. It's the way of nature and nature is not fair.*

COULD YOU PUT SOME OBSTACLES IN THE PATH TO BREAK IT UP? MAYBE YOU COULD MAKE A FEW FAKE PATHS AND COVER THE OLD ONE WITH BRANCHES.

"I guess." Danny said listlessly, a vision of Leo Peal, invisible in the front row of the classroom, leaked into her head. *Hide in plain sight,* she thought. "If you make signs I'll put them up on Saturday."

TOMORROW IS SATURDAY.

"Oh, yeah." Danny had forgotten.

For Fred's mother, February was the longest month. She had spent much of it at Fred's bedside, horrified by what an allergic reaction to a common woodland plant could do. For the first few days of treatment, her son looked like a monster, swollen from the steroids they gave him to help with the itching and oozing with blisters. He raved about bugs crawling on him and snakes sinking fangs into him. The situation was so out of control the doctors said he could go into shock at any moment and die. They put him on a respirator, in case.

The swelling slowly went down and Fred seemed to rest easier. The breathing tube was removed. She watched the blistered skin peel away each time her son's damp dressings were changed and knew the scarring from poison-ivy could be severe.

Doctors cut back on the sleeping medications. Fred's mother watched his bandage-wrapped face, trying to remember what his greenish eyes once looked like. Every now and again her son would moan, but mostly he was quiet.

Fred was dreaming; He dreamed about 3-Ring. In his dream he was part of the circus. He had just met Sky and her brother Crow and decided to reveal his own superpowers. "I can swell up like a blowfish and float." he told his new friends. Part of him thought that was a pretty weird superpower, but Sky and Crow seemed impressed...

They took the bandages off Fred's eyes when the blisters finally went away. Fred twitched a lot that night, but in the morning he opened his eyes and said, "What's for breakfast?" His mother fed him like she had when he was a child and her heart broke when he cried and begged, "Please, mommy, scratch my back. It's driving me crazy, please!"

On March first, the doctors promised Fred's mother he'd soon be out of the restraints. Fred's case, she was told, would be written up in medical journals and become the new standard for treating severe poison-ivy without scarring. They assured her that, with two more days in the hospital and another painful skin peel, her son would be good as new.

Thankful and relieved, Fred's mother went home to get the house ready. As she stepped from the car, she saw the girl from a few doors away open the door. "Good news!" Fred's mother said.

Fred's skin felt patchy and pink and tender, but at least it no longer itched. He was so happy to be back in his own room with his own things that he forgot to complain when his mother said she had to run up the road and did he want anything?

As soon as she closed his bedroom door, he remembered he had missed a whole month and maybe some new comics were out. He walked a bit shakily down the stairs to try and catch his mom before she left, but was too late. Turning to go back up he stopped when the doorbell rang.

A very, pink, frail looking Fred answered Danny's ring. He jumped back a little when he saw it was her.

"What do YOU want?" Fred was angry, but also a little afraid, of the visitor.

"Hi Fred. I brought someone I thought you would want to meet." A figure stepped from behind Danny. "This is Oxo. He is the author of 3-Ring."

The boy's mouth fell open as he stared at the dark boy with long sleek hair and a silver chain draped from his ear to his eyebrow.

Oxo stepped forward with a flourish. According to Danny, this kid was his biggest fan and Oxo had never had a fan before so, he was a little excited himself. After Danny told him about the 3-Ring fan club Fred was starting before he got poisoned and hospitalized for almost a month, he agreed to meet the kid. "Hi Fred. I brought you something." Oxo felt like a rock star as he handed his thunderstruck fan the first copy of the latest edition of 3-Ring.

Fred gulped and looked down at his new treasure. Across the front in black marker Danny had written at Oxo's request:

For Fred, my #1 Fan! OK

The sight of Fred's outraged body and patchy skin was never far from Danny's thoughts. Determined that no other person suffer the same fate, she decided her early efforts to 'people-proof' the trail were not enough.

The first step was to *warn,* and now that she was thinking more clearly she realized the **DANGER: POISON IVY** signs she'd posted around the perimeter of the woods were too vague. Danny made new signs with color pictures, descriptions of the plant, and graphic descriptions of the rash. Then she sealed each in a protective sleeve of plastic and posted one every twelve feet. Mister Al could see several from his deck and said they looked very professional.

Mister Al said people needed a compelling reason to veer from an established path, so Danny's next line of defense was to obliterate both the start and the finish of her well-worn path. The work was so easy, with all the storm damaged logs, limbs and brush still littering the woods, that she felt a rush of guilt. *If I'd only done this before, Fred would have never been able to figure out where I'd gone.* Of course without a clear path, she wouldn't have been able to drag the weed killer into the woods in the first place—but that didn't seem important now.

Finally, Danny reinforced the blockages and false trails she'd added several weeks before and discovered the forest residents had already found ways over and under and around the barriers she'd erected. *Well, the Fortress IS their home and this is their woods...come to think of it...*

With a sigh, Danny recognized that the only part of the trail she could permanently change was where she entered the woods. *I'll just have to enter the woods at different locations and keep reinforcing the blockages when the animals wear them down. I need a work-around,* she thought, and then, ***around.*** *That's it! A nice wide, accommodating path that circles around on itself.*

Danny felt more and more in control as she dragged a heavy log along the newly created trail. *Follow THIS path and before you know it, you will be back where you started,* she congratulated herself. The return of self-confidence brought a tumble of new ideas. *How about another path that goes in the woods near Mister Al and comes out on Cumberland Road? A path like that might come in handy for me as well. I'll have to start working on it...but not today...*

She was tired and dirty, and craving a long soak in her woodland hot tub, when she returned to camp that evening. She'd spent the last seven days at Mister Al's, but was none the less surprised to discover an odd looking vine had wrapped itself around the tent in her absence. The thing was almost twelve feet long; *it must have grown over a foot a day.* Danny unsentimentally yanked it up by the roots and squirted the hole with the last of the weed killer. Then she stood and looked around.

It felt good to be back—somehow right. The fog from the hot spring skimmed the surface of the grasses. Here and there flowers poked their heads out of the mist. An odd splashing at the stream caught her interest and she walked over for a look. A very fat little raccoon stood in the sand munching on what appeared to be a crayfish. The animal looked up at her with mild interest as she stared down at it.

Rosemary? She couldn't be sure. Rosemary hadn't been around for weeks and weeks and this raccoon looked really, really fat. "Rosemary? Is that you?"

The little raccoon chattered a soft response before dipping back into the stream and flipping over a rock. She pulled out another crayfish and began to munch.

Danny thought the stream looked pretty good, waded across to her hot tub area and sunk slowly into it streaming waters. From her vantage point she saw the raccoon turn over several more rocks before giving up and waddling off.

"Bye Rosemary!" Danny said and drifted into a peaceful reverie.

Since Rosemary had returned she seemed to always be hungry. The area around the hot spring kept her fed with early bulbs, fat juicy grubs, snails and lizards, and the stream itself had a good amount of crayfish—if you knew where to look. There were no fish in the hot stream unfortunately, but Rosemary didn't have too far to travel to find them; another stream was nearby.

She had spent some time trying to break into the tent but something smelled funny around it and so she'd given up. When she saw the girl, she remembered the other place she could find food and went to find it.

The old man was surprised to see a raccoon on his deck. He wondered if it was sick or something since it was daytime and raccoons were basically nocturnal animals, but no, this one was way too fat to be sick. It wasn't until the animal walked over to the patio door and put her hands and face against it, that he recognized Rosemary.

"Well, hello!" he said delighted to see his old buddy, "How was your winter? I thought you had left town." The old man rolled into the kitchen and hurriedly fixed a PB&J for his visitor. When he returned minutes later he saw Rosemary pacing back and forth in front of the door. *She must be really, really hungry.* He slid open the door and placed the sandwich, a bowl of water and a marshmallow just outside the door.

Rosemary was completely focused on the food and the smells of nuts and fruit mixed with something sweet. Immediately she sat down and began tearing off pieces of the sandwich and stuffing them in her mouth, all the while keeping her black eyes on the old man.

Al watched, surprised when the little raccoon ignored the bowl of water. He knew raccoons could carry rabies and that one of the signs was the fear of water, so he was relieved when she finished the sandwich, picked up the marshmallow and dunked it in the water—where it promptly dissolved into a sticky glob that glued itself to her paw. Not much liking the goo between her fingers Rosemary bit at it—transferring some foamy white to the fur around her mouth. She tried several times to flick the gunk from her paw and—when she finally succeeded—watched it fly up and hit the deck railing. There it stuck. She had to get up to retrieve it.

Next, Al handed over a big ruffled piece of fresh Kale. She sniffed it and washed it, sniffed it again and tossed to off the deck. "Good for you, my girl! I feel the same way."

Rosemary was a junk food addict and Al approved. "I bet you will like THIS though." He handed Rosemary a crème filled cookie and she took it right out of his hand. The sandwich cookie didn't go in the water until AFTER Rosemary had unscrewed the top and licked away the crème.

Al had just rolled into the kitchen to fix his visitor a bag of popcorn, when the doorbell rang. *Danny's back already?* He checked his watch, surprised to discover most of the day was gone.

The doorbell rang again, a little longer this time. *Not Danny.* He rolled to the door and opened it. There stood the woman Danny had pointed out as Fred's mother. Al blinked in surprise.

Fred's mother didn't know what to make of this silent man in a wheelchair. "Hello," She said and waited for a reply that didn't come. Fred had mentioned the old man was a little loony, so she decided to just give him the gloves and leave. "Here you are. Fred told me he found these and they belong to Danny."

The old man took the gloves and closed the door as soon as his unwelcome visitor walked away. He held up the gardening gloves and looked at them, remembering he'd stuffed them into one of Danny's pockets the day she took the weed killer into the woods. *Could Fred have been following her so he could return these gloves?* But no, from what he had seen of the boy, Fred was not particularly helpful. He scratched his gray head, shrugged and rolled to the laundry room to toss the gloves on the pile of used gardening clothes Danny had not yet washed.

Beatrice was pleasantly surprised when the first note from her father arrived. The notes and cards kept coming. She lined them up on her desk at the office, where for some reason they kept her focused. Sometimes she propped them up without even reading them, *that's okay,* she told herself, *I'm very busy.*

The cards stopped coming in February; she noticed in March and thought peevishly, *that girl would have called if something happened, if she wants to get paid, that is.*

It had been quite awhile since Beatrice checked her father's on-line banking statement but she did that now. *If you want to know what is going on just follow the money.* She soon discovered that her father had moved all his banking to another account; an account she could not access.

What is he up to?

At first the old man found himself idly scratching at his wrists. Then he began to rub the inside of his fingers. Blisters appeared that night and he understood the mistake he had made in touching the gloves.

The oil from poison-ivy could remain dangerous for up to a year and the gloves had absorbed a great deal of it.

He found a bottle of bright pink Calamine lotion and rubbed it into the blisters. It was alright, he thought, he could stand the tickling if it stayed confined to his hands. *But I can't let Danny see this.* It had taken almost the entire month of February for her to recover from what happened to Fred. *One more reason to be happy the kid is okay now.* Truth was, for awhile he didn't even enjoy Danny's company, she was so glum and unsure of herself. *I am so glad she is back.*

Al had just reached up to scratch what felt like something crawling through his hair, when Danny rang the doorbell, then knocked. He quickly moved to the kitchen and put both his hands into the sink full of scalding, soapy water. As he heard the door open he fought away the desire to scratch his head. The poison-ivy had obviously spread there as well.

"Hello Mister Al! It's me. Did you know Fred and his mother were moving? I just saw the van outside their house and Fred's mom said she wanted to move Fred as far away from the woods as possible! What do you think of that?" As Danny spoke she walked through the house and into the kitchen.

The old man began to wash the tea cups and he thought, *so that's why Fred's mother brought the gloves back today. She is clearing out the house.* A sudden uncontrollable itch started in the web between his thumb and finger. He thrust his hand deep below the subs and gave the area a good long scratch. He must have broken the skin because the spot began to sting and the soapy water turned a light pink.

Danny bustled around making the tea. "You could have left those dishes Mister Al. You know I do them before leaving every night. Gotta earn my money you know." Her voice was light.

This isn't going to work, thought the old man. *How will I keep her from noticing my hands?*

"Guess who I saw by the stream today? Rosemary! Boy, has she gotten fat. You should keep an eye out for her since I bet she'll be here looking for a hand out soon enough."

The kettle whistled and Danny turned away to pour the tea.

He pulled his hands from the water, sat abruptly in the chair and rolled himself into the living room where he pulled down the blinds. By the time Danny brought in his cup of milk-tea and plate of cookies he was leaning back on the daybed pretending to watch a golf tournament. He looked up and put his finger to his mouth "Shhh" he motioned and pointed to the television.

Danny was in such a wonderful mood she wasn't the least curious about Mister Al's dismissal. It had been a glorious day, and seeing Fred and his mother packing to go had made it perfect. She felt like a prisoner released from a life sentence. *Things are working out again!* she thought, *the mojo is back.* "Okay then. You watch the game and I'll stop in tomorrow after school. Looks like you've already eaten, since a half a loaf of bread is gone." Danny didn't even try to keep the affection out of her voice as she looked at the old man who had become her best friend.

Please leave... please leave...go...just go! The old man screamed, struggling with every fiber of his being to ignore the crawling, tickling sensations between his fingers, the top of his hand and both wrists. He turned to Danny briefly and smiled, hoping to encourage her exit.

"Bye then!" she started for the door, "Keep an eye out for Rosemary tonight." Danny said stepping out into the already darkening afternoon.

Inside the house the old man was back in his chair and racing for the kitchen. *An old remedy for poison-ivy is whiskey and salt.* Far under the sink he found a bottle of expensive whiskey left over from his drinking days. Shaking with need he took the bottle to the sink, broke the seal, and poured the vintage spirits over his cupped hands. The burning started immediately. Again, he washed his hands in the stuff—feeling as though his fingers were being attacked by a million angry bees. He reached for the salt shaker, unscrewed the top, dumped the contents into his palm and started to rub, rub, the gritty salt into the blisters.

This poison ruined my childhood dream; now it's back to stomp on me some more. The thin skin over the breaking blisters began to peel. Blood welled up from the abrasions.

Salt was supposed to dry the oily blisters and the alcohol in whiskey was supposed prevent infection—but it was as though he'd thrust both hands into fire. Tears ran down his face as the most satisfying pain he'd ever felt stopped the itching. Grimly, he poured on more whisky and ground in another handful of salt.

Thin, old, skin is very, very slow to heal.

Danny wrote:

A Friendship is like a treasure chest. There is no need to look inside to know the contents are worth protecting.

I am curled in my sleeping bag with the little heater on low. The temperature still drops at night but during the day the weather is mild and sometimes even warm. Dinner tonight was Ramen Noodles, which are yummy and easy to make now that I can just plug in the electric pot. All my gadgets work off battery juice now, and all I do to keep the battery charged is jump on the bike for a few hours. Another thing I have to thank Mister Al for. I hate to say it, but I don't think I could do any of this without his help.

I stayed at his house for two whole weeks, and he didn't ask any questions about my family. I think he knew I needed to be in the neighborhood, so I could keep tabs on Fred's recovery—Mister Al probably feels guilty too.

Fred came home yesterday, so I got Oxo to come help me surprise him and it turns out Oxo seemed to actually LIKE the kid—why, I just don't understand. The kid is, what my mom used to call, a loud-mouthed, know-it-all.

I was worrying about how I would handle having Fred in my business when I stopped by Mister Al's and found out he and his mother are MOVING!!! Yippee! I was worried Fred's mother would report the poison-ivy as a public health risk. I NEVER thought she would MOVE away just to avoid it!

I think Fred will be much happier in the city. It was a great day! I will write more tomorrow.

Beatrice was not happy about wasting her frequent flyer miles on a ticket home to check on her father, but it couldn't be helped. She told her co-workers that she had a daughter's sense that something was wrong.

The clack-clack of Bea's stilettos on the sidewalk sounded very efficient as she walked from the taxi to her father's front door. She stalled at the door to dig for house keys before remembering she still didn't have a set. She rang the doorbell. Waiting, Beatrice approved the neatly trimmed grass on the postage stamp sized lawn. She noticed the heavy buds on the cherry tree and thought, *that thing needs to be cut back, or cut down.* And then, *where on earth IS he?*

This time she rang the bell for a very long time.

The old man heard it this time, and roused himself. Perhaps he had taken too much pain medication, but it had been a very, very, long, mostly sleepless night.

She heard sounds from inside the house and thought, *I will certainly remember to get keys made this time. .*

The old man opened the door and was horrified. *Beatrice! Of ALL the times to visit.* He glanced down at the athletic socks he'd pulled over his bandaged hands before tucking them quickly beneath the lap blanket he'd had the presence of mind to add to the chair. Al looked up at his daughter with a guilty expression.

Beatrice smelled it right away. *Booze! He's drinking again!* Her sense of outrage knew no bounds. *He lost a good corporate job because of the bottle and ended up a BUS driver! Mother never recovered.* Beatrice didn't notice the odd, gray look in her father's face because she didn't look at him. She simply grabbed the handles of his chair and began pushing. "How COULD you?" her voice was high and pinched with fury.

The old man was confused. *What now? What is she talking about?*

"You promised mother you would never, ever, take another drink and now, here you are lying in bed, drunk, in the middle of the day! I suppose you think I have nothing better to do than sort YOU out?" She looked around for something to complain about and noticed the laundry room door was open. *There!*

Beatrice deposited her father in the living room and turned to face him— hands on hips—indignant. "Just look at this place!' she tossed her head, "Unmade beds. So much laundry you can't even shut the door! Mother was right about you! You can't do anything right!"

This time it was the patch on his head that itched, but his hands were too muffled up to provide a good scratch. *Maybe a fork?* Half listening to his daughters rant he thought, *Blah-blah-blah, something about laundry and something about being useless.* He'd certainly heard all that before and from the original source—what he was really interested in was scratching his head.

Beatrice continued to complain loudly as she made up the day bed and arranged the throw pillows decoratively. "You expect me to do everything. I can see that the girl I hired has her hands full, but why she didn't let me know you were back to drinking is beyond me!" Plumping one errant pillow she finally turned back to her father. Her eyes slid over his slumped form and returned to the open door of the laundry room.

The old man had just begun to move toward the kitchen to get a fork when he saw his daughter head for the laundry room. Through the open door he saw the pile of work clothes Danny had abandoned. *Oh great heavens! NO!* he screamed silently and took off toward the her as quickly as the chair could roll— shouting silently *Don't! Don't DO IT Bea! Don't TOUCH those things!* But he could make no sound.

Fortunately, or maybe unfortunately, the shoes Beatrice was wearing were not designed for moving quickly. With one step to go, her father's wheelchair cut in front of her and her ankle turned in her shoe. Bea had rather thick industrial sized ankles, so no harm was done—but she was livid just the same. *What was the old drunk doing anyway? Is he actually STANDING up?*

All the old man could do was put his arms around the entire bundle of clothing and stand up. The bundle was so big he couldn't see over it. He reached the washer as quickly as possible, but knew it could never be quick enough. Keeping his back to his amazed daughter, he crammed the soiled coveralls, long sleeves shirts, socks, gloves—even the goggles—into the machine, added detergent, a whole bottle of bleach, put the machine on Hot Wash/Hot Rinse, and turned it on. *That should kill it,* he thought, and this time his tears were for what was to come...

Beatrice would never know how close she'd come being covered in urushiol oil—but her father knew. He remembered restraining the little girl as she tried to scratch the poison-ivy rash she had picked up when he had taken her to the park—his little Bea was just as allergic as he was.

Now what? He thought, *I just wait for it to happen?* He remembered Danny talking about treatments for people who'd been exposed. *If Bea could get me to a doctor...how can I make her understand that?* He looked down at the hopeless mess he'd made of his hands. *Can't type...not that she'd read what I typed anyway.*

His daughter continued to rage, but at least she'd moved to another room. He heard the 'glug-glug' sound of his whiskey going down the drain. *She's in the kitchen.*

Finishing up in the kitchen to her own satisfaction, Beatrice clack-clacked up the stairs to her room where she was again outraged. *Can it just GET any better?!* Someone had been using her bedroom, and sleeping in her bed. *So now I have to do something about this GIRL who obviously has decided this is her home to do as she pleases.* It hadn't escaped her notice that the exercise bike was now prominently placed in front of the window.

She thought about the new, non-profit, Senior-Residential group client she had landed. The CEO of that organization had urged her to enroll her father in the Florida facility for rehabilitation and care—free of course. Beatrice thought at the time that it would be a good business move, but having her father so close would mean she'd be expected to visit often—and that put her off. *Well, I can't let the old drunk go on like this.*

Danny hadn't expected to hear from Mister Al that morning—and certainly not in the middle of a school day. When the phone chirped, she casually glanced down at the one word message before jumping up and dashing from the room.

It read: HELP

Middle School is not an easy place to escape, Danny was to discover.

The power of suggestion is a remarkable thing, the old man tried telling himself, *I shouldn't have symptoms for at least three more hours.*

Maybe. But the skin around the old blue eyes was swelling fast; the tickling had begun on his neck and arms—and his heart was beating way too fast.

This will kill me.

He had managed to undress in the shower and use his bandaged hands like washcloths to slather himself with anti-bacterial soap. He had coated his clothes with the soap too, clogged the shower drain with a washcloth and left it—shoes and all—to soak in the pool of scalding, soapy water.

It was the best he could do. *There has to be a way to get help,* he told himself. *I can't stand the thought of what comes next, where the ants start crawling everywhere and no amount of scratching will stop them from tickling and tickling and, oh please God!* He remembered, *when I picked up those clothes I got it in the face. My eyes!*

He was losing his grip. Panicking. *Stop! Stop!* He told himself. *Breathe. Slowly...breathe.* He forced his heart rate down and swallowed hard. The trick, he knew, was to keep the mind busy. *I can figure this out. There has to be a way to communicate. I need a work-around.*

Beatrice had changed to flat shoes and her trip down the stairs was much quieter than her trip up had been. She entered the living room and was surprised to see her father with a pencil sticking from his mouth. He appeared to be using the pencil to type something on the computer keyboard.

She watched in morbid fascination as he made attempt after painstakingly attempt to maneuver the pencil eraser across the touch pad. Finally he seemed to have gotten it right, because he tapped the Enter key and sat back. *Drunk. Why else would he type with a pencil in his teeth when he has two perfectly good hands.* She didn't notice the heavily bandaged hands held uselessly in his lap and when he finally looked up, she didn't notice how swollen his left eye was...

Danny didn't know where to go. All the doors were alarmed from the inside and even if she left, how was she to get to Mister Al's? *What should I do? I can call someone. I should call 911 but what do I tell them? It doesn't matter. Just so they get there before something worse happens.*

She realized she needed an adult.

Standing in the hall calling 911, Danny had just made contact when someone yanked the phone from her hand.

"What do you think you are doing young lady?! I will take this." Missus Schneider snapped the phone shut and glared at the small girl with the braid. *She doesn't look very good,* Schneider saw and felt a little bit mean and a little bit old.

"Oh no! Please! Please! It...It's...my Grandfather! He's in trouble and I have to call 911!"

"Reeeally...?" Schneider's voice dripped with sarcasm. Danny was one of the school's foster children and the whole administration knew it. *So what's the kid up to that she needs to make up a grandfather?*

Less than a block away, the determination had been made by the director of the Emergency Call Center to take the last call seriously—even though the caller had been cut off. It had been traced to Roosevelt Middle and the Columbine shootings were never far from anyone's thoughts. Within minutes the siren ripped a hole in the afternoon quiet and Kenilworth Fire and Rescue responded.

Danny jumped at the sound and allowed herself a moment of hope. When the sirens erupted Misses Schneider adjusted her grip on Danny's elbow and continued dragging her toward the Principal's Office. "We will SEE about this young lady."

"Ms Schneider, please," tears squirted from Danny's eyes; her nose was running and desperation threaten to choke her, "He needs help!!" she sobbed.

Don't whine! Stand your ground. Danny gasped. That had been her mother's voice as clear as day! Schneider hesitated and for a second Danny thought she too, had heard the voice.

Danny! Do not argue with these people. Explain. State facts.

Danny breathed deeply and forced a quiet, measured voice, "Missus Schneider. I take care of an old man at Rockaway Estates and he just text messaged me the word HELP."

Schneider stopped and looked down, startled by Danny's sudden maturity. Although her cheeks were tear-streaked, her jaw was very determined. *Hello,* Schneider thought, *where did THIS one come from?*

Thanks Mom. Danny cleared her throat and pointed to her cell phone. "Just look at the message."

HELP, Schneider read and frowned. The sirens were getting louder, "Did you...?"

"Yes. I did. I called 911. I said I needed help immediately. Then I was cut off." She tried to keep accusation out of her voice. "That is probably them now. I need to make sure they get to Mister Aldo Smith's house at 11314 Rockaway Estates." Danny took a deep and steadying breath before adding what she most feared, "He may have had another stroke."

Aldo Smith couldn't unwrap the gauze covering his hands; it had dried into the wounds once the leaking stopped. He gritted his teeth and pulled, and thought it would help if he could scream out loud—but of course he couldn't.

Fresh blood immediately welled up as both gauze and scab ripped away, and he examined his hands—they did indeed look quite awful. Now that the wounds were exposed, even the movement of the air in the room caused great pain. *That is okay, it takes my mind off the ants and it's the only way Beatrice might notice.*

Sirens sounded in the distance and Aldo Smith straightened. He knew his only hope was to reach the door before his daughter did. *Must move now.*

In his urgency, he gripped the wheels of the chair but when the naked, raw and bleeding hands made contact with the knobby rubber tread, the pain was so intense the world went white. He passed out.

The doorbell rang.

"Yes?" Beatrice had opened the door to find an anxious police officer. On the street, flashing lights and frantic activity made it obvious something awful had happened.

"Ma'am. Is someone here in need of assistance? We received a 911 call." as the officer spoke he tried to look around the woman at the door. There certainly didn't appear to be an emergency, but procedure was procedure.

"No officer, I did NOT call 911. Are you sure you have the correct address?" *Save me from incompetent bureaucrats. Some poor slob around the corner is probably dying and they turn up at the wrong house.!*

What a nasty piece of work SHE is. "Well Ma'am does a person with a medical condition," he paused to carefully read from his card, "name of Al...Al-doe...Aldo Smith live here?"

From the living room came a loud **CRASH**.

Beatrice gasped.

"Step aside!' the police officer shouldered Beatrice out of the way and rushed into the darkened living room.

An old man lay where he had apparently fallen from his wheelchair. It appeared his body was convulsing. "Get a medic in here right now!" Officer Spencer roared. He rushed to the old man's side to check for breathing and saw the man's hands—they looked like they'd been dipped in battery acid. *That evil, unspeakable woman! SHE had something to do with this!*

Beatrice was just collecting herself, when two more of them pushed by her. *What is wrong with these people?* She thought, *I know I didn't call the police and certainly my father couldn't have!* This was one of the rare times Beatrice was at a loss as to what to think or say. She simply stood aside and watched with some interest, finding it a bit thrilling. *Like watching one of those hospital dramas.*

Mister Aldo Smith had obviously been abused. Both eyes were swollen shut and there were red abrasions on his face, neck and arms. He was bleeding from small head wounds, and no one knew what could possibly have happened to the hands. He was unconscious when they wheeled him out.

Officer Spencer had no qualms about taking the woman who'd answered the door into custody. He didn't listen to a word she said. As far as he was concerned—if SHE personally wasn't guilty of abusing Mister Smith—she certainly WAS guilty of turning a blind eye as someone else did. *I don't care what she has to say, so why doesn't she just stop **talking**?"*

The only way the school would agree to let Danny leave was if her guardian came in and signed her out personally.

Danny broke down again after the police had taken the 911 information. She honestly tried to explain WHY she needed to go along and why the old man needed her to be there. It didn't matter. No one was listening. She was a kid and that was all there was to it.

She tried to be grateful; at least they sent someone to the home of Aldo Smith to check to see if he needed help. *But they didn't act like it was urgent or anything. Did they even write down that Mister Al can't talk?* She didn't think they did so— after the police left and she was alone with Schneider and the principal—she asked to "please," let her call a taxi.

"No," they said. That's when she discovered they expected her to go back to class and finish the day. *As if nothing had happened!*

So she'd lost it. Who wouldn't? *He's my best friend and the only person in my whole world I can really count on.*

Fortunately, part of Danny remained alert—when the principal whispered something to Schneider and Schneider scurried off only to return with a file, Danny noticed. When the principal opened the file, noted something and picked up the phone to dial, Danny had enough sense left to stop him. She knew he was dialing Roxanne Laird.

Danny returned to class and bided her time. The next period was lunch. She walked through the kitchen and out the cafeteria door. *Act like you are supposed to be doing what ever it is you are doing.*

It worked. She cut across the playing field to a bus stop she'd looked up on Google and the bus came right on time. She climbed on, her thoughts full of worry and fear.

"Well, hey there girl! I haven't seen you since the first snow. How's that Granddaddy of yours?"

It was Jamaal.

Danny lifted her head to the shaggy haired Bus Driver, her eyes glistening with tears. "Jamaal..." she choked.

Jamaal was naturally friendly and talkative, and he was used to being treated as sort of friendly background noise. He was stunned when the kid remembered his name, and his big heart moved.

"Oh Jamaal, I am so glad to see you! I'm going to Grandfather's house right now. The paramedics wouldn't let me ride with them. He's in trouble Jamaal, he sent me a text message that said HELP! I am so scared!"

"Oh girl, you poor thing!" Jamaal glanced behind him at the empty bus and made a quick calculation. "Let's go." He pulled away from the curb and within minutes the old bus was clattering down Cumberland Road. He knew a shortcut to Old Cumberland and knew he could make up time later but right now, Jamaal was most definitely off route.

See Mister Al, she thought, *I'm not the only one who loves you.*

SPECIAL DELIVERY

anny walked through the empty house trying to make sense
of what she was seeing...

The moment Jamaal opened the bus door, she'd run to
Mister Al's and used her key without knocking—hoping she'd
misinterpreted the message and called in a bogus 911 report.
But...the house was most definitely empty.

Mister Al's wheelchair was abandoned in the center of the
living room. *I guess they have their own wheelchairs at the
hospital...but THIS wheelchair has his computer and without it
he can't communicate.* Danny knew Mister Al would have
insisted they at least take his computer—*unless he COULDN'T.*
She tried not to think of Mister Al being carried to an ambulance,
mute and helpless.

An old volume of World Book Encyclopedia had tumbled to
the floor next to the chair. *P through Q*—she saw as she picked it
up and smoothed pages apparently wrinkled by the fall—the
pages were about poison-ivy.

Is he still thinking about poor Fred? It hurt her to think
Mister Al worried over something she'd caused. *Worrying can
cause a heart attack...or a stroke.*

Danny imagined the scenario: Mister Al sitting in his
wheelchair with the heavy volume in his lap reading about the
poison-ivy allergy. *Just remembering how awful it was for him
as a child might be enough to give him heart attack.* She
pictured the old gray head slumping forward and the book
tumbling to the ground and tears sprung to her eyes. She shook
them away. **No.**

*No! It couldn't have happened that way—he text messaged
me.* Puzzling over the sequence of events she looked around for
more clues. It seemed terribly important to fit what she knew
into some sort of timeline.

A wadded pile of odd rags on the floor beside the coffee table
caught her eye. She stepped over for a look. *Looks like dirty
white ribbons of something.* Placing the Encyclopedia on the
table, she knelt to examine the material. *Gauze!*

The yards of gauze were tangled around a dishtowel and a pair of white athletic socks—blotchy with brown and red stains. *Is that blood?!* She lifted a ribbon of gauze and found torn skin adhering to yellow, pus-like smears. Danny's stomach began a slow, sickening roll. *What happened?*

Moving her search for answers to the kitchen, she found it unusually clean. A dishcloth was folded beside the sink, not draped over the faucet as she and Mister Al always left it. A large clear salt shaker was on the counter—empty. She opened the lid to the trash can and was surprised to find an empty bottle of whiskey. *Huh. Maybe he had a friend over?* she thought and felt a blaze of hope, *maybe something happened to his friend and not to him.* Moments later she saw the flaw in that logic.

No. Only family members are allowed to ride along in an ambulance and Mister Al isn't here.

Danny kept looking.

In the bathroom she discovered an entire change of clothes, even slippers, soaking in the bottom of the shower stall. *Why didn't he use the washer?* She wondered until she saw that the washer was full of her work clothes. *Huh!?*

Danny felt like she had slipped into some other world and it was making her dizzy. Again and again she assured herself that only 16 hours ago, Mister Al had been sitting on the couch watching golf. *How could things have gotten so weird so quickly?*

Upstairs, the strangeness continued. Someone had moved into her room and it took but a moment of snooping to see, who that 'someone' was. *Beatrice!*

Beatrice's handbag lay open on the bed with her fancy touch screen phone blinking beside it. *She must have left in very big hurry, maybe because her father was sick?* But Beatrice's suitcase was empty and her clothes neatly hung in the closet. *She'd been here long enough to get settled...* Danny found a boarding pass for a flight that had arrived that morning. *Beatrice was here when he called me.*

Back downstairs, Danny returned to the encyclopedia. Things weren't all lovey-dovey between Mister Al and his daughter—but for him to call Danny when he needed help meant he couldn't make her understand something. The only other time he had needed to communicate with Danny and couldn't, he had resorted to a dictionary. She shook P through Q and a pencil rolled out. She caught it as it was about to go off the edge of the table and looked at it. *This pencil was never sharpened,* she saw something else—the lead end was badly chewed up. *Who chews on the wrong end of a pencil?* As she put the pencil aside, her fingers felt sticky. There was a smear of something on her hand.

Blood!

Blood was on the pencil. Actively looking now, she found more traces it on the book and on the arms of wheelchair. When Danny ran her fingers across the knobby tires, both came away wet with mostly uncongealed blood. *He used his hands to roll the chair.* Somehow, Mister Al had cut both hands—cut them badly. *His hands were messed up so bad he couldn't type, and couldn't communicate with Beatrice.* Again the scenario almost worked. But there was a problem. *Mister Al had typed the word HELP.*

Puzzles within puzzles. Her eyes wandered this time to the pencil. She and Mister Al once watched a TV special about a paraplegic who used a special stick held in his teeth to peck out words on a computer. *That's it! He used a pencil!* She pictured the old man biting down on the wrong end of a pencil to peck out a message. *To me!* She shook off another round of tears—there was no time for that. *I'll cry later,* she told herself, *after I figure this out. What else?*

Her eyes fell on the encyclopedia and she thought, *if he couldn't use a keyboard, he couldn't use the internet—so he looked it up.* She picked up the heavy volume and it again opened to the pages on poison-ivy. *He was injured but instead of taking it easy, he was reading the encyclopedia—there was something in here he desperately needed to know—and chances are it was about poison-ivy...*

Danny moved to the dining table where the light was better and stared down at paragraph after paragraph of information. *A lot to read and I've got to catch the next bus to the hospital.* Then she noticed certain parts of the entry were lightly stained by brown smudges. *Blood smears. The important parts are marked with Mister Al's own blood.* Whether he'd left the marks unintentionally or as intentional signs to Danny didn't matter; she was certain she was right and focused her attention on the highlighted text.

Come on Mister Al, tell me what happened. Help me, so I can help you, she thought as she checked the time yet again...

It was dinner hour and the doctor was determined to ignore the young girl with the braid who'd suddenly materialized at his elbow. He looked down at her in annoyance, and felt a nudge of recognition—she looked like a much younger version of the girl who had hung around the boy with poison-ivy while he was in intensive care—but it didn't matter, he honestly didn't have time for this, the police needed him to answer a few questions about an old man recently checked in.

"Doctor Muir?" the girl said, "Doctor, I need to speak to you. There is something you must know about your patient Aldo Smith."

"Sorry dear, I don't have time." Muir tried to slip by, but the girl was having none of that. She moved to plant herself directly in front of him.

"Mister Smith has been exposed to a very virulent crop of poison-ivy and he is highly allergic. Do you understand? You must do something right away! Please listen to me!"

This kid sure knows how to sling the crap! 'Highly virulent' indeed. Muir looked down impatiently at the child blocking his way. "See here young lady, I'm busy and you are in my way. Should I call security?"

"I am telling you something you need to know. I'm sure you remember the kid you treated who had poison-ivy? Fred McCarty? Well, I just discovered Mister Al handled that boy's clothes, and you know —of course—that urushiol oil can stay active for up to a year. Aldo Smith will be breaking out any minute—if you don't DO something!" she stamped her foot.

Danny could see the doctor wasn't listening. She raised her voice trying to impress him with sincerity. "Mister Al still has scars from a horrible run in with poison-ivy as a child, when his blisters became infected. If you don't pump him up with some of your steroids right away, THIS time, he's old and he'll probably DIE! It would be your fault if that happened!"

She had the good doctor's attention—*Kid knows too much about this to be ignored*—but when he saw a security guard walking toward him he made a quick decision, "Security! Security! This young person is not allowed in the hospital unescorted. She is making quite a nuisance of herself and I want her out of here."

The big security guard ushered Danny to the exit and Doctor Muir turned on his heel and stalked back down the hall to the wards.

Shaken and angry, Danny thought, *How could this be? How could that doctor just blow me off like that? THINK Danny! She* tried to mentally shake off the insult, and to focus. *The encyclopedia said there is a very small window after exposure. Time has probably already run out.*

The only person left who might be able to intercede was Mister Al's daughter, Beatrice—she must be somewhere in the hospital waiting for news of her father. *I have her number, but she doesn't have her phone! It's at Mister Al's.*

The hospital speaker system suddenly crackled to life, **"Paging Doctor Jose Segunda, Dermatology! Doctor Segunda please call reception, immediately!"**

The announcement gave Danny an idea. Dialing reception from her cell phone she kept her voice low and modulated. "Could someone please page Ms Beatrice Smith? She came in the ambulance with her father, Aldo Smith several hours ago and I have been watching her son. I'm afraid there was a playground accident and her son was cut very badly. Her signature is needed right away on some hospital forms. Could you please page her immediately?"

In seconds, a voice on the loudspeaker announced: **"Paging Beatrice Smith. Would Beatrice Smith please call reception? Ms Beatrice Smith, please call reception right away, you have an urgent message."**

Danny kept the phone clapped to her ear, betting the next voice she heard would be Beatrice's. As minutes ticked by she ran through what she would say and how she would say it.

A kindly voice came on the line, "I am so sorry dear. No one is answering the page. Let me get your number and I will page Ms. Smith again every few minutes until she turns up. Don't worry dear, we will find her if she is in this hospital!"

"Thank you", she said in a hollow, helpless voice, and hung up. *It doesn't matter anyway, it's too late. Too much time has passed.* The poison-ivy timeline laid out in the encyclopedia had been very specific—urushiol oil binds to skin cells five to fifteen minutes after exposure. *The oil bound to him when he put my clothes in the washer, by now he'll be covered in blisters and unable to explain what is wrong.*

All she could do was hope Doctor Muir would remember what she'd said and realize the blisters on an old man who hadn't been outside in almost a year were caused by poison-ivy.

If something happens to him I will never forgive myself.

At first Beatrice was frustrated beyond belief. *Are these local cops ALL idiots?* No would listen to her, or even LOOK at her, nor would they explain WHY she had been manhandled into the back of a police cruiser. She assumed, of course, that she was being taken to the hospital to be with her father.

Not so.

Beatrice was taken to the police station, told to take a chair in an empty room and left to wait. The longer she waited, the more furious she became; by the time an officer did arrive to question her, she was in a full, towering, rage—and quite uncooperative.

The interviewing officer took only a few notes before shutting the door behind him and leaving Beatrice to stew. He took his time checking the claim that she'd only just arrived in town.

The airline confirmed.

So, her flight information combined with the doctor's statement that both initial wounds and the secondary infection were 6 to 12 hours old, left the Police no choice but to release Ms-Beatrice-Renee-Smith-if-you-please, from custody.

Beatrice was told to go home.

How!? How do they expect me to get home when I have no car, no money and no friends or relatives? Beatrice would not give these stone-age fools the satisfaction of asking for a ride; only by standing her ground and demanding an answer, was she even told which hospital her father was in. *Great!* She thought, *something else to sort out.* Her first priority was to collect her phone—being without it made her feel naked.

Beatrice called a taxi, which of course took entirely too long to arrive.

Danny was trying to sleep between bouts of crying and pleading for her mother to please let her presence be felt, when the phone ran. She snatched it up without glancing at Caller ID.

"Daniela?" said a cold, but familiar, voice, "You are fired."

Danny felt like she had been punched in the stomach. All she could do was gasp. *He's dead! Mister Al died!* The struggle to stop the world from wobbling on its axis took only a second, but in that second Danny clearly saw a doctor pull a white sheet over Mister Al's face. She burst into tears, "When did he die? What happened? Please!" hysteria rose, "Please tell me what happened!"

Beatrice was startled by all the drama. Certainly no one had acted this way when she fired them before. *What makes the silly girl think the old man died?* "Young lady, my father is NOT dead, thanks only to a brilliant diagnosis by a local doctor...but he does have blood poisoning on top of a systemic case of poison-ivy of all things—and he will no longer need your services."

Relief washed over Danny like a wind off the ocean on a hot humid day. "Oh thank you for telling me! Thank you. Thank you! I was so worried..." she stopped, too choked up to speak another word. *Again with the tears?* Emotions kept hijacking her.

"Yes, well. He is quite old, but appears to be in surprisingly good physical shape."

All that bike riding. Danny smiled fondly.

"...we will see how much more damage has been done to him mentally..."

How much MORE damage? She acts like he was senile or something—and Mister Al is one of the smartest people I know...but, Oh!... Could they think he had another stroke?....Oh!...he would hate losing his smarts the WORST! I just KNOW him.

"...whatever the outcome, I have arranged for him to be moved to a Residential Senior Center in Florida."

Danny could not speak. There was a rushing, like standing close to a passing train, that canceled out everything.

"You may have done your job in the past, but it does appear you are the one responsible for my father coming into contact with poison-ivy. I will not involve the authorities in this— although you were clearly negligent—but do not expect a reference..." Taking a short breath Beatrice added, "...or to receive any payment, be it salary or severance."

Danny found she was tightly gripping a dead phone. Beatrice had hung up.

Danny struggled to write:

WHY!? I feel like my insides are bleeding. I cry and know I shouldn't because Mister Al is going to be okay and that is the most important thing. I should be happy! But I'm not and I wonder if I am just feeling sorry for my self.

When I imagine Mister Al trapped and pushed around in the hospital it breaks my heart and all I can think is I need to see him. I MUST see him before she takes him to Florida. But then I remember, I DID THIS TO HIM! He is in the hospital because of ME. Like he said—the Fortress of the Vines is a giant poison-ivy patch—and I live there. The Encyclopedia, said once the stuff becomes a systemic infection, you are hyper-sensitive for ever more. Just being around me is dangerous for him.

Danny put down the journal and began to sob. She hadn't eaten, or gone to school in days, nor had she moved from where she was, curled in the corner of her cot. She was confused and hurting in ways she had never thought possible.

On the third day, the patient Aldo Smith 'turned the corner' as they say and the antibiotics beat back the infection. Doctor Muir and a team of dermatologists were encouraged. The patient's system was strong and his will to live undiminished by age. After much consultation and whispering the decision was made to keep Smith sedated. The poison-ivy rash had appeared on much of the man's body—and even though they'd pumped him full of steroids—they didn't want his traumatized body to have to deal with the itching sensations.

Doctor Muir reported the good news to Aldo Smith's daughter, (a sour looking woman if he ever saw one), who nodded curtly and asked if that meant he could travel by the following month.

"Why not?" Muir said off handedly, offended by the lack of gratitude from this family member.

"Good. I am having him transferred to a nursing home."

That seemed rather rash to the doctor. The old man appeared to be in excellent shape—unlike most of the residents of nursing homes, it appeared this old fellow exercised. *Oh well, if he comes out of it with all his mental abilities intact, it isn't like Aldo Smith can't tell her 'no!'*

After a few nights, Danny's tent grew cold and she crawled like some sick animal, under the covers. She hadn't eaten or had anything to drink in days—so maybe she wasn't thinking clearly—somewhere along the line she had decided to give up...*do nothing...absolutely nothing*, least she hurt someone else she loved. She was beaten, completely alone and planned to stay alone for ever and ever...her very presence could kill people.

Depression was like a drug, able to shut down the big, painful stuff. But Danny couldn't shut down the little, physical annoyance of something digging into the soft skin of her stomach each time she moved. She'd shift and it would wake her. Finally, she yanked off the blanket to see just what was keeping her awake and in the present.

It was her cell phone. How it came to be under the covers she couldn't remember. She started to drop it to the floor just as it signaled an incoming voice message. Old habits are last to die, Danny opened the phone, keyed in her password and listened...

"Danny? It's Oxo. Where are you? Someone from your school called here TWICE, to find out where you were. I told Lady Lard to tell them you were sick. You better be sick and not just playing hooky! AND you better get back to school...or you will ruin everything!"

Yes, Oxo, I DO ruin everything. Danny tossed the phone and curled into a tight ball.

An hour later, her sleep was again disturbed by the sensation of fingers rubbing her face. *I'm dreaming.* The sensation intensified. Now she could feel little hands patting at her cheeks and her eyelids. The hand reached her mouth.

I'm dreaming. She again told herself, until tiny fingers begin to pry apart her lips. *Too much!*

Danny's eyes flew open as fingers tugged at her bottom lip, to find herself looking up at Rosemary. The little raccoon didn't notice Danny's shocked expression; she was too busy staring into space, using only her sense of touch to explore Danny's face.

"Bleeck!" said Danny sitting up.

This dumped the intruder onto the floor.

"How did you get in here?!" Her voice sounded rusty and faraway to her own ears. Sitting up suddenly had made her giddy and the room seemed to sway and flash in the light streaming through the open tent flap.

Rosemary wasn't fond of sudden movements and the only other time she'd been thrown to the ground was when the tree collapsed. She retreated to the corner, but stood her ground and loudly chirred, managing to sound both angry and offended.

"Oh ALRIGHT!" Danny leaned over and popped the seal on the large, wheeled cooler. "You want food." she grabbed a Yoo-Hoo. The clear bottle filled with chocolate drink was cold and slippery in her hand; condensation dripped down the sides. Danny's hands and arms felt weak and it was a bit of a struggle to twist the cap off—but she managed.

A tantalizing chocolate smell rose from the open bottle. Rosemary caught the scent and left her corner.

It smelled good to Danny too, and without a second thought she raised it to her own lips and guzzled the entire contents as her fascinated guest looked on.

"Ah!" she wiped her mouth with the back of a hand, "That IS good!" Danny reached for another bottle.

Soon both were sharing a bag of potato chips and Rosemary had her own personal Yoo-Hoo. The raccoon hadn't spilled a drop. She didn't look as fat, but that couldn't be because she was going hungry because Chips and a Yoo-Hoo seemed to fill her up; she headed right for the door.

"Oh well," Danny said to her guests retreating backside, "Rosemary's got things to do and people to see I guess." The visit had managed to lift some of the darkness and she found herself wearily collecting her things and then shuffling off to the hot spring.

It was time to soak away some of the funk and soon enough, she was sinking into the stream's always welcoming embrace. *I could just slip under the water and float away...no one would miss me.* That just didn't feel right, so she thought instead about tomorrow. She would return to school. She figured she could do that much for Oxo. *No need for both of us to have lives that suck.*

There were still the little pleasures—like the feel of scrubbing the soles of her feet in the clean creek sand or the smell of hundreds of wildflowers blooming on the creek bed. She was out of shampoo and so lathered soap into her long, untended hair. Holding her head in the water, she let hot currents comb out the worst of the tangles.

The little rituals took a long time and cleared her head just enough to think about her responsibilities. Tomorrow she decided, must be Friday. *Mister Al has been in the hospital four days already and his daughter says he's better now. I can't visit, but there must be some way I can let him know I won't forget him...*

Beatrice had a lot to do to get the house ready for sale. It was a good thing she wasn't the sentimental type, since there were piles of memories in the attic— **Baby Bea, Toddler Bea, Our Schoolgirl Bea**—boxes neatly labeled in her father's hand were stacked to the rafters. She opened a few of them to find old toys, forgotten clothes and every childhood drawing and clever thing she'd ever written, saved and cataloged.

Beatrice tossed all of it.

In the rest of the house, she found even more items of questionable value that she packed off to the local shelter and thrift store. First to go was the obnoxious contraption her father had let that girl set up in the living room. Then came the books. *Nobody wants books.* Most went to the landfill.

A few items gave her pause. An old looking bottle she'd never seen before went in the give-away box. She found a framed pirate map, or whatever it was, and thought it was quite clever; she considered taking it back to Florida where such things were very popular. But in the end she tossed it, too, in the box.

Beatrice was very efficient.

It was obvious by Danny's wan, hollow-eyed look, that the child had indeed been sick. The principal decided to just let it be. The girl was a good student after all and he guessed she hadn't meant to lie to Missus Schneider about having a grandfather. Skipping out of school was a whole lot more serious—but the kid didn't have any parents to care one way or another so, really, what was the big deal?

Missus Schneider was also thinking about Danny Smith. Schneider had asked her niece, who volunteered at the ER about Danny's story and found out that an old guy named Smith had been brought in by the police the day Danny called 911, and his hands looked like they'd been dipped in battery acid. *The girl was right to be concerned, and I was wrong to give her such a hard time,* Missus Schneider privately acknowledged. So, when Danny asked for permission to take the school bus that serviced the east part of Old Cumberland Road instead of the bus to Kenilworth Estates, guilt made her a bit more flexible and she agreed.

"Oxo, I get it! I'm asking too many favors and you've helped me out too many times already. But PLEASE! I don't have anyone else to ask and I will promise to help you, no matter what, if you EVER need it—no questions asked!"

Oxo was really enjoying his new role as benefactor and granter of favors. He knew he would help Danny the minute she asked—but it was pretty cool watching her get all worked up.

Danny couldn't help it. She started to cry. *It's like I have a leak somewhere these days.* She was disgusted with herself.

Maybe she SHOULD just figure something else out. She had money after all. If she couldn't ASK someone to help, maybe she could buy someone's help.

Oxo saw her cry and immediately felt awful. "Ah, sure I'll do it Danny! You know I will. CSD kids stick together right?" *Poor kid,* he thought. Somewhere along the line, Oxo had begun thinking of Danny as younger, and of himself as wise and mature. *I AM almost 18,* he reminded himself. *It's about time I grew up.*

Danny sniffed and looked up, dark eyes pink rimmed and puffy. Her hair was dull and coarse, the usually braid was haphazard. "I can pay you. I have money."

Oxo felt like one of his superheroes, "Nah! I don't need money! I have plenty."

He did too, his local comic sales were booming. There was also money rolling in each month for the care and feeding of Roxanne's three non-resident foster children. *Money really IS no problem.*

"So, you will meet me in front of the hospital Sunday morning?" she asked, not yet convinced he really meant to help.

"Yeah. I should dress the part don't you think? I think it would be more believable if I looked like an official flower delivery guy." Oxo loved costumes. *Do those guys wear white? No, that's the ice cream man. Brown? I think that's the parcel deliver guy.*

"Maybe..."

But Oxo was getting in to it now. "I can go by the thrift shop tomorrow and put together something. You wanna go?"

"Okay..." *I don't want to go anywhere, but I'm asking a favor.*

"Great!" *This could be fun.* "Do you want me to pick you up?"

Now Danny was confused, "Pick me up?"

"Oh I got my license. And I got a motor scooter—like the ones you see in those foreign movies. There's room for two." He was rapidly warming to the adventure, "Come on! It will be fun!"

"Sure. It will be fun" Danny echoed with zero enthusiasm.

"Where should I pick up?"

"Oh...I'll meet you here. What time?"

"Ten?"

At ten sharp, Oxo and Danny zipped away on the shiny new motor scooter his agent Bull had given him in trade. It was drizzling and Danny's helmet sloshed around on her head as she tried not to hold Oxo's waist too tightly.

She was scared to death.

The thrift store had only been opened ten minutes when they pulled up. Oxo locked up the bike. "You can just leave your old helmet on the seat," he said.

She noticed he was carrying his with him into the store. "Won't someone steal it?"

He smiled jauntily, "Nobody's that stupid!"

Danny found herself smiling for the first time in a very long time as Oxo opened the door and they walked into the store that always smelled like someone's attic.

"What do ya think of this?" Oxo said minutes later. He was holding up a tan work shirt with the name Arnold embroidered in script over the pocket.

"That looks pretty official." she agreed and added, "if you don't mind being called Arnold!"

"There are worse names." Oxo spoke as he turned the shirt around for a look at the back.

Printed there, shoulder to shoulder, was the jolly proclamation: **What you flush, we brush!** <u>Arnold's Toilet and Cesspool Service</u>

Danny started to giggle.

Oxo started to laugh, and it sounded just like a dog barking.

Now Danny was in fits. She snorted and held her sides. It felt absolutely marvelous to laugh!

For the next hour, barks and giggles cropped up regularly as they sifted through rack after rack of uniform shirts. They found Pest Control, Parcel Delivery, Computer Repair, and a white silk chef's shirt Oxo was particularly partial to, that announced: **We**

Cater to your Tastes.

Oxo was still looking when Danny wandered off to check out the books. She ran her finger across the spines of the fiction. *Mostly paperbacks.* The non-fiction volumes were on the bottom shelf. She knelt for a look, *old college textbooks.* A slim volume caught her eye. It looked familiar and she pulled it out—not quite believing her luck. *Yes! This is the <u>History of the County</u> like the one Mister Al showed me with the story of Rockaway 'as told by Aldo Smith'*

The book fell open immediately to the Rockaway chapter, delighting Danny further.

Oxo appeared with a simple beige shirt—the words **Acme Florist** embroidered over the pocket and across the back. He also picked up a pair of Khaki pants, with **HARMOND** written in magic marker on the inside tag. *Nice material too, probably from some rich kid's closet. .*

Danny clutched the 25-cent book to her chest as they carried their purchases out to the bike. The book made her feel closer somehow to Mister Al. *It's the story of our quest.* She thought. It was a connection—knowing she had a book just like the one he treasured.

On Sunday morning, Acme Florists delivered an enormous bunch of flowers to the sleeping Aldo Smith in room 214. It was an unusual bouquet, partly for its size, but mostly because there wasn't a single blooming flower in it—only buds.

Hospital staffers like to swap stories and the story of some poor slob, ordering flowers but getting nothing but buds, smelled enough like a rip-off for the tale to spread quickly. Flower delivery was expensive and certainly whoever had paid money for such a substandard bunch was entitled to money back. After all, who could say if the buds ever WOULD open? The Good Samaritans among the staff wanted to complain to the Florist, but Acme Florist could not be found and no one recognized the delivery man. Instead they decided to contact the sender of the flowers, but the card was sealed, so the identity of the sender remained a mystery.

We will just wait and see, was the consensus. Then the staff broke the boredom by establishing a hospital betting pool to guess the date the first of the buds would open.

FAREWELL MY FRIEND

It was another mild, spring-like morning. Danny waited for the bus, her eyes fixed on the cherry tree in Mister Al's front yard.

Overnight it had erupted in blossoms and in the early morning light it resembled a pink cloud. *He would love to see that.* Just thinking about Mister Al caused pain, so she shut down her thoughts and returned to the self-imposed numbness she used to cope.

The door of 11314 opened and Danny had her first glimpse of the woman who must be Beatrice. Her first instinct was to hide. *But she doesn't know what I look like.*

Mister Al's daughter stalked down the steps to the front of the small yard. Under the frothing cherry tree, she bent to pick up a wooden stake from the grass. It had fallen over. Pursing her lips she jammed it back into the ground—working it back and forth to force it deeper into the earth. Then she marched back into the house and slammed the door.

Danny swallowed hard and willed herself not to be curious. *I don't care. It's nothing to me.* But she did care—*everything reminds me of Mister Al...even this bus stop.*

When the bus arrived, Danny took a moment to tell the driver she would use the bus stop on the next block from now on. *It will be easier.*

About the time the loaded school bus left the neighborhood, Beatrice opened the door and stepped from the house. This time she carried a large staple gun and had a stiff, laminated sign tucked under her arm. She stalked across the yard and stapled the sign to the wooden stake. *There!* she thought and stepped back to admire the effect. *That should do it,* she decided, returned to the house and again slammed the door.

The sign in Aldo Smith's front yard read: FOR SALE

On the morning Al woke up, the only thing he saw were daffodils.

They were hard to miss. The big bouquet was in full bloom—a bar of sunlight turning each cup-and-saucer shaped blossom a sonic yellow and filling the room with the fresh scent of spring. The old man breathed in the display—and easily transitioned from sleeping dreams of a shaded glade, chuckling stream and little stone shed to day dreams of walking among the flowers there. *So pleasant...*

"Good morning Mister Smith!" a cheerful voice broke in.

The voice startled him. He looked up and did not recognize the speaker, or his surroundings.

The moon-faced nurse continued talking as she bustled over, "We wondered when you would wake up. You have had quite a time of it! But Doctor decided you were just about 100% and stopped all your meds just yesterday." She paused to give the patient time to speak, charging ahead when he didn't. "Your daughter has visited a few times.... I'm sure she will be relieved to find you awake when she gets here. Let me tell you, we were all real worried about you! Yours was an even worse case than the one we treated last month." She stopped plumping his pillows and waited again for a comment that didn't come.

Even worse case of what? Al's mind seemed muzzy, more comfortable in the dream world where he now remembered he had a friend; *she was a girl a little older than me with a long braid.* His eyes wandered the room—trying unsuccessfully to sort things out—the only thing worth seeing was the explosion of yellow daffodils. There was a nurse—so he must be in a hospital—*but why? Why is she calling me Mister? Where's mommy?*

The nurse adjusted the patient's bed to a sitting position, "Would you like a little something to eat?" She asked.

Al Smith looked down at the white sheets and his breath caught at the sight of wrinkled, blue-veined hands, crusted with scabs, laying atop the coverlet. Shocked, he stared in bewilderment. The hands moved. *My God,* he realized, *those are MY hands! But how? How did I get old?*

The nurse watched the confusion in her charge's unfocused blue eyes. *Uh-oh! This is more than just coming off medication. There's been some damage here. Poor old thing is confused and not speaking. This will disappoint the doctor.* She slowed her speech for the benefit of the old and infirm. "Not to worry Mister Smith, dear." Noticing his intensity as he stared down at his hands she added, "you were admitted with damage to your hands."

Damage to my hands? What kind of damage makes hands look old? Al's thoughts spun in all directions as the nurse babbled on.

"...and of course we caught the poison-ivy before you started showing further symptoms but, by then it was in your bloodstream. So Doctor let you take a little vacation, while you healed." She smiled down at him.

Poison-ivy! The nurse's words brought his situation into focus. *So it was poison-ivy again!* The remaining mental cobwebs lifted, *I remember now...I sent a text to Danny.* He frowned, *where IS Danny? It must be a school day. Otherwise she surely would be here, probably all broken up and riddled with guilt.* He knew both he and Danny would have to deal with that later. At least his hands were healing, maybe enough to type. *Where is my laptop?*

The nurse noticed the patient begin to fidget and to cast restless looks around the room. *Maybe he is looking for his daughter, and of course SHE'S not here.* She found Mister Smith's daughter's lack of concern for her father's well-being quite shameful. To soothe him, she murmured "Don't you worry, dear, she will be here soon."

Danny will be here soon.

The nurse's heart squeezed, as a peaceful look passed over the old face—and she disliked the daughter even more. Catching sight of the flowers now in full bloom, she thought, *at least SOMEONE seems to care about him!*—and crossed the room to pick up the sealed card. Holding it up like a winning lottery ticket, she trilled. "Look at these flowers! My, my! Somebody loves you!!" Then added, "I'll open it, shall I?"

Without waiting for an okay, she slipped a finger under the flap and tore it open. Like everyone at the hospital, the nurse was curious about the sender of the mystery flowers.

The old man kept an eye on the nurse who had begun to seriously annoy him. *It's okay. I can sort all this out and go home once Danny brings me my laptop.*

The nurse pursed her lips and read:

> I picked these for you. You were right about
> spring coming early by the stream. I wish I could
> visit, but you know why I can't. Please forgive me.
> I will miss you. D.

The nurse put down the note, more puzzled than before. *What was THAT all about? Somebody actually picked all those flowers, and then got a FLORIST to deliver them? That's just crazy! And what kind of signature is 'D'?*

The effect the note had on the old man was immediate. The nurse saw what looked like a storm cloud cross the blue, blue of his eyes as he slumped back into the pillows. She rushed to take his pulse—which was much too fast in her opinion—then scurried off to see if she could locate the doctor.

The old man couldn't shake the last sentence; *I will miss you.* The words lodged in his heart along with the memory of something he'd once told his young friend, "Remember, Danny, the Fortress is a giant poison-ivy patch."

Danny was telling him she had to stay away.

The worst of it was—it was true—unless he could work something out...

The familiar clack-clack of stiletto heels on hospital linoleum interrupted Al's thoughts. *Forgot about her,* he winced, *and she's coming this way.* Al feigned sleep—he needed to think and was not prepared to listen to his daughter's nonsense.

Beatrice didn't notice that her father's eyes were closed—she'd been told he woke up, so certainly he was awake now. She charged up to the bedside. "It is about time you woke up! You don't know the trouble you have caused me. But never mind, the doctor says you will be fit enough to fly next week and I've got everything ready." Beatrice followed this earthshaking announcement with, "You will be much better off in Florida!"

The old man's eyes flew open, focused on his daughter's brittle smile, and felt his sadness change to desperation. *She is burying me alive!* He reached out to touch his daughter's wrist, *please.* he begged silently.

She stepped away with only a glance in his direction and made a half-hearted attempt to explain, "I pulled some strings and got you a spot in a new senior residential facility—which you are going to love. There are lots of people like you there—and it's not like there's anything for you, here, anymore."

He grabbed at her wrist but she avoided him. He tried to catch her eye but her gaze was focused on a spot over his eyebrows. His weak hand fell to his side and his blue eyes snapped with rage, *LOOK at me*.

I know he's my father and all—but if he touches me again with those scabby hands I shall scream. Beatrice needed something to occupy her energy and spotted the flowers. They were drooping—in her opinion. She grabbed them up and marched out.

After dropping the bouquet in the trash can, she returned to the room. It appeared the old man was asleep. *Good enough reason to get out of here.* She'd left her purse on the table when she'd collected the flowers, and as she retrieved it, spotted the small card. She read it—twice.

The note told Bea one thing, *whoever brought the flowers was too cheap to go to a florist.* Wanting more information, she stopped at the nurse's station on her way out, to ask if her father had any visitors.

"No," the nurse on duty said, feeling no obligation to tell the unpleasant woman about the mysterious flower delivery, or the odd, daily phone calls from a young person wanting updates on Aldo Smith's condition.

In room 214, Mister Aldo Smith had watched his daughter march away with Danny's flowers and closed his eyes to consider his future of trackless days and pointless routines. *She is putting me in an Old Folks home, and I can't even explain that I am not ready, that there are things I still have to do!* But when the image of a young girl with a long braid offering him a poison-ivy branch flashed through his mind unbidden, he shivered. Salty tears burned the tender new skin around his eyes as he admitted to himself; *I can't go through that again...I just can't...* The admission seemed to block any hope of escape. *What difference does it really make? There ISN'T anything left for me here, Bea is right.*

Danny is quarantined, and so am I!

The depression the old man fell into was blacker than the hole he'd fallen in following his stroke. When the doctor finally arrived, he found his elderly patient unresponsive.

Neurological tests were ordered but, there seemed to be no physical reason for the patient's apparent relapse. It hadn't been a stroke, or a heart attack—the old man was losing muscle mass at a fast rate, but from inactivity, not sickness. Aldo Smith was physically in decent shape.

Because it takes seniors much longer to bounce back from anesthesia, the doctor decided his patient would benefit from mental acuity exercises.

That afternoon, the nurse tried to get her patient to focus on a flash card; again and again she asked in a sugary, baby-voice "What is this picture of, dear? Come now, you must know what this is? See the shape and the lovely red color? It is something yummy!"

The old man simply ignored both the cards and the nurse. *What is the point?* His life was over.

At the end of the second day, the doctor prescribed anti-depressants. The medication put the old man to sleep, which was great because his drugged dreams were scented with daffodils, the music of a chuckling stream and always, the stone shed.

For the next three days, Al Smith had no visitors. The nursing staff found this both sad and scandalous—he did have a daughter after all! The doctor told them that while the daughter had never contacted him, her lawyers had, and while he didn't like the idea of releasing his patient into the woman's custody, there was nothing he could do because she had a full power of attorney.

Beatrice was circling. *Like a vulture,* the hospital staff thought.

If it hadn't been for Rosemary, Danny would never have found the energy to hike to the store for groceries—but that is what she was doing, yet again. The little raccoon stopped by the tent every night for a hand-out and, although she appeared to have regained her figure, Rosemary was still a bottomless pit.

Only in Rosemary's presence did Danny feel connected to the world. The rest of the time she plodded along, doing only what had to be done to exist. Enjoyment seemed to have disappeared from her life—along with any desire to talk.

Danny's silence was fine with Rosemary. She ate what was offered and left, taking no time to play or indulge any of her natural curiosity.

Rosemary had more important things to do.

One night—after pulling up the most aggressive vines, washing out her sweat pants, and fixing herself and Rosemary a peanut butter and jelly sandwich—Danny picked up her treasured copy of the History of the County. The book opened immediately to the Rockaway chapter and the possibility that, somewhere, right now, Mister Al was also looking at the same page in his own copy—crossed her mind. She sighed and paused for a moment before remembering her plan to read the book all the way through.

She flipped to the title page, surprised to find an inscription. In faded—but still beautiful—handwriting that read:

To Aldo Smith,
One of the finest storytellers I have ever known.

Her heart leapt. *This is Mister Al's book! He treasured this book!* Like heartburn, anger rose to burn in the back of her throat, *SHE just gave it away, like it was nothing. I bet he doesn't know she is getting rid of his things. I hate her!!*

Danny shoved the book into her backpack and stormed from the tent—it was time for a showdown with Aldo Smith's evil daughter.

This was not a young person's anger—this was the kind of rage a mother bear feels when her cub is threatened—it was murderous.

I have to stop her. There was a rushing, like the ocean in her ears; *I have to stop her right now.* Danny wasn't aware of making the trip through the woods, she was blinded by a desire to confront the person who represented everything awful in her life.

When she reached Mister Al's house and saw the glow of the cherry tree's final blossoms under the full moon, she heard the voice.

Bloodlust? said her mother.

Danny stopped, suddenly angry with her mother too—but mother was inside her head and wouldn't shut up.

Hate? Is this what you want inside you, Danny? Hate eats people alive.

Why do you suddenly care so much? YOU haven't been around and I needed you. Just leave me alone. The short sidewalk of 11314 was all that now separated Danny from the woman who had stolen Mister Al's life.

No lights showed in any of the windows.

Nobody's home. Danny's fury flattened like a leaky balloon, but she refused to just go home. *I'll go knock anyway—maybe she's asleep and I'll pound and pound until I wake her up.*

Danny started for the door; once so familiar, tonight it looked different. Something white and out of place flashed at the edge of her vision. It was a sign, big and bright and staked in the front yard.

FOR SALE, the sign proclaimed. A smaller sign hanging beneath it rocked in the night breeze.

SOLD!

"What should we tell the kid when she calls?" the junior nurse asked as she started shift.

"Only tell her—the kid's a girl by the way, I got that much out of her—just tell her he appears fully recovered and was released today. But for goodness sake, DON'T mention he was released in his daughter's custody!" the senior nurse saw no reason to upset the caller. They had all warmed to the polite, concerned, girl who called every single day.

The younger nurse felt she owed the old man a kindness—she was pretty certain she'd upset him that very morning by mentioning money she'd won by predicting the date his daffodils would bloom. She should learn to keep her mouth shut! Turning to the head nurse she asked, "Can I tell her we have a forwarding address in case she might want to send something to the nursing home in Florida?"

"Absolutely, not! That daughter of his was perfectly clear. No one but the hospital can have that information. Besides, why upset the girl?"

"Wouldn't YOU be upset if someone you cared about just disappeared like that?"

Life gives clues. Dreams give answers, the old man mused as the airplane rushed him toward his fate. He'd surfaced from a drug-induced doze in a first class seat, with something important rolling around in the bleak landscape of his head...

If he could only remember.

It was something the nurse said. Something he paid no attention. *But it was something important. Something that's the key.*

Time had warped for the old man since he'd been sick. It was hard for him to know when, and even IF, things he remembered had actually happened. Most recently he'd begun to wonder if the whole Girl in the Woods thing was fantasy from start to finish. Maybe he was still in the hospital from his first stroke.

Still...there IS something! He bore down on the thought, determined to think it through. *Not the moon-faced one who called me 'dear', and never shut up.* He squeezed his eyes tight. *A different nurse...*

He tried to recall the most recent set of events. *A soapy smell...someone washing me up to leave the hospital... Not a real nurse...this one was an assistant and had dirty looking fingernails. She said she had a garden and grew only flowers native to North America.*

Al felt his brain engage as he moved ever closer to an important revelation. *Okay, something about North American flowers.* He shook his head, *no, no NOT about North American flowers...about flowers that AREN'T North American. Tulips...the Dutch got them from Turkey and brought them to America. Daffodils...did I know about daffodils? Daffodils came from England.*

That's it! That's what she said "Daffodils don't grow wild—if you see them, somebody had to have planted them!"

Al was terribly excited as thoughts fell into place...*Danny brought daffodils. She said she picked them by the stream. Oh great God!* The old man gasped. *They don't grow wild, Rickenbocker planted them. That's the key!*

Hollow. The damp air blew through her. She was wet, slogging toward the store, avoiding the public bus stops because she just couldn't face running into the sunny Jamaal. All she knew was Rosemary expected to be fed when she arrived that evening.

Danny kept walking.

A car on the opposite side of the road swerved slightly to avoid something. She looked to see what it was. Across the road, near the gutter, there was a shape in the road. Danny crossed over to take a look—premonition fluttering under her ribcage...

The animal had been hit more than once. Stomach ruptured, its insides spilled red on the black of rain-soaked asphalt. A car veered to avoid the girl standing on the road then passed in a rush of air that lifted the dead animal's spiky fur—heavy though it was with highway grit and puddling blood.

It was Rosemary.

Oxo heard the sound before he topped the small hill. He recognized it. Someone had reached the end. *The bottom.*

Rain made the road slick. The motor scooter fought for traction as Oxo came up over the hill and hit the brakes. He put his foot down and brought the little bike around beside the bedraggled form staggering down the middle of the road.

Cars whizzed by on both sides, beeping at the scooter before accelerating at the sight of the rain-soaked girl cradling the torn, bloody, carcass of an animal.

Oxo forced Danny, still gripping the bloody mess in her arms, to straddle the bike. She was shorter than he, so he put her in the front and jammed himself on the seat beyond. His arms were only long enough to reach around his passenger and touch the handle controls. It was dreadfully unsafe. He had discarded his helmet on the side of the road and now fought to see, as strings of wet hair blew in his eyes and stuck to his cheek—but he managed. Slowly. Thanks to the little platform at the base of all motor scooters, he was able to keep Danny's feet from dragging the ground, stabilize the bike, and eventually move from the center of the road to the shoulder. Then—using equal parts to push and accelerate—he guided the scooter the mile to the Laird's.

She hadn't stopped keening.

THE DAFFODIL RULE

They buried Rosemary just inside the tree line in the pouring rain.

Oxo wasn't much of a nurse, but he did his best for the girl. He pushed her up the stairs and into the old room she'd once occupied. He gave her some cleaner clothes and his cleanest towel and told her she needed a shower—which was pretty funny really, since they'd just spent hours outside in the rain.

Danny did as she was told.

Oxo thought she might not even know where she was.

He was right.

But the following afternoon when she woke to the smell of cigarette smoke drifting up from the living room vent, she knew exactly where she was. Rising quickly Danny began to pull on her soggy sneakers. What had happened was too horrible to even think about. So she wouldn't.

Oxo knocked. When there was no answer he opened the door to see Danny finish cinching the bow on her laces. "Here. It's coffee. I drink it black so you will too."

Grateful for the small kindness, Danny slurped the scalding brew. The hot mug was big enough to wrap both hands around. She held it close to her face and breathed the steam. "I'm going now. Thank you, Oxo. You rescued me yet again."

Relieved, Oxo smiled. "Sure." He watched her clatter down the steps still clutching the coffee mug. After what he had seen yesterday, he'd been afraid he was going to be stuck with a real, full-time, basket case. *And I have another edition to get out.*

Danny drained the mug and left it on the top of the porch step where Oxo was sure to find it. No matter how bad things got she'd once promised herself she would never go back to the Laird's. That pledge now seemed like the only anchor she had in life—so she would stick to it. *Last night wasn't intentional,* she decided, *it didn't count.*

Even the glade was soggy and miserable looking. Danny snapped and zipped the tent closed the minute she entered. Her once inviting space smelled moldy and damp. She realized she'd lost her backpack at some point yesterday. *Yesterday.* The events of yesterday flooded in, threatening to overwhelm her shaky emotional hold. She backed off. Shut down.

It was gloomy inside the tent—she'd run out of kerosene days ago. No lamp, no heater—the battery hadn't been charged in over a week. Tired, but resigned, Danny climbed on the bike and began pedaling. The bike was just one more thing she couldn't let herself think about. *There isn't anything left I can think of that doesn't remind me of someone I will never see again.*

Danny vowed to not think at all. *"Just DO it"*, wasn't that what the commercial said?

Beatrice didn't hear the dislike in her lawyer's voice—she was used to people sounding that way—but she DID hear his unwelcome message.

"Ms. Smith, as I told you several times before, there is nothing I, or any other lawyer for that matter, can do until your father's death." The lawyer paused, thought about the woman on the other end of the line and added with emphasis, "Mister Aldo Smith's passing must be confirmed and documented, and I must have a signed and notarized death certificate IN MY HAND, before I can authorize the sale of his house AND before I can authorize a search for other accounts in his name."

"But I..."

"Yes, I KNOW you have a General Power of Attorney—but under new rules passed to protect Soldiers coming back from war, you can make health decisions, pay bills, suspend or start up services, but you CANNOT sell homes or raid accounts without another separate, specific Power of Attorney."

"Look here, I..."

"NO! No. There is nothing more I can do." He was no longer concerned that he might lose a client, he didn't want her business. "Goodbye."

Beatrice ground her teeth in frustration.

Danny wrote:

Rosemary is dead.

Mister Al is gone.

I can't change anything so I am closing the book on the past. I don't think I'm numb, I think I'm empty, and it feels like forever.

This is my last entry—I just don't want to write anymore about anything.

Even in the rain, the hot tub was Danny's only solace. Inside it she could let her thoughts drift and simply BE, much like the stream itself. It was as though the stream's ever present fog had taken root in her brain—life felt unreal and time had no real meaning.

She leaned against the rough bark of Rosemary's tree and listened mindlessly to rain drumming on the tight nylon of the umbrella she'd propped above her. *How many days has it been raining?* Gazing blankly into gray mist, thinking about rain and no rain, she burned time...

The relentless pounding slowed to a drip and finally stopped altogether. A chorus of buzzes, cheeps and chirps kicked in, as the insects, birds and creatures of the forest began to rouse themselves. Danny listened without hearing.

But when a strange high, thin, mewling wavered through the damp air— feeble, intermittent and easy to dismiss—Danny heard. *What IS that sound?*

Minutes passed—the cry came again—closer, louder and more insistent.

Sounds like a lost kitten.

Danny sat up, hardly daring to breathe least she miss it. She strained to pinpoint the source as the cries continued; they seemed to be coming from the tangle of limbs and branches in the fallen tree she leaned against. When the pitiful mewling came next it was accompanied by the rustle of leaves somewhere behind her right shoulder.

Standing, Danny wrapped in a towel and stepped barefoot

into the damp brush. She tiptoed forward, carefully and quietly placing each foot. The thin cry sounded very close and she heard a sniffling.

A baby is lost.

The confusion of branches and leaves offered no clues. She wanted to help but was afraid any movement would scare whatever it was away, so she stood stock still, waiting, listening and staring. She heard it struggling but until the tiny pink mouth opened in a cry, the little creature remained invisible in the mass of brush.

Danny dropped to her knees, murmuring endearments. The little creature was frightened. She could see its small body shake. "You must be cold you poor little thing" she soothed and cajoled, reaching out a hand.

Is it a baby squirrel? What color are fox cubs? Baby rabbits are smaller than that. Could it actually BE a kitten? Or maybe even a dog. It could be a puppy.

Defenseless and confused, the baby let Danny scoop it from the damp leaves and cradle it in her cupped hands. Immediately the small nose began pushing at her hand, nuzzling between her fingers. *It wants to be closer; it's trying to snuggle as close as it can.* Her heart broke.

Cradling the shivering form with both hands, she hurried across the stream and into the tent, rejoicing she'd spent enough time on the bike to charge the battery.

With the heater on high, Danny soon had her small charge warm and dry. As she soothed and caressing its fluffy fur, she saw it was a light color—but not until it stopped shivering did she make out the dark mask-like fur around its eyes.

It's a baby raccoon! Rosemary didn't leave me.

All her thoughts centered on the animal's well-being. A life depended on her; she didn't question whether she was equal to the responsibility since she had no choice... It felt good to be needed.

The first challenge was feeding the tiny kit. It was much too small to eat on its own. It was obvious this baby wanted to suckle but—until Danny got hold of a baby bottle—some other way would have to be found.

She thought of poking a hole in the finger of a rubber glove, like she'd seen in countless cartoons—but she didn't have a rubber glove.

She could use an eye dropper—but didn't have one of those either.

Finally, desperate to get something in the hungry little mouth, she unscrewed the top to her water bottle and the baby managed to swallow a few drops. Thinking milk would be more nutritious, she opened a box of the shelf-stable kind—added a teaspoon of sugar—and mixed it with the water in the bottle. She screwed the top on extra tight—planning to give the mixture a good shake— noticing as she did that the lid was the kind with a pull-up, drinking nub. She never used it, but knew that with one pull and a twist, a thirsty athlete could squirt water in his mouth and never miss a step.

Will it work for a raccoon?

Turns out a sports nozzle makes an acceptable baby bottle. Perhaps because the kit was very, very hungry it clamped on the knob and began sucking up the sweet, milky concoction as quickly as Danny could squeeze it out.

Unfortunately, as Danny squeezed, the sides of the bottle collapsed; time and time again she had to pull the nipple back to let the bottle re-inflate. Each delay made the baby frantic.

The bottle forms a vacuum when I push the air out.

She tried poking a few pinholes high on the side of the plastic bottle so that incoming air displaced out-flowing liquid and kept the bottle from collapsing. This seemed to work. As long as she kept the holes pointing up—gravity let the contents drain out— and the tiny raccoon began taking long, greedy pulls.

The kit exhausted both the bottle and itself and drifted contentedly to sleep with a full tummy. Danny looked down at her fluffy charge. *So adorable!* He—she saw it was a he—lay on his back, arms and legs splayed, nestled in the crook of her arm and making odd little purring sounds.

Danny fell asleep too, and slept better than she had in a very long time.

Al sat almost prone in a first-class window seat. He wanted to laugh, and he wanted to cry. The giddy joy of realizing a childhood dream and the plunging despair of not being able to tell the only person in the world who cared as much as he did, had his insides aquiver.

Danny!! I've GOT to tell Danny! I've got to find a way. Sensing Beatrice's had turned his way, he forced himself to be still. If Beatrice saw he was awake she would insist they knock him out and he didn't want any more medication. He needed a clear head.

Beatrice leaned across to yank the window blind closed before returning to her magazine.

Good! Al thought; for the first time he was grateful his daughter never looked directly at him. He opened his eyes a slit to check out his surroundings. Maybe an idea would present itself.

From his position he had a view of Beatrice from the knees down. He could clearly see the open briefcase on the floor beside her. Inside the briefcase a tiny, electronic, red light blinked. *The phone.*

The old man's heart began to pound as he estimated the distance to the briefcase. Knowing his daughter, she'd have the latest in cell phone technology and he would have to hope he could figure out how to send a text message—IF he could get a hold of it in the first place. *GO somewhere.* He willed his daughter, *move!*

DONG.

The sound of the seatbelt sign going off did the trick. Beatrice immediately unbuckled her belt and stood to stretch. Then she stepped into the aisle and began to make her way to the restroom.

He had at most seven minutes.

First, he pressed the button to raise the seat back; the motion caused the large scab on the back of his hand to break loose but he had no time to worry about that. He unfastened his seatbelt, lifted the armrest separating his seat from his daughter's and leaned across the space. He was shockingly weak, but by kicking at the briefcase was able to topple it in his direction.

The contents spilled out.

Considering it something close to a miracle, the old man had his hand on the phone less than a minute later.

Bea's phone was little bigger than a deck of cards and about as thick. It looked self explanatory. *A touch screen.* Al's mood lightened even more. *Piece of cake.* He thought.

It had been a long and dangerous recovery, but the old man was back in form.

Beatrice returned to her seat and to find the contents of her briefcase spilled across the floor. In her annoyance at having to pick up everything she didn't bother to wonder how it had happened in the first place. There had been no turbulence.

Spring break was longer than usual—fortunate for both the raccoon and its new mother.

The first few days Danny rarely left the tent. Her raccoon only wanted to snuggle, sleep and eat—that was fine with her. Just weeks old, the kit's eyes were still light sensitive and may have even opened prematurely in the desperate search for its mother. *And you saw **me** when you opened your eyes, didn't you? I'm your mommy now.* Danny rained kisses on the little thing. It squeaked and attempted to worm under her arm.

She giggled.

It was time to add a bit of bulk to the little boy's diet. *I wish I could ask Mister Al,* Danny thought with a stab of regret, "I'll feed you stuff your mother, Rosemary, liked. I don't think you are old enough to eat a crayfish. It will have to be cereal."

A few drops of warm water reduced a tablespoon of oat cereal to a thick mush. Danny offered it to the hungry kit on the tip of her finger. It only took one good sniff for a tiny hand to direct that finger to his little pink mouth. The baby latched on and sucked Danny's finger clean.

Soon they were out of cereal.

Watered-down peanut butter was next on the menu. "Come on little orphan, your mommy used to love this stuff." The baby opened its eyes wide in ecstasy the moment the salty, nutty, taste touched its tongue.

She named him Gabriel, and even before spring break was over, they were tumbling around in the clearing and paddling in the shallows of the stream.

Worried about the kit getting enough variety in its diet, Danny spent one morning turning over rocks in the shallow part of the stream. She was ready when a small crayfish tried to scuttle away and snatched it from the stream bottom. The baby raccoon was immediately intrigued.

Danny dropped the tiny, inoffensive, lobster-looking thing beside him and watched to see what would happen.

The kit's black nose nudged the back end of the crayfish, causing it to dodge and weave and flash its itty-bitty pinchers. This delighted the kit, and before Danny could stop him, he bent to sniff the new toy—where upon the crawfish promptly latched onto his little black nose.

The baby squealed in outrage and swatted at the nasty thing, so the crayfish closed its other very small pincher on the baby's finger.

Certain the crawfish was causing only a light pinch, and highly amused by the battle of the two tiny titans, Danny watched the little kit hopping up and down, chattering and squealing. She was about to come to the rescue when the small crustacean went sailing through the air to splash back into the stream.

Victorious, but traumatized and in a tizzy, the chattering raccoon climbed Danny's leg, leapt into her arms, put its arms around her neck and burrowed deep under her heavy hair.

Laughter was back in the glade.

On the second to last day of Spring Break, Danny ventured into town to pick up the cage she'd ordered for Gabriel. Actually, it was a crate designed for a medium sized dog, and the pet store owner promised her it was roomy and secure—*of course he doesn't know about raccoons.*

She hated the idea of locking him up, but while she was in school she knew he had to be contained. *He is already into everything,* she remembered the day before when she'd noticed him smacking something around under the cot and was surprised by what she found when she bent to investigate. Tucked away was full stash of stolen goods! Gabriel had taken and hidden her hair brush, five or six quarters, a set of keys to Mister Al's old house, an empty jar of peanut butter—and Danny's cell phone.

Retrieving the phone was like touching a relic; she hadn't used it or thought about it in what seemed like forever. The battery was so dead it didn't respond when she put it to charge for the night. Although there was no real harm done, she would remember his thieving tendencies and check under the cot every so often.

She thought about those busy little hands now as she watched Gabriel climb over the cage top and fiddle with the door. She sighed, *even if I could figure out a way to smuggle him into school, there would be no hiding him.*

"Gabes you will be fine without me!" she said, knowing she was really reassuring herself, "I'll make sure you have toys and food and water. You won't miss me at all!"

Gabriel seemed to freeze in place. His ears twitched as he strained to listen, so intent he swayed as though in a very slight breeze. Seconds later, he began running in excited circles. Danny was mystified—until she heard it too.

A buzzing sound.

The sound was coming from a far corner. *The phone.*

The phone. It was still connected to the charger and instead of ringing it was dancing in a crazy circle each time it vibrated. The sight delighted Gabriel. He rushed over and he threw himself on top of it. Apparently, the vibration tickled his belly because he jumped up in surprise.

Danny laughed and lifted him. "Sorry little fella, it's not a toy!" Putting Gabriel on the cot she retrieved her phone and flipped it open.

It was a text message, and she briefly wondered how long ago it had been sent before she read:

IN FL. AM OK. FOLLOW DAFFODILS TO FIND STONE SHED. WILL TXT U. DO NOT USE THIS # AL

It was like hearing a voice from the grave and for a long time Danny simply stared down at the message.

Gabriel didn't like this at all and climbed up on her shoulder.

His new trick was to push his nose into her ear and snort. It always made her laugh.

Not this time.

He had never seen her cry.

"Gabriel..." she squeezed him and said in a funny voice, "Gabriel, it's Mister Al...Mister Al's okay! He's alright, and he doesn't hate me and, oh Gabriel!"

Gabriel squirmed free before she could squeeze him again. He moved to the middle of the bed and stared at her suspiciously.

"You would like Mister Al, Gabes. Your mother visited him all the time when she was alive...I'm so happy, you just don't know!" She moved toward the little raccoon, saw him flinch, and stopped. "Okay, I'm sorry. I'm acting silly aren't I?" Danny sniffed, wiped at her eyes and picked up the cell phone. "Alright Mister Al. What's this about daffodils?"

Wiping at her eyes again she considered the message, "Mister Al says to follow the daffodils." Danny patted her shoulder to show him they were going somewhere, "Come on Gabriel, up you go! We've got a whole hill of daffodils to follow and only a day and a half left before school starts."

Gabriel climbed up on her shoulder and Danny made sure he was securely seated before leaving the tent and heading for the stream. She stopped at the edge. "Could it really be that simple?" she wondered out loud as she stared into the unknown on the other side.

The only time she'd ventured to the opposite bank was to collect Mister Al's bouquet from the buds at the water's edge; now it was ablaze with daffodils in full bloom. Her eye followed the carpet of yellow flowers as they disappeared into the dense, wiry tangle of leafless vines. Far, far into the woods Danny could see winks of color. Hundreds and hundreds of daffodils, but not a single one on her side of the stream. Why had she not noticed?

"Look Gabriel, right there, see the yellow color?" she pointed toward the tangle. "That's what we are following, Mister Al says the daffodils lead to the stone shed and I can see gobs of them in the woods. We've got to go through those vines," she said and thought, *but how?*

Danny used Rosemary's tree to cross to the other side without getting wet and Gabriel loved the novelty of it. He was glad her eyes had stopped leaking but wished she'd talk some more. She hadn't said a word since she'd picked up the pace.

She was concentrating on the scene before her. More vines; how would she get through them this time? There was no freeze on the horizon to help her out and she had returned Mister Al's clippers long ago; the only thing she knew with absolute certainty was that Mister Al was right; in that big patch of daffodils was the stone shed. She would head toward the densest concentration of flowers and hope for the best.

Heading into the undergrowth where the flowers grew the thickest, she warned, "Hang on tight Gabriel! This isn't going to be easy."

But to her great surprise it WAS easy. The tangled long-dead undergrowth simply crumbled at her touch.

Danny had entered the heart of the Fortress, where it all began nearly one hundred years before with the death of twin Chestnut trees. When the mighty shade trees died and sunlight touched the earth for the first time in many decades plants of every type flourished. But vines fought hardest, climbed fastest, and suffocated every scrap of vegetation below them before turning on each other. By the time Danny showed up, everything was dead except the ancient canopy of poison-ivy and the delicate daffodil. These flowers lived, reproduced and died in the few weeks of warm weather before poison-ivy leaves again blocked out all light.

In less than a week, the granddaddy vine would return the forest floor to a dark, dry desert-state, but for now little, woody pieces pattered down amid the nodding daffodils as Danny moved forward. For once she wasn't trying to figure out the scientific reasons for her good fortune, she was just too excited. *I'm actually going to find it!* Her heart sang.

The smell of bruised daffodils mingled with scent of dust.

Beatrice insisted her father be first to deplane. She was ready the moment they touched down in Florida and walked beside the attendant pushing her father's wheelchair, pleased with the arrangements so far. She hazarded a look down at the scrawny, scab-covered hand clutching the chair arm and was repulsed by the bright blood oozing from a particularly thick, dark scab that had cracked and lifted. She averted her gaze thinking, *Who could stand to have someone like that around?*

The clack-clack of Beatrice's stilettos on the airport tile almost drowned out a light tinkling tone. The tone sounded repeatedly before Beatrice connected it to her own phone. *Why is my alarm going off?* She didn't remember setting it. *Could I have missed an appointment?* Just the possibility sent a squirt of adrenaline coursing through her veins and sent her digging in her briefcase.

Retrieving the phone she checked her appointment schedule, puzzled to read: RETURN FATHER'S LAPTOP

When had she written that?!

Al smiled grimy. He'd scheduled the same alarm for four consecutive days. *If that doesn't work, I'll get to another computer.*

He was determined to reach Danny.

The hunt for the stone shed was most definitely on.

Gabriel was enjoying the search and tumbling noisily through the undergrowth, ignoring tunnels and paths made by other animals because it was way more fun to make his own, and still keep Danny in sight.

Danny herself was keeping her head down—scanning the ground for the green stems and yellow buds. Being surrounded by a dim, uniformly nondescript confusion of tan and brown was disorienting, and she was finding it hard to gauge both depth and distance.

The only way I'll find the stone shed under these conditions is if I run right into it... Danny sighed. She kept moving although disheartened.

Breaking deeper into the brittle barrier and keeping an eye on the cluster patterns of the flowers, Danny kept an ear tuned to Gabriel cavorting and chattering nearby. Occasionally—because she knew he liked the sound of her voice—she offered words of encouragement. "Can't be long now Gabes" she said. Mister Al is going to be so excited!" she said.

Danny had just stumbled over a tree root when she heard

Gabriel squeal. It was an odd cry—more surprise than hurt—but she responded immediately, abandoning her own search and rushing toward the sound.

"Gabriel!" she hollered and was rewarded by a much more conversational chatter. His voice sounded hollow—like he'd fallen inside of something. Relived she thought, *What IS that rascal up to?*

As she waded through a strip of ground lush with the deep green of unopened daffodils a particularly loud burst of chatter and the frantic scrabbling of claws on stone made her stop and look down.

Only this saved her from stepping into a wide, dark, hole— much as Gabriel had done only minutes before. She dropped to her knees and looked down into the gloom.

"Gabriel? Are you down there?" Concerned, she lay on her stomach and peered over the edge, only to find two round eyes staring back from the darkness. She reached out and Gabriel wasted no time climbing into her arms from the not very deep hole. She hugged him and made him squirm and snort by raining kisses on his head. "You scared me!"

He was excited and very vocal.

"What a time you had, you little rascal!

Gabriel struggled to get down. It had been frightening when the ground went out from under him and sent him into the dark, but he'd landed on soft leaves and rubble and wasn't hurt—just VERY curious. All those new smells.

Danny held him a few more seconds before surrendering. "Now what have you found? Show me. You found a big, dark, hole didn't you?" *Not all that deep but surely dark...all shadowy and mysterious.* Trying to figure the dimensions of the hole, she stepped to the right and her shoulder bashed into what felt like a tree trunk—so she moved left and her other shoulder met resistance. *Like a doorway between two trees*, she smiled at the thought and ran a hand over one of the trees.

It's NOT a tree. "Its stone, Gabe, GREEN stone, a green stone wall!" The thrill of discovery made her giddy. "Oh yes, yes, yes!" she muttered and began to frantically scrape away vegetation. "It COULD be...maybe."

Gabriel used the occasion to jump off Danny's shoulder and scamper out of reach. He watched suspiciously as she worked to reveal more and more of the structure, and when she stood on her tiptoes to clear sticks from above her head his ears caught her excitement.

"It's a doorway, Gabe. It's got to be the front door to the stone shed. You found it!"

She braced her hands on either side of the door jam and leaned far inside to look around. *Not so many vines here, mostly shadows.*

The roof was gone and the floor had collapsed but Danny was pretty certain all four walls were standing. She would have to do more clearing to be sure, but from first glance it appeared the stone shed had weathered the years quite well.

Just like Mister Al always thought it would.

Running her hand appreciatively over the cool green stone of the door frame and breathing in the mysterious, loamy air of the interior, she let herself admit there were times she thought the quest was futile. "But we found it," she whispered as though to the old man, *I wonder when he'll get in touch, I have so much to tell him.*

Aldo Smith's hands felt stiff but comfortable on the keyboard. I WANT OUT OF HERE IMMEDIATELY, he pecked, MY DAUGHTER HAD NO RIGHT TO PUT ME IN HERE! When he paused to glower at his new doctor, he was encouraged to see interest in the young man's brown eyes. But interest wasn't enough, Aldo needed ACTION, so he hit delete and started over, searching for the words to make this doctor understand his situation and do something. *How much time do I have left?* Al reflexively checked the time display in the right corner of his laptop. *Ten minutes.* He was permitted an hour on the computer each day, but allowed no internet access. Swallowing currents of fury, Al typed...

Doc Rogers watched carefully. As one of the new breed of geriatric specialists and the newest member of the staff, (the facility had only been opened a month so that hardly mattered), he'd been assigned the most difficult patients. Aldo Smith was certainly that...records showed he was: surly, sneaky and uncooperative, refused to participate in speech therapy, attempted to lift an orderly's cell phone and was twice intercepted trying to break into the computer at the nurses station and gain access to the internet.

The cause of Smith's behavior problems was listed as "Stroke, trauma and age related", but Doc Rogers had read all of the old man's records and had his doubts...

Al turned the screen toward the doctor and hoped for the best:

SINCE MY STROKE OVER A YEAR AGO I'VE BEEN MUTE AND HAVE BEEN COMMUNICATING VIA COMPUTER. I'VE JUST SPENT WEEKS IN THE HOSPITAL RECOVERING FROM AN EXTREME REACTION TO POISON-IVY DURING WHICH I WAS KEPT HEAVILY SEDATED. IN THAT TIME MY DAUGHTER USED A POWER OF ATTORNEY TO MAKE DECISIONS ON MY BEHALF. SHE SOLD MY HOUSE AND ALL MY THINGS AND PUT ME IN HERE; WITHOUT A VOICE I COULD NOT STOP HER. Al watched the doctor's eyes as he read; best to see the reaction before making demands...

Doc Rogers scanned the paragraph thinking, *well written, well reasoned,* then he read it again more slowly. The old man's words would explain much of his bizarre behavior, but the brain works in mysterious ways and paranoia is quite common in Alzheimer patients so he'd need tests and more time to observe before invalidating the daughter's Power of Attorney. He could make the old man's life easier though, certainly allowing him to keep his computer—with conditions of course—would diffuse some of his anger.

Al watched the doctor and thought, *the boy is still too young to learn how to hide his thoughts.* When Doc Rogers' face softened he thought, *he's not fully convinced but he's made up his mind about something...*

"First of all Mister Smith, welcome to Sunnyside Senior Residential Care Facility." He reached out a hand, dropped it on the old man's shoulder, felt a jerk of surprise and mentally noted, *the old guy's got some muscle tone there.*

Startled, Al glanced up. The words hadn't been at all what he'd expected to hear.

Doc Rogers continued, "I can see you don't think you should be here and I understand why the inability to make your feelings known is frustrating." He saw the old man nod slightly.

It had been a very long time since anyone had spoken to Al as a fellow adult and he felt an enormous tension leave him.

"I hope you understand that because I want what is best for both you and this facility I can't release you on your own recommendation; I must be medically certain you can function independently."

The old man's eyes hardened as he pivoted the keyboard and typed, AND JUST WHAT WILL IT TAKE TO CONVINCE YOU OF THAT?

Ah, the doctor thought when he read the screen, *negotiation! The fellow's wits seem intact.* "Time and tests, I'm afraid," he spoke as gently as possible, observing the flash of anger in his patient's eyes.

I'LL DO ANY TESTS YOU LIKE, BUT I KEEP MY LAPTOP.

Doc Rogers pursed his lips as though considering the request, "You keep your laptop...IF you participate in Speech Therapy."

NO POINT IN IT, BUT OK. Al was sort of enjoying himself, the kid doctor was pretty sharp. INTERNET?

"Can't do internet in this part of the facility I'm afraid, but residents in the independent living section have both internet and cell phones."

HOW DO I GET OVER THERE?

"Earn it like everything in life. Cooperate. Go to therapy. Do your water aerobics, bio-feedback sessions and speech therapy. Stop frowning and use this time to get stronger and you'll be out of here before you know it." It was gratifying to see the impact of his words reflected in the old man's surprisingly blue eyes.

MY DAUGHTER WILL TRY TO STOP YOU.

"She can try all she wants but it actually isn't up to her..." the doctor hesitated, *how much to say?* "To interfere with the course of your care she needs medical proof that you are irreversibly incompetent. Then and only then can she take full control of you and your assets."

HOW COULD SHE SELL MY HOUSE AND HAVE ME COMMITTED LIKE THIS THEN?

The conversation was not going in the direction Doc Rogers wanted and he was becoming increasingly uncomfortable,

"Hemm...well you aren't committed first off and second, she didn't sell your house..."

Al was already tying.

"...the house is being rented, with the sale pending. She wants us, I...uh... mean ME to document your incompetence."

Al stopped. Was this kid threatening him?! Warning him?! Did he want something? *Money? A cut of the inheritance? My gold teeth?* One crooked finger hit delete and he typed: DO YOU BELIEVE IN GHOSTS, DOCTOR?

Okay, THAT was completely out of left field! The doctor thought, *Ghosts? Maybe the old boy really has slipped a rail.*

BECAUSE IF YOU DO HELP THAT WOMAN I'LL COME BACK TO HAUNT YOU. I SWEAR, I'LL STICK TO YOU LIKE GUM ON YOUR SHOE AND I WILL MAKE YOUR LIFE A LIVING HELL.

Doc Rogers laughed. *Quite clever,* he acknowledged even as a tiny chill raced across his shoulders. The afterlife was the only thing the old man had left to threaten with. "Please don't worry, Mister Smith. I play by the rules, and so far you seem very sane and healthy to me."

CAN I SEE A LAWYER?

"Well, again I have to say no, you can't, but you can write to one. I'll even print and mail the letter for you."

CAN I USE YOUR CELL PHONE?

"You just told me you can't speak. What use is a cell phone?"

TEXT

Text! Of course...what a stupid, last-century question! Doc Rogers could feel embarrassment burning the tips of his ears and without further thought blurted, "Oh...certainly...here," and handed over his newest plaything.

The phone felt warm and alive in Al's hand. He touched the screen and it sprung to life with possibilities.

Regretting his lapse in professionalism, the doctor watched nervously, "Do...do you...um...do you know how to...?" But the old man was obviously no stranger to technology. "Keep it short. Just one call," he mumbled as he watched his patient manipulate the touch screen.

Al typed Danny a message: DID YOU FIND IT!? TEXT BACK TELL AL YES OR TELL AL NO I'LL GET THE MESSAGE. TILL I GET INTERNET WRITE SUNNYSIDE SENIOR RESIDENTIAL CARE FACILITY, CLEARWATER FL. XO ~AL

Danny knew Mister Al would want a full report, but with vines so insinuated into the stone work that even the distinctive outline of a straight, solid, wall was completely obscured, she could only guess at the state of the structure beneath. The area would have to be cleared and all the vines pulled down and at this time of the year there would be spiders—lots of them. Just thinking about bugs made Danny's skin crawl, so she was thrilled when her shoulder brushed against an imposing knot of vegetation and it crumbled to dust. *Well if it's that easy,* she thought, *maybe I can use a stick or something.*

A short search of the area turned up a few promising looking sticks, but the second she put any pressure on them they broke to pieces. She backtracked to where she'd left off her own search and saw Gabriel batting at something in the undergrowth. "Now what? Did you find what I need?"

Gabriel, indeed, had found exactly the thing—a trash mound of discarded equipment with a coil of pipe sticking out of the dirt. A tug dislodged a tangle of other items buried there: remnants of glass tubing, a rusted-out copper kettle and a variety of small bottles and jars and—finally—a long, metal rod. Although several layers had rusted away Danny could see it was still strong.

Perfect!

The rod was like a magic wand; when she ran it over the stone the vines shattered and crumbled away, revealing the perfectly intact art of a master stone mason. No mortar was visible— stones were shaped or chosen to interlock perfectly with its neighbor. She was amazed to find window glass still intact in two of the three windows and when she pulled vines from the top of the wall she got another surprise—a 12 inch thick main ridge beam connecting the roof points still stood and it looked as sturdy as it had the day it was erected.

The orange rays of sunset turned the air a warm peach as Danny completed her efforts. Night was coming fast. Gabriel had long ago grown tired and cranky with hunger and finally fallen to sleep nearby; he woke when he sensed she'd stopped working and ambled over to tug at her pant leg.

"I know Gabe, you are STARVING! But just look at what we did!" Danny stood back, hands on hips, shoulders tight and sore with the day's labor and allowed her self to feel great. It was as though the stone shed had been released from a spell that had kept it invisible. Now it was free. It had no roof and no floor but it had all four walls—and it was well and truly beautiful. The sight of the perfectly proportioned cottage stirred a long forgotten memory.

"Gabriel," she spoke slowly, thinking about each word before she said it, "I must have been really, really little when daddy told me stories about a magic family of frogs living in a forgotten house in a town covered over by Kudzu vines—because I'd forgotten all about it until just now"

Her recovered memory was clear. She couldn't have been more than a toddler, because every morning, she'd run into her parent's room and hold up her arms so her father could lift her into the big bed. There she would snuggle between her parents and listen as her father spun fantastic stories of the frog family's secret life under the Kudzu. How could she have forgotten?

The green stone walls seemed to glow mysteriously in the evening light, as though they were somehow part of that memory.

"Its like the frog's secret cottage." Danny mused, "I wonder..." She stared at the shed imagining what it once was...what it could be again. "Kudzu Cottage!" she said as her imagination caught fire. "Do you like the way that sounds Gabriel? Could we call it Kudzu Cottage?"

Gabriel had climbed to his favorite perch on Danny's shoulder and he responded to her words with an extra gusty poke in her ear.

"Kudzu Cottage it is then!" she smiled. "I like the way that sounds and I think Mister Al would like it too...at least I hope so. We can't just keep calling it the Stone Shed, after all" Danny's eyes began to sting as she turned to go. *I really miss you Mister Al,* she thought, *thank you for sharing your beautiful dream with me.*

It had been a magical day and as a last slanting ray of sunset touched the corner stone of the Kudzu Cottage, letters chiseled deep in the rock one hundred years before revealed themselves one by one...

BEAUTIFUL DREAM

RICKENBOCKER

1868